About the

Lydia San Andres lives and writes in the tropics, where she can be found reading and making excuses to stay out of the sun. Lydia would love to hear from her readers, and you can visit her at lydiasanandres.com or follow her on Facebook, Twitter, and TikTok @lydiaallthetime

The Historical Collection

The Historical Collection:

Caribbean Courtships

LYDIA SAN ANDRES

MILLS & BOON

First Published in Great Britain 2023
by Mills & Boon, an imprint of HarperCollins*Publishers* Ltd,
1 London Bridge Street, London, SE1 9GF

www.harpercollins.co.uk

HarperCollins*Publishers*
Macken House, 39/40 Mayor Street Upper,
Dublin 1, D01 C9W8, Ireland

ISBN: 978-0-263-32113-5

This book is produced from independently certified FSC™ paper
to ensure responsible forest management.

For more information visit: www.harpercollins.co.uk/green

Printed and Bound in the UK using 100% Renewable Electricity
at CPI Group (UK) Ltd, Croydon, CR0 4YY

COMPROMISED INTO A SCANDALOUS MARRIAGE

Chapter One

San Pedro de Macorís, 1904

Sebastian Linares had always felt more at home in the sugarcane fields on the outskirts of town than among the ornate masonry houses of San Pedro de Macorís. The only thing he liked about being in the bustling port town, in fact, was the sea-fresh breeze that swept through the buildings, dispelling the heat and disporting itself with hats and hems and tree branches.

The breezes were the furthest thing from Sebastian's mind as he dismounted from his horse and tied it to the hitching post outside the red-and-white building that housed the town's fire brigade. Warm, humid air pressed against his skin, and Sebastian was in the act of reaching into his pocket for a handkerchief with which to mop the rivulets of sweat running down his temples when he noticed a coach rolling to a stop on the opposite side of the street.

The coachman jumped down from his perch and opened the shabby black door to reveal a flash of white fabric, even brighter than Sebastian's freshly laundered handkerchief. A small brown hand appeared out of the darkness of the carriage, and after it followed a wide-brimmed hat that even Sebastian could tell was not fashionable.

And then, like a budding rose unfurling its petals, a woman emerged from the carriage, unbending and straightening as the coachman helped her down. Her white skirts, full over a nipped-in waist, danced slightly in the stifling air when her heels struck the paving stones. Though she wore no beads or jewelry or anything that would catch the light, Sebastian felt as though he'd been dazzled.

He was fairly sure he hadn't made a sound, so it must have been the strength of his gaze that drew the woman's attention. She tilted her head, and when her hat brim moved to reveal her smile, it was as if the sun had broken through the clouds.

Paulina Despradel. She had been a quiet, unobtrusive figure in the background the two times Sebastian had visited the Despradel *quinta* to complete his business dealings with her brother, Antonio.

There was nothing unobtrusive about her now.

It was clear from her expression that she had recognized Sebastian. Belatedly, he doffed his hat and inclined his head in greeting. Her face brightened, and she started across the street, turning to tell her protesting maid, "Surely my brother wouldn't object to my stopping for a neighborly chat."

The hand she extended toward Sebastian was encased in a glove made out of fine netting and ringed at the wrist with a profusion of lace; resisting the urge to linger over it, he squeezed it briefly between both of his own as they both inclined to press their cheeks together.

Sebastian was far from an expert in women's fashions, but even to his untrained eye her frock seemed overly laden with frills and furbelows. A shocking quantity of lace had been employed liberally throughout, frothing each ruffle and flounce and giving the effect that she was being swallowed by fabric.

"Good morning, *vecina*," he said, making sure to use the formal *you* when he added, "It's a pleasure to see you. What brings you to town on such a stifling morning?"

The property Sebastian had bought the year before was far enough away from the Despradels' home that he rarely saw Paulina and her brother. Although he had come across Antonio in the streets of San Pedro a time or two before, this was the first time he had seen Paulina in town.

"I'm on my way to Don Enrique's store to buy some things for a little gathering my brother is hosting tonight in honor of my birthday." The brown skin of her cheeks looked a little flushed, and Sebastian would have thought it was from the heat if her eyes hadn't been shining.

He inclined his head. "My kindest regards to you."

"Thank you, Señor Linares. My apologies for not issuing a formal invitation, but I would love it dearly if you could stop by the house and celebrate with us."

"Please, call me Sebastian," he said and hesitated. Being neighborly was all well and good, but he did have a lot of work left to do at the mill. "As wonderful as that sounds, I'm afraid I won't be able to attend. I was, however, also on my way to Don Enrique's. Shall we walk together?"

"That would be lovely," Paulina said, and they fell into step along the narrow sidewalk, the maid trailing behind them. "I must say, it's so nice knowing that we've neighbors again. Particularly in Villa Consuelo, abandoned as it's been for so long. I'm glad there's finally someone to breathe life into it once again."

"I was hoping to do just that," Sebastian said. The house, at least a hundred years old and built solidly enough to withstand earthquakes and hurricanes, was still empty of furniture, the property as dilapidated as it had been when he'd purchased it almost a year before. He had big plans for it, though. And he'd get to them, soon, maybe, when he wasn't so busy at the mill…

Paulina glanced at him from under the brim of her oversize hat. "How are you liking our little town?"

It took a second for Sebastian to realize that she had taken him for one of the many Cubans who had settled in San Pedro after fleeing the war at home. When he did, he didn't bother to correct her—he *was* recently arrived from Havana, after all, and as far as he was concerned, the less the townspeople knew about his past, the easier a time he would have fitting in among them.

"There's nothing little about it," he replied. "It's grown remarkably in the last few years—or so they tell me."

"Is it anything like Havana?" she asked curiously.

"In some ways." Sebastian had given little thought to the differences between both cites, save for the fact that he'd been part of a happy family in one and of a diminished one in the other. He forced lightness into his tone. "Havana is like an old dowager countess—grand and glamorous and secure of her place in the world. San Pedro is beautiful, to be sure, and growing more prosperous by the day, but it wasn't that long ago that the town was a fishing village."

Her face lit up with a sudden smile. "Can you imagine the conversations they would have if they could meet? The venerable old countess and the little fisherman?"

Sebastian couldn't help echoing her smile at the fanciful thought. He made no response, however, as they had reached the corner.

All six of the tall, thin doors leading to Don Enrique's store were open to let in the light and breeze. Paulina paused in one of the doorways, as if to savor the sight of the neatly arranged shelves and gleaming display cases. Don Enrique dealt in imported wares, and the array of beautifully packaged goods must have captured her imagination.

Sebastian was well aware that this was where he ought to bid her a good day while he continued on about his business. He had half a dozen things to do in town, most of them more important than stopping at Don Enrique's for some candied pineapple for his business partner's widow.

It still stung, thinking of Dilia as a widow. Sebastian glanced again at Paulina's face, as if the wonder in her expression could arrest his sudden onslaught of pain.

"Will you look at those feathers?" she said suddenly, nodding at the counter that held what looked like odds and ends for trimming dresses or hats.

Taking off his Panama hat, Sebastian followed her through the store as she made her way to the counter and pointed at it. The feathers were half as long as his arm and tinted in brilliant jewel tones. "What kind of bird do you think could have produced such things?"

"Not one I'd ever like to meet," he assured her.

To the right, a laugh rose from a trio of young women as they held silk flowers up to their hats. Sebastian couldn't help but notice how Paulina's gaze flew immediately to the trio and lingered, growing wistful. One of the girls glanced over and caught Paulina's eyes; though she gave Paulina a curious smile, none of them came over to say hello. Not acquaintances, then.

"The ribbons are wonderful," Paulina said, half to him and half to the young clerk lounging against the ladder fixed to the shelves. She pointed at one of the spools under the glass of the counter. "Might I have a look at the red one?"

The clerk obliged, and Paulina wound one end of the velvet ribbon around her fingers, rubbing it lightly with her thumb. The scarlet looked festive against the golden brown of her skin.

"That color would look lovely on you." One of the young women had broken away from the rest and was regarding Paulina with a frank, open smile. "I can't wear it myself, but it suits your complexion."

"Do you really think so?" Paulina asked, looking pleased.

"If it's not too forward of me, I concur," Sebastian said. "As a matter of fact, I was just thinking that—"

A hand reached out and clamped around Paulina's wrist. "We won't be needing any ribbons today, thank you."

Antonio Despradel, Paulina's brother, was one of those men who thought their money and their standing in society conferred on them the authority they otherwise lacked. Sebastian had met the man only a handful of times while in the process of purchasing the sugar mill Antonio had inherited. Carlos, Sebastian's business partner, had once remarked that Despradel reminded him of a rooster. Not the fighting kind, but the kind that lorded over the chicken yard, pecking at the hens and puffing out its chest.

It had been an apt comparison.

Without releasing Paulina's arm, Despradel began to stride to the other side of the room, saying, "Heavens, Paulina, sometimes I wonder if you aren't twelve years old. This is why I don't like leaving you on your own, you know. You've scarcely more discipline than a child."

Sebastian was nobody's hero, but neither was he enough of a cad as to let a woman be mistreated in his presence. He reached Paulina and her brother in two long strides, reaching to tap the shorter man's shoulder.

"That's no way to touch a lady," he said when Despradel turned, thin lips parted in surprise.

Sebastian didn't want to fight. Not here, among these luxurious and fragile-looking wares. The best way to avoid that, he'd learned from experience, was to inject the promise of violence into his voice. "In fact, that's no way to touch anyone at all. I'd let go of her if I were you."

Despradel's lips spread into a genial smile, even as his gaze flickered from side to side as if to ascertain if other people were looking at them and how much he could get away with. Sebastian had spoken quietly, but sure enough, almost all of Don Enrique's patrons had stilled in anticipation of a dispute. Silence hung over the store for one long second, then Despradel released his sister's wrist and ostentatiously stepped away, his hands raised.

"No need to get upset," he said with ringing bonhomie. "Just trying to hurry my sister along—we've a lot to do before her party tonight, and she is awfully prone to distraction."

"All the same," Sebastian replied with exaggerated politeness that almost certainly did not match the look in his eyes, "that's no reason to handle a woman so roughly."

The mutual dislike crackling between the two men was broken as Paulina, now freed, swept past them. "I'd just as soon not be handled at all," she said tartly. "Come, Antonio, if you're in such a hurry."

The spectators, realizing there was to be no bloodshed, returned their attention to their shopping.

Sebastian stepped back, letting the menace in his gaze serve as warning to Despradel. The other man responded to it with a smile so insolent that Sebastian felt something inside him snap.

Despradel's eyes widened at whatever he saw in Sebastian's eyes, but all Sebastian did was brush past him on his way to his sister.

"Paulina?" he said when he reached her. "I've changed my mind—I should be pleased to attend your party."

"Tío Sebas!"

Few things in Sebastian's life were as gratifying as the enthusiasm with which the four little boys greeted him as he approached the elegant pink house at the end of the street.

They'd been tossing the ball around in front of the house, but at Sebastian's arrival the boys, whose ages ranged from twelve to a tender four, clustered around Sebastian. Experience had taught them to look in Sebastian's pockets for treats; he let out a bark of laughter as eight eager little hands dug into his pockets with more enthusiasm than finesse—to the detriment of the sturdy black fabric of the suit he usually wore into town. It took them mere seconds to extract the marbles and *pilones* he'd bought at Don Enrique's, and he knew that it would take even less time for them to finish off the red sucking candy shaped like miniature mortars and pestles.

It was a heartening—and welcome—change from the wariness with which the boys had regarded Sebastian since the day he'd ridden into town with news of their father's collapse at the mill. David, the youngest and Sebastian's godson, had acquired a most disturbing habit of bursting into tears whenever he saw Sebastian, as if he was a herald of death, come to announce the passing of another loved one.

"Tío Sebas, will you take us to look at the *corriente*?"

asked David, who already sported a red border around his mouth to match his flushed cheeks.

The current? "Erm, what?"

"He wants to go see the workmen who are putting up the posts for the electrical wiring," José, the oldest, explained. "Mamá said it's dangerous to be around the men while they're working, but she won't mind if you take us."

Sebastian must have walked past them, but he'd been so intent on Paulina that he hadn't even noticed them. He laid a hand on José's curly head. "I'm afraid I can't today—I've some business with your mother. Is she home?"

"She's inside," David piped in. "Trying not to melt from the heat because these damn people think everyone should dress like they're in Europe instead of on a damn tropical island."

That sounded like Dilia, all right.

"I see." Sebastian managed to say it gravely, though it took plenty of effort to hide his smile. "Will you go and ask if I can come in? I wouldn't want to intrude if she's, ah, not dressed as a European."

David scampered up the steps. Sebastian leaned against the slim white columns that supported the arched porch and watched the other boys as they played with their new marbles.

A peal of laughter from inside the house let him know that David had delivered his message. "Come in, compadre," Dilia called, poking her head out of an upstairs window.

It was cooler inside the house, though not by much. Dilia was sitting so close to the window, it was debatable whether she was inside the house or out. She was indeed fully and very properly dressed, in a black skirt and a high-necked shirtwaist. The painted fan in her hand was her only concession to the heat, though her gray-streaked curls were plastered to her temples.

"Hot, isn't it?" he said as he dropped a kiss on her cheek and the box of candied pineapple on her lap before taking the seat opposite hers. The mahogany armchair with its embroidered cushion had once graced the parlor of her Havana house, and the familiar sight never failed to make Sebastian feel a little wistful for old times. "Feels like it'll storm today."

"I don't doubt it," Dilia said, setting her needlework on the round table next to her. "I sent for some ice water. Will you stay for a cup of coffee?"

"Don't go to any trouble on my account." Sebastian set his Panama hat on his knee. "I've got to get back to the mill. I only came into town to make a deposit into your account. There should be enough in there to carry you through the next couple of months."

"That's right." Dilia's grin might have made her eyes sparkle, but it filled Sebastian with apprehension. "Why waste your time having coffee with old widow women when you could be strolling with pretty girls? I saw you walking with the Despradel girl earlier."

He gave a brief nod. "She invited me to a party she's having tonight."

"And you accepted? Well, well…" Dilia's right eyebrow arched.

Sebastian shrugged. "It would have been rude to decline the invitation."

"That's never stopped you before," Dilia observed. "Oh, don't get me wrong—I think it's perfectly delightful that you're finally getting acquainted with your neighbors. I'm just surprised that you consented to a party. You act as if you took a blood oath to spend all your time at the mill, you know."

Antonio Despradel had driven the mill to ruin through mismanagement. It had only been with great effort that Sebastian and Carlos had been able to turn a profit in the first year—and there was still so much to be done. He lay awake at night thinking of it more often than not. It wasn't only that Carlos had invested his entire fortune in modernizing the mill to Sebastian's exacting specifications—a fortune that would have been at Dilia's disposal if it weren't for the labor-saving but ruinously expensive cane-processing machinery Sebastian had been convinced he needed to turn the mill around. No, it was the people who weighed on Sebastian's shoulders. The workers at the mill, most of whom had mouths to feed. Carlos's family. All the people who depended on Sebastian's ability to eke out enough of a profit from a crowded market.

"I have an obligation to you and the children" was all that Sebastian said.

"Yes, and where will we be if you work yourself to death?" Dilia snapped her fan shut and struck Sebastian lightly on the arm with it. "You are barely twenty-five years old, Sebastian, with no family of your own. Talk to pretty girls. Go to parties. Heaven knows you deserve to enjoy your life."

"What I deserve is to enjoy this delightful ice water without having to fend off an arranged marriage," Sebastian said, smiling at Dilia's enthusiasm. "Save the matchmaking for someone else, my friend. The last thing *I* need is a wife."

Chapter Two

The scent of the ocean, so strong in the center of town, receded sharply as the Despradel carriage sped inland. At Paulina's feet were the numerous parcels Antonio had acquired for her party—his preferred brand of champagne, as well as the imported nuts and dried fruits that he favored. On the seat opposite hers, her brother scowled at the correspondence he had picked up at the post office while she'd been speaking with Sebastian.

Absently, Paulina rubbed her sore wrist. Her brother's grip had left a mark just above the lace that edged her detestably frilly gloves. She would have preferred much simpler ones, but Antonio purchased all her clothes, as he had since she was a child, and he insisted on as great a quantity of frills and furbelows, as if to communicate to anyone who saw her that the Despradel family's coffers were as full as they'd ever been. The more dire their financial situation became, the more lace sprouted on Paulina's clothes. It was the same twist of logic that had made him spend a ruinous amount in Don Enrique's store, though it had only added to their already massive debts.

"Have you ever thought about selling the *quinta* and buying a house in town?" she asked her brother. "Particularly now that it's being wired for electricity. Just think, not having to go to the bother of filling oil lamps and—"

Antonio glanced at her over the papers in his hand. "Trust a woman to put her petty conveniences over a centuries-long legacy," he remarked. His eyebrow quirked in the way it always did when he was about to say something sarcastic or mocking, and Paulina immediately regretted her remark. "By all means, let us abandon our ancestral home and lands just so you won't have to go to the bother of filling a lamp or two."

Paulina didn't bother to point out that Antonio hadn't bothered to hold on to the rest of their inheritance— namely, the money left behind by their parents as well as the sugar mill that had been built by their father when he converted what used to be pastureland for the family's cattle ranch into sugarcane fields. The Despradels' fierce opposition to the use of enslaved people for the hard labor required by the sugarcane industry was one part of her family's legacy she could be proud of.

She tugged again at the lace bordering her gloves and started when it tore away from the white netting. She glanced up quickly to see whether Antonio had noticed and was surprised to see that he had not gone back to his correspondence but was watching her through narrowed eyes.

"Are you carrying on with Sebastian Linares?"

Paulina blinked at the sudden change in subject. "Carrying on? Of course not. Why would you say such a thing?"

"Why wouldn't I, after seeing how you were simpering over him at Don Enrique's?"

"I was only inviting him to my party tonight. It's about time we got acquainted with our only neighbor. He's lived there for an entire year and we've never made any social overtures—I didn't want him to think we're ill-mannered recluses. In any case," she added, "he might not come."

Sebastian hadn't seemed particularly inclined to when she'd issued the invitation, and though he'd accepted it firmly enough after the altercation with Antonio, Paulina knew better than to get her hopes up. It had been months since she'd gone into town, and longer still since a handsome young man had paid her any attention. That Sebastian Linares had any interest in furthering their acquaintance beyond the strictly neighborly seemed like a schoolgirl dream.

Still, she couldn't deny that the prospect of seeing him again was making her heartbeat quicken.

Antonio's lip curled disdainfully. "I don't know if I care to associate with someone like that—and I won't have you doing it, either."

Paulina knew better than to argue with her brother when he was in one of his moods, but she couldn't help asking, "Like what?"

"Can you really be so naive? You're twenty-one years old, Paulina. It's time you learned a little about life." Carelessly crumpling the letter in his hand, Antonio leaned forward. "Sebastian Linares is not our social equal. In fact, I have every reason to believe he's been lying to conceal the fact that he's of inferior birth. None of the respectable Cubans who've come over have heard of him. Nobody knows who his people are."

It might have been naive of Paulina, but she could scarcely understand why it mattered. Even from their short acquaintance, it was clear that Sebastian Linares was a much better man than her brother, for all his proud lineage, could ever be.

Antonio had gone back to his correspondence without waiting for or likely even expecting a response from

Paulina. She turned her head to look at the sugarcane fields speeding past.

The rest of the morning passed nearly as fast, what with all the preparations for this evening's festivities. Changing out of her one good frock and into her thin, shabby everyday dress, Paulina arranged flowers in vases, nailed bunches of greenery over the missing paintings in the parlor and helped polish the few remaining pieces of silver. She'd been barely seven years old when her parents died, but she remembered clearly the bustling excitement that used to permeate the rambling old house whenever her parents held one of their frequent parties. They had plenty of servants then, almost a dozen of them, all kinder and more energetic than the pinched-face maid and sullen man-of-all-work her brother employed. Even so, her mother would always plunge elbows-deep into whatever needed to be done.

"The preparations are half the fun of a party," she would tell Paulina as she arranged Castilian roses in a cut-glass vase.

It wasn't all that long ago that the Despradels' *quinta* had rung with cheer and music, but one wouldn't know it to look at the dingy chintz on the upholstered chairs or the scuff marks on the once-polished mahogany tables. Even the wicker and rattan chairs she had lined up along the house's back veranda looked the worse for wear. Paulina was grateful for the lush green landscape beyond the veranda, which the guests would face while sitting. It was much more beautiful than any of the paintings Antonio had sold over the years.

In the parlor, through which the guests would pass on their way to the veranda, the flowered wallpaper had proven no match for the tropical humidity; great patches of it had begun to peel away from the walls. Paulina sur-

veyed it critically and decided that it wouldn't be noticeable once the afternoon light began to fade.

The fact that she was wearing the same dress as that
morning, however, *was* unfortunately noticeable. The
high neckline was unfashionable for evening wear—it
had been ages since Paulina had attended any parties,
but she knew that much. No matter. The house was clean,
there were fresh flowers in her hair and Sebastian Linares had promised to come. Paulina could hardly ask
for anything more.

Except perhaps for clear skies.

Smoothing down one of the many ruffles that be-
sieged her dress, Paulina seated herself on the veranda
and peered up worriedly at the overcast sky. No one
would come if it looked like it was about to storm—the
roads out here weren't paved, and carriage wheels didn't
take kindly to mud.

The first guests began to trickle in before Paulina
could work herself into too much of a state over the in-
clement weather. Antonio emerged from his chamber
before long, freshly bathed, his hair slicked back with
oil, and set about performing his duties as host. He could
be quite charming when he wanted to, and before long
the elderly Garcia sisters, all spinsters, were simpering
over his outrageous compliments.

Having never been to a proper school—because Antonio didn't believe in educating women—Paulina hadn't
any friends her own age. Most of the guests at the party
were friends of the family, acquaintances who remembered her parents fondly and wished to pay their respects.
Paulina didn't care. She'd been looking forward to this
party for weeks, and she didn't intend to let anything
spoil her enjoyment—not even being cornered by Tío
Ramon, her grandmother's second cousin, who spent a

quarter of an hour describing in exacting detail the flock of parrots that seemed to have settled into the mango and cashew trees on his property.

"It's a splendid cacophony," he said. "You ought to come see them the next time you're in town."

After what had happened earlier that day, Paulina was sure it would be a long time before Antonio allowed her to leave the *quinta*. "I certainly will," she told Tío Ramon.

He wasn't appeased by her comment. "You should be going into town more often, my girl. A pretty girl like you ought to have friends and beaus and liveliness. You'll end up an old maid if Antonio continues to keep you out here all the time."

It might have been true, but Paulina couldn't help but feel a flash of irritation. Here was another relative—another man—dictating what she needed rather than taking the time to ask her what she wanted. In any case, Tío Ramon was wrong in one respect. She was not a girl. As of today, she was twenty-one years old and long past the age at which women gave up dances and beaux for housekeeping and babies.

As she had been trained to do, Paulina hid her irritation with a smile. "Oh, I couldn't possibly be married right now," she said lightly. "What would Antonio do without me to keep house for him?"

"Hire a housekeeper," Tío Ramon replied dryly.

Antonio wouldn't, even if he could afford one. Paulina's brother might not be a shrewd businessman, but even he knew the value of the free labor she provided him. She had no intention of being his unpaid housekeeper forever, but finding the means to leave had proved to be difficult enough when even Antonio could scarcely lay his hands on enough pesos to keep the household supplied with lamp oil.

Clasping a glass of champagne by its delicate stem, Paulina drifted from one sparse group to the other. The conversation around her wasn't especially thrilling, but she soaked it in just the same, feeling a curious fluttering in her stomach whenever there was a flash of motion at the corner of her eye.

It was only when she saw him standing in the doorway that she realized she'd been waiting for Sebastian Linares.

He shouldn't have come.

Sebastian stood at the open door to the Despradels' *quinta*, trying his hardest to keep from running down the long list of reasons why he should stay away from that house—the main one being that he had far too many troubles of his own to borrow someone else's.

He couldn't say what it was that finally compelled him to cross the threshold and venture inside. The expression on Paulina's face when her brother had grabbed her by the wrist, perhaps. The long sweep of her eyelashes as she'd studied the ribbon. The sensation that had crackled through his limbs like an electrical current the instant she'd lifted up her gaze to his and curved her lush lips into a smile.

It was hard to say.

Although similar in construction, the Despradels' *quinta* looked nothing like his own empty house, stuffed as it was with what looked like a hundred years' worth of furniture and pictures, all exhibiting the sort of shabby elegance that came with generations of wealth. For all they were clearly expensive, the velvet drapes and chintz-covered chairs had faded with time; against their pale tones and that of the papered walls, the large oil painting hanging from the far wall stood out in marked contrast. Seated in front of rich green draperies, a dark-haired man and a woman who shared Paulina's snapping dark eyes gazed solemnly back at Sebastian.

With no servants to show him the way, Sebastian followed the sound of voices past the parlor and into a terrace where far fewer people than he'd expected sat on chairs lined up against the wall. There was no music. Antonio and a handful of other men had gathered in a corner of the terrace in what looked like a card game, and their exclamations pierced the low buzz of conversation. All five of the men gathered around the card table looked like disreputable rogues, despite the fact that two of them were dressed in the navy blue uniforms of the civil guard. Odd though it seemed to Sebastian for those roughs to be among those invited to a party celebrating a lady, it wasn't any of his business whom Antonio Despradel chose to associate with.

It wouldn't have been difficult to pick out Paulina even if the terrace had been ten times more crowded. The sky had grown dark with clouds, and the tangled foliage beyond the terrace waved ominously in the breeze. In the white dress she had worn that morning, Paulina was a bright spot against the gloom as she bent slightly to allow an older woman to whisper something in her ear.

When she caught sight of Sebastian hovering in the doorway, her smile was so bright that he once again had the momentary impression of a shaft of sunlight breaking through the clouds.

"You came," she said, pressing his hand between both of her own. Sebastian couldn't help noticing how slender her fingers were when compared to his large, sundarkened hand.

"I can't stay long." Sebastian slid his hand into the pocket of his trousers and clenched it, hardly knowing whether he wanted to erase or preserve the memory of her light touch. His fingers brushed against something soft. "I only came to give you this."

The ribbon, when he extracted it from his pocket, lay curled and limp on his palm. Sebastian suddenly felt foolish. Making sure that Paulina hadn't been further mistreated by her brother had seemed like a noble enough reason for coming to her party, but standing here in front of her, holding out his pitiable excuse for a birthday present, he had to admit to himself that there was nothing noble about why he'd come. He wanted to see her again, plain and simple. Firm as he was in his belief that he did not want or need a wife, it clearly did not prevent him from acting like a love-struck fool.

"Thank you," Paulina said, her fingertips brushing Sebastian's palm as she wound the ribbon around two of her slim fingers. To his surprise, she sounded genuinely happy over his paltry gift. "It really is a beautiful color."

As if on impulse, she swiftly wove the ribbon into her hair and tied it into a bow, smiling at Sebastian as she did. "Will you stay for a glass of champagne?"

Sebastian had done a lot of difficult things in his life, but saying no to a beautiful woman was not one of them. He assented and a few moments later found himself seated at the far end of the terrace and being peered at by half the guests. Having been subjected to many of those curious glances since his return—mostly from young ladies and their matchmaking mothers—Sebastian had made a point of rejecting all the overtures that followed. It wasn't only, as he'd told Dilia, that he had too many burdens weighing down his shoulders to saddle himself with a wife. Sebastian was fairly sure that his chance of being recognized by these members of San Pedro society was slim, but he couldn't risk it. Not quite yet.

Turning away from the curious gazes, he nodded toward the garden stretching beyond the terrace's balustrade. It was encircled by a stone wall and bordered with bougainvillea hedges. The red flowers stood out against the glossy dark leaves, the same shade as Paulina's ribbon. "What beautiful gardens," he said politely. "I would ask you to take a stroll down there, but it would feel a bit like being put on display."

Paulina perched on the edge of the chair next to his, as skittish as the little brown birds that sometimes ventured through his open window. "They can be awful gossips, I know. Particularly— Well, it sounds conceited to say it, but I know many of them are curious about me. I don't blame them, you know. I suppose I *am* something of a curious specimen."

"Are you?"

"I feel like it sometimes. I'm sure you've been in town long enough to hear the whispers—how the Despradel girl was allowed to grow wild out here. How I've spent most of my life roaming barefoot in the sugarcane fields instead of learning about Cervantes and how to embroider flowers with other girls."

"It doesn't sound like a terrible way to grow up."

"A trifle lonely, perhaps," she admitted. "Particularly…"

"After your parents passed?" Sebastian supplied. "I've heard about their legendary house parties."

"What I remember of them was wonderful, but most of their guests had no use for little girls such as myself. I was always told to run along and play." She captured her lower lip between her teeth for a second. "There was a little boy. His mother was a washerwoman who came to the *quinta* once a week to help with the laundry. He made a few cents running errands or performing small tasks, but mostly…mostly he played with me. He taught me how to suck the nectar from *coralillo* stems and captured the prettiest green lizards for me to pet." Her lower lip, slightly reddened from her teeth, stretched into a smile. "Very few people have taken the time to know me as he did."

Sebastian took a slow sip of champagne, careful to keep his gaze on the bubbles breaking on the surface of the liquid. "Did something happen to the boy?"

"I don't know," Paulina said, and he heard the frustration in her voice. "His mother died shortly after my parents, and he was taken away by relatives, I think. I never was able to find out much about what became of him, though I asked everyone I could."

"I'm sorry."

"So am I," she said. "Sometimes I wonder what would have become of me if he'd stayed. I have no reason to believe anything would be different, save for… Well, I did always feel braver whenever he was beside me. Stronger, too. A foolish notion, perhaps, to think that a child could have changed the course of my life, but…"

"It isn't foolish," Sebastian said, thinking that Carlos had been a child himself when he'd taken Sebastian under his wing, back in Havana. "Having someone to stand shoulder to shoulder with can make all the difference in the world. It's a shame that was taken away from you."

"I still hold out hope that I might have it someday."

Sebastian found himself wanting that for her, as well, and not only for her sake—whoever found his place beside her was sure to benefit from the quiet strength running through her like a vein of gold. He wasn't given to impulsive gestures, but if he had been, he would have surely reached over to clasp her hand in his own. Not only to offer her comfort, but because her disarming honesty felt too raw in the face of all he couldn't tell her.

Sebastian glanced away, and his gaze fell on the card table where Antonio still sat. Paulina's brother was staring at them, his thick brows knitted in speculation. There was nothing explicitly menacing about the look, but it made Sebastian's blood run cold with unease.

A distant rumble of thunder interrupted his next words. As if the sound had been a signal, Paulina's guests rose from their chairs and began to take their leave, a process that usually took hours but was accomplished in mere minutes under the threat of incipient rain. Wineglasses were set down, used napkins set aside, cigars snuffed out, and the guests began to surge around Paulina.

Sebastian hesitated, knowing he should stay and say a proper goodbye. But he had never been any good at goodbyes, and in any case, it wasn't as though he had anything more to say.

He had come to make sure she was all right. That was all.

The first drops were beginning to dot the dirt path, joining the deep ruts left behind by carriage wheels. Sebastian unhitched his horse and was swinging himself over the saddle as the partygoers started to pour out through the doors without bothering to linger over conversations. A heavy drop landed on his shoulder as if in warning, but he nonetheless paused and glanced back at the house. Paulina was still standing in front of the open door, the endless ruffles on her dress fluttering in the rising wind. Her slim brown hand was raised in a wave as her guests rushed for their respective carriages, and although they were separated by the bustle, it felt like she was looking straight at him.

Chapter Three

Antonio had had too much to drink.

The warm glow that had kindled inside Paulina's chest during her conversation with Sebastian was extinguished the second she returned to the veranda to begin cleaning up the detritus from the party. It took a single glance at the expression on her brother's face to know that she should remove herself from his presence. Antonio didn't drink often, but when he did, he didn't fly into rages—his sarcastic tones grew cold and hard, and he would start in on Paulina, taking her to task over any perceived infraction or defect of character.

In the time it had taken for Paulina to close and bolt the front door, the skies had broken open. Heavy rain battered the tiles on the terrace roof, so loudly that she almost didn't hear Antonio speak from the corner where he sat lounging on a rocking chair, a hand cupped around a snifter of his usual expensive brandy.

"I thought I warned you to keep away from that man," Antonio was saying. His tie was slightly crooked, as if he had started to loosen it. "Do you know what you looked like, panting over him?"

The maid seemed to have vanished—gone to bed,

most likely. The servants' quarters were in an outbuilding by the kitchen, cut off from the rest of the house by the curtains of rain streaming down and far enough away that she wouldn't hear if Paulina called for her help with the dishes. Not that she was likely to come out in the rain.

"It was positively indecent," Antonio said. "I was embarrassed for you, and so was everyone who noticed."

"What are you talking about?" Paulina asked, though she had an idea of whom her brother meant.

"Sebastian Linares." Their neighbor's name roiled out of Antonio's mouth, charged with loathing.

The napkins would stain if they weren't soaked overnight, but the washing up could wait until the next day. Paulina emptied wineglasses over the railing, placing them on a serving tray to be taken to the kitchen in the morning. "It was a party," she said wearily, though she knew he was in no state to be reasoned with. "I won't ask him again if you don't wish me to, but I could hardly turn him away at the door."

"You wouldn't turn him away from your bed, either."

"Antonio, what on earth has gotten into you?" Paulina recoiled in shock. "You're acting as if I—as if I—"

"Look at you, pretending to be virginal when half the town just saw you making a fool of yourself over that man. I wouldn't be surprised if you'd—"

"I'm going to bed," Paulina said loudly in an attempt to drown out her brother's vulgarity. Though he always enjoyed making sure she was aware of her faults, Antonio had never spoken to her with such ugliness. She wiped her hands with a clean napkin and, despite the apprehension shooting through her chest, did her best to sound commanding. "I hope you'll be more civil in the morning."

She was halfway to the nearest door when Antonio stepped into her path.

His bloodshot eyes glared down at her, and Paulina fought the urge to turn her head when confronted with the full impact of his breath, strong enough to overpower even the scent of rain-drenched earth. "You're a disgrace to our family," he said. "Our parents would be ashamed to see you carrying on like a common tramp. You couldn't turn him away at the door? You had better hope he feels the same about you."

Paulina's throat tightened as, for the second time that day, Antonio's fingers bit into the soft flesh of her forearm.

Was it her imagination or did she see a flicker of amusement in his eyes?

Before she could decide either way, Antonio began dragging her into the house.

"What are you doing?" she protested. "Let go of me— *Antonio!*"

He paused, and Paulina hardly had time to register relief before realizing that he had opened the front door. A moment later, Paulina felt herself being pulled into the lashing rain.

Half bewildered at this development, she stopped struggling and simply stared at her brother. Surely he didn't mean to— Surely he wouldn't—

She couldn't seem to catch her breath. Her chest strained against her corset, and the water beating against her face made her feel as though she were drowning.

One-handed, he pulled open the iron gate at the end of the path and hauled her through. It wasn't until the gate clanged shut and she saw him turn the key in the lock that she realized what her brother was doing—and by then it was too late.

"Antonio!" she screamed as he turned back toward the house, but the rain and wind swallowed the sound.

A numb sort of shock was starting to settle over her as she stared at the locked gate. There was no question of trying to walk all the way to town, not in the middle of a storm and with darkness about to blanket the fields surrounding her. Sebastian. She would go to Sebastian.

Evening was starting to fall, but the sky was white with clouds, and there was just enough light for Paulina to see the path before her. The hard-packed dirt, rutted from carriage wheels, had softened into mud. She could feel it sucking at her heeled shoes with every step she took. The tooled leather would be ruined—but then, so would she.

A flash of lightning crackled just ahead of her, lighting the path with startling clarity. Paulina had a moment to make out broken branches and fallen palm fronds before the world was plunged back into darkness.

Paulina didn't waste time screaming. Seizing handfuls of fabric, she raised her skirt as best as she could and ran the rest of the way to Sebastian's house.

Villa Consuelo was smaller and more run-down than the Despradel home. She'd explored its outbuildings as a child, and though she hadn't ventured that way in years, Paulina's feet still remembered the way.

The lantern by the door was still burning, protected from the driving rain by a rather ramshackle overhang. Though it did not illuminate much more than the weather-beaten door, its glow was a welcome sight. She stumbled up the slick, muddy steps, heaving one breath after another as she reached the relative safety of the overhang.

Briefly, she considered waiting for daylight out here, but a sudden cascade of water from the leaky wooden structure disabused her of that notion. She grasped the iron knocker and let it fall several times against the solid wood of the door, then wrapped her arms around herself, feeling the rivulets run down her ribs as she squeezed the sodden fabric of her bodice. Her voluminous skirts were too soaked to billow in the wind, but Paulina felt something cold slap against the side of her face—her new ribbon. Pulling it out of her snarled hair, she shoved it into her pocket.

A few moments passed before the door was flung open and Sebastian appeared in the doorway. It hadn't been all that long since he'd left the Despradels', but in the intervening time he had been divested of half his clothing. The upper half, Paulina couldn't help but note as the light from the swaying lantern fell on the sharply defined muscles of his arms.

"Pardon the hour," she said absurdly, as if this were a social call.

To say that Sebastian looked surprised would have been an understatement. "Paulina? Are you all right? Did you walk all the way here?"

"I— That is, my brother—" Paulina bit her lip to hold back the sob threatening to burst out. "Yours is the only house near here, and I—"

"I see," Sebastian said, though he couldn't have at all, because Paulina found herself unable to choke out any more words. His expression was inscrutable even as it was illuminated by another flash of lightning. "I would take you somewhere more suitable, but I haven't a coach, and it's not a night to be out on horseback. Why don't you come inside and get dry?"

The parlor he led her to could hardly be called that— the walls were covered in paper and a brass lamp hung from the wooden beams crisscrossing the ceiling, but that was it as far as furnishings were concerned. The pattern on the tile floor stretched unbroken from the entrance to the shuttered arches set into the far wall.

"You'll need towels and a change of clothing," Sebastian was saying. "My housekeeper has gone to visit her daughter, but I can go fetch some—"

"I'm sorry to be so much trouble," Paulina said and, to her horror, burst into tears.

She buried her face in her hands to spare him the sight. To her surprise, she felt herself being drawn against a warm, solid chest.

He smelled faintly of rum, which her brother never drank because he claimed it was common. The spicy scent was underlaid by the sweet, earthy smell of her childhood, the same one that clung to her father's lapels when he came home from a long day at the sugar mill. Paulina found it steadying. She gave a loud sniff and straightened away from the warmth of Sebastian's chest.

"It'll be all right," she said, and she was pleased to hear that her voice didn't waver too badly. Neither did her fingers tremble when she accepted the handkerchief he held out and used it to wipe her face clean of tears and rainwater. "When he sobers up in the morning, he'll realize that I've done nothing wrong and take me back in."

"Do you *want* to go back?" There was something unbalancing about his penetrating gaze. Rather than make Paulina want to shrink into herself, under his gaze she felt the need to stand up a little straighter.

"I— Well, it isn't as though I've got a choice," she said. "I haven't any money or relations, really, or…friends."

"I'm your friend," Sebastian said, so firmly that Paulina's knees felt a trifle hollow. "And I've money if you want it. Enough to get you to New York or Madrid or Paris—or even Constantinople if that's what it will take to get you away from that goddamned brother of yours. So I'll ask you again. Do you *want* to go back?"

The trembling in Paulina's knees seemed to have traveled upward. She felt almost dizzy as she contemplated the fact that, for the first time in her life, she might be able to do as she pleased. The notion felt thrilling—and slightly dangerous.

The shock was beginning to clear, and Paulina was able to remember the hardness in her brother's voice when he'd mentioned Sebastian's name. That Antonio had taken a dislike to this man was more than clear. Why was another question altogether. Surely he would have to know that she would seek refuge with Sebastian on a night when walking into town would be near impossible. Why would he cast her out if by doing so he was all but driving her into Sebastian's home?

"No." She lifted her chin. "I never want to go back there again."

"Then you won't," Sebastian said with a little shrug, as if it really would be as easy as that. He turned away, saying over his shoulder, "My apologies for the lack of furniture. I'm afraid I've been so busy at the mill I haven't been able to find the time for getting the house in order."

The parlor was not in fact as empty as it had seemed at first glance—an ancient cushion lay on the tile next to an overturned crate, which held a bottle full of water, a small cask of rum and an enamel mug. A single oil lamp sat on the floor beside the crate, its flickering light casting dancing shadows on a covered plate.

Crouching in one fluid movement, Sebastian poured some of the aromatic brown liquid into the mug and gestured at her to take a seat on the cushion. "Here," he said, handing her the mug. "You could probably use some fortification right now. Have some water, too, or your head will ache like the devil in the morning."

Paulina pressed the cool enamel to her lips and inhaled deeply before taking a tiny sip. "I'm sorry for interrupting your evening," she began, feeling the rum swirl down her chest and settle low in her belly.

"You're not interrupting anything," Sebastian replied swiftly. "I would have been at the mill right now if it weren't for the storm, and since I'm not, all I've been able to do is sit here and think about all the sugarcane that's being ruined by the rain or scorched by lightning. Nobody told me that the life of a sugar mill owner held all the worries of a farmer and a merchant put together." He gave her a crooked smile. "I welcome any distractions."

"Well, I'm happy to provide one. A most dramatic one, at that." She cocked her head. "Do you often go to the mill at night?"

The covered plate on the floor held several half circles of fried dough. Sebastian held it toward her, and though her first instinct was to demur politely, the first whiff of fried dough and beef had her almost snatching at the plate. Only the fact that Sebastian had begun to talk kept her from closing her eyes to savor the first blissful bite.

"I can't seem to stay away," he said ruefully. "The machinery we installed requires constant attention, and I'm the only one who knows how to coax it into working correctly. I studied engineering in Havana, and I find machinery easy to understand, but the bookkeeping is another matter." He shook his head. "We've half a dozen ledgers, and I've found that they're liable to get into a snarl if I don't pore over them day and night. And with my partner gone…"

"Oh, yes," she said, swallowing and wiping her greasy

fingers on her skirt. "I did hear about the passing of your partner. That must have been devastating."

"He was my brother," Sebastian said quietly. Having caught sight of her surreptitious gesture, he dug into his pocket and offered her his handkerchief again. "He believed in me like no one else ever has, and I refuse to fail him."

"You won't." Paulina wiped her fingers clean and impulsively laid a hand on his bare arm. Wiry hairs brushed against her palm as she squeezed his arm gently, the sensation as intoxicating as the rum coiling through her belly.

Several droplets fell from her sodden sleeve to join the rivulets pooling on the tile around her dirty skirts. The pool had expanded slowly, and Paulina realized that the water must have been seeping through Sebastian's trousers for a while.

"Oh, but I've made you all wet," she exclaimed as Sebastian jolted to his feet.

"I'll get you a towel," he said, "and something dry to wear."

He returned in a few minutes, his expression so calm it was almost blank, carrying a stack of linens in one hand and a basin full of water in the other. "I seem to have run out of clean shirts, but I've enough towels and sheets to drape the new fire station. I don't imagine there's anything respectable about it, but at least you'll be decently covered until we can get you a new dress."

A new dress—and a new life. Paulina let out a breath.

"I'll step into the other room while you wash."

Paulina thanked him and waited until the door had closed firmly behind him to look down at herself. The water in the basin would not be nearly enough to do away with all the mud and broken leaves coating her feet and legs, though the worst of it would probably come off with her stockings. She needed a full bath—longed for it, really—but for the moment she would settle for wiping off the muck.

She set the linens down, and as her hands rose to unfasten her clothing, she remembered that unlike the plain cotton dresses she wore for everyday, this lavishly ruffled frock was held closed at the back by a dozen minuscule mother-of-pearl buttons traveling from the nape of her neck to the small of her back, all of which had been fastened by the sour-faced maid. Her stomach sank as her fingers met the limp flounces at her chest. There was no housekeeper here, and no maid.

She would have to ask Sebastian for help.

The rest of the house was dark, but the flickering glow of a second lamp guided Paulina through an open door at the side of the house. She stepped out onto a colonnaded terrace and had no trouble locating Sebastian even in the dim light. Facing the howling storm underneath one of the brick-bordered arches, he stood unflinching as a violent wind ripped fronds from the cluster of royal palms several feet away.

A sudden flash of lightning illuminated the rippling muscles of his back, the deep indentation just above the waistband of his trousers and the pale, fluttering cloth he held in a tight grip. Hungrily, she drank in the sight of his broad shoulders, set against the punishing breeze. There was something dashing about him even in relative stillness—a certain grace and strength in the way he performed even the most mundane tasks.

The white thing in his hand was a shirt. He pulled it over his broad shoulders and made short work of the buttons, then turned around—and caught Paulina staring at him.

"Did you need something else?" Sebastian asked.

"Oh, I—I need help with my buttons. And my—well, my laces." She tried to say it matter-of-factly—what room was there for blushing hesitancy after all that had happened?—but Paulina was aware of the embarrassment coloring her voice.

Sebastian nodded, and she turned her back to him, touching the place where the lace on her dress met her neck to indicate the row of buttons. Having just seen him doing up his own, it didn't surprise her that his fingers were as nimble as they were gentle and as warm as his chest had been. His knuckles brushed her sensitive skin, and to distract herself from the sensation, she asked the first thing that popped into her head.

"Do you not hate it? Living out here alone?"

"It's peaceful enough," he said after a brief pause. "And close to the mill."

"I've always dreamed of living in town," she confessed. "In one of those houses by the square, with a great balcony from which I could look at the couples strolling in the park and businessmen hurrying to the bank."

"We lived in town in Havana. On a busy street, not far from the cathedral. Carlos and I liked to sit out on the balcony and smoke cigars and drop coins and sweets to the street urchins down below. Then Carlos convinced me to rig an elaborate pulley system with two buckets, and he and Dilia, his wife, had great fun sending down all sorts of things." His soft laugh danced like a gust of wind over her exposed shoulder blades. "Dilia had gotten it into her head that she needed to practice her embroidery before having children of her own and sent down many a fancifully decorated suit of clothes. Those must have been the most colorfully dressed urchins in all of Havana."

She could tell when he reached the end of the buttons, because his fingers grazed the linen covering her bottom. Her undergarments were worn almost through, as Antonio only cared to spend money where it would be seen. Despite the warmth of the evening, Paulina felt her flesh pebbling.

She must have made a small noise, because his fingers stilled.

"My apologies. I think the laces are too wet to untangle—the knot is proving beyond my abilities."

"You'll have to cut it, unfortunately." Paulina craned her neck. "Have you a knife handy?"

Most men of her acquaintance—what few men she knew—carried knives on their person. Sebastian was no different, though she'd interrupted him in a state of dishabille. Paulina heard his noise of assent, then felt her laces being pulled tighter.

Abruptly loosened, both corset and dress sagged around Paulina. Her hands shot up reflexively to clasp the wet fabric to her bosom. A properly brought up young lady would surely scurry away at once at this breach in modesty. If there had been anything proper about her upbringing, perhaps Paulina would have done so instead of turning to thank Sebastian.

She was close enough for her filthy skirts to swish over his bare feet and brush the knees of his trousers, close enough that she couldn't fail to see the gleam in his dark eyes. Over the sound of the rain, she heard him draw in one deep, ragged breath.

The lantern hanging from a nail by the door was swinging wildly; even the glass cover around the flame couldn't keep it from going almost horizontal in the wind. It may have been the light, but Paulina was sure that what she saw in Sebastian's eyes was desire.

The skin of Paulina's back still sang with the memory of his touch. Every fiber in her body longed desperately for more—more, Paulina suspected, than she had any right to want.

Sebastian squeezed his eyes shut. When he opened them again, it was to give her a smile, even as he stepped away from her. "There," he said lightly. "You're done. I'll wait here until you've had a chance to wash."

She'd been holding her breath. Paulina let it out slowly as she gave a nod. This was an honorable man, who would commit no improprieties while she was under his roof. It was no cause for disappointment, but nonetheless Paulina felt her loneliness follow her back into the house.

Chapter Four

Sunlight pressed against Sebastian's closed eyelids. He had never been in the habit of sleeping in, and it was the brightness of the light that alerted him to the fact that he had done just that.

His eyes blinked open, and he found himself looking not at the whitewashed ceiling of his bedroom, but at the sturdy wooden beams that held up the ceiling of his parlor. The bare tile was uncommonly comfortable. Only... the softness was all down his side, not underneath him.

All the events of the previous night flooded Sebastian's mind, and he glanced down to see the woman clasped in his arms.

Paulina's hair was still in its arrangements of braids, but it was no longer neat. Dozens of tiny ringlets had escaped from their confines to ring her head and catch the light like a halo. They brushed softly against his chin in the gentle wind coming from the open doors and windows. Her lashes, which had glistened with tears the night before, fluttered and parted. In the warm morning light, her eyes were the exact shade of the rum they had shared the night before.

"Good morning," he murmured quietly, so as not to

startle her. He must have fallen asleep without meaning to—he'd had every intention of offering her his bed while he made himself comfortable on the rocking chair on the terrace. But then she'd cried, and when he'd rubbed her back as he used to rub little David's, she had collapsed against him, her body trembling with sobs, and he had gathered her close.

And apparently hadn't let her go.

She lifted her head slightly, and Sebastian felt the breeze waft over the slightly sweaty spot on his shoulder where her cheek had rested.

"Oh," she said, and licked her lips. "I— Good morning."

"How's your head?"

"It doesn't pain me. I suppose drinking all that water worked."

"It usually does," he agreed. One of his arms still pinned by Paulina, Sebastian folded his free one beneath his head and regarded her calmly, as if it hadn't been years since he'd awoken next to a woman. "You'll be wanting to freshen up. I'll make us some breakfast, and then we'll go to my friend Dilia's. She'll see about getting you something to we—"

The door, which he'd left ajar the night before, slammed into the wall, as loud as a gunshot.

Keeping a protective arm around Paulina, Sebastian rose onto his elbow as Antonio Despradel burst into the parlor, two men in civil guard uniforms at his heels.

"I told you she'd be here," Despradel said, his heavy black boots leaving behind mud prints on the patterned tiles as he strode to where Sebastian and Paulina lay, his chest puffed out like a rooster's.

Paulina sat up, clutching the sheet around her, and let out a soft noise of protest as Despradel hauled her upright. Even from the floor, Sebastian could see the way his fingers dug into her soft brown skin.

Sebastian sprang to his feet. "What's the meaning of this?"

It wasn't unreasonable to assume that Despradel had come with the intention of making trouble for his sister, and perhaps even Sebastian, not just to fetch her home. The man seemed to delight in little cruelties, and Sebastian had surmised that getting Paulina away from him wouldn't be as easy as Sebastian had made it out to be the night before. Still, he wasn't expecting the words that came out of Despradel's mouth.

"You can see it for yourselves," Despradel told the guards. "This man is a kidnapper and a despoiler of innocent young women."

Sebastian's mouth dropped open. "Kidnapper?"

"Half the town saw you cavorting with my sister at Don Enrique's store," Despradel informed him coldly. "Trying to tempt her with cheap ribbons, as if she were a common tart. It didn't work, so you resorted to stealing her away in the dead of night—and plying her with spirits," he added, looking pointedly down at the cask of rum on the overturned crate.

Sebastian let out a bark of laughter at the ridiculous fabrication. "You don't really believe that."

"What should I believe?" Despradel said, his gaze raking over the exposed flesh above the blanket Paulina held tight against her bosom. "Your word, or the ruined dress discarded outside? These gentlemen—" he gestured at the guardsmen with his free hand "—can attest to the fact that it was ripped open and the laces on the undergarments cut. What need would there be for such brutishness if nothing untoward had taken place?"

"Nothing did," Sebastian snapped. "I provided a

neighbor with shelter during a storm. If you're quite finished with whatever it is you're trying to do, I'll thank you—all of you—to get off my property."

One of the guardsmen took a step forward. "I'm afraid you'll have to come with us, Señor Linares. On orders of the magistrate."

"The magistrate?" Sebastian echoed with a sense of dawning horror. This was more than making trouble. Getting hauled in front of the magistrate with an accusation of kidnapping…

As far as the residents of San Pedro knew, he was a stranger in these parts, with no one save Dilia, another newcomer, to attest to his character. That Paulina had spent the night under his roof and in his arms was more than evident. And now there were witnesses, one of whom was all but leering with triumph, clearly insensible to the blow to his sister's reputation.

This was more than scandal. This was ruin—for Paulina, for Sebastian and for the dozens of people who depended on him, including Carlos's widow and children.

Sebastian forced his tensed shoulders to straighten. He'd find a way out of this—if not by reason, then by bribery. Failure was not an option, and though nothing Paulina said would restore her damaged reputation, the kidnapping charges would be dropped once she gave her account.

He turned to her. "It will be all right. All you have to do is explain—" Sebastian stopped dead.

He had no way of knowing if it was her brother's cruel grip that prevented her from speaking, or the fact that she was a party to the deception. Her face had gone ashen, and tears glimmered in the morning sunshine as they dropped from her eyelashes to her cheekbones, but she remained silent as she turned her face away from him.

Her betrayal rolled over him like a wave of nausea. Without meaning to, Sebastian took a staggering step backward. The guards' hands went to the pistols at their belts, and they started to close in as if to prevent him from fleeing.

Despradel was watching him closely, and whatever he saw in Sebastian's expression made his lip curl with a smile that was slight but so gleeful it made Sebastian's hand clench into a fist.

"You will please refrain from trying to coerce my sister into lying for you," Despradel said, and Sebastian *would* have struck him if two sets of hands as unyielding as iron bands hadn't seized Sebastian by the arms.

He knew better than to struggle, but he couldn't prevent the involuntary twitch in his shoulders, his body's attempt to throw off their grip. Holding himself with rigid dignity, he crossed the room in his bare feet. He didn't turn his head once, not even when the sound of Paulina's tremulous breaths followed him out the door.

It had been less than a day since he'd stopped to say hello to Paulina outside Don Enrique's store, and already she was well on her way to ruining his life.

They weren't taking him to the magistrate at all.

In his shirtsleeves, his bare feet sliding first over drying mud and then over cool tiles, Sebastian followed the guardsmen out of the blazing sunshine and into the cramped darkness of the Palace of Justice. Only when they tugged him through the courtyard did he realize that the guardsmen meant to put him directly into one of the stinking jail cells at the back.

As if anticipating that he would run, their hands tightened on his biceps. Jeers, shouts and the pungent odor of unwashed men followed them as the guards dragged

Sebastian past a holding cell. It was too bright outside for Sebastian to get much more than a glimpse of half a dozen faces pressed up against the bars before he was shoved into a cell of his own and the cold clang of the iron lock alerted him to the fact that his day had just become infinitely more complicated.

"Wait," Sebastian said before the guardsmen could walk away. The word burst out of him with more desperation than he'd meant it to, so he took care to modulate his voice as one of them glanced at him curiously. "I have money. A great deal more of it than Antonio Despradel. I would be more than happy to make it worth your while if you should release me."

The force they'd held him with had been cold and impersonal—the smirk on the guardsman's face, however, made it clear to Sebastian that he was getting some enjoyment out of it. "Would you now?"

Sebastian didn't like the look on the guard's face. "If you were to speak to the magistrate on my behalf..."

The guard laughed. "You hear that, Pedro? He wants us to pay a call to the magistrate himself."

The other guard, Pedro, the one with the tense shoulders, gave him a hard look. "Leave off, Juan. I don't want to miss my breakfast."

He set off without another word, and his partner followed him at a more leisurely pace, hands in his pockets, leaving Sebastian with only the chickens for company.

Despite the bars that made up most of one wall, the interior of the cell was dank, dark and devilishly hot. Perspiration streamed down Sebastian's temples—it wouldn't be long until he reeked as sharply as the slop bucket in the corner.

The thought sent another wave of sweat down his back. How long *did* they mean to keep him here, if they didn't mean to take him to the magistrate? And what the devil did Despradel mean by having him locked away?

It struck him, suddenly and with some violence, that no one save Despradel and the guardsmen knew where he was. Even if someone at the mill noticed his absence—which would likely happen sooner rather than later, given Sebastian's penchant for spending the better part of his day there—no one would know where to look for him. Despradel could have him held for as long as he wanted.

An expletive exploded past Sebastian's lips. His foreman at the mill was more than capable enough to hold things down for a day or two, if it took that long for Sebastian to get out, but his employees needed to be paid at the end of the week, and the money for that was all locked away in Sebastian's safe.

He had to get a message to Dilia. Neither she nor Sebastian had any powerful connections among the townspeople, but she was the one person who could advocate on his behalf in front of the magistrate—unless he, too, was involved in whatever game Despradel was playing at.

The bars separating him from the courtyard were warm, almost the same temperature as his skin. Beyond them, all Sebastian could see was the bare dirt of the courtyard and a pair of chickens scrabbling in a patch of sunshine.

Filled with a sudden inclination to smash his fist through something, Sebastian's fingers tightened around the unyielding bars, hard enough for his knuckles to ache. Then, breathing hard, he hauled off and leaned against the grimy wall.

He'd talk to the guardsmen when they returned. Dilia would pay for news of his whereabouts, and if Sebastian couldn't bribe them into freeing him, maybe they would take a few pesos for a message.

Unfortunately for him, when the guardsmen came back—so many hours later that the patch of sunshine had traveled past the iron bars and was beginning to climb up the far wall of the cell—they brought Despradel with them.

Flanked by his henchmen, Despradel scattered the chickens as he strutted through the courtyard. He stopped when he reached Sebastian's cell and gazed down at him with the vaguely amused air most people reserved for zoo animals. "I'm grieved to say that prison doesn't suit you, Señor Linares."

Sebastian wasn't in the mood for games. "Are you ready to enlighten me as to why I'm being held captive?" he asked, not bothering to rise from his spot on the ground. The heavy rains from the previous night hadn't finished soaking into the dirt, but what was a pair of muddy trousers, under the circumstances?

"It's a matter of incentive. I've found that a little solitude makes men more amenable to cooperating with my suggestions."

"Suggestions?" Sebastian snorted at the gross misuse of the word. "What is it you want, Despradel?"

The other man leaned forward so that his face was framed between two iron bars. "I want you to marry Paulina."

It wasn't surprising, not after what Despradel had said that morning, but Sebastian couldn't help but think there was an ulterior motive—if only because there was nothing in their short acquaintance that indicated that Antonio Despradel had ever done a thing for his sister's sake.

"Go to hell."

"I don't believe I will," Despradel said after pretending to consider it. The bastard was enjoying this far too much. "Not just yet, at any rate. Look," he added, sounding almost reasonable, "I've plenty of resources, and more than enough time and patience. You can either have a nasty few days in here, or you can spare yourself the trouble and say yes now."

A memory flashed through Sebastian's mind—Dilia and Carlos, leaning against the iron railing of the balcony in the Havana house, silhouetted against a blazing sunset. On the street below, elegant carriages heading to the house on the corner had begun to pile up as a mule laden with saddlebags refused to budge from the middle of the street. "That mule has nothing on Sebastian," Carlos had said, laughing. After that, every time Sebastian was being particularly stubborn, Carlos would make a teasing remark about holding up traffic and they would all laugh.

His lips tightened at the memory. "I will not say yes," Sebastian said. "Not now, not tomorrow, not if you keep me here for five months."

"That can be arranged." The mocking tone was gone from Despradel's voice; it was hard and flat as he said, "You'd rather take the hard road? So be it." He started to turn away. "Perhaps another day or two in here will make you reconsider."

"Why are you doing this?" Sebastian asked. "What could you possibly want from me?"

Something flickered over Despradel's countenance, and for a moment, Sebastian thought he might tell the truth. The moment passed swiftly, though, and Despradel's voice was hard and cold when he said, "To keep you from besmirching my family's honor." He jerked his chin at the guardsmen. "Put him in chains. No food until he cooperates, but be sure to give him water—the last thing I want is for this dog to perish before he makes amends with my sister."

As Despradel made his own way out of the court-yard, the guardsmen let themselves into Sebastian's cell.

The guard who had smirked at him earlier, Juan, was the one to put the irons on him. Sebastian tried to ignore the heavy bracelet being clamped around his ankle and directed his words to the second guard, the one who continued to avoid Sebastian's gaze.

"If you won't free me, will you at least get a message to someone in town for me? Dilia de Gil. She'll be more than happy to arrange some payment for any news of me."

The guard remained quiet, his eyes fixed on the manacle he was fiddling with.

Sebastian pressed on. "I will personally make sure that you're handsomely rewarded for any assistance you might be able to—"

A fist cracked against his jaw, and Sebastian reeled backward, almost tripping over the big iron links, as pain exploded over the lower half of his face. He managed to catch himself before he fell, but not without catching the back of his shoulder sharply against the bars.

The guard at his ankles was, for once, not smirking, but gaping up at his partner.

Sebastian followed his gaze. The other guard was cradling his fist in a large hand, something that looked like fear glinting in his eyes.

"Shut up about messages," he said. "Shut up about all of it."

The expression on Juan's face was quickly shifting from surprise to glee. "Want me to gag him, Pedro?"

Pedro started like a spooked horse, then jerked his head into a nod. His partner grinned and pulled a grimy handkerchief from his pocket.

Pressed against the bars, the manacle tight around

his ankle and the chain binding it to the ring on the wall pulled as taut as it went, Sebastian squared his shoulders and said, quietly but distinctly, "No."

The advantage ought to have been entirely on their side—but Sebastian had desperation on his, and that made him more reckless than he otherwise would have been.

Sebastian had dealt with his share of bullies when he lived on the streets. Loath as he had always been to get into scuffles, he knew how to handle himself.

One of his hands hadn't been bound yet. When Sebastian caught Juan eyeing it as he approached, he made a show of shuffling his feet enough to make the chains rattle, hoping it would make the other man cocky.

"I would prefer to handle this like the gentlemen we are," Sebastian said.

The guard grunted. "Listen to this one. Gentlemen. Cowards, more like."

Sebastian waited until Juan was close enough to smell his breath, then launched himself to one side and pushed the other man from behind, pinning him against the bars. The guard wrenched himself free and came at Sebastian with a snarl.

Sebastian used the momentum to twist him around. One swift kick behind the leg and Juan was kneeling in front of Sebastian while Sebastian hooked his manacled hand around the other man's head and pulled the chain taut against his unshaven throat.

Juan strained against his hold, gasping, even though Sebastian had a firm hold on the chain to prevent it from digging into his throat.

"You can finish putting the irons on me," Sebastian said as he stood over the guard, trying to keep his breaths shallow, "but I won't be gagged. Do we have that clear?"

The lout was in the act of jerking his head in a nod when something tumbled from his pocket and hit the dirt floor with the jangle of metal.

The keys.

Less than five centimeters away from Sebastian's bare toe.

For one long second, all three men in the cell held their breath.

Sebastian could have pounced for it—but with bound ankles and one bound wrist, he wouldn't have gotten far before the guardsmen overpowered him. So instead, he nudged it toward Juan with his dirty toe and unhooked the chain from around the other man's neck. "Are we agreed, then, to act like gentlemen?"

There was no need for threats. Without bothering to answer, Juan snatched the keys from the floor and stormed out, barely waiting for Pedro to exit the cell before slamming the door shut with a clang.

Chapter Five

Overhead, the sky was blazing a bright blue. Inside Paulina's chest, however, another thunderstorm was raging.

"I won't help you ruin that poor man's life," she said.

She was back in the house she'd thought she had escaped for good. Antonio had hauled her, numb with shock, there that morning before disappearing for the next several hours—just enough time for Paulina, whose sole pair of shoes aside from her house slippers had been ruined in the storm, to search through the trunk containing her mother's things in the hopes of finding a pair sturdy enough to withstand the long walk to town.

She *would* talk to the magistrate. It didn't matter how hard Antonio's fingers had dug into her arm that morning—the abject disappointment on Sebastian's face had made her chest seize with shame at her cowardice.

Antonio had found her before she'd even reached the gate, and now here she was, gripping the back of a chair while he pulled a steaming plate of rice, beans and pork toward him, paying her as much mind as he would have a bothersome mosquito. There was a plate for Paulina, too, but she couldn't countenance eating. Her stomach was still roiling, both from the rum she'd had the night before and from the cruel trick her brother had played on Sebastian.

"I won't help you ruin his life," Paulina said again.

Antonio glanced up briefly. "You'll do as you're told for once in your life."

She lifted her chin. "I'll go to the magistrate and tell him you're lying—"

Antonio gave a bark of laughter. "And just what do you think that would accomplish? The magistrate and every other guardsman in this town are indebted to me in one way or another. If I were in fact plotting to ruin Sebastian Linares's life, there's nothing *you* could do to stop me."

While Paulina often felt powerless when it came to her brother, she had never until that moment felt helpless. As much as she hated to admit it, she recognized the truth in Antonio's words—there *was* nothing she could do to stop him, no matter what he tried to do.

"It just so happens," Antonio continued, cutting a sliver of pork from the chop on his plate, "I have other plans for Linares. I mean to make him marry you."

"Is that why you drove me out yesterday?" Paulina asked grimly. "Why you cast me out during a storm?"

He raised a shoulder into a shrug. "I have it on good authority that Linares can never resist playing the savior. I knew it was more than likely that he would take you in."

"I could have been killed."

"Don't be dramatic," Antonio said coldly.

"Did you not notice the lightning? The falling branches?" Paulina could hear her voice growing higher as she recalled her panicked run through the gale.

Antonio forked up a mound of rice and beans and

looked up at her again. "Have you realized that you've never thanked me?"

"Thanked you?" Paulina echoed, her mouth dropping open.

"For everything I've done for you. I've kept a roof over your head for almost fifteen years. You've been fed, clothed in the latest fashions. You've wanted for nothing. And now I've even found you a husband."

Being urged, or even forced, into marriage to a near stranger was nothing unusual for a woman. It was, however, more than Paulina could countenance.

"But it's all right. I forgive your lack of gratitude, painful though I find it." His plate mostly empty, Antonio stood and chucked her under the chin. Though the gesture was casual, his eyes were dark with warning. "As long as you behave."

Paulina met his gaze steadily, though her stomach was still pitching. Behaving was precisely the last thing she intended to do.

Perhaps it was true that the magistrate wouldn't help her, but there had to be someone who would. And she knew just the place to find that person—the mill. It would mean avoiding the walk to town, too, for which she was grateful. It was barely past one in the afternoon, and the sun was hot enough to sear a person's skin.

Antonio always took his siesta out in the veranda, sprawled on a rocking chair with his booted feet up on the railing. It wouldn't be difficult to sneak past him and cut through the sugarcane fields to reach the mill without taking the main road, where she might be spotted.

For most of her life, Antonio had warned her away from playing in the fields lest she be snatched by an outlaw or a cane cutter, but she had only ever found friends there. Today would be no different.

It might have been, if she'd stepped directly out into the veranda and through the gardens. Instead, she went into her bedroom to fetch her hat.

Paulina thought later that despite all that her brother had revealed of his character and his intentions in the past day, a small part of her must have still believed that he couldn't be all that bad. That part was extinguished when Paulina, her hat in her hands, heard the soft *snick* of her bedroom door being pulled shut.

She dropped the hat and flew across the room to rattle the doorknob. Locked. Antonio had locked her in.

"Let me out," Paulina called through the thick wood, trying to keep her voice sounding steady and reasonable.

It wasn't her brother who answered.

"I'm sorry, miss," said the maid—not the sour-faced woman who had trailed her in town the day before, but the frightfully young girl who had been sweeping the steps when Paulina had been dragged home that morning wearing nothing but a bedsheet. Paulina had never seen the girl before, but that was no surprise, as Antonio fired and hired household staff at the slightest transgression. "I'm under orders from your brother not to open the door without his say-so."

"I understand," Paulina said, her mind churning. "What's your name?"

"Berenice, miss. I—I don't want to get into trouble."

Could she somehow persuade the girl into releasing her? Bribe her? There was a laughable idea—Paulina hadn't even a decent pair of shoes, much less anything that would suit as a bribe.

Turning, she leaned against the closed door...and found herself gazing at the shuttered windows of her first-floor bedroom. Here was a better idea.

The windows were far shorter in the bedrooms than in

the rest of the house, and they were set high into the wall
to discourage petty thieves. Paulina dragged her bureau
underneath one and cleared everything from its surface,
then climbed atop it without too much difficulty, despite
the fact that the leather soles on her mother's old shoes
were worn almost to slickness. Unlatching the shutter,
she peered out through the opening.

The sugarcane fields were bathed with sunlight. Beyond them, she could see the mill's thick smokestack.
The sky above it was a deep blue, unmarred by the steam
it belched whenever the machinery was in use.

Paulina, who had spent most of her childhood climbing trees, hefted herself onto the windowsill. It wasn't
until she was preparing to swing both legs over the side
that she saw the coachman lounging beneath her window, no doubt posted there by her brother.

Antonio had thought of everything.

She was trapped.

There was no help for it.

That was what Paulina told herself as she stood just
beside her bedroom door, clutching the heavy water jug
from her washstand.

Her temples were damp with perspiration, a product
of her nerves and of the heat that had been collecting in
her bedroom over the past two days. With both door and
windows shut tight for the past couple of days to prevent
her from escaping, there was no hope for a breeze to relieve the oppressive atmosphere.

The cheerful yellow flowers painted around the jug's
border were so at odds with what she was about to do that
Paulina almost burst into nervous laughter.

She swallowed it back and called through the door,

"Berenice? Would you mind refilling my water jug? I accidentally overturned it and I'm *so* thirsty."

Pressed against the door frame, she could hear the maid's muffled assent and the jangle of keys. Paulina hefted the jug and braced herself as the door started to slowly swing open. Paulina made as if to hand Berenice the jug but instead flung the water at the startled maid with all her force.

It was a few seconds before the maid gathered her wits and gave chase, and by then Paulina had pelted into the dining room and was pulling down chairs behind her to make it more difficult for Berenice to follow.

The four arched doors leading to the terrace were all open. Through them, Paulina could see a blur of blue and green—the cloudless midday sky and the garden below it, through which she could escape.

There was a crash behind her, and though it was likely Berenice stumbling over the overturned chairs, instinct made Paulina glance over her shoulder.

It was only for a second, but when she turned back, there was a dark figure blocking the doorway.

Antonio.

Paulina tried to whirl toward the other archway, but the soles of her mother's old shoes had been worn smooth. Skidding, she slammed into Antonio. He let out a grunt as the impact knocked the breath out of him, but he kept both his footing and his presence of mind—before she had time to peel herself away, he had trapped her against him with one viselike arm.

Paulina hadn't brawled a day in her life, but at some point she had stumbled across the notion that the only surefire way of stopping someone was to strike them between the legs. She tried to jerk up her knee, but her skirts tangled around her legs, so instead she dipped her head and sank her teeth into Antonio's forearm.

With an undignified yelp, he flung her into one of the rocking chairs on the veranda.

"You provoking little…" He rubbed the indentation on his forearm and gave her a baleful glare. "Just where do you think you're going?"

"Anywhere but here," she snapped. "What do you mean by keeping me locked in for days on end?"

"I wouldn't have to if you didn't keep trying to run away," he said, sounding aggrieved.

Berenice appeared in the doorway, soaked and flushed, and Antonio dismissed her with a flick of his fingers, scowling as he considered Paulina. "I thought you had more sense than to go against my wishes, Paulina, but clearly I have a habit of overestimating you. Here I am, doing my best to salvage your honor and that of our family, and all you want is to be left free to run after a man you've met twice. That's where you were going, isn't it? To find Linares?"

"It's none of your concern where I was going."

She lunged to her feet and he caught her by the arm. "You want to go to him? Well, then, let's go."

He had been drinking the night he cast her out into the storm, but today he was sharply sober. His fingers were like iron against her arm as he pulled her toward the carriage, pausing only to say a word to the coachman, who grunted in response.

Refusing his help, Paulina scrambled onto a seat. "I won't marry him."

Her voice was firm but low, and for a moment, Paulina wasn't sure if Antonio had heard her over the rattle of the carriage wheels.

"It will be worse for him if you don't," Antonio said.

"You'll cost him his reputation. Is that what you want? To have Linares disgraced for life because you were flighty enough to spend the night under his roof?"

After the events of the previous day, Paulina had begun to think that nothing her brother did, however vile, could shock her. His words, however, made her mouth drop open. "You would really try to blame me?"

The grave expression he put on might have fooled anyone save for Paulina, who had never seen true sincerity on her brother's face. "If anyone's to blame for this situation, it's me. I have done my best to raise you to be an upright young lady, but it's clear I have failed you, Paulina. Even my maid and coachman would attest to the fact that I had to keep you locked in your bedroom to prevent you from running after Linares for a second attempt to compromise your virtue."

"You're reprehensible," Paulina told him, and she wasn't surprised when he laughed at the emotion in her voice. "How can you play with people's lives so cavalierly? Haven't you a conscience?"

Antonio shrugged. "Haven't found much need for one. Money's a far more useful thing to have. Here's some free advice for you, little sister—the world rewards money and those who have it, not scruples." He chucked her under the chin with another laugh, and she turned away, disgusted and a little shaken.

He had never really mentioned marriage before, at least not in regard to her. She'd always assumed he meant to keep her at the *quinta* as some sort of unpaid housekeeper. For him to be so insistent about marrying her off to Sebastian…he must have figured out a way to wring profit out of it.

It certainly wasn't for her benefit.

The carriage rolled to a stop, and she and Antonio alighted in front of the Palace of Justice.

"What have you done?" she whispered, but Antonio wasn't paying her any attention. He was speaking to a group of guardsmen in uniform who were smoking by the entrance. One of them came forward, and, giving her brother a respectful greeting, he led them inside.

The jail cells at the back of the Palace of Justice were a wretched sight. Most were crowded with prisoners, foul-smelling and dark, and the dirt yard that formed a sort of courtyard before them was smeared with chicken droppings.

The guardsman stopped in front of a cell, and Paulina let out a cry when she saw Sebastian through the bars. Clad in a shirt that looked like it had been used as a cleaning rag for months, his face streaked with grime, he was chained to the bricks at his back.

Bitterness welled up inside her. He wouldn't have been here, looking like this, if it weren't for her.

The guardsman unlocked the cell, and Antonio hauled her in through the open door, saying with disgusting cheerfulness, "Good morning, Linares. Have you given any thought to my offer?"

Sebastian's eyes flicked toward Paulina, but there was no acknowledgment in them. "Go to the devil," he said through parched lips.

"Must we really go through all this again?" Antonio let out an exasperated sigh. "I didn't want to do this, but as everyone here can see, your lack of cooperation forces me to take extreme measures." Stepping closer—though Paulina noticed he remained just out of reach of the latter man's powerful arms—Antonio spoke down to Sebastian. "You will either marry my sister to make up for your dishonorable actions, or—"

"What?" Sebastian croaked out. "You'll starve me? Withhold water? Whatever it is you want, Despradel, you won't be able to get it if I die."

"I'm grieved at such an accusation," Antonio said, though he only looked annoyed. "I don't mean you any harm, Linares. All I want is restitution. And since we all know that a woman's virtue, once taken, cannot be put back…"

Without conscious thought, Paulina had been edging back, away from Antonio and Sebastian. The warm, damp bricks at her back, filthy though they were, were much preferable to Antonio's punishing grip.

"Men never have to face the consequences for such things," Antonio remarked, hauling her forward. "It's always up to women to deal with society's shame and condemnation. Would you really allow Paulina to be ruined when a single word from you could save her from being repudiated by every respectable person in San Pedro? She'd be out on the street—a man of virtue such as myself can't be expected to countenance such goings-on under his own roof. And what will happen to her then? Do you really want that on your conscience?"

"Don't believe anything that comes out of his mouth," Paulina said furiously, struggling against his grip.

Antonio smirked. "Something tells me that Linares is not likely to trust either one of us. As well he should— we all know how treacherous females can be, and especially when it comes to snaring themselves a husband."

"Sebastian…" Paulina began, but her words were lost in her own cry when Antonio dug his fingers into the soft flesh of her upper arm.

"You'll both be disgraced," Antonio said. "Tell me why I shouldn't shove her into a group cell and let the prisoners do with her what they would?"

Paulina couldn't see Sebastian's face—his head was bowed, and he was silent as well as motionless. Her stomach clenched. Part of her wanted him to continue refusing Antonio, who had surely been lying when he said he would cast her out into the street. Or worse, into another jail cell.

But part of her wanted Sebastian to be the honorable man she believed him to be—the honorable, upstanding, heroic man she had built him up to be in her mind.

Paulina forced herself to keep her gaze on that bowed head, almost holding her breath as she waited for his response, though she didn't know whether she was willing him to say yes or no. Her stomach was pitching as if she were on a ship about to wreck—which, in a way, she was. Whatever Sebastian's response, her life was about to change.

She couldn't help thinking about the night of the storm and how he'd given her strength when her emotion had worn through what she'd believed to be the end of her resilience. When she'd awoken in his arms, even knowing the upheaval she was facing, she'd been almost…happy.

And while it was probable that he hadn't felt the same way, surely she hadn't imagined the gentleness in the way he'd held her. There was something between her and Sebastian, some unspoken sense of possibility. Maybe marriage, a treacherous part of her insisted, would give her the opportunity to find out for sure.

Antonio's fingers were digging painfully into her arm, and Paulina's own were clenched around folds of her skirt.

And still, Sebastian's silence grew around them.

"So be it," Antonio said finally. He nodded to the guardsman, who moved at once to open the cell.

Paulina wrenched her arm out of Antonio's grip. "Let go of me. I can walk under my own power."

"Stop," Sebastian rasped, lifting his head. He swallowed. Even from where she stood, her knees loosening with relief, Paulina could see what it cost him to say what he said next. "Stop. I'll marry her."

It was over in minutes.

Sebastian and Paulina's wedding was as brief as it was joyless. One of his manacles was removed so that he could sign the marriage act. His hand left streaks of dirt on the thin, grayish paper of the clerk's ledger. The man had been summoned from the civil registry and presented with the suitable papers—how Despradel had acquired them, Sebastian did not wish to know.

Paulina was ashen, her face a pale brown smudge in the gloom of the cell.

A handful of nights before, she had cried on his shoulder, and like an absolute fool, he'd believed every damned word that had fallen from those pretty lips. This wasn't the first time that Sebastian had been taken in by a beautiful woman pretending to be in trouble—but he would make damn sure it was the last.

Even the clerk looked troubled as he oversaw the proceedings. "This is most irregular," he had muttered as he'd entered the cell and caught his first glimpse of the bride and groom. Any protest on his part was quelled by a warning sound from Juan, who had begun wearing a pistol that he stroked ostentatiously whenever he was around Sebastian.

As for Sebastian himself, he kept a tight rein on his emotions. There was no need for any of them to see the dread curdling in his stomach. It didn't seem right that his entire life should be destroyed by something as inconsequential as two signatures on a piece of paper.

The only person who seemed jubilant was Despradel. As soon as the ink was dry on the marriage certificate, he folded it and slid it into his pocket. "I'll keep this safe, if that's all right with the happy couple," he said with a leer.

He left the cell first, a companionable arm slung firmly around the clerk, who looked as if he were about to lose his breakfast. Only when they had been gone for a while did the two guardsmen release Sebastian from the wall, though they kept him in shackles until they had shoved both him and Paulina into a waiting coach.

As the iron around his wrists was yanked free, one of the guardsmen slapped the side of the carriage to signal the coachman. The horses set off at once, halfway down the street before Sebastian could so much as think to swing a fist toward either guard.

Paulina had pressed herself into a corner of the carriage, as far from Sebastian as she could get in the enclosed space. Whatever her role in this godforsaken mess, she was clearly planning on playing the innocent until the bitter end.

Sebastian had had plenty of experience with that kind of playacting, and if there was one thing he knew, it was that he'd rather take up residence in that filthy jail cell than fall again for such tricks.

"Thank you for what you did back there. I should have been in dire straits if you hadn't—"

"Don't touch me," he snarled, and the slender hand that had been reaching toward him was instantly jerked away.

He felt like a wounded animal that had just been released from an iron trap—raw and broken and more than willing to snap his teeth at anyone in his sight. "I don't know what it is you two want from me. I don't know what made you target me in this way, and I certainly don't pretend to know what else you have in store for me. Your brother wanted you respectably married? Congratulations. You are now my lawfully wedded wife. You will live in my house and eat at my table. But make no mistake—I want no part in this sham of a marriage. You will not touch me again."

She reared back against her seat, as if struck by the force of his words. Everything inside Sebastian burned with the urge to apologize, but he forced himself to keep still.

Silence pressed in around them, and it went unbroken as the carriage rattled its way out of town.

Chapter Six

When Paulina was six years old, her parents had hosted a wedding at the *quinta*. The party had been one of their largest and most extravagant—close to a dozen houseguests had arrived the week before the wedding, and still more people streamed in from nearby towns on the day itself. The bride had been a distant cousin of her mother's, and she had worn white gardenias in her hair.

Paulina had pictured her own wedding countless times since then. But what she had never imagined was arriving to the end of it, perspiring and ragged and miserable, next to a husband who could barely bring himself to look at her.

Damn Antonio for robbing her of yet another dream.

The carriage came to a stop in front of Villa Consuelo. Wearily and slightly awkwardly, Paulina hopped down from the high perch without waiting for Sebastian. After what he'd said, and the heavy silence that had settled between them, she was certain he would have no interest in helping her down. And yet here he was, coming around the side of the carriage, grasping her arm when she stumbled as the fabric of her skirt snagged on a splinter. It was true that he released her arm like he'd been burned the very instant she was steady on her feet, but the small kindness heartened Paulina.

"Sebastian! There you are!"

The cry was uttered by one of the two women who stood in front of the steps and was quickly followed by a muttered, "*Santísimo!*" when Sebastian walked into the pool of light cast by the hanging lantern.

"What happened to you?"

"We were so sure you'd had an accident, but your horse is in the paddock—"

Paulina hung back. Both women wore black and were older than her, one by a handful of years and the second one by two or three decades, judging by the gray in her hair. They reached out for Sebastian like a mother and a sister would, though there was no resemblance between them.

He allowed them to fuss over him, murmuring something that made them smile despite the worry furrowing their brows. It made Paulina think about the way he'd looked at her in Don Enrique's store, and later when he'd handed her the red ribbon. She could have basked in his quiet warmth all day, and her chest tightened at the thought that she might never get to. Whoever these women were to him, they were lucky that they had no cause to worry about losing his regard.

With a start, Paulina realized that their gazes had turned to her.

Sebastian, who had just patted the older woman's shoulder, stepped away and gestured toward Paulina. "This is…" His eyes flashed. "This is Paulina Despradel. My wife."

Paulina could hardly miss the stress he laid on the word, nor the way the women's mouths fell slightly open when they heard it.

Half expecting their shocked expressions to turn into hostility, she was taken aback when the younger of the two women brushed past Sebastian and came to Paulina's side, leaning in to kiss her cheek.

"I'm Dilia, a good friend of Sebastian's." Her dark brown eyes were quick and curious but also kind as they swept over Paulina. "It's a pleasure to meet you. A pleasure and a surprise, if you'll forgive my saying so."

"For us both," Paulina said, and she was gratified when Dilia laughed.

Sebastian made a low noise at the back of his throat. "She'll need a bedroom."

"And a good meal and a bath, I imagine," the older woman said briskly. "Come with me, my dear. I'm Josefa, the housekeeper. I'll get you settled in."

Paulina murmured the requisite pleasantries as she was guided into the house. She couldn't help but sneak a glance backward. Sebastian's shoulders were slumped beneath Dilia's hand, and the two stood close together, speaking in low voices.

When she turned back toward the house, Doña Josefa was waiting at the far end of the front room, something like pity and suspicion mingled in her expression.

Paulina couldn't blame her.

"Will your belongings be brought later?" Doña Josefa asked. "We've a boy that can help with any luggage, but he'll be on his way home soon."

"I haven't any," Paulina said, surprised to realize this was true. "No luggage, I mean, and no belongings."

And nothing she wanted out of her family's *quinta*, save for the few things of her mother's inconsequential enough to have escaped Antonio's notice when he was scouring the house for things to sell.

Doña Josefa didn't seem perturbed by this admission.

"Your husband isn't much for having too many things, either, and let me tell you something—it makes housework a sight easier. Less polishing and dusting, you know."

"I would imagine so," Paulina said, having seen what passed for furnishings in Villa Consuelo.

She wouldn't have minded if their path through the house had included a detour to the overturned crate and Sebastian's rum cask, but the housekeeper didn't slow down as they passed several closed doors.

When they reached their destination, Paulina waited by the doorway as Doña Josefa bustled in, unlatching the louvered doors at the far end and pulling them open to reveal a dim chamber furnished with a bed and a table that looked too rickety to hold more than a water jug. It was scrupulously clean, though, as was the rest of the room—not a single dust mote drifted in the shaft of light coming in through the open shutters.

A mosquito net hung limp from one of the bedposts. The bed itself was surprisingly luxurious, considering the bareness of the rest of the house, its crocheted coverlet heaped with silk and embroidered pillows.

It was also large enough for two. Of course, Paulina would not be sharing it with anyone.

She bit her lip, trying not to show how disappointed she was by the prospect.

A large chest in the corner contained bedsheets, all bleached a bright white by the sun. The ones Doña Josefa pulled out smelled fresh, as if they had been laundered only days previously. "I'm sure you'll want to have nicer ones made, but these will do for now."

Paulina hastened to help her make the bed. "I don't need fancy blankets."

"Hmm." Doña Josefa's iron-gray brows drew together in obvious skepticism. "I expect you'll want to make changes around here, regardless. It's only natural for a new bride." Easily lifting a corner of the heavy feather mattress Paulina was struggling with, Doña Josefa tucked a fold of the bedsheet under it.

Paulina made a noncommittal noise in response.

"I'll bring you something to eat while the water for your bath warms up," Doña Josefa said, adding, as she caught Paulina glancing toward the door, "I expect he'll want to clean up, too. He'll come to you when he does."

Would he? Paulina had a feeling that Sebastian had said all he meant to back in the carriage.

Still, the tiniest spark of hope flared to life inside her chest. Sebastian was her husband now. Certainly he didn't mean to ignore her for the rest of their lives. That would be impossible, not to mention impractical.

Yes—he would definitely come to her. And then she would have the opportunity to convince him of her innocence, and perhaps even convince him that being married to her might actually be a good thing.

"What the devil happened?" Dilia asked the moment they had stepped into the front room. "You look like you've been through a war or two."

Sebastian closed the door behind her and scrubbed a hand over the bristles covering his jaw. "I feel as though I have. Nothing's broken, though, I don't think," he added, feeling that the assurance should have eased at least some of the creases on Dilia's forehead, not deepened them.

The overturned crate with his rum was still in the middle of the room, though the guardsmen's muddy footprints had been wiped off the tiles. If it weren't for the fact that he was now saddled with a wife, Sebastian could almost pretend they had never been there.

Sebastian poured a hefty slug into the enamel mug and offered it to Dilia, who declined with a moue of distaste.

That small attempt at hospitality was all Sebastian had in him. Raising the mug to his lips, he drained every last drop of rum in it and cast it aside before sinking to the floor, his head in his hands. "I'm married," he said to Dilia.

"Legally?" she asked.

"I think so." Briefly, Sebastian outlined the events of the previous three days.

In response, Dilia grew thoughtful. "I wonder why you." At his raised eyebrow, she elaborated. "Not that I don't believe you wouldn't make a good match for anyone short of a royal princess—half the matchmaking mothers in town have tried to claim you for their daughters, after all. But it isn't as though wealthy, handsome men are scarce around here. There must be a reason why Despradel targeted you specifically."

"I've been wondering the same thing myself. Wealth and devastating good looks aside—" Sebastian scrounged up a smile for Dilia and was relieved to see the crease on her forehead soften. "I can't help but think it had something to do with what happened at Don Enrique's store. Whether because I embarrassed him by challenging his treatment of Paulina, or because half the town having witnessed it would have made it easier to convince them of an entanglement between us. Or maybe it's just that he knows I haven't any well-connected relations to intervene on my behalf." He sighed. "But speculating isn't going to do me any good. What I need is to figure out what to do now."

"Get an annulment, for one," Dilia said briskly. "There's not a judge in his right mind who wouldn't grant you one."

Sebastian wasn't so sure about that—not after seeing

how readily Despradel had persuaded the guardsmen and the clerk to do his bidding, but he didn't say so out loud. There was no need to alarm Dilia any further. It had been bad enough seeing the consternation on her face when he had come into the house. He rubbed his face again, glad for the stubble that covered the bruise on his jaw.

Dilia had paused, clearly wishing to say something and just as clearly hesitant to offend him. From experience, Sebastian knew he had to wait for her to speak in her own time.

Her question came a handful of seconds later. "Do you think this is anything like what happened with that woman, back in Havana?"

Sebastian tried to make his shrug look careless. "It wouldn't be the first time a beautiful woman has tried to swindle me. At least she didn't go so far as to marry me."

"Fortunately," Dilia muttered. She fetched the mug from where it had rolled, halfway to the door, and poured him some more rum. "You'll need a lawyer. We'll go into town as soon as you get cleaned up."

"I have to get to the mill first."

"You're in no condition to be going to work," Dilia told him, and Sebastian had to admit—to himself—that she wasn't wrong.

"I've never been away this long," Sebastian said, but he made no effort to stand. He was already light-headed from the rum, and he would have been hard-pressed to pull himself up on the saddle, never mind stay upright all the way to the mill.

"And yet the mill is still standing."

"As far as you know," Sebastian muttered mulishly.

Dilia shook her head in fond exasperation. "This may come as a shock to you, but the walls of the mill will not in fact tumble to the ground without you to prop them up."

Perhaps not, but the mill had held up Sebastian when he'd needed it the most. For weeks after Carlos's death, he had taken refuge among the machinery and the paperwork, infernally dull though the latter was. Each entry into the ledgers had been a small reassurance that dozens of people would be taken care of, at least for another month.

"A cool bath and a hot meal," Dilia told him, in a tone that brooked no argument and that Sebastian had often heard her employ on her unruly boys. "That's my condition for letting you out of the house."

"That doesn't seem entirely unreasonable," Sebastian agreed grudgingly.

"Good boy. Wait here while I go help Josefa heat up the water and rustle up something to eat. And Sebas?"

He softened at the sound of his old nickname.

"It will all be all right—as long as you refrain from sharing a bed with her. It would invalidate an annulment, and if she were to get with child..."

The notion, or perhaps it was the rum's fiery fingers, made Sebastian feel suddenly flushed. "Don't you worry about that," he said, as firmly as he could manage when the world around him was wobbling like warm *majarete*. "I have no intention of sleeping with my wife."

The word tasted bitter. Sebastian took another sip of rum.

He must have fallen asleep right there on the floor, because he awoke some time later, his head reeling. There was still some light streaming in through the shutters, but he couldn't tell if it was evening or very early in the morning.

He staggered out in search of the promised sustenance.

The kitchen was out back, and rather than walk through the house and risk encountering Paulina, he made his way through the length of the terrace.

Sebastian was so used to being alone in the house, save for his housekeeper, that when he caught a flash of motion through one of the shutters out of the corner of his eye, he paused on instinct and peered through the wooden slats.

Josefa must have settled Paulina in the room next to his, because there she was, stepping out of the tin bathtub, droplets of water catching the light like beads as she stretched languidly and reached for a towel to wrap around herself. Her hair was wet and swept over her shoulder, revealing the slender nape of her neck and the cluster of tight ringlets plastered to her dark skin.

Sebastian hadn't thought about women—not in this way—in...his aching head couldn't remember how long. He hadn't *wanted* to.

This sudden arousal flaring in him at the merest glimpse of Paulina's back was as unexpected as it was unwelcome. He'd meant it when he'd told Dilia that he had no plans to sleep with his wife. He sure as hell wasn't about to lust after her, either.

Even if the sight of her dark skin gleaming as beads of moisture rolled into the deep indentation at the small of her back was sure to follow him into his dreams.

Damn, but she was beautiful. Maddeningly so. Inconveniently so.

Intolerably so.

Mostly because it reminded him of being a scrap of a child, trudging alone through the streets of Havana, craning his neck for a glimpse into windows full of things he thought could never be his.

Of being even younger and being instructed to play

with the young lady of the house while his mother worked, the girl with satin bows and crisply starched pinafores that showed every mark of his muddy hands so clearly, he didn't dare touch her.

Abruptly, Sebastian turned away. If his heart was racing, it was only a product of the rum, and of having been startled.

He bounded down the steps and found himself striding to the outdoor kitchen as if there were wild boars after him.

The tantalizing smells wafting from the large pot on the *anafe* almost made him stumble. Josefa liked to cook over wood instead of coal, and the pleasantly smoky scent billowed out past the three wooden walls surrounding the cook fire. The other side was open to the yard and held the collection of rickety stools and upturned buckets that served as the dining room—Sebastian had been meaning to get himself a table, but he hadn't gotten around to it yet.

Thank heavens he'd enough beds and mattresses.

The three-legged stool Sebastian sank onto rocked alarmingly—or perhaps that was just him, still reeling with exhaustion and hunger and the remains of the rum.

"You look like something chased you here," Josefa observed as she heaped a large serving of rice and pigeon peas onto a tin plate.

"You put her in the room next to mine."

"Should I not have?" She raised an eyebrow as she handed him the plate. "Would you rather your wife slept in the horse paddock?"

Sebastian winced at the word *wife*.

"Like that, is it?" she remarked, but she refrained from questioning him. Josefa had many fine qualities, among them her excellent cooking skills, but by far the one Sebastian appreciated the most was her discretion.

The slice of avocado on the side of his rice glittered in the evening light as if it had been dusted with moonlight and magic instead of salt. Sebastian dug his fork into its tender side, pausing with it halfway to his mouth. "Has she eaten?"

"She ate, all right," Josefa grumbled. "She may be a slip of a girl, but she's likely to eat you out of hearth and home if her dinner was any indication. You might want to talk to Leo about planting some more yuca and plantain if we're to keep up with her appetite."

Sebastian muttered something incomprehensible through the spoonful of rice and avocado he had just shoved into his mouth, then followed it with a change of subject that was guaranteed to make Josefa forget all about Paulina's appetite. "Did your daughter have her baby?"

Josefa brightened and began to tell him all about her newest grandson.

The shadows cast by the outbuildings were beginning to lengthen. Sebastian shoved heaping spoonsful of rice into his mouth, Josefa requiring little of him in the way of conversation save the occasional grunt to indicate he was still listening.

"And the others?" he said when he had cleared his second plate. "Is everyone all right?"

"As fine as Candida's goat. He got out of his pen again and went romping through the fields. Ate up half the *auyamas* Leo's mother had planted, too. That animal is going to end up in someone's pot before long." Taking his plate, she tossed him a clean, damp rag that he used to wipe some of the grime from his face and neck.

Slowly, some of the tension in his shoulders started

to ease. They were all fine. Either Despradel was more honorable than Sebastian had given him credit for—doubtful—or he hadn't known to target them.

"The water's almost ready for your bath," Josefa told him.

Sebastian nodded. "I'll bring in the buckets so you don't have to carry them."

"Leo can do it. You look tired enough to fall over, but I put freshly laundered sheets on your bed and you're not getting any of that filth all over them."

Sebastian glanced down at the rag on his lap. It was streaked with dirt, as were his hands and forearms. "Filth?" he repeated. "You call this filth? It's just a little dust."

He lunged after Josefa with his hands in the air, as if he meant to wipe them on her spotless black dress. She snapped her apron at him with an indignant, *"Mira, muchacho!"*

Before long, the two of them were howling with laughter. Josefa lowered herself onto an overturned bucket and wheezed, waving a corner of her apron in dismissal when Sebastian offered her a glass of water.

"You'll be the death of me yet, mark my words." She dabbed her apron on her corner of her eyes as her wheezing subsided and her gaze grew serious. "We were worried about you."

"I know," Sebastian said, giving her a firm pat on the back. "But I'm here now. And I'm all right."

He cast a look back at the house. Villa Consuelo wasn't much to look at, not yet. Leo didn't usually come at night, but there he was, quietly going around lighting lanterns and hanging them from the hooks outside the doors. He must have given Paulina a lamp as well, because a warm glow spilled through the louvered shutters of her bedroom.

Her temporary bedroom, he amended silently. First thing tomorrow, he would go into town and pay a call to the lawyer who'd assisted him and Carlos in the purchase of the mill. With any luck, by this time next week, Sebastian would no longer have a wife.

Chapter Seven

The birds were singing at the top of their voices when Paulina awoke in an unfamiliar bed the following morning. Before she had even wrenched her eyelids open, she was reaching across the mattress...and finding nothing but a cotton-covered expanse of bed.

She propped herself up on her elbow and regarded the empty space beside her.

Something more bitter than disappointment welled in her chest. Pressing a hand just below her collarbone, Paulina willed the pain winding around her heart to recede. She was not going to give in to the tears gathering just behind her eyes, not after all she'd been through. And certainly not because of her misguided expectation that Sebastian would relent.

The chances that he would were slim, of course. Still, knowing that hadn't stopped her from arranging her curls enticingly on the pillow, wishing she had pearls or diamonds to wink at him in the darkness. She had even fiddled with the shoulder of her nightdress, leaving its satin ribbon undone so that it slipped invitingly off her shoulder.

She'd been as foolish as a schoolgirl.

Flinging the thin blanket aside, she sat up. What did it matter that Sebastian hadn't come to her bed the previous night? He'd been tired and hurt and so had she. Maybe he hadn't wanted to disturb her. After all, they'd both had a long, hard day, and heaven knew they'd needed some rest. He might even be outside her door now, waiting for her to awaken.

With that encouraging thought, she sprang out of bed and rushed through her ablutions, using the last of the lukewarm water in the clay jug.

The clothes she had worn the day before had been taken by Doña Josefa to be laundered, but she had washed her undergarments in last night's bathwater and laid the shabby linen on the cane-backed chair by the door. To her surprise, there were two clean blouses and a cotton skirt folded over her combinations—Doña Josefa must have brought them while Paulina was still asleep. Both blouses were a trifle plain, but well-made, much finer than the frilly white monstrosities Antonio had purchased for Paulina. She chose the plainer one of the two, enjoying the sensation of the soft fabric slipping over her skin.

There was no mirror in the washstand—in fact, there was no washstand at all, only a chipped enamel basin on a rickety table, next to the jug—so she gathered her hair into a twist and pinned it up as best she could, hoping that it looked presentable.

And then, her stomach fluttering with nerves, Paulina walked out into her new home.

Which was as empty of people as it had been of furniture.

It wasn't until she ventured outside that she found Doña Josefa standing over a cauldron the size of a bathing tub, muscular arms submerged to the elbow as she scoured an enamel bowl.

"Good morning," Paulina said. "Did—? Is—?"

Doña Josefa gave her a shrewd look as she wiped her hands dry on her apron. "He's gone to the mill. He'll be there most of the day, I expect, so you needn't be on the lookout for him."

With a start, Paulina realized she had instinctively glanced in the direction of the mill. "Oh."

The short word didn't come close to conveying the depths of her dismay. So he did mean to stay away. He did mean to pretend that she wasn't his wife—that she didn't exist.

Her hand clenched into a fist. He had the right to be angry with their current circumstances, she would give him that. It wasn't like she herself wouldn't have preferred for things to have happened differently. But they hadn't, and ignoring her wasn't going to change the fact that they were now married.

Doña Josefa didn't remark on Paulina's lackluster response. She bustled to the table and began to pile food onto a plate. "You'll be wanting breakfast, I expect. Would you like me to bring a tray to your bedroom? I can have Leo bring it to the terrace if you'd rather take your coffee there."

"There's no need to trouble yourself on my account," Paulina said, perching on a three-legged stool. "I can see you've plenty to do without having to tote trays in and out of the house."

The housekeeper's eyebrows rose, but she handed Paulina a tin mug without comment. Though tepid, the coffee was excellent, and Paulina had downed half of it by the time a plate of eggs and sliced avocado was placed on her lap. There were hot roasted *batatas*, too, and another mug full of milk so fresh it was still warm. A far cry from the linen tablecloths, bakery buns and hot chocolate Antonio insisted on, but all the better for it.

The kitchen itself was similar to the one at her old home, with its three wooden walls surrounding a central brick-ringed cook fire—aromatic wood, she noted, rather than sooty coal or even the dry sugarcane pulp often used in the region. The scarred worktable standing against one of the walls was piled with reed baskets full of eggs and *víveres*, some with dirt still clinging to their tough exteriors.

As Paulina ate, Doña Josefa pulled down a bulb of garlic from the bunches hanging from a large iron nail. Breakfast may have been over, but the next meal would be soon in coming.

Paulina took one last sip of her now-cool coffee. "Does he always work through lunchtime?"

Doña Josefa frowned as her large thumbs worked off the garlic's papery skin. "A dreadful habit, mark my words, and one I haven't been able to break him out of. I was hoping that would no longer be the case, now that there's a fetching young lady waiting for him at home."

"He won't want to see me." Paulina touched the tines of her fork to the smear of yolk that was all that remained of her breakfast. She glanced up to see that Doña Josefa was giving her another one of her incisive looks, her eyes sharp beneath her wrinkled lids. Paulina returned it with a steady one of her own.

But all Doña Josefa said was "I wouldn't be too sure about that." She dropped the denuded cloves into a large wooden mortar before adding, "Your husband has a heavy load on his shoulders that he thinks he has to carry all by himself. He'd spend entire days up in that office of his if we let him."

"We?"

"His foreman, myself and most everyone who works in the mill or thereabouts. His foreman once threatened to throw him over his shoulder and haul him home when he caught him sleeping at his desk for the second time in a row."

Paulina couldn't help a smile at the image of broad-shouldered Sebastian being carried home like a tired child. "It sounds like he has a lot of people looking after him."

"He does his share of looking after us, so it's only fair," Doña Josefa said. The glance she cast at Paulina over the rim of her mortar felt like a warning, and Paulina answered it the only way she knew how.

"I won't hurt him," she told the housekeeper. "Not intentionally, in any case. He did me a kindness and has paid horribly for it. I would hate for him to suffer any more on my account."

Doña Josefa nodded in what looked like approval, but all she said was "I can't imagine you'll have much of a choice in the matter. There never is when it comes to love."

There were a lot of things between Sebastian and Paulina, but love was definitely not one of them.

A sharp intake of breath from Doña Josefa made Paulina glance up from her empty plate.

"Sebastian?" Paulina blurted out. Her heart was fluttering, and not just at having been startled—from the way Sebastian was frowning at them, she had the uncomfortable feeling that he might have heard what the housekeeper had just said. "But I thought… Doña Josefa said that you never come home for lunch."

"I'm not here for lunch," he returned immediately. "I came to make sure my house was still standing."

The knot that had been tightening her stomach had

all but dissolved at the sight of him. Still, she rose and set her plate next to the basin, then made a show of putting her hands on her hips. "What exactly did you think I would do? Dismantle it stone by stone the minute you had your back turned?"

Behind her, the housekeeper excused herself and slipped away.

"I wouldn't put it past you," Sebastian said.

It was such a ridiculous accusation that Paulina couldn't help but scoff. "Should I be flattered that you think me capable of all sorts of villainy?"

He raised an eyebrow. "Is that the sort of thing that pleases you?"

"No, Sebastian!" Good heavens, this man could certainly try her patience. "What in the world do you think I'd have to gain by destroying your home?"

"Far be it for me to know what goes on in that scheming mind of yours."

"I am not the unscrupulous scoundrel you think I am."

"And I am no fool."

To make up for the difference in their heights, he had unconsciously leaned forward, and he was now so close that the angular slope of his nose was in danger of brushing hers.

So close he could have kissed her without having to do much but tilt his head down.

A most inconvenient frisson down her spine made her take half a step back.

"No, not a fool," she told him, adding in a rush, "but it is foolish to insist on putting a wall between us when we should—"

"A wall is all there will ever be between us," he snapped. "And don't you forget it."

With that, he turned on his heel and stalked out of the kitchen yard, leaving her once again.

Sebastian didn't come home until late in the evening. Paulina had gone into her bedroom to bathe before dinner, and when she stepped out, it was with a jolt of surprise to see him sitting on the floor of the terrace.

His back was turned to her, and it was bare.

Paulina stopped abruptly, her foot coming down hard on the tile beneath it. The breadth of his shoulders was outlined in flickering lamplight, in echo of the way he had been highlighted by lightning on the night of the storm, when he had stood in the same place, gazing out into the lashing rain.

The sky behind him was mild tonight, but Paulina was filled with the same longing to spread her palms on that sweat-slick expanse of skin and feel the flex of his muscles. Had their circumstances been different, she would have knelt behind him and pressed her body against his, her hands on his bulging arms and her lips following the drop of perspiration making its way down the back of his neck…

A shudder slid over her.

As if he could feel the waves of heat radiating from her skin, Sebastian glanced backward. "Is anything the matter?"

Paulina grasped at the fraying threads of her composure. "I know you don't want me around, and I'll stay out of your way if that's what you wish. But before I do, there's something I wanted to tell you."

All she wanted was to finish giving voice to the thought that had been circling her mind since the day before. She'd tried it that morning, before he had stalked away, and she was going to give it one more try, if only to show Sebastian that she didn't intend to be put off that easily.

His shirt had been flung over the railing, and Paulina was almost overcome with the impulse to press it to her face and see if it still smelled warm and spicy. Or better yet—bury her head in the crook of his neck.

He must have noticed her looking at the shirt, because he yanked it off the railing and pulled it on, shrugging the white cotton over his shoulders. It wasn't until his head popped out through the neck hole and his eyes met Paulina's, eyebrows raised in inquiry, that she realized she was staring.

Tearing her gaze away, she said the first thing that came to mind. "I— What are you doing?"

"Carpentry."

"In the dark?"

She saw his chiseled shoulders move into a shrug. "I rarely have the opportunity to work on it in the daytime. Besides, I've a lamp."

Paulina studied the back of his head. "The mill does seem to take up much of your time."

Neither Antonio nor her father, when he still lived, had spent such long hours at the mill. Then again, neither of them had contrived to eke much of a profit from it, either.

"A great deal of people depend on it remaining a profitable enterprise," he answered flatly and turned back to his work.

Using the back of a hammer, he pried off the remains of a broken baluster. Instead of casting it aside, he fit one splintered end against another piece he must have dislodged earlier, as if in preparation for joining the two. As Paulina watched with growing fascination, he set one piece down and clamped the other one between his powerful thighs before using both hands to run a small tool over the ruined edge.

Wood shavings tumbled from his trousers to the floor in pale curls as the broken end of the baluster grew smoother.

Paulina couldn't help but contrast Sebastian's painstaking restoration to the careless way her brother hauled his boots onto his railing, not noticing or even caring that it was starting to come apart from the wall.

"Was it damaged by the storm?" she asked, perching on the edge of the rocking chair.

"It's been broken for years." Sebastian's hands swept over the wood as if he were caressing it, and Paulina tried not to imagine that same hand running over her bare leg. "It's a beautiful old house—or it was, once. I had grand plans to restore it to its former glory, but all I seem to have repaired is part of the roof and half a meter of this balustrade."

His voice drifted off, then he seemed to shake himself, as if recalling that he had no interest in having a conversation with Paulina. He cleared his throat. "What was it you wanted to tell me?"

He reached for the jar of nails next to the hammer as Paulina started to answer. The cuff on his shirt pulled back slightly, showing the deep violet bruises around his wrist that must have been left by the manacles. Even in the dim, unsteady light of the lantern, the brutal discoloration looked painful.

Paulina stifled a gasp.

He caught her look and, scowling, yanked his cuff over the bruise. "What?" he demanded again, in harsher tones.

"Oh, I—just wondered if you were ready for dinner."

"I already ate," he replied in clipped tones, turning back to his work.

Paulina nodded and started toward the kitchen in silence. She was on the top step when she paused and studied the top of Sebastian's head. His tight curls had been cut short, leaving his ears and nape looking oddly vulnerable. What she wouldn't give for the freedom to graze them with her fingertips as she passed and have her gesture met with a smile.

"I had nothing to do with it, you know," she murmured.

"I know nothing of the sort," he said coldly.

She nodded. "You've no cause to trust me. I know that. And I know you mean to dissolve this marriage—"

He snorted as if finding offense in the very word.

"—as soon as the law will allow. But if I'm to live in your house and eat at your table—"

He started at hearing his own words said back to him.

"I will do my best to gain what little trust you can afford me. Not because we've been forced into a marriage, but because I'm as much a victim of my brother as you are, and fighting each other will do neither of us any good."

He gave her an irritated glance. "Didn't you *just* say you meant to stay out of my way?"

"I changed my mind," she said, lifting her shoulders into a shrug. "I've spent far too long making myself small to appease my brother. If that's what *you* want, you'll have to find yourself a different wife. I won't make a pest of myself, but neither will I cower in a corner. I'm tired of feeling like I ought to tiptoe around everyone."

She said it quietly enough, but Paulina surprised herself with the force behind her words. She cocked her head. "Who knows? I might even try my hand at being contrary, just for the fun of it."

She had gone down the steps and was halfway to the kitchen before Sebastian spoke again, so she didn't quite hear what he said, but it sounded awfully like, "Good for you."

Sebastian set down his spokeshave and yawned so hard his jaw cracked. He'd woken before dawn in order to ride into town and borrow some clothes from Dilia, as Josefa had pointed out that her own dresses would swamp Paulina's shorter frame. Josefa had been busy frying eggs when he arrived, and rather than drop the clean frocks into the basket with the dirty laundry, he had taken them into Paulina's bedroom himself, holding his breath as he folded them on the chair by the door.

In the dim light of dawn, Paulina was a series of curves under the thin blanket. The hinges had let out a soft whine of protest when he eased the door open, and she had stirred, the long column of her bare arm moving over the pale cotton.

He hadn't taken so much as a step into the room, but the sweet floral scent that seemed to cling to her had followed him all the way back to his horse and down the well-worn path leading to the scattered handful of wooden houses between Villa Consuelo and the mill.

He had stopped in to see Doña Candida first. The elderly woman's intrepid goat had broken out of its pen again, and Sebastian took the time to mend the enclosure with some sturdier wood before hauling the bleating beast back into its confines. Before leaving, he slipped a handful of coins into the half-rusted can where she kept her life's savings and tucked several bills into the bottom, in case he should run afoul of anyone else—though he hoped there weren't many people in San Pedro who would resort to kidnapping.

Sixteen-year-old Leo's widowed mother was next. He'd taken her a tonic for her debilitating headaches and another book for Leo, who consumed them as voraciously as Sebastian did the crisp *cazabe* he was offered. Sebastian had offered to pay for Leo's schooling, as well as a small house in town for him and his mother, and with only a few months until the school year began, the pair were in a flurry of preparations for their upcoming move.

There were several other houses on the way to the mill, and Sebastian visited them all, eager to reassure himself that their inhabitants were as well as Josefa had claimed they were.

If anyone had noticed his absence, none remarked on it, and Sebastian breathed a sigh of relief at not having to explain the events of the past several days.

As much as it pained him to admit it, the mill had indeed fared well in Sebastian's absence. His foreman was more than competent, the workers all well trained by Carlos. In their care, the mill ran as smoothly as the still-shining machinery into which Carlos had invested most of his fortune.

Nothing seemed to have caught fire, at any rate, and the cane itself had gone unharmed in the storm.

"I was beginning to worry," his foreman remarked when Sebastian swung down from his horse outside the large wooden structure. He grinned at Sebastian from under the brim of his woven reed hat. "Finally decided to take in the sights in San Pedro?"

"Something like that," Sebastian replied, half amused at the foreman's suggestion that he'd been carousing in brothels. It saved him having to explain what had happened, though, and for that he was grateful.

A note from Dilia had been waiting on his desk when he reached it. Knowing that Sebastian would never agree to be so far from the mill, she had offered to put up Paulina at her house in town. Sebastian had meant to tell Paulina when he got home—he would have, if she hadn't utterly disarmed him with her remark about not cowering in corners. It had made him recall, in painful detail, all he'd said to her in the carriage on their way home from the Palace of Justice.

Sebastian cast a glance at Paulina's door. Her light was still glowing through the narrow slats. He hesitated, nudging his spokeshave aside, then suddenly recalled the way those beads of water had cascaded over the pronounced dip of her lower back and thought better of risking those treacherous slats. He'd tell her tomorrow after he returned from town.

But when he arrived the following evening, after a disappointing visit to a lawyer who claimed to be too busy to take his case, he found her clambered up a stool on the terrace, her braid swinging slightly as she twisted one of his turnscrews into the hinge of her bedroom doors.

The plain frocks he had borrowed from Dilia on her behalf suited her far better than the ridiculous white dress had. Without the overabundance of ruffles and flounces to obscure her figure, she looked lithe and shapely as she stretched onto her tiptoes to reach the top hinge.

It wasn't only her braid that was swinging.

"I've been meaning to do that," Sebastian said, rubbing the back of his head as he watched her deftly remove the old iron fittings. The new ones he had purchased were lined up neatly on the floor. "I would have gotten to it, eventually."

"You've enough to do. I thought you might appreciate some help."

"I don't need your help."

"The words you're looking for are *thank you*," she said a little tartly, twisting to look at him. "And I didn't say you needed my help, only that you might appreciate having one less chore waiting for you in the evenings. Will you hand me the chisel?"

He obliged, feeling bemused as he took the turnscrew she passed him.

"Where did you learn to do all this?"

She gave a slight shrug. "I lived in an old house, too, you know, and I've a brother who hates parting with his money unless it's for something he believes other people will admire. I had to either learn how to do household repairs myself or live in a permanent state of dilapidation."

Sebastian absorbed the news of Despradel's miserliness with little surprise. A glance at their *quinta* had told him as much, and even if that hadn't been the case, Antonio's decision to sell the mill could have only come from deep financial need.

If Despradel had found himself unable or unwilling to bear the cost of his sister's upkeep, marrying her off would have certainly seemed like a reasonable course of action. That he had chosen Sebastian for it was likely convenience.

The way he had done it, however…was it merely some sort of innate cruelty, or perhaps just repayment for having felt slighted by Sebastian that day in town?

The dislodged hinge clattered to the stone floor. Paulina hopped down lightly from the stool and turned to face him.

Her eyes were astonishing. Not only because of their rich brown color, or the way they seemed to catch and hold all the light around them until they were as luminous as lanterns. It was the expressiveness of them that made Sebastian catch his breath.

He must have been staring. She cocked her head at him.

"I assure you, I know how to put it back together," she told him. "You needn't wait to make sure I do it—heaven knows you could use some rest."

Vaguely disconcerted, though he couldn't say exactly why, Sebastian picked up the spokeshave he had been using to smooth down the broken baluster. "I'm not tired," he lied. There was no need to admit that his thighs ached from the long ride into town and his shoulders still felt cramped from the irons. "And that door's too heavy for you to manage on your own. I'll hold it up while you get the last hinge."

She looked briefly startled, as she did every time anyone showed her the slightest kindness—as if she was unused to even the most basic courtesies.

Unsurprising, considering that damn brother of hers.

Working together, they made short work out of swapping the old, rusted hinges. Sebastian held the shutter in position, trying not to let on that his muscles were screaming in protest, while she leaped up onto the stool once more and screwed in the new hinges.

"These doors really ought to be painted," she was saying from above him. "The old paint is coming off in my hands. Would it be all right if I asked Leo to help me sand them down tomorrow? I saw some cans of paint behind the kitchen that might do, though you might want to purchase some the next time you're in town—how do you feel about a bright, cheery yellow?"

As a matter of fact, Sebastian was partial to bright, cheery yellows. What he didn't like was the desperate panic beating at his ribs as she smiled down at him, for all the world as though she and her brother hadn't conspired to keep him bound in a stinking cell for days.

"This isn't your home," he said abruptly, releasing the secured door.

"I know that," she told him from above, flint in her eyes. "I know it better than you possibly could. I'm reminded of it at every minute of the day—that I live in a house that will never be my home, and that I'm wed to a man who despises me. Forgive me for trying to make the best out of a wretched situation."

As she stepped down from the stool, it gave an alarming wobble and sent her flying.

Sebastian caught her reflexively, his aching arms wrapping around her slender waist and pulling her against his chest as if his body remembered the last time they had stood that way and was eager to repeat the experience.

And like the last time they had stood that way, his body felt seared from the inside out, though he hadn't had so much as a sip of rum.

It was made even worse by the image that flashed into his mind. He didn't have to close his eyes to see again Paulina stepping out of the bath, the pronounced curve of her lower back glistening with beads of water right where Sebastian's hands were now placed.

Her lips pouted in an approximation—or perhaps anticipation—of a kiss. Her front tooth was ever so slightly crooked—endearingly so, he would have called it, had it been anyone else's. He couldn't let himself find anything endearing in Paulina Despradel.

"I don't despise you," he said softly. Too softly. He forced ice into his voice. "I don't…feel anything for you. As a matter of fact, I don't think about you at all."

He was protesting too much. She ought to have been

able to see right through him. If she did, she didn't show it. Her only response was to stiffen in his arms.

He'd hurt her feelings. Yes, well, he'd meant to. He didn't need her getting any ideas about what her being in Villa Consuelo meant.

It would do him well to keep that in mind, as well.

"And I would appreciate it if you could manage to remember that you're a guest here. It's not up to you to paint my doors or repair my shutters, and it's definitely not your place to order my staff about."

Gently, he set her on her feet. And then, feeling as though her touch had scalded him and needing to put enough distance between them to keep himself from burning, he walked off into the night.

Her eyes were as luminous as they were expressive, and the image of them followed him all the way to the darkened mill.

Chapter Eight

A fallen log wasn't the most comfortable place for Sebastian to have his morning coffee, but peaceful spots were in perilously short supply these days and sitting at the edge of the cane field with only a flock of birds for company was the closest thing he could get to peace.

He couldn't really see the house from here, save a glimpse or two when the wind parted the leaves in the right way. It was just as well.

Setting down his enamel mug, he snapped open his newspaper and stared at the sun-dappled page. He had paid visits to almost all of the lawyers advertising there and had been turned down by all of them. Their reasons for doing so were varied, mostly inconsequential…and utterly fabricated.

Sebastian was on fairly good terms with the few townspeople in his acquaintance, and he knew he was considered a respectable businessman, if a trifle distant from society. He hadn't any debts, and he paid his bills on time.

Why, then, would every lawyer in San Pedro, prominent and disreputable alike, decline to take his case?

Sebastian had thought that plunging into action would

go a long way toward restoring at least some measure of peace, but this entire situation only continued to make him feel desperately helpless. It wasn't a sensation he was accustomed to, or one that sat well on his shoulders.

With no one around to see it, he didn't bother to stifle a yawn. He'd stayed late at the mill the night before, creeping into his bedroom a scant few hours before dawn. It had made him irritable—not just the lack of sleep, but the indignity of having to sneak into his own home like a common patio thief.

He'd ride into town again today, after a brief stop at the mill, and see about the rest of the lawyers in the directory. First, however, he needed at least five seconds' worth of quiet while he finished his coffee.

Evidently, that was too much to ask.

A flock of tiny black birds detached itself from the branches above Sebastian and set off across the sky, chattering. As if in response, the tangle of vegetation separating Sebastian from the fields gave a violent tremble. Sebastian had an instant to hope for a wild beast, or even Candida's confounded goat, before something much less desirable emerged through the parted leaves—Paulina.

"What are *you* doing here?" he asked ungraciously as he lowered his newspaper.

She looked surprised, and tired, and Sebastian felt a pang of something that felt uncomfortably like guilt even as he reminded himself that he was doing this not for his own sake, but for those of everyone who depended on him. Then she seemed to draw up, as if she could pull strength around her like a cloak.

As if she could tower over him in spite of the considerable difference in height between them.

"I was going for a walk," she returned. Her hair had been woven into braids and wound around the top of her head, an arrangement that made her cheekbones look more prominent and her gaze more intense. "That is, if I am in fact allowed to go for walks and not expected to wait somewhere convenient for the next time you feel like telling me how unwelcome I am in your home."

Defiance suited her. Her hands were on her hips, her hair was half-unbound and blowing in the breeze, and she was glaring at Sebastian with enough heat that he could almost feel it curl around him and settle low in his belly.

It was damned unwelcome.

"I'm not the kind of person who holds people prisoner until they do his bidding," Sebastian pointed out, the words coming out more harshly than he intended as he tried to cover up the frisson of desire.

"One can only hope there aren't many of those around here," she muttered and started to turn away.

"In a hurry to go conspire with your brother?"

Her hesitation made his shoulders tense. "You don't have to look at me as though you've caught me with my hands on the dough. I *was* on my way home, as it happens. Not because I'm in league with Antonio, but because there's something I want to fetch."

"A set of irons?" he said sarcastically.

"My mother's portrait." Her sharp reply made him feel slightly chastened.

He tried to cover it up by raising an eyebrow. "Do you really think your brother will let you stroll out of the house with a painting under your arm?"

"It's not a painting." She let out a breath. "A few months before she died, my father had a miniature of hers painted by an acquaintance who attended one of their parties. It was set into a locket." She lifted her chin in the half-defensive, half-defiant manner he was beginning to recognize. "I took the locket from her jewelry box because I was angry that they were leaving again, to attend a cousin's wedding in Puerto Plata, and they didn't mean to take me along. I took it and hid it in my bedroom, and it was still there when they died. Antonio doesn't know I have it, or he'd likely try to sell it, though it isn't all that valuable."

Sebastian nodded. He didn't have anything of his own parents' save for a few faint memories, and he'd often wished that the adults who'd taken over his care when his mother died had thought to save something—anything—for him to remember them by. He couldn't fault them for not doing so, however—they'd had no choice but to be ruthless about their practicality.

Setting the newspaper next to the remains of his coffee and the jacket and hat he had cast off, he stood from the log. "I'll take you."

"Take me?" she asked warily.

"Surely you don't think I would let you go to your brother's house unescorted. If he's the villain you say he is, capable of forcing you to do just about anything—"

"Oh, you—" With a low sound that might have come from anger or just plain frustration, Paulina turned away from Sebastian and began walking in the direction of the Despradels' *quinta.*

She had a right to be angry. He knew he was being insufferable. More than that—he was being outright mean.

Women's clothes not being conducive to moving with any sort of speed, it took only a few long strides for Sebastian to catch up with Paulina.

"Why don't you just send me away?" She was looking straight ahead, as if navigating the overgrown path required all her attention. "Take me to the harbor and put me in a boat and send me to New York, or Madrid, or Paris, or even Constantinople, like you offered on the night of the storm. I would do it myself if I had any money."

"Don't think I won't do it," he said grimly. He'd thought of nothing else since Dilia had suggested that Paulina stay with her, and he had ultimately discarded the idea. He needed her here, if only to ensure that she signed whatever document was drawn up to dissolve the marriage.

"Trust me," she said, pushing a palm frond out of her way. "I would far prefer it if you did."

"We don't all get what we want."

"I'm aware of that." She could have said it bitterly, but there was only weariness in her tone.

"Yes," he said after a long pause. "I suppose you are."

The words were hardly out of his mouth when a breathless Leo popped into the path in front of them, having come through the brush. "Don Sebastian? Will you come to Doña Candida's? There's…a situation." He looked desperately apologetic, though Sebastian could have told him he wasn't interrupting anything of consequence.

"The damned goat got out again?" Sebastian said, sighing in resignation, already turning to follow Leo to the elderly woman's house.

"Not exa—"

"Did you hear that?" Paulina asked suddenly. "It sounded like a scream."

Sebastian cast a sharp glance in the direction she was looking at, but all he could see was the tangle of vegetation that surrounded them. "The goat, I expect. The determined little ba—beast keeps breaking out of its pen and chewing through his ropes. I've half a mind to put *him* in irons."

"It was a human scream," she said and darted down the path.

Swearing under his breath, Sebastian pelted after her, Leo at his heels.

Vines and branches whipped at Paulina's face as they raced toward what, yes, did sound like a woman's shrieks.

Sebastian began to run in earnest, overtaking her in a couple of bounds of his long legs. Paulina kept pace with him easily enough, though her long skirts were swirling around her ankles.

The screams subsided, and by the time they reached a clearing by a steep embankment, it had been replaced with something that sounded distinctly like scolding.

It was coming from a girl, whose bare feet were planted firmly in the packed dirt of the clearing as she yanked a rope out of a young man's hands. Looming threateningly over her, the young man raised a hand as if to slap her. Rather than cower, the girl stood her ground.

"Berenice?" Paulina was startled into saying out loud.

"You know her?" Sebastian asked, sparing Paulina a glance.

"She works at my brother's house." The last time Paulina had seen her, the girl had been acting as his assistant jailer, keeping Paulina locked in her bedroom. Warily, she followed Sebastian toward the group that had gathered around her and the young man.

Sebastian seemed to be something of a local hero—or, if not hero, at least enough of an authority figure that Paulina caught the expressions of relief as the group parted respectfully to let him through.

"What seems to be the problem?" he asked mildly.

Berenice spoke up first. "I was on my way to work when I caught this boy trying to steal Candida's goat!"

"I wasn't stealing anything," the young man said immediately, and he was promptly backed by one of the bystanders.

"That's Candida's grandson," said a man with a graying beard, spitting out a stream of tobacco into the ground. "And if you ask me, he's got more of a right to dispose of her property than the little busybody."

Berenice's brow rose. "*Busybody?* How dare you?" she said furiously, but was forestalled by Sebastian.

"Candida's grandson?" Sebastian directed an agreeable smile at the boy. "I've never met you before, have I?"

"I've been in Moca, trying to find work," the youth explained reluctantly.

"Ah, you must be Alfonso, then. I'm Sebastian Linares. I'm a friend of your grandmother's."

From the look on the boy's face, Paulina could tell he doubted Sebastian's claim to friendship.

"I'm no great friends with her goat," Sebastian added, though his attempt at humor wasn't well received by Alfonso, "but I do know that your grandmother's awfully fond of him. She wouldn't happen to be here, by any chance?"

"She went to visit a friend in town," Berenice put in. "And he was taking advantage of her being gone to sell it without her consent."

"I don't see how it's any of your business what I do with my grandmother's livestock," Alfonso told her. Paulina, looking at the scraggly specimen at the end of the rope, wasn't sure she would have used that word herself. "Don't you have anything better to do than to meddle in something that clearly doesn't concern you?"

Berenice's brows drew together. Before she could say anything in her own defense, Paulina stepped in. "That's no way to speak to a young woman," she said sharply.

"Particularly when she's looking out for your own grand-mother's interests."

The young man turned to Paulina as if noticing her presence for the first time. His expression morphed into a sullen scowl. "I'm only trying to do right by the old lady. She needs money more than she needs a useless old goat that's always causing trouble."

"I see," Sebastian said, flicking a glance at Paulina. "And does Candida agree?"

Alfonso's scowl deepened. "She doesn't know what's good for her. I found a man who's willing to take the goat off my hands for twelve pesos. It's a good deal. And this one—" he jerked his chin toward Berenice "—probably just wants it for herself."

A murmur from the people gathered made him cocky, though Paulina wasn't sure they were in agreement with his pronouncement.

Alfonso gave a sudden lunge for the rope Berenice was still holding. The goat, which this far into the pro-ceedings had been content to gnaw on it, suddenly saw an opportunity to escape. He wasted no time—snapping the frayed rope with a single bound, he leaped away, but not without first kicking Berenice aside.

The spectators scattered as the goat went right through the crowd, heading straight toward the low branches of a nearby tree. Dodging the goat's horns, Paulina threw herself after Berenice, who had crashed to the ground right at the edge of the embankment behind them. Her fingers grazed the girl's dress, but she couldn't reach her in time before Berenice went tumbling down.

Only Sebastian's arms around Paulina's waist pre-vented her from following Berenice down.

He gripped her against him, hard enough to make Paulina's pulse roar in her ears.

"For heaven's sake, Paulina," he said irritably, though she had noticed the hitch in his breath, "have some care for yourself."

She pulled away. "I'm perfectly fine."

The incline was only about twice Paulina's height, but it was damnably steep, and she could see no clear path down. Some distance below Berenice, a narrow stream tumbled over a series of rocks.

"Don't worry," Paulina called down. "We'll find a way to get you up. Are you hurt?"

"My ankle," Berenice called back. "I think I broke my ankle."

Behind her, Sebastian was telling the men to fetch a longer rope with which to haul the girl up. Paulina was the only one who saw Berenice sit down suddenly, like a marionette whose strings had been abruptly cut.

"*Santísimo*, she's going to faint," Paulina exclaimed. She didn't think twice about it. Seizing one of the long vines dangling down from a tree growing right at the edge of the embankment, she tested it with her weight. It would hold her, but not any of the men clustered behind her.

"Paulina?" Sebastian sounded bemused. "What—?"

She didn't waste time to hear his protests but used the vine to let herself down onto the ledge where Berenice had fallen. Paulina had spent much of her childhood shimmying up trees and swinging from vines, but it had been a while since she'd last done such a thing, and her descent was not as smooth as it should be—the vine scraped the skin of her palms as Paulina slid down a little too suddenly, forcing her to let go and leap down lightly onto the wide ledge.

Berenice was conscious, but her breathing was ragged

and her face screwed with pain. Paulina put an arm around her. "You'll be all right."

Sebastian's head appeared over the edge, brows knit together into a thunderous frown. "Leo went to fetch a longer rope. You could have waited."

"Berenice was feeling a little faint," Paulina said up to him. "I thought she'd appreciate some company down here."

"By all means. Would you like a pot of coffee and a cake for your visit? Or perhaps a bottle of port?"

Was it her imagination, or did he look slightly admiring under the disapproving frown?

Not that it mattered.

"Sarcasm doesn't suit you," Paulina called, and she was rewarded with a smile before he withdrew.

Heedless of the mud and broken leaves, she sat herself beside Berenice. "It won't be long before they find a rope long enough to pull us up."

The girl nodded. "Thank you for coming down here. That was...brave."

"Or foolhardy, as I'm sure Sebastian will waste no time in telling me." Nonetheless, Paulina offered the girl a smile. "It was brave of *you* to try to keep Alfonso from making off with his grandmother's, er, livestock."

"Doña Candida has been good to me since my parents died," Berenice said softly. "And she loves that wretched beast. I didn't think she'd appreciate coming home to find the goat gone."

"And she won't, thanks to you. You did right to stand up to that grandson of hers."

Berenice pressed her lips together, but a smile managed to find its way past them. "Just wait until Doña Candida gets back. *She'll* have a lot more to say to him. She doesn't have a lot of patience for Alfonso's schemes for getting rich quick—I know she was hoping that he would find enough work in Moca to keep him occupied for some time."

"Maybe Sebastian will be able to help in that regard," Paulina said, though it wasn't Alfonso she was concerned with. "Are you still in my brother's employ?"

Berenice gave Paulina a sudden glance, then hung her head before saying softly, as if admitting to something wretched, "I am."

They had no opportunity for further conversation just then. A good length of rope having been secured, Sebastian and the other men above prepared to haul them both up. Paulina made sure Berenice went first.

Once the girl was safely over the edge of the embankment, Sebastian cast down the rope again for Paulina to tie around her own waist. Seizing the rope in her scraped hands, she scrambled up the embankment as quickly as she could—and almost cried out when her foot slid on a patch of slick vegetation and she found herself face-down in the mud, her arm scraping painfully over a protruding root.

Only the rope squeezing her midsection kept her from plummeting all the way down to the rocks poking out of the water below.

"Paulina!" Sebastian shouted. His face came into view, and he looked ready to vault over the edge himself. "Hold on tight. I'm coming down."

"No." She couldn't have explained the sudden panic that gripped her at the prospect of him rescuing her again, but it was enough to make her lift herself out of the mud, a trifle shakily, her fingers tight around the rope. "I can pull myself the rest of the way."

"Are you—"

"I can do it," she said grimly, half to herself.

Sebastian was waiting for her at the edge, his powerful arms clasping her tightly as he pulled her up. She was not ashamed to admit that she clung to one of those arms for the second it took for the hollowness in her stomach to dissolve—thick and hard as branches, they felt reassuringly solid.

He made no move to dislodge her, and Paulina wondered if he could feel the hammering of her heart against his arm. "Are you all right?"

"Fine," she said shakily, then essayed another, firmer, "Fine."

She stepped away from Sebastian to find Alfonso looking at Berenice's ashen face with a troubled frown. "I didn't mean… My grandmother, she— I really didn't think she would mind me selling the goat."

"Maybe it would be better if we let Doña Candida be the judge of that," Sebastian said gently. "In the meantime, if it's work you want, why don't you stop by the mill tomorrow? I'm sure we can find something for you to do."

Paulina could see the gears grinding in the boy's mind. On the one hand, whatever deal he had struck for the goat must have been profitable enough that he seemed reluctant to abandon it.

On the other, it was clearly not the best idea to rebuff Sebastian outright. One had only to look at him to know he was prosperous as well as respected, and even if the young man had no interest in a job at the mill, anyone with a little foresight would try to keep in Sebastian's good graces.

He gave a grudging nod.

"Why don't you and Leo take the goat back to its pen while I see to Berenice?" Sebastian suggested, clearly not trusting the young man to go on his own.

Another nod, and both young men departed.

Paulina, who had crouched next to Berenice, was probing at her ankle. "It *is* broken," Paulina said. "I'm not expert, clearly, but it looks like a bad break."

"Oh, your poor hands," Berenice cried, grasping the objects in question, and Paulina realized she had left smears of blood on Berenice's leg. "Your palms are torn to shreds."

The cuts were fairly nasty, Paulina saw, but it was Berenice's ankle that worried her. It was puffed and swollen, the dark skin around it badly discolored. They would need a doctor. She lifted her head to tell Sebastian, but he was already crouching beside her.

"We had better get that seen by someone at the Municipal Hospital," Sebastian told Berenice, but the girl wasn't paying him any attention. Her lips were trembling as she looked at Paulina, and it didn't seem to be from pain.

"I'm sorry about helping your brother lock you up." Berenice's voice broke, and she buried her face in her grimy hands, though not before Paulina saw, with considerable surprise, the tears running down her cheeks. "He said he would hurt my little sister if I didn't follow his orders."

"I won't let him do anything to either of you," Sebastian said fiercely. "I'll find a place for you to stay until your ankle heals. In the meantime, I'm taking you to the hospital."

"Don Antonio will be waiting," Berenice said, looking apprehensive.

"Let him wait," Sebastian said grimly, adding softly, when he saw the girl's brows knit together, "You won't be able to work in this state. We'll send word that you'll be indisposed for a while."

Paulina put her arm around the young woman's shoulders to help her up. Sebastian put a stop to that by scooping up Berenice. "I can manage."

It wasn't until they had returned to Villa Consuelo, much later that morning, that Sebastian turned again to Paulina to voice what he had clearly been turning in his mind for the past several hours. "He locked you up?"

"Only so that I wouldn't go to you," she said, as matter-of-factly as she could.

Sebastian gave her a hard nod, more an acknowledgment than an expression of gratitude. Still, she couldn't help but notice the slight shift in the way he was looking at her—less like a thorn that had gotten wedged into his side, and more like someone he was trying to figure out.

Paulina stepped out of her muddy clothes, all too aware that in the next room, Sebastian was doing the same. She tried to summon up some of the irritation that had propelled her on her walk earlier that morning, but all she felt was tired.

And curious about the look he had given her when he'd asked about Antonio locking her up. It was as if he had still believed that she'd been Antonio's conspirator, and Berenice's testimony had begun to disabuse him of that notion.

It was as if he was seeing her in a different light.

Paulina unbuttoned her mud-caked blouse and pulled it over her shoulders, the abused muscles in her arms aching from the effort. The cotton garment whispered to the floor to join the skirt she had already discarded.

Mud had seeped through to her undergarments, staining them faintly with brown. She wiped them as best as she could with a clean rag, then began dressing in her spare frock. It couldn't be helped—Paulina had the one chemise and pair of drawers, which she laundered each night and hung by the louvered doors to dry, and in the pale yellow dress their lack would be noticeable.

She would have to stay in the sun until she'd dried out, that was all.

Once more presentable, and with her clothes bundled in her arms to be soaked before the stains could set, she strode into the kitchen yard. Several large tamarind trees shaded the area, though here and there sunlight filtered down through the protective canopy. Paulina paused in one such patch, soaking in the brightness and the heat.

She closed her eyes and tipped her head back. The morning sun was always warm, rarely as searing as it became as the day wore on.

When she opened them again, it was to see that Sebastian, not Doña Josefa as she had expected, was standing in the kitchen.

And he was looking at her.

Unaccountably flustered, Paulina shifted her light bundle of clothes to her front to hide the way her chemise and dress were molded damply to her chest, and hurried the rest of the way to the kitchen.

Sebastian had also changed clothes. His pristine shirt was buttoned at the cuffs and the neck, though he wore no necktie, and the droplets of water glinting in his close-cropped curls attested to his own ablutions. Trying to pretend that she was not flooded with awareness—of the faint scent of soap wafting from him, or the fabric clinging to her hardened nipples—made her clumsy.

They reached at the same time for the blouse she had dropped.

Their fingers tangled on the muddy cotton, hers slim, his broad and blunt. There was absolutely no reason for the simple contact to make her heart race—no sensible reason, at any rate.

Paulina yanked her hand back, remembering to keep her hold on the blouse. "I'll thank you not to manhandle my clothes."

He lifted an eyebrow. "You're welcome."

The sardonic tinge in his voice sent prickles up and down her spine. She turned her back to him. She could hardly ask him what he was doing in the kitchen, it being his property and all, so she settled for asking about Doña Josefa, who was nowhere in sight.

"She went to the Municipal Hospital to make sure the doctor knew what sort of poultice to apply to Berenice's foot. She'll have the entire hospital following her orders before nightfall."

Paulina couldn't hold back a smile. "That sounds like her."

The tub they used for laundry was too large for just her skirt and blouse, so she looked for the enamel basin— and found it in Sebastian's hands.

"I needed that," she said.

"This will only take a moment. Give me your arm."

She narrowed her eyes at him. "Why?"

"Because it's badly scraped, and I've something that will make it feel better."

"Why should you care?" Paulina said.

It came out more forcefully than she'd intended; rather than look taken aback or annoyed, Sebastian merely met her eyes.

"I care," he said, so seriously that Paulina had to look away.

She shifted her gaze from him to the basin, which was filled with clear water.

Her skepticism must have been written all over her face, because he gave an impatient sigh and set the basin down on the table, then showed her the contents of a covered mug next to a clean rag. "I'll clean out the dirt, then put some *remedio* on the scrapes. Josefa brewed it, if it makes you feel any better. Will you give me your arm now?"

Mildly discomfited, she complied, extending her right hand in his direction, palm upturned as if she were offering him something. The sleeve of her dress ended just below her elbow, very close to one edge of the scrape. Very gently, he folded up the fabric so that it wouldn't get in the way, then dipped the rag into the clean water and began to bathe her wound.

He did it confidently, and Paulina would have thought he were used to this sort of thing were it not for the fact that she knew that was how he did everything.

Paulina was no stranger to longing. In fact, she was acquainted well enough with it to know that the sensation twining around her limbs was something...different. Something deeper.

Something that made her wonder what it would be like if he were to trail the backs of his fingers over the soft, unmarred skin on the inside of her arm. If he were to lower his head and press his lips to the tracery of veins on her wrist. And perhaps venture farther, following the line of her arm all the way to her neck and the hollow beneath her ear.

It was just as well that Sebastian had no idea how his touch affected her—or the thoughts currently searing their way through her mind.

In order to distract herself from his confident hands, she looked straight ahead and found herself staring at his chest instead, which didn't help matters any. The wide expanse of his shirt was bisected by light brown suspenders, which were daubed with spots of mud.

"There's mud on your suspenders."

Sebastian glanced down. "Yes, well, I only have the one pair."

"They'll get your clean shirt all dirty. Here." She plucked the damp rag by a clean corner and briskly began to brush off the worst of the dirt.

"Paulina." His large, warm hand rose to cover hers, pressing it lightly against the center of his chest. It felt so natural that, for a moment, Paulina's world tilted and rearranged itself and she had to remember that they had never, in fact, stood together in that way.

She didn't want to look up into his eyes—not for fear of what she might see there, but for fear of what she might not. "That's a little better, but you'll have to soak your suspenders overnight," she said, concentrating very hard on a spot near his left shoulder.

"Paulina," he said again. "You…ah… What's that in your arms?"

"My clothes," she said after a brief pause. He had clearly changed tracks in the middle of speaking, and even though she had been ready to bolt a moment before, she felt a burst of disappointed curiosity. "I only have the one change of clothes, so I need to wash the mud right away if they're going to dry by tomorrow."

He frowned. "I should have sent you to the dressmaker to have more clothes made. My apologies. I know I've been remiss in—"

"It's fine," Paulina said, cutting him off. "I don't need more clothes, not really. And I wouldn't want to take advantage of your hospitality."

"You haven't. Also, you never did get your mother's portrait," he said gruffly.

"I suppose I didn't."

"Would you like me to go fetch it for you?"

She shook her head. "I don't think it would be a good

idea for you to go there on your own. Antonio is sure to get into one of his moods when Berenice fails to arrive, and we both know what that can lead to." She lifted an eyebrow and finally looked up into his eyes, confident that there was nothing but a dark sort of humor in hers. "It's just as well. Going to the *quinta* was probably a bad idea. Even for the portrait—it's probably more trouble than it's worth."

"I doubt that," he said with the gaze of a man who was intimately acquainted not only with grief, but with loss.

It made Paulina wonder if he was also an orphan. He'd told her a little about Carlos, and there was Dilia, the woman who had been waiting for him when they'd returned from the Palace of Justice, but Paulina was reasonably sure he hadn't mentioned any relations, at least in her presence.

He hadn't released her hand. Looking down at the scraped skin, the furrow between his brows deepened. "I haven't any bandages, but I can have someone fetch a doctor—"

"That's all right," Paulina said. "I'm fine."

"Paulina, I—"

His thumb grazed the back of her hand. If he had done it intentionally, it would have been a shockingly intimate touch—but of course, Paulina thought wildly, trying her hardest to keep her face from betraying her, it had probably been involuntary. A mere jerk of the muscles. Not a caress.

Definitely not a caress.

"I didn't know he'd locked you up. If I had…"

"You'd have believed me when I told you I had nothing to do with his plans? Doubtful."

His eyebrow quirked. "That morning when he burst in on us. You didn't say anything. I thought…"

Paulina gave a little sigh. "I should have come to your defense, I know. I was numb with shock. And embarrassed. And not wearing any clothes, if you might remember."

"Oh, I remember," he murmured.

"That puts one at a disadvantage. Honestly, I think I'd grown a little too used to giving Antonio his own way. It was…easier." She shrugged, looking down at their joined hands. "Maybe I'm as weak as he thinks I am."

"There's nothing weak about you, Paulina," he said, and her gaze skipped up to his. He gave her fingers an absent squeeze and released them, sliding his hands into his pockets. "I think I was perhaps a bit hasty in putting any blame on you for…all this. I should apologize."

"Yes, you should," she said tartly.

"I misjudged you."

"You certainly did."

To her surprise, he smiled down at her. "You aren't going to go easy on me, are you?"

She found herself smiling back. "Not in the slightest." A tiny sigh escaped her. "At first I was hurt that you could think me capable of such duplicity. But then I realized—you don't know me. Not truly. Otherwise, you'd have realized that this kind of marriage is the last thing I would want. I had always thought that if I did ever marry, I would marry for love. Like my parents did. They found such joy in each other. I couldn't help but want the same."

"I don't know if I can give you that. But I do owe you an explanation." Sebastian stepped away then, but only far enough to lean against the worktable, his solid hands gripping its wooden edge tightly enough for Paulina to see that whatever he was about to say wouldn't come easily.

"Before we left Havana—before I convinced Carlos and Dilia to leave, that is—I became entangled with someone. I—don't think it's necessary to go into the details. Suffice it to say, she told me everything I'd ever wanted to hear. She made me believe…"

He made a dismissive gesture, but Paulina saw the ghost of an old wound flickering in his eyes. "That isn't important," he continued. "The point of this story is that I was very young and very foolish and fancied myself some sort of chivalrous knight or something equally as ridiculous, and she did not hesitate in taking advantage of my romantic notions. It was little things at first—minor domestic disasters that I could avert with a handful of pesos, earnest pleas for small loans for her ailing father… Before I knew it, she and her father had swindled me out of what little I had."

He didn't seem to hear the low noise of distress that escaped Paulina's lips. She should have suspected that Antonio was not the first person to take advantage of Sebastian's giving nature. That Sebastian had been justified in his suspicion of her… Paulina didn't know why that made her chest feel so tight.

"And then, the moment she realized that I was not Carlos's true brother, and therefore not about to inherit half of his parents' estate, she left. Literally left the island, without so much as a note to let me know that she'd gone." His lips lifted into a humorless smile. "I don't want to say that she left me with nothing, though she stripped my bank account almost bare, and for months afterward I felt like she'd stripped my heart right out of my chest, too. I know I've been suspicious of you—"

"You had a good reason to be." Paulina was still holding her bundle of clothes in the crook of her right elbow. She laid it down on the table and began to empty the water from the basin. Something was simmering in her chest, some strong emotion she couldn't quite name. "I'm not her, you know. I wouldn't— I didn't want any of this to happen."

"I know that now," Sebastian said quietly.

He was close enough that his breath grazed her ear. Paulina looked up at him, and her breath caught at the emotion in his eyes.

Unbidden, her hand rose to land lightly on his jaw. She breathed in sharply and would have snatched her hand away at once had he not trapped it with his own much larger one.

His touch was electrifying.

Tingles zinged down Paulina's arm, collecting somewhere just beneath her breastbone and speeding up her pulse.

Sebastian's head inclined toward hers.

"We shouldn't," she murmured.

"I know," he answered.

With those words hanging over them, their lips met in something that was surely more than a kiss. Something more vital than an exchange of breath. Something more intimate than an exchange of souls.

Paulina's heart was racing when she pulled away, gasping. Sebastian looked as stunned as she felt.

Unfortunately—or perhaps fortunately—before either of them could say a word, a voice came from behind them.

"Don Sebastian? You're needed at the mill again. One of the men had an accident."

Letting out a sharp breath, Sebastian dropped his hand from Paulina's and turned to face the messenger boy who was standing at the edge of the kitchen yard, looking apologetic at the intrusion.

Paulina took advantage of Sebastian's distraction to slip away with the basin, the soap and her dirty clothes. The splotches of mud had begun to dry. It would take a great deal of scrubbing to get them all out, but that was for the best.

Maybe the exertion would make her forget just how good his touch had felt.

Chapter Nine

After sleeping in for three days in a row, Paulina finally managed to awaken before the sun had brightened enough to send bars of light through her shutters.

She hurried into her clothes, making a perfunctory attempt to tidy her hair, and rushed out so fast she nearly collided into a tree. No—not a tree. Sebastian, who had just emerged from his own chamber, the faint aroma of soap wafting from his person. In his shirtsleeves, framed by the dark lines of his now-clean suspenders, his arms were as thick—and as hard—as branches.

He had vanished for much of the previous afternoon and had returned after dinner looking out of temper and smelling distinctly like goat. When questioned, he had muttered something about having ruined two shirts in a single day and dragged the tub into his bedroom. He hadn't emerged by the time she had retired, but Paulina, awake and restless with memories of the kiss they had shared, had heard him fussing with the railing long into the night.

"You don't sleep much, do you?" she said in lieu of a good morning, hefting the bundle of fabric she had tucked under her arm.

Sebastian shrugged. "I don't need to," he said, but he belied his own words with a yawn so wide his jaw made an audible popping sound.

Paulina limited her remarks to a skeptical, "I see," as they began the walk to the kitchen.

He let out a breath that sounded like a laugh. "Dilia makes me take naps," he confessed. "Orders me, in fact, as if I were one of her boys."

"I can see why," Paulina replied. In the time she had known Sebastian, the crinkle of exhaustion hadn't left his eyes. "Have you ever thought about taking some initiative and *not* waiting for someone to bully you into napping?"

"I've a lot to do," he said simply.

He didn't seem inclined to mention what had happened between them the day before, and Paulina thought it was probably for the best. It wasn't likely to happen again, after all. Sebastian was probably already regretting that it had happened at all. Both the kiss and his confession.

Through the tamarind trees that canopied the yard, Paulina could see the sky beginning to lighten with pale bands of light. Below the sprawling branches, however, it was still fairly dark. Paulina could barely see the hulking shape in the middle of the kitchen yard—and judging by the way Sebastian almost walked into it, neither could he.

"What's this?" he asked warily, eyeing the shape as though it were one of the wild boars that lurked in the mountains rather than a harmless old door laid out on trestles.

"Our new dining table." Paulina shook out the clean bedsheet she had tucked under her arm and laid it over the peeling wood. "Doña Josefa helped me set it up before we went to sleep last night."

"It was about time, too," the housekeeper remarked

from behind the cook fire, which was already roaring beneath a pan of frying eggs and onions.

"I hope you don't mind," Paulina said, glancing up at Sebastian. "We thought it would be fun, and the door didn't appear to be in use…"

"It's a ridiculous idea," Sebastian replied as Leo came up behind them with the milk pail, saying a soft good morning.

Paulina's heart sank. "Oh, all right, I—"

Stuffing a hand into the pocket of his trousers, Sebastian pulled out a wad of bills, two of which he handed Leo. "Go to Ronaldo's workshop and buy the biggest and finest table he has." He scowled down at the overturned bucket at the head of the table. "And chairs. At least eight of them."

Leo nodded and made as if to leave right then, but Sebastian caught him by the back of his shirt. "After you've eaten."

Paulina, who had opened her mouth to say the same thing, snapped it shut.

Sebastian turned to Paulina with a glower, which she met with the sunniest smile she could muster.

"Are you trying to look forbidding?" she asked, fetching the jar of flowers she had left by the water barrel and placing it squarely on the center of the table. "Maybe you ought to furrow your brow a little more. Or growl. That'll do it."

He shook his head, clearly trying not to laugh. "I've got to get to the mill."

Coming up behind him with the coffeepot and two mugs hanging from her little finger, Doña Josefa pressed him down onto the three-legged stool. "You have time to eat breakfast before you go."

"And you are as bossy as a general," Sebastian said

with a good-natured grumble, but he submitted to Doña Josefa's orders.

Briefly, Doña Josefa laid a hand on top of his head before heading back to the cook fire.

It was a curiously familiar gesture for a housekeeper to make to her employer. Paulina tilted her head and looked at the pair more closely. They looked nothing alike, though they were both large and broad in their own ways. Doña Josefa had soft, blunt features, while Sebastian's looked like they were chiseled out of stone. Was there a similar cast to their shoulders? Did they hold their heads the same way?

The kitchen yard began to lighten as she and Leo helped Doña Josefa carry the rest of the breakfast things to the table. Through the branches, the sky looked freshly laundered, a bright blue with clouds like frothed soap. It reminded Paulina of the lather she had worked up the day before, trying to erase her memory of Sebastian's touch. The scrubbing hadn't helped, and even if it had, it would have been for nothing—Paulina could count at least half a dozen times their fingers tangled over the eggs.

Perhaps the table had been a bad idea.

Sebastian reached across the table for the pitcher of milk Paulina had just taken hold of, and when his fingertips brushed the tender skin on the inside of her wrist, she gave up on breakfast and lifted the folded newspaper by Sebastian's plate. It wasn't recent, but Paulina didn't care. Humming under her breath, she discarded the first half until she came to the advertisements, which she perused with quiet contentment.

There were three houses for sale in town and two for rent. Not for the first time, Paulina wished they came with pictures, though the short descriptions were satisfying in their own way.

"Has there been a murder?" Sebastian asked.

Paulina cocked her head. "A murder?"

"It must be a shocking one, the way you're poring over the paper."

"Oh! No, I'm just looking at the houses for rent."

Raising an eyebrow, Sebastian said, "Houses for rent? I hope our hospitality hasn't been lacking."

"Doña Josefa has been wonderful to me," she said pointedly. "Leo, too. This is just a habit I have. I suppose it amuses me to pretend like I'm looking for a house. I've always dreamed of living in town."

"Why is that?" he asked, looking at her as if he really were interested in the answer.

Paulina gave a little shrug. "It's so lonely out here in the country. I'd much rather be close to other people and be able to go to frolics at a moment's notice and strolling on Sundays. It's a silly notion," she added firmly, folding the newspaper back into a tidy rectangle.

"There's nothing silly about not wanting to be lonely," Sebastian said, frowning down at the tin mug cradled in his long, strong fingers. "I enjoyed living in town back in Havana, though it did get a trifle hot and noisy sometimes. There were plenty of afternoon strolls and all sort of frolics, too." He nodded at the newspaper. "Which one would you choose?"

With the advertisements hidden inside the fold, the only words visible were the name of the paper and the banner unspooling beneath it reading *Noticias, Variedades y Anuncios*.

Even without a visible reminder of what she had just read, Paulina didn't have to think long to make a decision. "The masonry house on the corner of Calle El Retiro. Or—no. I'd buy an empty lot and have a house built to suit my tastes. Large, airy rooms with high ceilings and whitewashed walls and boxes full of white bougainvillea in every window. And two long galleries, one upstairs and one down, with plenty of room for guests and dancing."

Paulina made herself stop, suddenly aware that she had gotten carried away. "It sounds overly grand, I know. The truth is, I'd be just as happy with a shack if it was mine and mine alone."

Sebastian's brow was furrowed. "Sounds like you've given it a lot of thought."

"Yes, well. I've never been able to make any decisions for myself. Not about where to live or what to wear or who to befriend. Thinking about those things was just the only thing I *could* do, so I was apt to do plenty of it." She spread her hands. "Dreaming is free, after all."

He gave her an odd look. "You've never chosen your own clothing?"

She shook her head. "Antonio picked out every scrap of lace on those awful frocks he made me wear. My hair ribbons, too."

Paulina didn't know what to make of the sudden stillness that came over Sebastian. "Did he...mistreat you?"

"He wasn't violent, if that's what you mean. He just made himself so disagreeable to be around that it was always easier to let him have his way." Paulina shrugged. "His main complaint seemed to be that I was too much of an expense for him. Maybe he thought I would ruin him if I was allowed free rein at the dressmaker."

Over the years, Paulina had grown used to answering every flare of Antonio's temper with a turn of her head. She had looked away or left the room or otherwise found a way to keep from confronting the fact that her brother had grown up to be hard and mean and greedy.

There had always been a part of her that had been

uncomfortably aware of just how much she depended on Antonio. When her parents died, and none of their friends or relations had offered to take her in, Antonio had been quick to make her understand that as the new head of the family he held not only the purse strings—he held the reins of her life. Not only was he going to make all the decisions from now on, she had no right to question him, or to even offer her opinion.

The only thing that had gotten Paulina through those stifling years was dreaming about how one day she would be free. And now she was, in a way. No closer to that house in town, perhaps, but free nonetheless.

"Seems to me he's done a better job of emptying out his coffers himself," Sebastian remarked. He took a swig of his coffee. "I asked around town, and word is your brother's mired in countless debts. Losing at cards being much more of an expense than a few hair ribbons."

She felt her lips tugging upward as she recalled the red length Sebastian had given her for her birthday. What a pity it had been ruined in the storm. "I wouldn't be so sure about that. Do you know how many hundreds of pesos I could spend just on the ribbons Don Enrique carries in his store? I'd buy yards and yards of every color and hang them from my dressing table like streamers." She laughed at herself, tracing the rim of her mug with her fingertip. "A silly aspiration, perhaps, but a tad more attainable than purchasing an entire house."

Sebastian looked thoughtful—even a little forbidding—and Paulina wished she hadn't said quite so much. She began to gather the empty plates from her side of the table.

She had gotten so used to the way her sharp longing for companionship had lodged inside her chest like a particularly prickly burr that it hadn't occurred to her until now that her dreams would sound pitiful to someone else. It had been that way for as long as she could remember, even when her parents had been alive. She had never been able to find a place among the grown-up guests that crowded into their *quinta*, or among the girls of their set that she rarely saw. The little boy who had played with her among the sugarcane had been her one true friend—until he, too, went away.

At some point, she had come to believe that heart-wrenching loneliness was all life had to offer her. Save for the scant handful of hours when she had waited in bed for Sebastian that first night, when she had allowed herself to picture something different, for once.

"It isn't the worst hardship anyone's had to bear," she said as she piled the plates together.

"Don't make light of what you went through," Sebastian said with sudden heat, reaching for her wrist. His shirt cuff pulled away again, but this time he hardly seemed to notice the flash of discolored skin it revealed, or to care that she saw it. "You may not have worn manacles, but your brother kept you captive as surely as he did me, and for much longer. Denying you even the scant freedom due to you as a woman? It's nothing short of villainous."

Paulina stood as if frozen, captivated by his vehemence.

"You were locked up for only a few days. But Paulina, you've been trapped for most of your life."

Sebastian rose and, seizing the dirty crockery from her arms, carried it to the washtub where the housekeeper was already beginning to warm up water. "I should be on my way," he said. He started to add something else, then seemed to change his mind. "I won't be back until late."

She nodded her acquiescence, offering him a faltering parting smile.

* * *

There was a vase on his chest of drawers.

And there were *flowers* in it.

Sebastian eyed it as warily as he would have a snake.

He had come directly into his bedroom after a long, hot morning at the mill, intending to rest for a few minutes before lunchtime, and the little pitcher crowded with fiery red hibiscus blossoms was the first thing he'd seen.

He ought to resent this evidence of her intrusion into his home, his *life*. Maybe he would have, if he hadn't been filled with a grudging respect for the way she was managing to make Villa Consuelo into more of a home than it had been in the time he'd owned it. The business with the table, earlier that morning, had filled him with embarrassment at how thoughtless he'd been toward both Paulina and Josefa, who'd uncomplainingly made do with the little he'd provided them in the way of accommodations.

Well, he was about to change all that.

Quickly splashing some water onto his face and wiping off the excess moisture, he went in search of Paulina.

She, too, deserved better, and not only in the way of furniture.

Her brother had treated her abominably. That had been more than evident from the moment he'd met her. But every time Sebastian thought he knew the extent of that ill treatment, it turned out that he'd only scratched the surface.

Sebastian had known his share of tightfisted men who enjoyed a little begging and pleading from the people who depended on them. The ones who needed to be flattered before they'd part with a single *chele*. Antonio Despradel, Sebastian suspected, wouldn't relinquish so much as a dust mote for his sister's sake if it somehow didn't benefit him.

It wasn't begging he wanted, or flattery—it was control.

A few days ago, nothing could have persuaded Sebastian that he had anything in common with the youngest daughter of a wealthy household—a woman who kept to her home and only emerged swathed in yards of lace and finery, delicate as the rose he had compared her to when he'd first met her in town. A pampered woman, he would have called her.

He couldn't have been more wrong. She'd endured privations, just as he had. Only Sebastian had had two things she hadn't—family and freedom. In his darkest days, when getting a crust of bread to soothe his growling stomach seemed like an impossible dream, he'd still had more than her.

Anyone might have pitied her for it, but Sebastian was filled only with admiration at her resilience.

Paulina was fetching water from the barrel when he found her. The barrel was almost as tall as he was, and the water must have been low, even after all the rain that had fallen the night of the storm, because she had clambered onto the damn stool with the wobbly leg and was leaning so far into the barrel that all he could see was the roundness of her bottom above the rim.

The sight of it reminded Sebastian of how Carlos used to tease him for his single-mindedness when it came to the business. Sebastian hadn't only eschewed the company of the fine young ladies of the town, he'd kept mostly to himself for the better part of two years.

"You've got to have someone to come home to," Carlos had told him one evening as they pored over figures, teasing having given way to the serious tones Carlos adopted whenever he gave Sebastian some much-needed brotherly advice. "Knowing you, that's the only way you'll ever leave this confounded office."

"I've got all I need right here," Sebastian had told him, gesturing at the ledgers and diagrams scattered over his desk. "What woman could compete with all these beauties?"

No distractions until the mill was a success. That was what he'd told himself whenever he awoke in a panic in the middle of the night, sweating over the way Carlos had risked his family's future on Sebastian's word. No distractions. He needed them still less now.

And yet he was having a hard time remembering why as he watched Paulina's full bottom swaying beneath her plain brown skirt. He wasn't in the habit of ogling women's backsides, but there was nowhere else for him to look as he neared her.

She went on her tiptoes, apparently straining to reach the water. It had the effect of lifting her bottom even higher, for all the world as if she were trying to show it to its best advantage. Another man might have pressed up against her, taking it for the offer it wasn't, but Sebastian had been taught better.

He cleared his throat to warn her of his presence. From the depths of the barrel, he heard an exclamation, followed quickly by a splash, and the next thing he knew, she had kicked the stool out from under her own feet and was clinging to the lip of the barrel.

Even flailing inside a barrel, she managed to be graceful.

There was no help for it—and there was no avoiding her bottom as he seized her by the thighs and helped her down.

"Let me guess," she said when she emerged, drenched

and sputtering slightly. "You've been meaning to put in a spout?"

"I will eventually," he said defensively. He'd bought it, at any rate, though it was getting rusty as it lay unused among his tools.

"Hopefully before someone drowns in there." Paulina smoothed back her wet ringlets. Water clung to her long eyelashes like tiny diamonds, making them shimmer in the midday light and making Sebastian wonder what she would say if he asked her to close her eyes so he could kiss the drops away. "I'd do it myself, but as a guest here, I wouldn't want to presume."

"I deserved that," he told her ruefully as he dug into his pocket for the square of linen he had tucked in there earlier. "I'm sorry for startling you."

He handed her his clean handkerchief, which she waved away, along with his apology.

"It was that dratted stool. I was going to try and fix the wobble, but Doña Josefa needed water to finish mopping the house. I've half a mind to throw it into the cook fire instead, before anyone else becomes its victim—that's the second time you've had to rescue me from falling off the wretched thing."

"Lucky I came home when I did, then."

"Why *are* you here? I didn't expect you home for lunch," she said, and damn if she didn't sound exactly like a wife would have. She must have realized it, because she blinked and added, "I mean, I thought you spent all day at the mill."

"I had something to tell you."

"Oh?"

Striving for nonchalance, Sebastian said, "I sent word into town and set up an account for you at Don Enrique's store, should you need to procure anything for yourself or the house."

"Why would you do that?"

He shrugged, feeling slightly embarrassed. "I haven't the time to see about buying drapes or furniture, and Josefa has far too much to do for me to pile yet another thing on her plate. Of course, you needn't do anything if you'd rather not. I just thought…"

"Oh, no, I would like to."

"I would like for you to be comfortable while you're in my care. Don't stint on anything, no matter how much it costs. I should hate for any of you to want for anything. And Paulina?"

"Yes?" she asked softly.

"Get yourself a length of ribbon in every color that strikes your fancy."

Her answering smile filled the hollowness in the pit of his stomach. Sebastian cleared his throat and nodded at the water barrel. "Would you like me to fetch you the water you needed? My arms are longer."

"I can do it myself if you tilt the barrel. It's half-empty, so it shouldn't be too heavy."

"Oh? You don't think I'm strong enough to move a water barrel myself?"

She raised an eyebrow. "My apologies—I didn't know I was in the presence of Hercules. By all means, go ahead and shock me with your feats of strength."

Even as he laughed, Sebastian was struck with a sudden pang. Carlos would have liked her. He would have been aghast at the situation Sebastian had found himself in, but Carlos definitely would have liked Paulina.

Sebastian was about to reply with something equally—and recklessly—flirtatious. He managed to stop himself just in time—but the words that popped out of his mouth instead were no better. "Will you come into town with me? I've somewhere I want to take you."

Surprise lifted her brows. "Right now?"

"Unless you're too busy taking impromptu baths in the water barrel," he said, flicking away a drop of water dangling from one of her ringlets, for all the world like an infatuated schoolboy.

The slight widening of her eyes stopped Sebastian short.

He was aware that he shouldn't get too friendly with Paulina, or give her the wrong impression. Not because he still harbored any suspicions when it came to her character, but because it had taken him only a couple of days to find out how closely to the edge he was skirting. Another kiss, another invitation from that intoxicating mouth, and he would find himself in a most uncomfortable position.

Sebastian may have been a lot of things, but he wasn't the sort of cad who took advantage of women under his protection. And for better or for worse, Paulina was now someone else he had to take care of—at least until he found a way to annul the marriage.

Making her his wife in more than name would not only ruin his chances of doing so, it would bind them together in ways he couldn't allow himself to be bound, given his responsibilities toward so many others. The very thought made his pulse roar in his ears.

Giving in to the attraction tugging at them both, however tempting, would only end in certain heartbreak.

Then again, he couldn't bring himself to push her away, as he'd tried only a few days before. Particularly not after having glimpsed that haunting loneliness in her eyes when she'd spoken about longing to live closer to town. It would have been too cruel, and Paulina had been the recipient of enough unkindness.

Sebastian was no longer a schoolboy—and neither was he the naive youngster who had let himself be used for the sake of a pretty smile. The lesson he had learned then was a hard, bitter one, and it was still so raw, Sebastian doubted he was likely to fall for such machinations again. No matter how beautiful Paulina's smile might be or how luminous her eyes, he knew better than to let himself be seduced again.

As impossible as the prospect would have seemed even days earlier, there really was no reason why Sebastian couldn't be friends with his wife.

He examined her face. The trace of wariness was gone from her eyes, though he could still sense some sort of reserve. No doubt she was making the same sort of calculations he just had.

"We can go another time if you'd rather," he offered, in case she had come to a different conclusion.

"I'd like to go." Paulina pushed back a strand of wet hair. "But I should freshen up first. I'm sure I look an absolute mess."

He wiped her face dry with the handkerchief she had declined, then tucked two of her curls behind her ears, trying not to linger on their delicate curves. "You look beautiful," he said firmly and took her hand to tug her to where his horse was hobbled. After a moment, her fingers curled around his own, and she consented to be led.

Sebastian had never seen the need to purchase a carriage when the saddlebags on his horse were capacious enough for anything he needed from town. He didn't realize his mistake until he had helped Paulina up onto the saddle and swung himself behind her and found his thighs nestling into hers.

And then, when he reached over her shoulders for the reins, effectively wrapping her in his embrace…well.

She kept her back very straight, which was effective in keeping their upper bodies from touching but would prove painful by the time they arrived in town.

"It'll be more comfortable if you settle back against me," Sebastian suggested. "Just…pretend I'm a chair."

"I wouldn't want to incommode you."

"You won't," he told her firmly. "If you sit like that all the way into town, your back will be stiff for days."

There was no need to think of anything else that might grow stiff on the ride, particularly not when her bottom was pressed so firmly against him.

More distracting than that was the little sigh she let out when she leaned back against Sebastian, her head resting on his left shoulder and the loose strands of hair around her temple tickling the side of his neck.

Realizing he was holding the reins in a grip so tight his knuckles were turning white, Sebastian forced himself to relax as he clicked his tongue and urged his horse toward the road to San Pedro.

Chapter Ten

"Are you going to tell me where we're going?" Paulina asked. They could have ridden all the way to the other end of the island for all she cared—seated in the saddle in front of Sebastian, his arms loose around her, she was in no hurry to get to their destination, whatever it was.

"It's a surprise," he said, speaking almost directly into her ear. Paulina suppressed a shiver of delight. "A token of friendship, if you will."

"Friendship?" She twisted as best she could to look at Sebastian's face. His eyes were shaded by the brim of his Panama hat, but his shapely mouth was forming what to Paulina looked like a cautious smile.

"If you're willing."

"To accept your friendship?" Turning back around, Paulina tried to smother some of the hunger in her voice. At least he couldn't see the sudden tears stinging her eyes. That wasn't the only thing she wanted from Sebastian, but it was a start. "I wouldn't object to that."

There was a pause behind her, and it went on long enough that she could feel his stillness at her back. "But would you like to have it?" he said finally.

"Yes. I would like it very much."

The sun was at its most potent when they arrived at a fairly nondescript house, a handful of streets away from the church at the center of town. Paulina blinked the brightness out of her eyes as a girl in an apron led her and Sebastian to a wide, bright terrace at the back. It was furnished with a worktable piled with bolts of fabric and a gleaming sewing machine set into a wooden stand. The woman sitting before it rose gracefully from her seat the moment she spotted them, a hand extended in greeting.

"This is Blanca," Sebastian said after he had introduced Paulina, "the finest modiste in San Pedro, or so I'm told. She's going to make you an entire wardrobe."

Sheer delight leaped into her chest, and Paulina couldn't help but show it, even as she protested, "Oh, but I couldn't possibly accept such extravagance."

"Not even for my sake?" Sebastian asked. At her questioning glance, he elaborated. "You're my wife now, and for better or worse, you represent me and my household. I'd rather not have it whispered around that I haven't done well by you. Or that my business is so unprofitable that I can't afford to clothe my bride. Really, you'd be doing me a favor."

"Oh." Paulina looked at the dressmaker, who had discreetly turned to sort through the fashion magazines on the table. "Well, I suppose, in that case…"

Sebastian smiled in satisfaction. "Thank you for being so agreeable." He inclined his head toward Blanca. "I'll leave you to your work, Señora. I'll return in an hour or so."

The moment he disappeared through the doorway, Blanca and her assistant fell upon Paulina, exclaiming over her shapely hips and long legs. Paulina submitted to their attentions and found herself growing absorbed in sorting through the scraps of fabric and lace on display.

Blanca laid out fashion plates on the table, picking out the ones she thought would be most flattering to Paulina's figure, and together the three women assembled combinations of fabric and trimmings to go with each.

It was overwhelming, in an entirely blissful way. Until that moment, Paulina hadn't quite realized how stifling it had been to sit idly by while someone else made all her decisions for her, large and small. Choosing her own clothes might have been inconsequential for anyone else, but going through the process of determining what she liked and what she didn't made Paulina feel like she had control over more than just her clothes—like maybe she could have control over her own life.

As well as the magazines and samples, Blanca had an array of finished garments that she pulled out for Paulina to inspect. Before long, one end of the table was heaped with silk petticoats, combinations made out of linen so fine it felt like gossamer against her skin, two night-dresses with satin ribbons and breathtakingly intricate lace bordering their immodestly plunging necklines and an assortment of crisp white blouses with eyelet embroidery and tucks in the sleeves.

Her attention drawn by an intriguing glimpse of yellow, Paulina extracted another blouse from the pile. The whisper-thin fabric was embellished with bands of creamy yellow embroidery on the bodice and the full sleeves.

"Bishop sleeves," Blanca explained. "It's the latest thing."

"They look very elegant," Paulina said. "And I love the embroidery."

"It would suit you splendidly. With a few tucks, here and here…" The dressmaker pinched a fold of fabric in illustration. "I could have this ready for you in minutes. I also took the liberty of selecting a skirt for it."

Gesturing for Paulina to follow, she pulled a dress form from behind a painted screen. The cambric-covered figure was wearing a day skirt the color of the late-morning sky.

Gently, Paulina touched the fabric with her fingertips. "It's beautiful. I don't think I've ever worn such a color."

"It's very becoming," Blanca said. "I've only to put in a dart or two for it to fit properly. Here's a bow for the neck."

The bow was made out of the same fabric as the skirt, and it made for a pleasing contrast against the crisp white of the shirtwaist and the twining butter-colored vines on its sleeves.

"Why don't you try them on so that I can make the adjustments right away?"

How could she have said no? Paulina stepped behind the screen and shucked off her pale yellow dress, which suddenly looked shabby and frumpy in comparison with Blanca's exquisite garments. The blouse felt like silk as she pulled it over her threadbare chemise, and the skirt fit as if it had been made for her.

"I don't think you'll have to make any alterations," Paulina called through the screen as she fastened the buttons at the waist.

The other women were so absorbed in their discussion of hat trimmings that they didn't realize Paulina had emerged until she cleared her throat. They turned and beamed immediately.

"I was right about that shade of blue," Blanca said, looking satisfied as she reached up to adjust the bow around the neck of the blouse. "It looks wonderful against your skin."

"I'll have to take your word for it," Paulina said, craning her neck for a glimpse of herself in the long oval mirror that was partially obscured with discarded clothes.

"Maybe not," the assistant said under her breath, and Paulina felt her pulse stutter to a stop as she followed her gaze to the far side of the terrace.

Sebastian was standing in the doorway, and he looked stunned.

Looking self-conscious, Paulina smoothed a hand over the sky-blue fabric hugging her hips. "What do you think? Do I do you credit?"

Sebastian started at her question, as if he'd been gazing at a painting that had suddenly burst into song. When he managed to formulate words, they came out softly. "It would take a far more eloquent man than me to answer that question."

He still would have tried, if he hadn't recalled that they were not alone. The dressmaker and her assistant, ever discreet, had retreated to the far side of the room to confer over a dress form, making a point of looking absorbed in pinning some sort of garment around it.

Sebastian cleared his throat. "Are you ready to go? I can come back later if you need more time."

"I think I've got everything I needed," she said. "And far more, besides. Are you really sure—"

"I'm sure," Sebastian told her, and he asked the dressmaker to prepare the bill.

Blanca jotted down some notes in a miniature notebook. "That's three day dresses, one tea gown for Sundays, two plain skirts and five shirtwaists. In addition to the blue-and-yellow ensemble."

Paulina frowned. "I have no need of so many clothes."

"Nonsense," Sebastian said firmly. "Dilia owns twice

as many, and she's been in mourning for a year. Blanca, how soon can these be ready?"

"Two weeks, I should say."

Paying Blanca and making arrangements for the clothes to be delivered to Villa Consuelo was the work of a few moments. Through it, Sebastian could feel his gaze darting toward Paulina, who was chatting with the assistant as the apron-clad girl folded a pile of delicate underthings into a satin-covered box. It wasn't the frilly garments that held his attention, but the light that had come into her eyes at his pale excuse for a compliment.

Privately, he resolved to offer her many more, if only because he liked watching her bloom under the attention, like a wilting plant that had been aching for sunlight.

From the way her fingers fluttered to the bow at her neck and continually smoothed down the fabric of her skirt, he could tell that she was enamored of her new ensemble. It was that more than anything that prompted him to say, as they emerged onto the scorching sidewalk, "I was going to take you home, but you deserve to be seen by all of San Pedro. Would you care for a stroll around the park? Later, I mean, when the sun goes down a bit."

"That would be lovely." Her eyes were shining. "What do you propose to do in the meantime?"

"You need hats and jewelry and handbags and any number of things that haven't occurred to me," Sebastian said, adding, as he spotted a woman in the distance who was shading herself with something pale and lacy, "Like a parasol. And neither of us have eaten. I'd say we have plenty to occupy us for the rest of the day."

"You don't need to return to the mill?"

"Not today," he lied, offering her his arm. It was the polite thing to do, but his body had quite a different idea about the hand innocently grasping his inner elbow.

Every brush of her knuckles against his rib cage, covered in layers of fabric as it was, sent ribbons of unexpected desire running through him.

He took her to La Belleza, José Oliva's hotel, café and restaurant. Sebastian wasn't personally acquainted with Oliva, but it was in his establishment that he, Carlos and Dilia had stayed upon their arrival from Havana. The restaurant on its ground floor had to be the most elegant in all of San Pedro, with its starched linens and crystal chandeliers that tinkled lightly in the breeze. Sweeping murals covered the high walls, and potted palms set at intervals in front of the floor-to-ceiling drapes highlighted their intense color.

San Pedro society was on full display in the crowded main dining room—ladies in white dresses frothy with pearls, men in fashionably cut suits that showed off their gleaming watch chains.

They made no attempt to hide their curiosity as Sebastian, Paulina on his arm, followed the maître d'hôtel to a table right in the center of the room.

Sebastian laid the immaculate linen napkin over his lap, watching with amusement the awe in Paulina's expression as she took in the entirety of the room. She wasn't quite gawking, but it was more than clear that her damned brother had never brought her to this kind of place.

There was a bustle around them as what seemed like a small army of waiters in black bow ties descended upon their table to fill their water glasses, hand them leather-bound menus and recite the day's specials. Paulina listened with endearing seriousness, concentration etching a fine line between her gently arching brows.

"It all sounds so good," she said. "I couldn't possibly decide."

Sebastian narrowed his eyes at her. "Oh, yes, you will. What's more, you'll order for me, too."

Her gaze flicked toward him, and she sat up a little straighter, as if to signal that she accepted his challenge. She perused the menu again. "For myself," she told the waiter, "I'd like the red snapper."

"A wonderful choice," the waiter said. "The fillet comes in a light cream sauce, which partners well with our Spanish Albariño, which we keep chilled—perfect for such a warm day. What will the gentleman like?"

An impish look came into Paulina's face. "Oh, I don't think he's very hungry. Perhaps some bread and butter?"

Sebastian growled, making Paulina laugh. "I'll take a bite out of you if you don't get me some proper food, you scamp."

"All right, all right. Let's see. San Pedro is known for its cattle, so why not *filete a la pimienta*?"

"That does sound good," Sebastian said, though she hadn't so much as glanced at him in confirmation. It did his heart proud.

The waiters retreated almost as suddenly as they had come, and Sebastian found himself, once again, sitting across the table from Paulina. Had it only been that morning that she'd confessed to never having selected her own hair ribbons? Was it too much to hope that a single shopping experience had helped her break free from those years of deprivation?

With her uncanny knack for divining his thoughts, Paulina leaned forward. "I wanted to thank you, Sebastian. For the clothes and—and all this," she said, gesturing around her. "It's all so grand and beautiful and…"

"And?" He raised an expectant eyebrow.

"And I could really get used to it," she said, her smile turning so wicked at the edges, it was all he could do to keep from knocking aside the carnations in their silver vase and lunging across the table to devour that curl with his own mouth.

Not exactly the sort of thing a friend would do.

"I hope you do," he told her, swallowing back the urge. "It's only a fraction of what you should have had growing up. I know that restaurants and new clothes can't come close to making up for all you've lost..."

"Having your friendship does." She looked at him with those clear eyes of hers. "I appreciate that as well, Sebastian. I hope you know I don't take it lightly."

"Neither do I," he said, and the arrival of the bread-basket prevented him from saying anything more.

The fish was followed by port and demitasses of strong, sweet coffee. At Paulina's request, there was even ice cream, served in delicate etched dishes and topped with sliced almonds. She kept Sebastian so distracted with her enthusiasm and curiosity for every item on the menu that when he finally glanced around, it was to find that the restaurant had emptied and the waiters were close to dozing as they leaned against the far wall.

By then, the shops had reopened for the afternoon. Fueled by wine and port and the sparkles in Paulina's eyes, Sebastian swept her into every one they passed— Manuel Lebron's shoe store, where he insisted she try on several pairs of fine leather pumps; El Lente de Oro, where he talked her into a painted fan and two parasols, one silk and dripping with lace and the other one sprigged with little flowers...

Lacking a carriage to haul their purchases home, Sebastian paid an additional fee for them to be delivered to Villa Consuelo the following day.

A startlingly colorful sunset was starting to blaze in

the horizon when Paulina laughingly begged off going into yet another store.

"You did promise me a stroll in the park," she said.

"So I did."

The park was only a few streets away. It wasn't Sunday, when afternoon concerts were traditionally held, but a handful of musicians were practicing in the gazebo set into the center of the park. The low notes wafted in their direction, borne along on the warm, fragrant breeze.

Paulina tilted her face up to the last of the sunlight. The sudden change in angle made her lashes cast feathery shadows on the lustrous brown skin over her cheekbones.

Sebastian tore his gaze away, making himself admire the freshly painted iron fencing around the flower beds.

Then she spoke, and he was obliged to turn back to her.

"If it's not too bold an observation to make…you don't seem to mind spending enormous quantities of money on providing me with a wardrobe. It makes me wonder…"

He made an encouraging noise, though he wasn't sure where she was going.

"Why haven't you done the same for Villa Consuelo? You've lived there a year, haven't you? Why," she said, and Sebastian braced himself, "are you depriving yourself the comfort of a decently furnished home?"

The breath he let out felt as gusty as cyclone winds. He would have been tempted to make light of his answer if he wasn't certain that Paulina wouldn't let him get away with that.

"I really was busy, in the beginning. Carlos and I had a devil of a time getting the mill to run smoothly after the state it was left in by your brother. But then…"

"Then he died?" Paulina supplied gently.

Sebastian dipped his head into a nod. "And suddenly

I was responsible not just for his wife and children, but for the mill and everyone who works there. If the cane caught fire or the machinery broke down and we didn't make enough in profits to cover everyone's salary... The prospect of spending money on drapes and chairs when doing so might have taken the food out of someone's mouth made my stomach curdle."

"I see." She walked in thoughtful silence for a few minutes. "Last year's *zafra* was unusually profitable for everyone, wasn't it? I remember reading in the newspaper that sugar prices rose worldwide."

"Your memory's impressive," Sebastian said. "And yes, the mill made almost double what Carlos and I had projected."

"And with there being no export tax, it stands to reason that this year's will be similarly profitable. After all, we're well past hurricane season, and the cane is ready to be harvested. Barring some sort of sudden catastrophe..." She bit her lip for a moment. "Would it make you feel any better if you were to establish some sort of trust that the mill and cane workers could draw from in case of an emergency? You could contribute whatever you needed to it and that would free up the rest of your funds—and your mental energy—for frivolous things like buying furniture for your home."

It shouldn't have surprised Sebastian that she had solved, in a matter of minutes, something that had been plaguing him for over a year. It was as Carlos used to say—Sebastian had a bad habit of getting so bogged down with worries that it often rendered him unable to notice the solutions that were right in front of his face.

"I'll speak to my bank manager about it first thing tomorrow."

"And in the meantime," she said, "I'll take you up on

your suggestion to procure some furniture for the house." In the late-afternoon sunlight, the smile she flashed him looked golden. "I'll be glad for a project to occupy my time."

Chapter Eleven

The following day found Sebastian riding into town again, this time to speak with his bank manager about Paulina's suggestion and to put in another order for the metal tracks he was having laid through the sugarcane fields to more easily transport the cane to the mill once it had been cut. It was an expensive proposition but one that would relieve the cane cutters of a great deal of labor.

He had never shared his saddle before riding to and from town with Paulina the day before, but he found himself missing the space she'd occupied on the leather seat. On the way back to Villa Consuelo in the falling dark the day before, she had drowsily relaxed against his chest, her head pleasantly heavy on his shoulder. What was it she had said at the restaurant? That she could get used to it?

Well, so could he.

The notion wasn't nearly as alarming as it should have been, and Sebastian paused to consider why. He'd enjoyed her company more than he'd expected. Maybe he had also been lonely. Maybe he, too, had needed a friend. Secure in his control of himself, and in no danger of letting himself be seduced, he had allowed himself to see her for who she truly was—a remarkably interesting woman.

And a damn desirable one.

Nor for the first time, Sebastian thought about Antonio Despradel's reasons for forcing them into marriage. It wasn't like it would have been so difficult to find Paulina a husband by conventional means. She was everything a man could want—everything Sebastian would have wanted, if his circumstances had been different.

Who wouldn't want to wake up every morning to the sight of those luminous eyes?

Or that round bottom pressed against—

Sebastian swore out loud, to the consternation of the two sparrows perched on a fence post, which took immediate flight.

Paulina had far more to offer than her beauty, of course. She was brave and intelligent and more skillful with a hammer than he could have imagined.

Sebastian had awoken that morning with every intention of fixing the shaky stool, only to find that the leg that had wobbled like a loose tooth was now perfectly solid. On it was a note, pinned down by a rock. It read, *My apologies for taking liberties, but I couldn't let the stool claim another victim.*

Then he'd gone to find the spout for the water barrel, and of course Paulina had taken care of that as well. She'd even managed to scrub away some of the rust that had accumulated on the metal in the months the spout had been lying among Sebastian's tools.

And damn if it hadn't felt like a weight off his shoulders. A weight he hadn't realized he was carrying until it had been lifted.

Sebastian sighed. He didn't like intrigue, and he wasn't particularly good at it—not just that; it made his head ache. He said as much to Dilia when he stopped by the pink house after his errands, a heat-induced headache pounding behind his eyes. She all but ordered him to take a nap on her stiffly upholstered settee, as if he were another one of her boys.

As pieces of furniture went, it wasn't the most comfortable, or even particularly beautiful. The only thing it had to recommend it was the fact that it had been placed close enough to the louvered doors that opened out into the front gallery that a most agreeable breeze wafted over his overheated body.

Dilia must have sent the boys out to play in the street, because the house was utterly quiet. Or perhaps Sebastian was just that tired. He fell asleep almost instantly, and when he dreamed, it was of a woman in a pale yellow dress, dancing in the sunlight.

Whereas Paulina's bedroom was overcrowded with all the previous day's purchases, the rest of Villa Consuelo was awfully bare. There were no lace curtains or oil paintings or fine silver candlesticks gleaming from a sideboard—there weren't even any sideboards, or much in the way of furniture.

Even Sebastian's bedroom, Paulina discovered when she ventured inside alone to sweep its floors, had only a bed and a chest of drawers. A small mirror hung from a single nail; below it a set of shaving implements had been lined up on a clean towel. Another glance around the room revealed a neat pile of clothing atop a crate.

She had seen a different side to him the day before, and not just because he'd been so extravagantly generous toward her. He was so devoted to everyone in his care, to his own detriment. When was the last time someone had taken care of him?

Trying for briskness, but falling short, Paulina tied the mosquito net to the side and began denuding Sebastian's bed of its linen. The light cotton blanket, folded and tucked underneath the single pillow, smelled faintly of him—laundry soap underlaid with the earthier scents of sugarcane and sunbaked skin. Paulina tucked the pillow under her chin as she stripped off its plain cover and caught a whiff of the spice she had smelled when she'd pressed her face against his chest on the night of the storm.

A sudden urge insisted that she do the same with his pillow. Paulina would never know if she'd have overcome it or not as, at that moment, a shout came from the parted doors.

"The new table's here! Oh, Paulina! Come see the new table!"

Abandoning the pillow with alacrity, Paulina snatched the sheets off the mattress and added them to the basket on the terrace, then hurried down the steps to see a pair of burly men with their shirtsleeves pushed up to their elbows carefully unloading the table from a large cart. The dining table in her family's *quinta* had been a massive hulk of dark, carved wood; this one was beautiful in the simplicity of its well-turned legs. She ran a hand over the smoothly polished top.

"Centenary mahogany," said one of the workmen.

The man beside him made an impatient noise, clearly straining under the weight. "Where do you want it, Doña?"

"The terrace, I think," Paulina said with a gesture. "To keep it out of the sun and rain."

In the space of several minutes, the men had finished unloading the new dining set and the cart was rumbling its way down the path while Leo and Doña Josefa clustered around the table. The chairs were wood and rush, but to look at their faces, anyone would have thought they'd been made of gilded wood.

It was a start, Paulina thought, recalling that she had thought those very words the day before in regard to the friendship Sebastian had offered her. A start—but why should any of them settle for just a start?

"We should have a feast," Paulina said suddenly. "To celebrate the new table."

Doña Josefa gave a swift nod. "I know just what to make."

"Stewed goat?" Paulina offered, and they all laughed.

"Leo, go to Candida's and see if she'll sell you one of her guinea hens." Finding several coins in her pocket, Doña Josefa pressed them into the boy's hand.

"We ought to have a proper tablecloth. I'll go into town to buy one—and a new vase and candlesticks," Paulina added, recklessly adding to the list in her mind. "We'll make an elegant occasion of it."

And so it was that less than an hour later, Paulina was arriving in town, freshly bathed and clad in one of her new shirtwaists, her hair wound into an intricate coronet of braids. Her modish straw hat cast a decent enough shade over the bridge of Paulina's nose; even so, she was feeling like a roasted chicken by the time she arrived in town. This late in the morning, the sun was blazing mercilessly overhead, without the merest scrap of a cloud to soften its potency.

She was passing a pretty, sherbet-pink house when a voice rose from the elegantly columned gallery shading its front door. "Paulina? Paulina Despradel?"

Glancing up, she spotted a familiar-looking woman on a rocking chair, wearing the same black dress she had worn the last time Paulina had seen her, on the day of her marriage. Paulina raised a hand as she bid Dilia a polite good afternoon.

The other woman set down her needlework and went quickly to the railing. "*Santísimo!* Did you walk all the way here?"

"I caught a ride part of the way on a vegetable cart," Paulina said, then wondered if she should have admitted to such unladylike behavior.

Dilia didn't look disapproving, merely friendly. "Won't you come sit with me for a spell and get out of the sun? It's scorching out there."

Paulina hesitated. "I would love to, but I came to town on an errand, you see…"

"I promise not to take up too much of your time—I would never forgive myself if I let you get on in such a state. Please, come up and have something to drink with me. I've some tamarind juice, or lime if you prefer."

Before she knew it, Paulina found herself ensconced in one of the rocking chairs set deep into the shade of the porch, a set of louvered white doors at her back and a cool glass of juice dripping condensation onto her lap.

Dilia hadn't resumed the seat next to Paulina's yet, having been called to the aid of a little boy with a badly scraped knee. As she waited for Sebastian's friend, Paulina gratefully sipped the juice, feeling slivers of ice slip past her lips.

A faint snore behind her made Paulina crane her neck in search of the person it had come from. The louvered doors, which had been ajar earlier, were pushed farther open by a stray breeze, revealing a sleeping Sebastian.

She'd assumed he'd gone to the mill, and so to find him here, asleep, in the middle of the day, should have been surprising. Anyone who had been paying attention to the shadows under his eyes, however, would have known how badly he needed the rest.

He hadn't attempted to fold his body onto the cramped settee but lay with his long legs flung over the spindly carved arm, a roll-shaped cushion under his neck. One of his powerful arms trailed to the floor, where it brushed the patterned tiles; the other was thrown over his forehead, as though shielding his eyes from the light pouring in from the gallery.

Poised and contained during his waking hours, in sleep Sebastian allowed himself the abandon he eschewed in the daytime. It was a glimpse at a side of Sebastian Paulina had never seen—and one that made her feel oddly flushed as she summoned up the memory of the one night she had spent in his arms.

If they were to share a bed again, would he let himself fall into a sprawl next to her? Fling his arm over her as a smile of contentment softened his lips?

She wanted the chance to find out.

The startling strength of her desire almost made her gasp out loud. As if he could feel it, Sebastian stirred.

Quickly, Paulina averted her eyes to find that Dilia had returned and was watching her.

"I try to make him sleep when I can, but I'm afraid one of these days he'll figure out that I can't actually force him to do anything." Dilia smiled briefly. "My boys have, at any rate."

"Your boys? You've four of them, right?" Paulina said in a blatant attempt to distract both Dilia and herself.

"Four little terrors that keep me in plenty of mending," Dilia said, smiling at Paulina as she reached for the needlework she had abandoned.

"Tell me about them," Paulina said, and Dilia obliged with enthusiasm.

Stopping just short of breathing a sigh of relief, Paulina sat back and allowed the sweet tartness of the tamarind juice to cool her down. All the while, though, she was aware of the certainty blooming larger and larger inside her chest—she was uncomfortably, inconveniently, irrevocably in love with her husband.

When Sebastian drifted back into consciousness, it was to the sound of Paulina's voice.

"I suppose we're getting used to each other," she was saying.

"He deserves more than someone getting used to him—he deserves love. From someone who means it."

"I hope he finds it," Paulina replied.

"But not with you?" Dilia's disembodied voice may have sounded cool, but Sebastian was sure it was accompanied by one of her probing looks.

It was an odd subject for a dream, even taking into account the fact that lately Sebastian's thoughts seemed consumed with Paulina. Which was only to be expected, he told himself hazily, seeing as she was always *there*—putting vases in his bedroom, standing in patches of sunshine and trailing that slight floral scent wherever she went so that his entire home seemed to be filled with her.

Opening his eyes and gazing straight up, Sebastian considered whether he was still dreaming or whether he had somehow been transported back to Villa Consuelo. But the white ceiling was dappled with light refracted from the small chandelier Dilia had brought from the Havana house, and he could hear the faint but unmistakable sound of little David wailing at his brothers.

Then he realized that the sound had come from the gallery, which meant that Paulina was sitting on one of the rocking chairs on the other side of the louvered doors—and that her conversation with Dilia was not one he should overhear.

In one swift movement, he had swung his legs to the floor and was pulling the doors open the rest of the way. Even though the lace-edged blouse she wore was bright white, he observed as he leaned against the door frame, there *was* something reminiscent of sunshine about her.

Even Dilia, clad as always in her mourning clothes, looked brighter for being beside Paulina. She glanced up at the sound of the hinges, and Sebastian was forced to step out into the gallery.

"Paulina?" he asked as if he had just noticed her. "I wasn't expecting you here. Did something happen at the house?"

Glancing up at him, Paulina set down the glass she'd been holding and wiped her hands on her skirt. "The new table arrived this morning, and I decided to go to Don Enrique's store for a new tablecloth."

He raised an eyebrow. "So you walked all the way from Villa Consuelo?"

"I caught a ride on a farmer's cart."

"I see. Well, we can't let your industriousness go to waste. I'll go with you to Don Enrique's and then I'll take you home. Dilia, my dear, I'm grateful as ever for your hospitality."

"Oh, but why don't you both stay for lunch?" Dilia said. "The cook is making *moro de guandules* and those *yuca arepitas* you love…"

"Another day."

Bending to kiss her on the cheek, he rescued his hat from a corner of the porch, where it was being employed as a receptacle for rocks by one of her little scamps, and set off down the street, Paulina at his side.

The streets were markedly quiet this close to noon, the

scents of garlic and *sazón* filtering through open doors and windows—so quiet that Sebastian was able to hear the growl of Paulina's stomach. She murmured an embarrassed excuse, pressing her hand to her midsection.

Sebastian glanced down at her. "We can go back to Dilia's if you're hungry," he offered. "Her cook's *arepitas* really are truly excellent."

"Oh, no," Paulina said hurriedly. "Doña Josefa is making a special meal for us. I wouldn't want to spoil my appetite or be late."

"Then maybe an *empanada*?" Sebastian nodded at one of the houses they were walking past. Half-hidden behind an overgrown hibiscus bush was a handwritten sign listing the foodstuffs for sale. "The Alvarez sisters make the best *lambí empanadas* in town."

Interest sparked in her eyes. *"Lambí?* I don't think I've ever tried it in an *empanada*."

"That really needs to be remedied," Sebastian said firmly. "They make *dulces*, too—we could get some *dulce de coco* for the others."

They went inside, and Sebastian watched her gravely consider all the options before selecting a jar of *dulce de coco* and one of stewed papaya to bring back home. Like he had the day before, Sebastian found himself egging her into getting more things, to the delight of the elderly sisters who were adding up the purchases with gleeful smiles.

Finally, they came out onto the front yard with a basket laden with jars hanging from the crook of his elbow and the last two *empanadas* of the day in each of their hands.

Sebastian had hardly raised the *empanada* to his mouth when he stumbled over a bootblack's box. Its proprietor, who couldn't have been more than a handful of years older than Dilia's younger boy, was crouched nearby, playing with a marble. He glanced up at the sound of Sebastian's boot striking the wooden box, but it was the aromatic pastry that captured his attention.

The boy looked nothing like Sebastian, but he couldn't help seeing another, scrawnier version of himself in the skinny limbs. He'd been lucky enough to have not gone hungry for long—thanks entirely to the kindness of people who'd barely had enough for themselves.

"*Amiguito*, want an *empanada*?" The words popped out of Sebastian's mouth before his brain had much of a choice in the matter, and a second later the boy had snatched the *empanada* from his hand and scampered off with a hasty thanks.

Paulina was watching him, a small smile on the corner of her lips.

He shrugged, though she hadn't said anything. "I wasn't hungry anyway. I was just keeping you company."

Of course, his stomach chose that moment to growl, not just audibly but embarrassingly loudly.

"I'm not that hungry, either," she said.

Splitting her *empanada* in half, she handed him a piece, which he consumed in a single bite. It was still hot, but he had always been partial to the tender conch meat, and here in this former fishing village, the seafood was always fresh.

Paulina took the time to savor hers. At the first nibble, her eyelids drooped closed, and she let out a sound that made Sebastian grateful that they were half-hidden behind the hibiscus bush.

Her plump bottom lip was slick with grease. A gentleman would have offered her his handkerchief, but Sebastian's was limp with perspiration and, in any case, despite how hard Dilia had tried to turn him into one, Sebastian wasn't a gentleman.

He wiped his thumb firmly over her lower lip, and even though Sebastian wasn't given to impulsive gestures—and this most certainly counted as one—he raised his thumb to his own mouth and swept his tongue over the salty smear.

Her lips parted. Her gaze was trained on his mouth, as intently as he had been looking at hers.

"You can do it, you know," she said, in a voice so low he could hardly hear it over the sound of two men arguing as they walked down the street. "You can kiss me again. It wouldn't have to mean anything you don't want it to. It wouldn't…mean anything at all."

It wasn't the disarming vulnerability in her tone, or the frank desire in her eyes, that struck Sebastian—it was that once again, Paulina had proven herself damn courageous for giving voice to their desires.

More softly than before, he grazed her lip with his thumb, slowly rubbing it back and forth over skin as soft as a rose petal. "It would to me," he told her.

And then he kissed her anyway.

Sebastian had never been the sort of man who found pleasure in the forbidden. But as he plumbed the depths of her eager mouth, he couldn't begin to imagine why. He knew he shouldn't kiss his wife. He knew that every minute he spent with her, every time he had to avert his gaze from her curves or her distracting mouth, took him one step closer to plummeting over the edge.

He knew it all, and yet he couldn't stop.

Her warm hands slid under the lapels of his jacket and traveled up to his shoulders before twining behind his neck. She clung to him as if to a life raft, her body pressed tightly against his and soft moans escaping her salty mouth as he dug his fingers into the boning of her corset and pulled her even closer, wishing there was a handy tree he could press her against.

They were half-hidden from the street by the hibiscus bush, but anyone who came around it would see them. They should stop before that happened. His brain was screaming for him to stop, though his hands and mouth refused to heed it. For her sake, if not his own— he couldn't let her be seen like this, with her clothes in disarray and her mouth swollen from his kisses. San Pedro may have been turning into a cosmopolitan city, but its residents would not take kindly to a woman behaving wantonly in full view of them all.

"Well, well, what have we here?" said a cold, cruel voice behind them.

When Sebastian recognized the man the voice belonged to, his first instinct was not to spring away from Paulina but to draw her even closer into the protective circle of his arms.

"The devil do you want with us?" he snarled at Antonio Despradel.

Along with a gray-haired man, Despradel had come around the hibiscus bush and was contemplating Sebastian and Paulina with a smirk.

"Is that any way to greet your new brother-in-law?"

"I know a better one, and it doesn't involve any words," Sebastian ground out. Just looking at Despradel's face brought the sickening memories of the days he had spent in the cell bubbling to the surface of his mind.

"Always the brute," Despradel remarked, flicking a glance at his companion. "But then, can I really expect better from a man who thinks it perfectly fine to accost my sister in the public streets?"

"I'm not getting involved in this," the gray-haired man muttered and hurried away.

If Sebastian hadn't already been convinced of Paulina's innocence, the way she was recoiling from her brother would have more than done the trick.

"We don't have to stay here and listen to this," Sebastian told her in a low voice, ignoring Despradel. Her hand slid into his, and she nodded. "Let's go finish our errand."

Despradel stepped in their way. "Not so fast. I require something from you, Linares."

Sebastian gave Despradel a contemptuous glance. "There's nothing I would give you, save for the blow or two you deserve."

"Funny you should talk about deserving," Despradel replied, unruffled, "because I was just thinking that I deserve some compensation."

"Compensation?" Paulina echoed.

Despradel didn't so much as glance at her. "For the pain and suffering of having my sister abducted from my own home."

For a moment, Sebastian was too surprised to be outraged. He barked out a laugh. "Do you really think I'd give you *money* after everything you've done?"

"I should think you'd be willing to pay any price to keep the good residents of San Pedro from finding out about your villainous proclivities," Despradel shot back. "I want a hundred pesos." He scraped a glance over Paulina then, taking in her crisp shirtwaist and the blue skirt. "You can clearly afford it."

It was astonishing how quickly that man could provoke Sebastian into a blind rage. He took a step forward, his free hand clenched into a fist. From the corner of his eye, he could see a couple ambling down the street toward them, but he didn't care if the president of the republic himself was about to witness the violence Sebastian was about to unleash upon Despradel.

Paulina had other ideas.

"If you're here for *empanadas*, you really must try the *lambí*." She slipped her hand through the crook of Sebastian's elbow—mostly, he suspected, to keep him from doing anything unadvisable. "Sebastian, do you have the *dulces*? We don't want to be late for luncheon."

Inclining her head graciously, she bade her brother a good day and all but propelled Sebastian into the street.

Chapter Twelve

Well, that answered the question that had been plaguing Sebastian for days—like the leech that he was, Despradel was planning on using Paulina to extract enough money from Sebastian to pay for his lavish lifestyle.

Paulina was still holding on to his arm, though Despradel was long out of sight. Sebastian had been walking so quickly—stalking, almost—that he hadn't noticed the fine tremble running through her limbs.

He slowed down and looked at her more closely. "Are you all right?"

"I will be," she said. "He's a damn bully, but he can't force you to give him any money, can he?"

"He can try to blackmail me," Sebastian said. "Or have his henchmen throw me in prison again. I'd give him the damn money if I thought it would satisfy him. But men like him can never have enough."

"It's the only way he can find value in himself," she said contemptuously. "Owning things and having people under his thumb."

Sebastian grunted his agreement. "Did you happen to recognize the other man?"

"Yes," she said, and she bit her lip lightly before saying, "That was the magistrate."

Sebastian limited his response to a nod, though a great part of him wanted to rage. Not only were none of the lawyers in town willing to support his claim against Antonio, there was no authority to report him to, either. "I should thank you for your quick thinking. I don't know what he or I would have done were it not for your intervention. Get hauled into prison again, most likely, only this time for murder."

"Don't say that even in jest." She shuddered. "I never want to see you in that place again."

"Me, either," he said, giving her a crooked smile.

Instead of returning it, she nodded at the open doors below the sign reading, *Enrique Rijo, Gran Bazar de Novedades.* "It's almost noon. We should go in before they close for lunch."

He touched her shoulder. "Before we do, there's just one thing I have to tell you. I will *never* let him hurt you again."

"I wish I could promise you the same," Paulina said softly and went into the store.

Looking fairly grim, she picked out a tablecloth and several yards of ribbon. Then, lifting her chin in that determined way she had, she said both to Sebastian and the clerk, "I should like a pair of candlesticks as well."

His worry melted slightly into amusement as she selected two long tapers and the ugliest pair of pewter candleholders he had ever seen.

"You do know I can afford brass or silver," he said, coming up beside her and setting the basket on the counter.

"I didn't want to presume," she said primly.

"Presume away," he told her. "If it's finery you want for the new table, pewter just won't do."

"If you're looking for something elegant," the clerk said, turning with alacrity to produce two monstrous silver pieces the length and girth of Sebastian's arms, "I have just the thing for you."

Sebastian was stupefied into silence, and from the lack of a reaction beside him, he suspected Paulina was, too. The candlesticks weren't merely large—they were atrociously misshapen, towering pillars of silver infested with vines and squat, ugly little cherubs, each candlestick with five ungainly arms to thrust candles into the air. Here and there, the silver was dotted with red glass globes that Sebastian thought were meant to simulate grapes.

"Imported from Spain," the clerk said, surveying the horrid thing with an air of pride.

"What do you think, dear?" Sebastian asked Paulina, manfully containing his laughter.

Paulina's blink gave Sebastian the impression that she hadn't often been asked that before—with or without the endearment he had appended to the question, as if there was something humorous about the two of *them* posing as a real husband and wife.

"They certainly are grand," she said thoughtfully. "Wouldn't they look perfectly elegant on a table by the door, where anyone might see them the moment they step inside?"

Sebastian's smile faltered. "I…ah…"

"Surely that would justify the expense. Of course, we'd have to redo the entire parlor to make it suitable. Damask curtains, velvet sofas and perhaps a crystal chandelier or two? Marble and gilt tables, to be sure…"

Sebastian caught the wicked glint in her eyes and almost sagged with relief. "I'm not sure that's advisable at the moment, dear."

She shook her head with fake regret. "If you say so." She winked at the clerk, adding, sotto voce, "I'll convince him eventually. In the meantime, we should probably take a look at something a little less…elegant."

The clerk turned around, and Sebastian pressed against Paulina's side for a brief moment, feeling her body tremble with mirth.

In the end, they settled for a pair of blue ceramic ones with a white design wreathed around their bases that went nicely with the white tapers and the blue embroidered tablecloth made by Don Enrique's daughter. Sebastian put in an order for new sets of china, and silver, too, from the shipment that would arrive the following week.

It was a welcome distraction—not only that, but every step he took toward making Villa Consuelo a home kindled a glow inside Sebastian. Carlos and Dilia's generosity had never made Sebastian long any less for a home of his own; slowly, and ever so surely, the pile of bricks and stone that had been Villa Consuelo was becoming just that.

He didn't say as much to Paulina, though he couldn't help thinking about her habit of looking at houses in the newspaper. As wildly different as their respective upbringings had been, they shared a longing for a true home.

"Are we going to discuss what happened before we were interrupted?" he asked as they left the store.

She glanced up at him, and Sebastian felt his gaze skipping away to focus on the newly erected lamppost at the end of the street. "Must we? Something tells me you're going to be utterly impossible about it."

"If by impossible you mean sensible. We shouldn't

have…indulged. And you know that we can't let that happen again."

"We're married," she said heatedly. "It was one thing when you thought I was conspiring with Antonio and you couldn't stand the sight of me. But now—"

"If we were to consummate the relationship," he said, still avoiding her gaze, "we wouldn't be able to have the marriage annulled. And only parties over the age of twenty-five can request a divorce without the consent of a family member, so you would be tied to me for four years."

"I don't want an annulment," she snapped. Looking a little startled at the admission, she bit her lip. Then, with that defiant tilt of her chin that he found so appealing, she added, "Or a divorce."

"You might," he said softly, willing her to understand. "And I would be as much of a villain as your brother if I took that choice away from you. You said it yourself— you've never had the independence to make your own decisions. I refuse to bind you to a marriage you didn't choose." He took a deep breath. "I offered you friendship, and that's all I'm prepared to give you."

Sebastian couldn't have made it more clear. Paulina had been foisted upon him, and even though he was clearly as attracted to her as she was to him, he did not intend to…what was it he'd said? Indulge?

A most unladylike snort escaped her as she pulled at the tablecloth so that its edges hung evenly around the tabletop.

The worst part was that he wasn't altogether wrong. She was no longer bound by Antonio's strictures. She was a married woman, for as long as she chose to be, and as such she had something much more valuable than anything anyone had ever given her—freedom.

The notion made a little thrill of possibility leap in her stomach.

She was savoring the word when the housekeeper came onto the terrace to admire Paulina's handiwork. As well as fitting fresh candles into the new candlesticks, she had twisted long branches of greenery into wreaths that she wove around the serving platters, dotting them with small, fragrant white flowers she had found growing by the path to the mill.

Doña Josefa, who never hesitated to let her opinion be known, went into paroxysms of delight. Unused to such effusiveness, Paulina felt herself flushing at the praise.

"If I'd known a handful of cloth and ceramic would inspire such joy, I'd have stopped by the store more often," Sebastian observed from where he was leaning against the railing.

"Making another person happy isn't usually a complicated thing," Paulina said, going to join him as the housekeeper excused herself to return to her cooking. "You seem to manage it well enough."

He gave her a questioning glance, at which Paulina elaborated. "The *empanada* from earlier," she said. "You noticed I was hungry and were willing to stop for food even though I'm sure you had plenty of other things to do. It was small, as gestures go, but I can tell you that *lambí* made me quite happy indeed."

No need to mention everything else she had felt as a consequence of that *empanada*. Her knees were still quivering—though that may have been a product of spending the better part of an hour pressed against Sebastian's warm torso, her head pillowed on his shoulder and his arms around her in something that closely resembled an embrace.

"Well, if it's small things that please you, I have something for you. Only a token of friendship," he hastened to explain. "A small one."

"How small?" she asked.

"Minuscule." He held out a hand, long fingers unfurling to show the tiny things on his palm. "You were so busy looking at tablecloths that I thought I should get some finery for you. They aren't as elegant as the silver candlesticks, alas, but…"

"Nothing could compare to those," Paulina agreed, plucking one of the earrings and holding it up to the light. From a slender gold stem dangled a single bead of amber carved into the shape of a rose. It didn't so much catch the light as look as if it had been crafted from it—sunlight made solid. "These, however, are just small enough to be perfect."

Looking unaccountably pleased, Sebastian took gentle hold of her face and slid the earring he still held into place. She fought a shiver as his fingertips brushed the curve of her ear. It should have been entirely impossible for a touch to her earlobe to inspire such an intense sensation.

"I'll try for something even smaller next time—ant-like."

Next time. The words hung in the air between them, heavy with a promise that Paulina knew he didn't mean to fulfill.

"I should go help Doña Josefa with the food," she said, touching the amber bead dangling from her lobe. "I… thank you, again."

Without waiting for a reply, she turned and headed for the kitchen, where the steam from the various pots and pans provided the perfect excuse for the heat flooding her face.

Doña Josefa had outdone herself. There was the guinea hen in a thick, red sauce scented with wine and spices. A mound of fluffy white rice sprinkled with bits of fried ripe plantain and flecks of parsley. A pineapple cut in half and hollowed out held the salad, which looked crisp and fresh despite the day's increasingly oppressive heat.

"It really is a feast," Leo remarked as he helped Doña Josefa carry the food to the table.

Paulina couldn't help but agree. The food was excellent, as everything prepared by Doña Josefa tended to be, but in Paulina's estimation, the best part of the feast came when they were enjoying small dishes of *dulce de coco* and Leo shyly asked Sebastian for a story.

From the way he worded his request, Paulina was given to understand that it used to be a regular occurrence, before Sebastian had acquired a wife and the sudden need to spend his days and evenings anywhere but home. It made Paulina sad to think that her presence had disrupted life at Villa Consuelo so drastically. If she had run anywhere else on the night of the storm, would they gather every evening to talk by the light of the lantern?

Paulina expected Sebastian to resist, or to insist that he had work to do, but he acquiesced easily enough to the boy's plea.

Sliding a spoonful of sweet coconut pudding into her mouth, Paulina watched Sebastian grow increasingly animated as he told the story of a farmer who had gone to water his *conuco* early one morning, only to realize that all his crops had begun to talk.

The story wasn't one Paulina had heard before. She almost forgot to listen to it, so absorbed was she in watching Sebastian's face grow mobile with humor. It only served to remind Paulina of just how short their acquaintance had been. She had thought him hopelessly serious when she'd first met him. Then he'd proved noble, and brooding, and responsible and desperate to protect everyone around him.

All that, and he was funny, too.

She wasn't sure she'd even heard Sebastian truly laugh before, and little wonder, what with everything that had happened. It was a bright, booming sound, underlaid with something like surprise, as if Sebastian himself had forgotten that he was capable of it.

Sebastian was in high spirits when he finished the story—the champagne they'd bought at Don Enrique's might have also had something to do with it—going so far as to tweak Doña Josefa's ear, which earned him a snap of her apron. He dodged it, still laughing, and fell to one knee in front of Paulina. "Will you join me in a dance?"

"But there's no music," she said.

Sebastian glanced at Leo, who obligingly began to drum on the table.

"There is now," Sebastian told Paulina, his hand still outstretched.

Sliding her palm into his, Paulina let herself be pulled from her seat. Sebastian seized her lightly by the waist and swung her into something that Paulina, inexperienced in such matters, thought might be a waltz.

"I don't think I'm very good at this," she said.

"It takes practice."

"And rhythm, of which I've got none. You do it wonderfully, though."

"I had a lot of practice in Havana. The secret is to look at your partner, not down at your feet. It also helps if you avoid treading on your partner's toes," he added with a grimace.

"I'm sorry!" she said, burning with mortification.

The problem with looking into his eyes instead of at her feet was that it felt like an extraordinarily intimate thing to do while his hand lay lightly on the small of her back and their palms pressed against each other's without the benefit of layers of fabric. The sensation did nothing to improve her coordination, and neither did the encouraging smile he was beaming down at her.

"No need to apologize. My toes were in want of a good stomping."

"How gracious. Is that what you told the debutantes in the ballrooms of Havana?"

A glint came into his eyes. "I didn't have to, actually. They were all good dancers."

Before she could laugh, the pressure of his fingertips on her waist heightened subtly, and she found herself being swept to the other side of the terrace, where a fluid twirl brought her up against the railing.

Paulina withdrew her hand from his and held it up in a silent plea for a moment's break, though she wasn't as out of breath as her panting indicated. After a moment's hesitation, Sebastian relinquished her waist.

"You seemed a bit quiet back there at the table," he said. "Are you all right? If you're troubled about what your brother said…"

"I'm not upset," she hastened to reassure him. "Just thinking."

"Oh?" Sebastian leaned against the railing, facing toward the house. "Anything you would like to share?"

There was no end of things she wanted to share with Sebastian, and that was part of the problem. "You may have been right, earlier. I hadn't really considered that now that I'm no longer under Antonio's control, I have the freedom to do whatever I want."

It might have been her imagination, but she thought she saw a flicker of pain in his eyes before he shifted his gaze to the sugarcane fields in the distance. "What *do* you want?"

"I want the *world*," she said, feeling as voracious as her words. She had always been reprimanded for wanting anything at all, so she saw no issue with wanting everything.

"You want to travel?"

"Oh, nothing as grand as that. I want to live, truly live in the world. I want to stroll down the streets on Sunday afternoons and sit on friends' balconies sipping juice and gossiping. I want to make a fool of myself flirting with handsome young men at balls and…and I want a home of my own. And a family to fill it with."

Her hands had clenched into fists. With some effort, she relaxed her fingers, placing them lightly on the railing, only inches away from Sebastian's back.

"Family," he said, and Paulina was taken aback by the intensity in his voice.

"Is that…not something you want for yourself?"

He shook his head. "I couldn't imagine wanting anything less."

"Not even children?"

Her heart in her mouth, Paulina watched him as he hesitated, then shook his head again.

Was that why he hadn't wanted a wife? Why he was refusing to share her bed? When he'd talked about giving her choices, did he mean himself? Of all the people she had ever met, she would have thought Sebastian was the least likely to desire the life of an unfettered bachelor— likely because he was so beholden to his responsibilities.

That only went to show how little she knew him.

Then he surprised her by adding fiercely, "I've seen too much misfortune in my life. I wouldn't be able to bear it if a child of mine had to go through even a fraction of what I went through as a child. Or you, for that matter."

She wrapped her arms around herself. "I was wondering, the other day, if you had any relations left behind in Havana. I take that to mean that you don't?"

"No," he said shortly. A furrow appeared between his brows, and he looked as though he was deciding whether or not to add something. "Josefa's my godmother."

Paulina's mouth fell open, even as she glanced at the table where the housekeeper still sat, chatting fondly with Leo. "I— She is?"

"She's my father's cousin. He was a cane cutter here in San Pedro. My mother was a washerwoman. She went from house to house helping with the laundry and the ironing, and I went with her, to perform small tasks for her and earn the occasional coin or two bearing messages for the mistress of the house." He looked at her, half defiantly and half expectantly.

Paulina's heart skipped a beat. "It was you, wasn't it? The washerwoman's son. You were the little boy I used to play with."

"I was."

The admission was hardly more than an exhalation, but it was still potent enough to wring a gasp out of her.

"Why did you never tell me?" she whispered. "The day of my birthday party, when I was talking about it..."

"Would you have treated me differently if you knew?"

She shook her head. "No, but..."

"I hardly knew you then. And I thought I had to hide the truth of where I had come from, because society wouldn't accept me otherwise, and I needed their help to make the mill a success. Business here relies so much on social connections—you can see it for yourself in how your brother operates." His voice sounded suddenly wry. "Although I didn't exactly go out of my way to secure their friendship. Maybe I'd have had an easier time of it if I'd done that instead of burying my head in my ledgers."

"I suppose that's true." Paulina bit her lip, then released it long enough to ask, "Why did you leave?"

"My father died, and my mother shortly after. Josefa did her best to look after me, but she had her own children and her own worries, and when an acquaintance of hers offered to take me along on her voyage to Cuba and later Spain, Josefa knew it might be my one chance at a better life. The acquaintance was a childless old lady, and I think Josefa was hoping that she would take me under her wing and provide enough schooling for me to make something of myself. But the old lady died on the ship, the night before it docked in Havana. And I arrived there alone." He made a small sound that under other circumstances might have been a laugh. "I wasn't penniless, not quite, because Josefa had taken up a collection among the cane cutters who had worked with my father, but I was swindled out of the money my first week there, and I was forced to live on the streets until Carlos's parents took me in."

Paulina felt a jolt as she recalled Antonio, in the coach home from town on the day of her birthday, saying something about how he suspected Sebastian of being of inferior birth. Her snob of a brother had been right about Sebastian not having come from a wealthy family, though not about the fact that he was concealing his identity.

Paulina hadn't been wrong, either—whatever his ancestry, Sebastian had proven to be far more noble than her brother.

"How old were you?"

"Eleven," he said.

Heartbreakingly young to have to fend for himself in an unfamiliar country.

"They all looked after me," he said. "The cane cutters, their wives, the washerwomen and the ones who worked as housemaids in the big houses in town. They all made their contributions so that I could have a better life. And I left them all to fend for themselves."

"You were a child," she tried to protest.

"When I first left, yes, I was. But I grew up. And as I was frittering my time away dancing and trying to flirt with fashionable young ladies, my people were going hungry. I don't know if I ever would have returned to San Pedro if it hadn't been for my own romantic failures and Carlos and his willingness to invest in the mill. He put in everything he had inherited from his parents—everything he might have saved for his sons' comfort and future. All of that is in the mill. In my hands.

"The mill was failing when I came back. Your brother had driven it to ruin, and everyone he employed was suffering for it. Their wages were so low as to be practically nonexistent, for backbreaking work, and Antonio kept threatening to lower them still more. And then there were the accidents, caused by your brother's neglect and his unwillingness to invest in better machinery. The foreman did the best he could, but your brother was no help at all. Did you know that Leo's father was killed in one of those accidents?"

"No," Paulina said, her voice quiet in contrast to his fierce tones. "I didn't know."

"They were my people, and they had been suffering while I danced my way through every ball in Havana."

"You're here now," Paulina said firmly, hoping Sebastian could take a measure of comfort in the fact. "You've done plenty for them—and for me."

"It's not enough." He scraped a hand over his face. "I don't know if it ever will be. I don't know if I—" Sebastian cut himself off before he could finish the sentence, but Paulina could fill in the blanks. He didn't know if *he* could be good enough.

If that was truly how he felt, it went a long way toward explaining why he claimed not to want a family. It wasn't bachelorhood he wanted, nor to be unfettered— what he wanted, Paulina thought, was to avoid feeling this way again.

Her heart broke for him. "You don't have to take care of everyone. Unfathomable though it may seem, you could even consider letting someone help *you*."

He stared at her.

"You have Josefa and Dilia and Leo," Paulina continued. "And, well, me. You could lean on me."

"I don't think anyone's ever said that to me before."

"Well, it was about time," she said firmly. She wanted to reach for his hand, but after all that had happened the day before, she wasn't sure it would be a good idea. Instead, she settled for lightly thumping the railing. "It isn't right for anyone to have to bear such burdens alone."

"I can shoulder them," he said with a twitch of his own broad shoulders, as if in illustration.

"I have no doubt that you can. That doesn't mean you should have to."

He was silent after that, his gaze distant as if he were looking far beyond the sunlit fields. Paulina knew she had given him a lot to think about. Falling into silence herself, she remained next to him long after the table had been cleared.

Chapter Thirteen

"It's not my place to say so, I'm sure, but it was nice seeing the both of you enjoy yourselves yesterday," Doña Josefa remarked the next morning as Paulina helped her clean the rice for the midday meal. "I thought the business with the table pure foolishness, though a pleasant enough diversion for you, but I can see that we were all in need of a little foolishness."

Like a candle being extinguished by a hurricane, Paulina had smothered the flicker of disappointment that had flared inside her when she'd tumbled out of her pallet from a dream of *empanadas* and horses and found that Sebastian had already left for the mill to make up the work he had missed the previous day.

"I remember your mother," the housekeeper added, holding a carrot and cutting it into perfectly even rounds without taking her gaze off Paulina.

"You do?" Eyeing her nervously, Paulina picked a piece of chaff from the white grains and flicked it into the bucket at her feet.

"A very elegant lady, with a laugh like silver bells and never too proper or too busy to help with a day's hard work. You resemble her, you know. And not only in looks."

Paulina's heart lifted. "It's wonderful of you to say so," she said softly. "I remember so little about her, sometimes I wonder if I made up the scraps of memories I do have."

She didn't have much of her mother's save the scant few items in the old trunk that Antonio had deemed not valuable enough to sell. There was the portrait, too, of course, though going to fetch it or asking Sebastian to do it seemed like a terrible idea at the moment.

Paulina's stomach clenched at the thought of her brother and his blatant attempt at extortion. Was there no limit to his dastardliness? It made her sick to think of all the people he had been winding around his web without her having noticed. Every fresh revelation made her wonder just how—or why—she hadn't noticed. It was true that she wasn't party to his life outside the house, but she had known, from the way he lorded over the *quinta*, that Antonio considered himself a man who was not to be crossed. He was a petty tyrant, and it stood to reason that he wouldn't limit his reach to just Paulina and the few people he employed.

She was stretching to rid herself of the kink in her lower back when the rumble of carriage wheels made her curiously head to the front of the house.

Even from a distance, the black-clad woman being handed down from her seat was instantly familiar to Paulina.

"I thought I would return your visit," Dilia said when she was within speaking distance, leaning to kiss Paulina on the cheek as if they had been acquainted for years. "I must say, I really should come out here more often. It's so peaceful—but then, any place is peaceful when there aren't twelve dozen little boys doing their best to use your finest linens as sails for their boats and generally tear your house apart for their amusement."

"I thought you had four sons," Paulina said.

"In theory. Sometimes I think they multiply when they're out of sight. They certainly eat enough for twelve dozen. In any case, I found myself in the mood for some companionship and remembered that I promised Sebastian I would call on you every once in a while."

It was on the tip of her tongue to ask why, but—somewhat belatedly—Paulina remembered her manners. "That's so kind of you. Won't you come sit down on the terrace?"

They went out to the kitchen first so that Dilia could greet Doña Josefa. Dilia was as inexorable as a cheerful cyclone, and Paulina found herself trailing in the older woman's wake, feeling slightly dazed.

As Dilia exclaimed over the new table—and the candlesticks that Paulina had lovingly dusted first thing that morning—Paulina set a chair next to the rocking chair overlooking the yard.

"He hasn't made a scrap of progress on the railing," Dilia said, running a hand over the stripped wood before taking the seat next to Paulina's. "I don't dare hope it's because he's actually taking the time to rest."

"He scrapes away at it sometimes," Paulina said. "I've helped where I could, but I'm not all that knowledgeable about woodworking."

"I'm sure the house will look infinitely better with your input. At the very least, I see that you've persuaded Sebastian to invest a little more in the way of creature comforts." Dilia drummed her fingers approvingly on the arm of the chair. "Are you settling in all right? I remember those early days of marriage—not a day would go by without me rushing home for advice or comfort or something I'd forgotten. I imagine you consider yourself equally fortunate to live so close to your childhood home."

Suspicion and defiance darted through Paulina's chest, and she found herself saying, with some heat, "If you're trying to ascertain whether I'm in contact with my brother, let me assure you I'm not."

Dilia gave a surprised laugh. "I wasn't terribly subtle, was I? If it's any consolation, Sebastian didn't send me to ferret out your secrets. He doesn't know I'm here, actually. And I really did need to escape my house before it was fully overrun by children."

"I *have* no secrets," Paulina said firmly. "And while I can appreciate your desire to look after Sebastian, I can assure you, he's more than capable of determining by himself whether his wife is plotting against him."

"You're right," Dilia said after a moment. "He's more than capable. Or he would be, if he weren't so softhearted." To Paulina, there was something impatient about her sigh. "He's been swindled more than once by people pretending to need his help."

"I know," Paulina said, gratified that for once she actually did know something about her own husband's past.

"Carlos was like that, too," Dilia said, a soft smile playing on her lips. "Generous to a fault, always ready to give whoever needed it the very shirt off his back." She rolled her eyes. "I can tell you, between Carlos and Sebastian, I had my hands full keeping them in shirts. And yet… I couldn't tell you how grateful I am that my boys have Sebastian to look up to. It may be selfish of me, but I'll do anything I can to keep the world from being tarnished for him and, by extension, for my boys."

"And for your memories of Carlos," Paulina said softly.

"For him above all. So, you see, I had to see for myself that you weren't taking advantage of Sebastian, particularly after the way the two of you hurried off yesterday."

"Nothing has happened between us," Paulina told her. "Nothing *will*."

"I wouldn't be so certain of that."

After that, the conversation turned to more prosaic subjects—the electric lines being put up in town, and whether nor not Dilia should make the switch from gas. The boys were fascinated by electricity, but was it really safe to have in the house?

It struck Paulina that perhaps Dilia was a little lonely, too, for all that she lived in town and had all those children to keep her occupied. She didn't have much time to dwell on the thought before they were interrupted by the sound of carriage wheels.

One unannounced visitor would have been odd enough. Frowning slightly, Paulina excused herself to go see who it was. The only other person with a coach she could think of was Antonio, and her heart started pounding at the thought that he might have come to finish what he had started the day before.

To her relief, it *wasn't* Antonio who was stepping down from the gleaming coach that had rolled to a stop next to Dilia's—it was Sebastian.

Paulina didn't do much but blink with surprise, but Dilia, who had followed her, brushed past her and regarded Sebastian with a hand on her hip. "Why, Sebas. Is that a coach?"

Sebastian jerked his head into a nod. "I've been meaning to get one."

"You only ever ride on horseback," Dilia pointed out, giving Paulina a conspiratorial look. "As a matter of fact, haven't you always said that riding inside a carriage feels as suffocating as being in a coffin?"

Paulina watched in delight as Sebastian's brows grew progressively thunderous under the onslaught of Dilia's ribbing.

"You should have gone into the law," Sebastian told her.

"Mothering my four mischievous little beasts has certainly prepared me for it. Five, if I count you, and I certainly should."

Paulina gave Dilia a curious glance. The other woman couldn't have been more than a handful of years older than Sebastian. There were faint lines on the corners of her eyes, it was true, and several strands of silver at her temples, but everything else about her was exceedingly youthful—particularly the way she was laughing at Sebastian.

"You didn't mother me so much as badger me until I had no choice but to relent to your endless commands." Sebastian glanced at Paulina, his lips curled into a grudging smile. "You're free to use the carriage whenever you wish," he told her a little gruffly. "I've employed a coachman, and he has instructions to take you wherever you want to go—so I'd be grateful if you avoided farmers' carts in the future."

Paulina received the news with something of a pang—while a carriage would be more comfortable, she hadn't exactly minded sharing a saddle with Sebastian. Feeling him nestle behind her had been almost as good as a true embrace.

Dilia's eyes were dancing with amusement, and Sebastian must have noticed them, too, because he added, with studied casualness, "Of course, it's mostly for Josefa. She's getting on in years, and with that new grandson of hers, she'll want to visit her daughter more often than ever. It isn't right that she should have to walk there or hitch rides in carts at her age."

"Of course it isn't," Dilia said in a voice brimming with laughter.

Sebastian gave her what for all intents and purposes ought to have been a furious glare, but it was spoiled by a sudden bark of laughter. "You rogue," he said, throwing an affectionate arm around Dilia and squeezing her to his side. He looked at Paulina over Dilia's head, and she softened when she saw the unvarnished affection in his eyes. "She never lets me get anything past her."

"It's my responsibility as your de facto older sister," she said, disentangling herself from his grip. "Now, I insist you take Paulina on a ride in the new coach."

A mixture of alarm and desire flashed through Paulina at the prospect of sitting in a small coach with Sebastian with their knees touching—or, worse, feeling the warmth of his body press all down her side.

"Oh, but don't you mean to join us?" Paulina asked Dilia.

"I couldn't possibly leave my little monsters alone for a minute longer—I'm sure to arrive home only to find the maid tied down and the cook tipped into her pot."

Before Paulina could point out that Dilia had just contradicted everything she'd told Paulina less than half an hour before, Dilia had bustled to her own coach in a flurry of blown kisses and twinkling promises to call on Paulina again.

Sebastian looked almost as dazed as Paulina felt when he turned to her with a quirked eyebrow, asking, "Shall we?"

Briefly, she considered telling him that they should take Doña Josefa with them. Then some tiny but insistent part of her gave a rebellious shake of its head. Paulina met Sebastian's gaze. "Let's go."

The memory of their last ride in a carriage was too recent for Sebastian to feel truly at ease as he climbed in next to Paulina, trying not to think of the raw anger and pain he had been filled with. That he had gone from that roiling mass of emotion to something so close to friendship was a testament to how hard Paulina had worked to make herself agreeable—not just to him, but to his entire household. He hadn't failed to notice the little kindnesses she did for Josefa, or the way Leo had started to turn to her with any problems.

Sitting almost diagonally to keep his long legs from tangling with hers, he had taken the seat that faced the rear so that she could look comfortably out the window.

The delicate lines of her face were outlined in sunlight. It gilded the curve of her cheekbones, lingering on the sweep of her brow and turning her plump bottom lip into something precious. It hardly seemed possible that just a day before he had kissed it with abandon.

Struck wordless, Sebastian was glad when she turned away from the landscape speeding past the window to abruptly ask him, "Do you regret having helped me on the night of the storm?"

He took a moment to consider the question. "I don't think there's much point in regret," he said finally. "Or dwelling on the past. I believe in looking forward and changing the things you *can* change."

"And when you feel like absolutely nothing is under your control? What then?" she asked with an intensity that would've been surprising to anyone who hadn't seen the steel beneath her placid demeanor.

Sebastian didn't have a chance to reply.

Against his better judgment, after the episode with Candida's goat, he had hired her grandson Alfonso as a coachman. The young man was only a few years older than Leo and something of a daredevil, judging from the speed with which he took the dirt road, still rutted deeply from the storm. To Sebastian, whose long limbs were cramped from how strenuously he was trying to avoid brushing up against Paulina, the rut felt more like a chasm.

The wheels bounced down, *hard*, and in the moment it took for the horses to pull the back wheels into and over the rut, Sebastian found himself with a bruise on his tailbone and a luminous beauty on his lap.

He had caught her reflexively as they were both jostled into the air by the seat's brand-new springs, shielding the top of her head even as his cracked smartly against the roof of the carriage. A swear escaped him, and he heard Paulina laugh breathlessly at the vulgar string of words that had left his lips.

He groaned. "I'd beg for your pardon, but I can't help but think that was justified."

"Unquestionably," she assured him.

Her fingertips grazed his forehead and continued in a gentle exploration of his scalp. Sebastian's eyes squeezed shut, and it wasn't only from the throbbing pain on his crown, or because her bottom and his thighs were once again renewing their acquaintance.

It had been a long time since anyone had touched him with such tenderness and care.

And even longer since he'd allowed himself to surrender to it.

Sebastian knew he'd done the right thing by telling Paulina that he wouldn't pursue a physical relationship with her. Unfortunately, his body was not as convinced.

He only had to turn his head a fraction of an inch before his lips were grazing the inside of her wrist, just above the healing scrape on her forearm. Even with the thunder of his pulse and the rhythmic pounding of hooves and wheels filling the carriage, he could hear her trembling exhale.

And then everything stilled, as if the world were holding its collective breath while Sebastian took on the superhuman task of pulling away from her and leaving her lips unkissed.

Her eyes were wide and a little grave when he looked up at her, still somewhat dazed from the blow and the gold on her gleaming brown skin. His gaze dropped to the tempting little hollow at the base of her throat, dipping lower to follow the shadow that deepened into another, much more dangerous chasm...

His tongue delved between them before he could think better of it. And when her nipples rose sharply to press against the fabric of her blouse, he circled one with his mouth, closing his teeth around her just hard enough to make her gasp.

"I shouldn't take liberties," he said roughly.

"You aren't." With excruciating slowness, Paulina undid the first several buttons of her blouse. "I'm giving them to you. I'm choosing to let you touch me. Isn't that what you told me? That I'm now free to do whatever I want?"

She brought his hand to her chest. "What I want is you."

He cupped her full, pliant breast, feeling it mold into his palm. The sound of her ragged breaths filled the carriage, and Sebastian's grew just as uneven when she ground herself against him, throwing her head back so that Sebastian had no choice but to follow the graceful column of her neck with his mouth, all the way to the warm lips waiting to receive him.

There was a bang on the outside of the carriage and Sebastian blinked, realizing that the world wasn't holding its breath—the carriage had stopped.

"Don, are you all right in there?" called Alfonso.

Sebastian swore again, under his breath this time, just loud enough for Paulina to hear. She dissolved into giggles.

"Fine," Sebastian snapped. "You can turn back now. And Alfonso?"

"Diga?"

"Go slower."

Inhaling deeply, Sebastian picked up Paulina and placed her back on her seat, from where she regarded him with mingled regret and mirth as she did up her buttons.

Sebastian ran a hand over the top of his head, wincing when his palm touched the rapidly swelling bump. "I suppose I can be grateful my head didn't split in half like an overripe *auyama*."

"That would be difficult, as it appears to be bone all the way through," she said teasingly.

He settled back against the upholstery, giving her a smile tinged with all the things he couldn't allow himself to say. "What makes you believe that?"

"Only an utter bonehead would purchase a coach without taking his own height into consideration—or his coachman's driving skills. I'd have that top padded if I were you," she said, laughing at him.

Sebastian had never wanted her more.

There wasn't a chance of his acting on that desire again. Fortunately—or unfortunately—the carriage came to an abrupt halt. A moment later, the door popped open, and Alfonso's anxious face appeared in the opening. Telling him to find Josefa for something to eat, Sebastian stepped down gingerly. Instead of firm ground, his feet sank to the ankles into something soft.

He didn't want to think about what would happen to the ache on his head if he looked down—fortunately, he could identify the pile underfoot from its vague scent of rotting vegetation.

"I've told Leo half a dozen times to burn those leaves before they molder," he said impatiently.

"I'd be surprised if he *had* heard you, with how he spends all day mooning over his books," Paulina said as he helped her down, lifting her by the waist to swing her clear of the rotting leaves. "Josefa told me that you're paying for him to go to school in town. That's awfully kind of you."

He waved the compliment away like he would a mosquito. "His mother has done more for me than I could ever repay. Even if she hadn't, I try to be good to the families around here. If only to make up for some of the indignities they've had to face."

"At my brother's hand?" she guessed.

"In part. He's not the only unscrupulous mill owner in the area, or alone in wanting to squeeze every drop of work from his workers without a shred of regard for their humanity." His voice had gone hard, as it tended to whenever Sebastian contemplated the injustice faced by cane workers.

"Is that what you're trying to do?" she asked interestedly. "Make up for how ill-used the people have been?"

"I don't think there's anything I *could* do to make up for some of the things they've been through. I just provide whatever little help I can."

"I'm not sure I would call all you do *little*," she said.

"I don't know how anyone around here would get along without you. Myself included."

The midday light filtering through the trees cast dappled shadows on her clear brow. Suddenly overcome with the desire to place a kiss just above her right eyebrow, Sebastian instead plucked off the tiny, elongated tamarind leaf that had fluttered down to catch among the curls haloing her face.

"I'm the one who couldn't get along without them." He cleared his throat. "Yourself included."

"I aim to be of service," she said lightly, turning toward the house. "In fact, if you've no objections, I think I'll ask Alfonso to take me into town to look at furniture tomorrow. I thought I would order some drapes for the windows, as well. Do you have time to walk through the house with me so I could explain how I'm thinking of arranging it all?"

When it came to her, he had all the time in the world. Experience told him that he ought to soak in every minute with her before she came to her senses and left, as everyone he'd ever loved had.

"Lead the way," he told her, trying not to let that thought show in his expression.

He hadn't quite realized it until then, but this was what he'd meant that day in town. Given the ability to make her own choices, and relieved of whatever misguided sense of gratefulness she felt she owed him, Paulina was sure to leave him. And when she did...

Sebastian was far too familiar with heartbreak, and with loss. Nothing, not even the promise of long, sultry nights with her in his arms—and in his bed—could persuade him to experience such grief again.

Chapter Fourteen

The *zafra* was finally underway.

All day, Paulina had heard the lowing of oxen as they pulled carts heavy with sugarcane through the dirt paths that bisected the fields. The mill must have been a hive of activity, with groups of men unloading the carts while others fed stalks of sugarcane through the machinery to be squeezed into pulp.

The familiar scent of burned sugar reached Villa Consuelo in clouds, as did the tiny vermin that raced to escape the fields that were now bristling with people. They took refuge in the rice barrel, inside the tin mugs that hung from nails by the kitchen table and, as they all realized when Paulina let out a bloodcurdling scream one morning, in the toes of her shoes when she discarded them before bed.

Doña Josefa had taken Sebastian up on his word and taken the carriage to visit her daughter and grandson, secure in the knowledge that Paulina would keep an eye on the house, and on Sebastian's unfortunate propensity for putting his work over meals.

The *zafra* having proven more interesting than food, however, Sebastian had spent all day at the mill or in the fields. Leo had gone home shortly before dinner, and after whiling away a few hours on the terrace, Paulina climbed into her bed.

It had taken a fairly short time for Paulina to grow attuned to the rhythms of her new household. In the mornings, she leaped from her bed the moment she heard its first stirrings, and she was more often than not lulled to sleep by the sound of Sebastian working on the railing each night.

Tonight, all was quiet on the terrace. Paulina turned on her mattress, straining to hear any indication that he had returned home.

Pushing her light blanket aside, she padded out to the terrace on bare feet.

The door to Sebastian's bedroom was ajar, and it swung open softly when she pressed her hand against the still-warm wood. "Sebastian?"

Silence answered her—Sebastian wasn't there.

The covered plate she'd left on top of his chest of drawers was untouched, except for a tiny brown lizard soaking up its residual warmth. Paulina felt her lips curl into a smile as she nudged its long tail aside with her fingertip. If Sebastian had not come to his dinner, then it would go to him.

She was closing the door behind her when a faint noise—the squeak of a floorboard, perhaps, or something just as innocuous—made her squint into the darkness. The hair at the back of her neck prickled with sudden alarm.

"Is someone there?" she asked sharply.

Her question was met by the usual nighttime noises— the soft whistling of a breeze making its way through the fields, the chorus of crickets and frogs, and the rustle of bats and other small creatures.

Once she had made sure that no one lurked in the deep shadows, Paulina dismissed the noise as having come from yet another creature seeking shelter from the cane cutters.

She placed the plate inside a basket and, with a glance back toward the quiet house, plunged into the sugarcane fields. Paulina would have been able to navigate the fields blindfolded, but fortunately a bright moon illuminated the way to the mill.

The night watchman, dozing on his chair by the door, didn't notice as she slipped into the mostly darkened building and followed the stream of light up a ramshackle set of wooden stairs that swayed slightly under her every step. At the very top was a small office with glass panes set into a window that overlooked the floor down below and a desk that faced the door. On a rickety chair that looked like it had been discarded from an old dining set was Sebastian, slumped over a snarl of papers and pots of ink.

He was sleeping.

Paulina leaned across the desk and touched his shoulder. "Sebastian?"

His lips parted in a smile of such uncomplicated tenderness and happiness it took her breath away. He must have still been dreaming.

"Sebastian," she said again, shaking him harder.

His eyes flew open.

His chair crashed to the floor as he flung himself backward. Leaping clear of it, he landed on slightly bent knees, looking frantically from side to side.

"It's just me."

He gave her a wild, uncomprehending look. "Paulina?"

"I brought you dinner," she said calmly, gathering his

papers and ledgers into a corner of the desk and not even flinching when she saw that at least two of the books were spread open to sections headed *Annulments* and *Divorces*. Sebastian was reading about how to dissolve their marriage.

Because he wanted to, or because he still persisted in the belief that she would?

She felt his gaze on hers but went on clearing the desktop, quickly and efficiently, until she had enough space on which to unpack the basket. "I thought you might be hungry."

Sebastian scrubbed a hand over his face. "I am. Thank you."

He righted his chair, then fetched her one from the pair under the window, which were holding still more books and his discarded jacket, slung over the back. The skin of his forearms looked dark against the crisp white of his rolled-up sleeves, and as he sat across from her, Paulina couldn't help but notice that he'd also unbuttoned his shirt at the neck.

The enamel plate Paulina set out was crowded with thick pieces of ham and boiled yuca topped with vinegary onions. By now familiar with Sebastian's appetite, she had added two round crackers almost as big as her face and a bottle of the tamarind juice Leo had made in the afternoon, now gone lukewarm.

Sebastian reached for the juice first and grimaced at the first sip. "Leo made this, didn't he?"

Paulina laughed, nodding. "You'll want to mix in a little water if you have any. I swear, if you didn't make sugar for a living, that boy would be the ruin of you."

She perched on the edge of the chair he had brought her and looked with interest at the large map of Havana tacked up on the far wall.

"Do you miss it? Havana, I mean."

"Sometimes I do," he said, breaking off a piece of the cracker and offering it to her. "More so the people than the city."

"And the young ladies who danced so beautifully?" Paulina asked, nibbling on the cracker.

Somehow, he contrived to smile through the large piece of ham he had just wedged into his mouth. "Not as much anymore."

It was silly how such a little thing could make her want to squirm with pleasure.

Busy scooping rings of onion onto his fork, Sebastian hadn't noticed her reaction.

Paulina propped her chin up on her upturned palm, casting in her mind for a subject that would make him keep talking. He always looked so happy when he talked about his life in Havana. "How did you meet Dilia?"

"Her family had lived next door to the Gils for as long as anyone could remember. I would run errands for her grandmother, sometimes—mostly because she would sit me down afterward with a warm bowl of *arroz con leche* to fill out my skinny frame." Sebastian heaved a blissful sigh at the memory. "Dilia hadn't many siblings, either, only one much-older sister, and I suppose it was only natural that the three of us should fall in together. Though I can't imagine how Dilia found companionship in two rascals such as Carlos and me." Thoughtfully, he speared a piece of yuca with his fork. "Now that I think of it, I'm sure part of the appeal lay in having someone to boss around."

"She does seem a trifle…"

"Like she ought to have an entire fleet at her command?" He grinned. "Her mother was a schoolteacher, and I think Dilia would have liked to be one as well if she hadn't been otherwise occupied bearing those little scoundrels of hers."

"I can definitely see her heading up an entire school," Paulina said. "Do you think she would ever go back to Havana?"

And take you along, she added silently.

"We discussed it, once," Sebastian said. His lips compressed for a moment, then opened to admit another forkful of yuca. "Her grandmother moved in with Dilia's uncle, and with Carlos's parents gone and their house sold off, there didn't seem to be much of a reason to return."

"Not to mention the mill," Paulina added. "I don't see you parting from it anytime soon."

"Heaven willing." He poured a stream of water into the tamarind syrup—Paulina could hardly call it juice—and shook the jug. "Do you want some?"

Her teeth ached at the prospect. "No, thank you." She brushed a crumb off the edge of the desk, watching as Sebastian shoveled in the rest of his meal.

He *had* been hungry. Tired, too—she could see it in the faint shadows under his eyes. Paulina felt a pang of guilt. She'd been taking up an awful lot of his time lately, and he surely had to make up for it by working far into the night.

And here she was, distracting him again.

She knew she ought to leave, but she couldn't quite face returning to the darkened, lonely house. Not yet.

Turning away, Paulina gestured to the shadowy mill beyond the dusty panes of his window. Even up here, the musky, sweet scent of the sugarcane was underlaid with a heavy metallic smell and something she thought was engine grease. "Have you thought about having someone come in to read to your workers, like they do in tobacco factories?"

Sebastian shook his head. "The machinery's too loud for that, and everyone is too busy to take much notice."

"Not everywhere, surely. And certainly not at midday."

He raised an eyebrow. "Do you remember what you said the other day about not making a pest of yourself?"

Paulina made a brief assenting noise.

"You're failing miserably."

Paulina's laugh made his brow furrow even more fearsomely, but she wasn't worried. There was no heat behind his words, and he hadn't said no to her idea, either.

"I should think you'd enjoy being pestered every once in a while," she said cheerfully.

She went to the window and stood gazing past her reflection at the grimy machinery. "I feel like I'm inside a clock. If the clock were the size of a large house."

The great wheels did look like the cogs inside a pocket watch, only they were almost twice as tall as Sebastian.

His nod came with a brief laugh. "It's as beautiful as clockwork when the gears start turning."

He wiped his mouth with his handkerchief and came to stand beside her, his reflection a darker smudge beside hers. "She's a noisy beast, but she's damn beautiful."

For the first time that evening, Paulina was very conscious of the fact that she was still in a nightdress whose fabric was so thin she fancied she could feel his breath right through it. "I can just hear you describing your wife that same way," she said, forgetting momentarily that *she* was his wife.

All it took for her to remember was Sebastian's murmur. "My wife?" he said, and she could tell from his voice that he was striving to sound casual. "There's nothing beastly about her."

"Does that mean you think her beautiful?" she asked his reflection.

His head dipped a fraction of an inch—just enough for his voice to caress the curve of her ear. "Not just that. She's luminous."

Her breath caught, and even though she knew better than to read too much into it, she said, "I could say the same about my husband. You, Sebastian, shine with an inner light that touches everything around you."

"That's funny," he said, and Paulina turned to look at him properly, noticing for the first time that in spite of the deep shadows under them, his brilliant brown eyes were still warm. "That's what I think about you."

Turning away from Paulina, Sebastian busied himself returning the dinner things to the basket she'd brought them in. His pulse was racing so hard inside his ribs, his chest felt like it had been fed into the mill and spat out into pulp.

Unlike *bagazo*, however, there was nothing useful about the way he felt for Paulina—not when he couldn't act on it.

It was his own damn fault. He had been the one to start it, after all, this delicate, impossible dance, buying her earrings and devouring her lips with wanton recklessness, like someone who meant to do much more than touch.

Like someone who had the right to want her.

He swallowed, hard, and said as steadily as he could manage, "I do appreciate your bringing dinner—if nothing else, for helping me avoid Josefa's wrath."

Moonlight and lamplight dappled Paulina with silver and gold when he lifted the basket from the table and turned to face her.

"What are you doing?" she asked when she tried to reach for the basket and he answered with a shake of his head.

"Walking you back to Villa Consuelo. You shouldn't have walked through the fields by yourself—it's not safe."

"Nothing will happen. I've spent half my life wandering these fields, and I've never gotten lost or robbed or whatever it is you imagine will happen."

"The *zafra* has started. There are dozens of men with machetes roaming about." He sighed. "You're my responsibility now, like it or not, and I never shirk my duty."

Something wavered in her gaze. "I don't want to be anyone's responsibility."

"I can respect that," he replied. "I can even understand it. But it won't make me feel any less wretched if something were to happen to you after I sent you back on your own."

They went down together, past the quiet, hulking machinery, the mountains of cane stalks and the lightly snoring watchman. The moon was round and full, and out of the pool of light cast by the mill's lanterns, the shadows were deep enough to make stumbling a likely prospect.

Clouds of mosquitoes buzzed in the air between them, but neither they nor the dark seemed to trouble Paulina as she stepped unerringly into the narrow path. The cane was almost twice as tall as Sebastian. The long, slender stalks waved gently in the breeze, turning the path into a tunnel as they met overhead. It was hard to believe that within the next three months, this forest of stalks would be stripped away, the ground laid bare.

"Did you know that all this used to be grazing land?" Paulina asked suddenly.

"Was it?"

"My ancestors were cattle ranchers for over a hundred years. They had a horror of slavery, opposed it fiercely and vowed to have nothing to do with any industry that relied on it. So they raised cattle here and built the small but prosperous ranch where my father grew up. Now, *he* had no interest in cattle, and since his sisters had all married and moved away, he used my mother's dowry to plant the sugarcane and build the mill."

"I know," he said softly.

"Oh? I imagine Antonio told you all this when he sold you the mill. He's obsessed with the history of the Despradels and will prattle on and on about it to anyone who will listen. And here I am, doing the same."

He found her arm in the dark and touched it lightly. "It's only natural that you should want to talk about your parents. You must miss them terribly. Particularly after…" He trailed off, even though he felt no compunction about calling her brother all sorts of names.

"After my brother proved to be a villain?" she said archly but followed it with something that sounded like a laugh. "I think I missed them while they were still alive. They were always gone, or busy with their guests or planning their next frolic. They were wonderful to me when they thought to include me, but most of their amusements were unsuitable for children."

"And you hadn't any playmates," he recalled. "Save for me."

"I still have a hard time believing that was really you. That I've known you all my life." There was a slight movement in the shadows next to him, which he thought was a nod. "I consoled myself by thinking that when I was grown, I would have a whole lot of children—a dozen, at least—and I would plan frolics for *them*."

She gave a slight laugh, as if to indicate that she now found this idea ridiculous. As well she might, Sebastian reflected. After all, she was now wed to a man who wouldn't touch her or share her bed, never mind give her a dozen children.

The overwhelming loneliness of her life made his chest ache again.

"Paulina—" The sound of her name on his lips felt oddly intimate here in the dark.

He didn't know what he was about to say—probably something foolish like offering to give her any number of children she wanted—so it was probably a good thing that he was interrupted by a soft cry of pain.

"What happened?" he asked, stopping abruptly.

"I stepped on a rock, I think. It's nothing."

"Let me see."

Kneeling, Sebastian set down the basket and reached into the dark. His fingers brushed her bare ankle before encircling it and gently lifting it off the ground. Paulina made a small noise, and he felt her hand land on his shoulder for balance.

The scents of laundry soap and sunshine clung to the folds of her nightdress, which billowed softly over her calves in the slight breeze sweeping through the cane. Trying not to remember how transparent the thin fabric had looked in the lamplight, Sebastian held her ankle firmly in his left hand and used his right to explore the rest of her foot. Her sole was gritty with dirt. He brushed it clean with the back of his hand, in a gesture that could have seemed nonchalant to anyone watching but that made sweat bead on the back of his neck.

Her sharp intake of breath made him glance up. "Did I hurt you?"

"No," she said, though her voice came out soft and tremulous. "Just…keep touching me."

How could he help but to oblige? How could he help but to trace the long line of her calf, bare beneath the thin white fabric cascading past her hips? How could he help but press a kiss to the indentation at the back of her knee and touch his tongue to her salty skin until their breaths turned ragged?

His hand traveled higher, grazing the spot where the back of her thigh began to swell.

Her fingers dug into his scalp, and for a moment Sebastian wished he didn't keep his hair cropped short, so that she might lace her fingers through it and tug at his curls. He leaned into her touch, burning with need.

And then he pulled away.

"I can't give you what you want," he said in a low voice. "I can't be your husband."

I can't love you, he wanted to say, though he was starting to suspect that he already did. And to him, at that moment, there was not a prospect more terrifying than that of falling in love with his wife.

"Can't or won't?" There was something fierce in the way she said it, and in the gust of wind that swept suddenly through the field, rattling the cane as if it, too, demanded an answer from him.

Silently, he tugged his handkerchief out of his pocket and bound it around the pronounced arch of her foot, then lowered it gently to the ground.

"Sebastian."

He pulled a fold of her nightdress so that its hem tumbled down over her knee, covering her almost to her ankles.

"Will you be all right walking—"

"Sebastian," she said again, this time louder, her fingers digging urgently into his shoulder. "Did you hear that? It sounded like—"

"A scream," Sebastian said and pelted toward the house.

Chapter Fifteen

The kitchen yard was silent when Sebastian burst through the edge of the field. Half expecting to find the house engulfed in flames, he didn't see anything at first.

Then, aided by moonlight and the lantern they usually kept burning overnight dangling from its hook in the kitchen, he caught a glimpse of what looked like a quickly moving shadow slipping down the terrace steps.

Not sparing a moment for so much as a thought, he charged toward the dark figure.

Alerted by the sound of Sebastian's boots pounding on the hard-packed ground, the figure broke into a run. Sebastian put on a burst of speed. The other man was fast, but Sebastian was faster—he slammed into the man with his full strength, sending them both rolling to the ground.

They fetched up against the crumbling bricks that surrounded one of the yard's largest tamarind trees and Sebastian, moving with furious speed, seized the man by the back of the collar and pinned him down with a knee to his back.

The night was filled with grunts and breathless swears as Sebastian tried to keep hold of the frantically writhing man. Then the intruder bucked underneath him, hard enough to send Sebastian flying backward. Immediately surging to his feet, Sebastian lunged for the man.

This time, the pursuit was brief. It ended just as they cleared the next tamarind tree, the one closest to the kitchen, as Sebastian grabbed him once again by the collar and flung him against the trunk. He was breathing hard by then, and sweat was pouring into his eyes, and the intruder must have been tiring as well, because he didn't try to run away again.

It wasn't until Sebastian saw the metal of a blade catch the moonlight that he realized why.

The intruder wielded the knife as if he knew how to use it and, moreover, as if he was determined to inflict serious damage. The blade slashed through the night—Sebastian managed to block the thrust with his forearm, but he miscalculated the next one and felt the sting as the knife dug into his upper arm.

Sebastian leaned into the sharp bite, roaring out an expletive. It wasn't a sophisticated bit of maneuvering by any means, but it caught by intruder by surprise and made him lose his footing long enough for Sebastian to push him past the dark stone ring of the banked cook fire.

Holding the other man by the base of the neck, Sebastian slammed him against one of the sturdy wooden posts that kept the kitchen walls upright, so hard that the knife went flying in a silver arc, disappearing amid the grass and fallen leaves. Above their heads, the lantern swung wildly, tossing disorienting shadows on the two walls of the kitchen.

Desperate now, the man clawed at Sebastian's face, then changed tactics and began pummeling his midsection with short but powerful punches. The first blow knocked the breath out of Sebastian, but the second one skidded off his ribs as Sebastian twisted to the side.

Sebastian's right hook caught the intruder by the jaw. Sebastian had a moment to feel greasy bristles under his knuckles before the man's face jerked upward with the blow, suddenly visible as the lantern arced to the other side.

The guardsman.

The shorter, stockier one with the mean little eyes, who'd been so eager to gag Sebastian. Juan.

Taking advantage of Sebastian's momentary shock, he wrenched himself out of Sebastian's grasp and reached above his head for the burning lantern. His attempt to dash it over Sebastian's head failed when Sebastian ducked to the side, causing the lantern to crash to the ground instead.

It would have likely extinguished itself upon contact with the dirt floor, if it hadn't caught the edge of a can of peanut oil. The oil cascaded to the floor, igniting as it came into contact with the flames and roaring up into a blistering cloud.

Sebastian pulled back at the sudden stinging heat, throwing up an arm to shield his face. With a loud grunt, Juan shoved Sebastian toward the flames and made his escape.

For a fraction of a second, Sebastian hesitated, torn between giving chase and tending to the rapidly spreading fire.

The house was mostly stone and wouldn't burn, but it would be all too easy for the fire to spread to the piles of leaves and palm fronds that Leo had neglected to clear away, not to mention the trees in the kitchen yard—and from there, to the sugarcane fields.

They must be kept from burning at all costs.

It was that thought more than anything that stirred Sebastian into action—he emptied a sack of rice over the spilled oil, then snatched a rag from the table just before it was reached by the flames and began to snap it at the fire as it crackled up the wooden legs of the table and the boards of the wall behind it.

The guardsman must've had a horse waiting nearby, because a moment later, the clomping of hooves came from the front of the house.

All of a sudden, Paulina was there, wrenching the lid off the water barrel and dipping what looked like a bedsheet into it. She tossed the sodden mass at Sebastian, and he used it to beat back the flames that had begun to crackle up the wooden wall.

"Stand aside!" Paulina cried, and she flung what must have been the entire contents of the cornmeal barrel at the flames.

The cornmeal smothered most of the flames, and Sebastian launched himself at the rest, raising his aching arm and bringing it down in swift, powerful arcs as he beat the wet cloth against the bright fingers rising from the wood, over and over again until a hand landed on his shoulder.

"It's over," Paulina said, panting. "The fire's out."

Sebastian's entire body was heaving with breaths. He staggered back, coughing, and wiped the sweat streaming off his forehead with the scorched cloth he was still holding.

Something tiny and blue caught his eye as he did and, belatedly, Sebastian glanced down at it.

It would have been unrecognizable if not for the remains of the embroidered band around one edge. Wishing it were a piece of paper he could crumple into oblivion, Sebastian cast the ruined tablecloth to the ashes and turned abruptly away.

There would be no more feasts at Villa Consuelo.

No feasts, no dancing and absolutely no more distractions.

"Who screamed?" Paulina asked hoarsely when they had caught their breath. "I thought no one was home."

"I asked Leo to stay here tonight so you wouldn't be left alone," Sebastian told her. "Have you seen him?

She shook her head, eyes wide.

Sebastian bolted toward the house, using his long legs to leap over the steps to the terrace. His heart leaped into his throat when he saw the young man crumpled in a corner, next to the overturned rocking chair.

"Leo!" cried Paulina, who'd followed on his heels.

The boy was already beginning to stir. Sebastian dropped to his knees beside him, calling over his shoulder for Paulina to light a lamp.

When it flared into life a moment later and the extent of Leo's injuries became visible, Sebastian sucked in his breath.

"He hit me from behind," the boy croaked. "And I fell against the railing. It's not as bad as it looks."

That wasn't exactly comforting.

Paulina, bearing a cloth and the basin of water from her room, nudged Sebastian aside and began to minister to the boy's cuts.

It occurred to Sebastian that he should go fetch the doctor, but the last thing he wanted was to leave them alone and unprotected in case the guardsman returned. Sebastian swore under his breath. Paulina had been right to call Villa Consuelo isolated. With no close neighbors to turn to, and no one to hear their screams if they were being murdered in their own beds.

It hadn't escaped him that with Josefa gone, Paulina

had been alone in the house all day. She could have easily been the one who was attacked.

Leo's fingers twitched.

"Don't try to talk," Sebastian said automatically, but the boy persisted. His fingers closed around the knee of Sebastian's trousers.

"I think he thought I was you."

It was an effort to keep still, his hand gripping the boy's in silent support, when all Sebastian wanted was to leap on his horse and gallop after the guardsman so that he could murder him with his own hands.

Paulina finished her ministrations, quietly winding another length of cloth around Leo's head. When she was finished, Sebastian carried the gangly young man to his own bed. At sixteen, almost seventeen, he was as tall as Sebastian and nearly as broad through the shoulders. No wonder the guardsman had confused them in the dark.

Paulina followed them inside, ostensibly to light the way with the lamp. Had Sebastian not grown to know her as well as he had, he wouldn't have noticed the tight grip she had on the lamp, or the way her eyes darted toward the deep shadows surrounding the house.

The fear in her eyes was like a knife digging into Sebastian's guts.

He helped Leo into a clean shirt, as his was rent and splattered with blood. Then, telling Paulina to give the boy some rum to drink from the decanter she had chosen to replace his cask, Sebastian slammed out onto the terrace, feeling choked by his own rage and fear.

Leo could have been killed, just because he'd been mistaken for Sebastian. Because Sebastian had once again put his compulsion to come to someone's aid above his own safety, and that of the people he was responsible for.

This was why Sebastian hadn't wanted a wife. This was why he couldn't let himself fall in love with Paulina even when his very limbs ached to twine around hers.

Loving someone—caring for them—only meant that it hurt that much more when that love was inevitably ripped away.

He didn't bother with a chair but slid down to the tiles and stretched out his legs, letting his spinning head fall back against the warm stone wall. His throat was raspy with the urge to cough out all the smoke he had inhaled, but he didn't want to leave his post, even for the few seconds it would take to fetch the water jug or the rum from his bedroom.

Presently, the door opened and Paulina slipped out, narrowly keeping herself from treading on Sebastian's stretched-out legs. Regaining her balance, she gracefully lowered herself to the spot next to him on the cool tiles, so close that he could have put his arm around her. He wanted to. He wanted to gather her against his chest and pull her long, silky legs over his lap and find comfort in the taste of her lips and the feel of her pliant body beneath his hands.

She wouldn't refuse him if he asked—and that was precisely why he couldn't.

Sebastian clenched his raw hands on his lap, but she didn't seem to notice.

"He's resting comfortably," she said.

"You should go to bed," he told her. "I'll stay out here until morning."

"I'm not tired," she said, drawing up her knees and clasping her arms around them. The thin white fabric covering her legs was scorched in places and had a long tear near the hem.

He started to ask if she was all right, but the words

stuck in his throat, and not just because of the lack of water.

Unaware of his inner turmoil, she continued. "I'm… confused. I couldn't get a good look at the man's face, but we both know he was no common thief. Am I mistaken in thinking you recognized him?"

Sebastian gave a brief nod. "It was one of the guardsmen from the municipal jail."

Also known as one of her brother's henchmen. He could tell when she registered the fact from the line that appeared between her delicately arching brows. He could also tell she was coming to the same conclusion as he had when Leo had said, *He thought I was you.*

"He was after me," Sebastian said bluntly.

"You think this may have been a warning? Because you didn't give Antonio the money when he asked for it?"

Sebastian shook his head. "No, not a warning. That blow to Leo's head…that was meant to inflict real damage."

Though left unsaid, Antonio's name hung between them. Paulina's brother might have been a lot of things, but it was clear that she had never thought him for a murderer and neither had Sebastian.

They'd both been wrong.

"He wants the mill back," Sebastian said.

Dawn was beginning to streak the sky with light, and though the terrace was still filled with shadows, Paulina couldn't fail to notice that the indentations under his eyes had grown even deeper. The skin above his eyebrow was split, grimy with blood and soot, and Paulina knew there must be bruises spreading across his ribs where the other man had pummeled him.

Paulina herself was tired, and hunger was beginning

to nibble at her stomach, but there was no question of making breakfast with the kitchen destroyed. And even though she knew she smelled strongly of smoke, she couldn't quite stomach the thought of lighting a fire to warm up water for a bath, either. Unobtrusively, she rubbed at a streak of grime on her arm.

"If Antonio has no money," Sebastian said, "and no way of acquiring enough to tempt me to sell, he must have realized that the only way was through you. That's why he went to extreme lengths to keep us from having the marriage annulled. Only it doesn't seem like he was planning to wait enough time for you to claim half my property in a divorce—not when he could kill me and have you inherit *all* of it."

"I'll divorce you," she said. "I'll do it tomorrow if that's what'll stop him."

"You can't. You need the consent of a relative if you're under twenty-five years of age, remember? Our best bet—our only bet—was an annulment. And your brother made that impossible by threatening or blackmailing or whatever he did to all the lawyers in town to discourage them from representing either of us."

"What will we do, then? If he tried it once, he'll try it again, and we can't sit around waiting for one of his attempts to succeed."

"I don't know," he said grimly.

Somewhere in the distance, a rooster began to announce the dawn. Paulina glanced at Sebastian, who was looking down at his clenched hands.

"I don't know how to tell Leo's mother that he was hurt while under my care," he admitted. "She's a widow, and Leo is all she has in the world. If anything worse had happened—if the guardsman had had a pistol..."

"It didn't," Paulina said firmly. "Leo told me that you

were putting them both up in town so that he could attend school later in the year. Why not send them now, ahead of time? I think you'll breathe easier if he's safely out of the way."

"That's a good idea."

"I've been known to have one, every now and then," Paulina said mildly. Sebastian didn't crack so much as a smile, which made Paulina frown. "Something else is troubling you."

He grunted his assent.

A sudden thought occurred to her. "You don't think I had anything to do with this, do you?"

"I don't blame you," he said, and she noticed that he hadn't said no. "I blame myself. I should have never left you all alone. I should have thought to hire someone to guard the house, or taken any number of precautions. I should have—"

"Been all knowing and all seeing? If you were to follow that line of reasoning, you should have known better than to take me in the night of the storm. You should have never walked me to Don Enrique's store, or even stopped to talk to me on the street. You couldn't have predicted that any of this would happen," she said, but she had the feeling that Sebastian wasn't listening.

She sighed. "Maybe you should leave town for a spell, at least until we can decide what to do about Antonio."

"*We* are not deciding anything. And in any case, I couldn't possibly leave the mill now, not as the *zafra*'s beginning."

Making an impatient noise, he hauled himself to his feet and started to make his way to the railing. It wasn't until Paulina saw the slight stagger in his step that she realized that the guardsman hadn't only punched him.

"You're bleeding," she blurted out.

He glanced down and, catching sight of the red stain on his bicep, gave her a shrug. "Just a scratch, I expect."

"A scratch? It's soaking through half your shirt. Here, let me—"

He reared as she advanced toward him, for all the world like a shying horse. "I'm fine."

She gaped at him. "Do you really mean to play the hero right now?"

"I'm not a hero," he mumbled.

"No, you're just trying your damnedest to single-handedly save half the population of San Pedro."

"You don't understand—"

"How could I, when you don't tell me a thing? When you spend your days running yourself ragged trying to solve everybody else's problems and refusing to see all the people who are trying to help you? I am trying to help you, Sebastian. I could, if you'd only give me a chance."

"I can't give you a chance," he snapped. "I can't afford any more distractions."

"Is that all I am to you? A distraction?"

"If we hadn't stopped in the fields—" he began wretchedly.

"You think that if I hadn't distracted you with my foolish talk about cattle ranching and dozens of children, you would have come home in time to…what? Be clubbed to death in your own bed? You were asleep at your desk," she said, and her voice sounded ragged to her own ears. "If I hadn't woken you up, would you have come home at all?"

Paulina stopped, breathing hard.

The silence that fell between them, so tense that it surely had to snap, went unbroken—until Sebastian said, in a voice that was hoarse with smoke and emotion, "I'm meant to be the one protecting this household. Not bringing danger to the doorstep."

Paulina sank into one of the new dining chairs, suddenly and thoroughly drained. "But that's not right, is it? You're not the one bringing danger to it—I am."

She waited for Sebastian to deny it, or to say something reassuring, but he remained silent, looking out over the fields. Bowing her head, Paulina let out a quavering breath. "I can't be responsible for anyone else getting hurt. Maybe I should be the one to go away."

"No," Sebastian said after a moment. "Your going anywhere won't stop your brother."

Whatever scrap of reassurance Paulina might have scrounged from his telling her to stay vanished at the second half of his sentence.

"I'll find another solution. Antonio is not getting my mill and I sure as hell am not letting him get away with hurting my people." He turned to face Paulina. "If the magistrate is crooked, the only authority that can supersede his is that of the governor of the province. I'll find a way to plead our case to him."

Rage tensed every one of Sebastian's limbs. Standing against the blazing sunrise, he looked like some sort of avenging angel, burning with righteous strength.

This was the man who had taken her in during a storm, the one who had agreed to marry her rather than let her be mistreated.

This—this was the man she had fallen in love with.

Chapter Sixteen

The smoke might have cleared, but the air between Paulina and Sebastian was more charged than ever. Paulina's heart ached as she stood in her darkened bedroom, watching from behind the shutters as Sebastian clattered down the terrace steps.

No one had been badly hurt and only the kitchen had been damaged in the fire, but one wouldn't know it from looking at the grim expression Sebastian wore these days.

It wasn't only Sebastian who was on edge. More than once, Paulina had caught herself jumping at shadows, growing tense every time a tree branch swayed unexpectedly or a bird took sudden flight.

Leo had been dispatched into town ahead of schedule and set up with books and tutors until school started. Sebastian wasn't confiding much in Paulina these days, but she had learned from Dilia that he'd sent word to Doña Josefa to stay with her daughter for another few weeks.

It wouldn't have been so wretched if she had Sebastian's company, but he had begun going to the mill earlier than ever, hours before the sky began to lighten, leaving behind two burly men to look after Villa Consuelo…and Paulina.

Paulina had never found any use in tears and she wasn't inclined to indulge now, but neither could she ignore the desperate loneliness curling through her as soon as she opened her eyes, the birdsong uninterrupted by the bustle of Doña Josefa's cooking or Leo's quiet voice. The men Sebastian had hired were nice enough but not inclined toward conversation.

The furniture Paulina had ordered for the house had arrived, and while the pieces were as beautiful as she'd expected, arranging and rearranging them only took up so much of the day. It was a relief when, after a couple of days of solitude, the rumble of carriage wheels in the front yard announced a visitor.

Paulina was on the terrace. The homely rocking chair had been replaced by a handsome new set, with carved backs and flowered cushions on the seats. They were grouped around a round table, which Paulina had laid with a silver coffeepot and a delicate porcelain cup from the service she and Sebastian had purchased on one of their jaunts into town. Similarly arrayed in her sky-blue skirt and a white blouse bordered with eyelet lace, Paulina thought idly that she would trade it all for the tin mugs and the shabby yellow frock if it meant having people around her again.

The guards hired by Sebastian had been lounging in the shade of the tamarind trees; at the sound of the carriage, they rose from their spots with such alacrity that Paulina realized their lethargic poses had been nothing but an act.

"It's all right," she said when she spotted the familiar coach. "It's only Sebastian."

It wasn't like him to come home in the middle of the day. Not anymore. Paulina tensed as she watched him alight with a single bound of his long legs, her hands crumpling the newspaper she had been reading.

Sebastian's face was tight, and he spared neither a greeting nor a smile for Paulina when he stopped beside her.

"I couldn't get an audience with the governor," he said without preamble. "But I did secure an invitation for a ball he's hosting tonight. He leaves for Santiago in the morning on a health matter, so it's our only chance to approach him."

"A ball?" Paulina echoed. "But I haven't got a—"

"I went to Blanca's earlier. She still had your measurements, so it was only a matter of hours for her to alter a gown to fit you."

As if in illustration, Alfonso lugged a satin box into the terrace.

"I asked her to select shoes for you, too, and whatever accessories were necessary. It should all be in the box." Without further explanation, Sebastian started to turn around.

A sudden wild panic gripped Paulina at the thought of being left alone again, and she had the irrational urge to plant herself in his path and force him to acknowledge her. "Wait!" she exclaimed, her hand fluttering in his direction, though she stopped short of touching his retreating back, half-afraid that he would shrink from her touch.

Sebastian glanced at her, and it was as if a door that had previously been left ajar had been shut in her face. "Alfonso will take you to the governor's residence when you're ready."

"You're not coming with me?"

"I have some business to attend to, but I'll join you there later."

Paulina scowled. "Is that really all you have to say to me? 'Get dressed, we're going to a ball, meet you there'?"

His back stiffened. "What else do you want from me, Paulina?"

"The friendship that you offered me, for one," she snapped, her temper flaring. "And for you to stop treating me as though I was the one who clubbed Leo over the head. Stop pushing me away, Sebastian. I thought we were long past this."

He didn't reply, and her irritation at his silence made her say, "I'll go to the governor's ball with you, but there's something I want in exchange—when we are no longer married, I want you to book me passage on the first train out of San Pedro, and provide me with some funds to make the journey. I intend to get far away from here the very second I can."

She was horrified with herself the instant the words left her mouth—both because it made her sound uncomfortably like Antonio, but also because she hadn't realized how much it would hurt Sebastian until she saw his mouth clamp shut.

He gave her a hard nod. "Yes." The despair in his eyes hollowed out her chest. "I had a feeling you would."

She sighed. "Sebastian, I—"

"I'll give you anything you want, Paulina," he said tiredly, not letting her choke out an apology.

"And you won't even miss me, will you?"

He smiled at her then, finally, but it was a sad, regretful smile. "I think you know me better than to think that."

"I thought I did," she told him, and it was she who turned away, walking past the discarded newspaper and coffee and into her room.

The nights were much cooler in town than they were among the sugarcane fields. A pleasant breeze, tinged with the saltiness of the sea and the slight brackishness of the river water, swept through the open louvered doors at the far end of the governor's second-floor ballroom.

Paulina shivered as the breeze touched her bare shoulders. The evening gown that Blanca had hurriedly adapted to fit her had sleeves—cascading wings of topaz-colored chiffon that fell softly around her elbows, suspended from heavily beaded straps that left her shoulders uncovered. The gown was cinched tight around the waist with a taffeta sash that bore still more beading. Along with the low neckline, it made her aware of her own figure, and of the way her body slipped through the crowd as she went in search of Sebastian.

An ostentatious topaz necklace had been included in the box with the gown, but Paulina had worn instead the rose-shaped amber earrings Sebastian had given her. She raised a hand to touch them now, nerves fizzling in her stomach like the bubbles in the champagne flute a waiter had handed her earlier.

Trailed by the thrilling notes of music coming from the musicians on the dais, Paulina circled the crowd once again. There were dozens of people in the ballroom and a handful more on the balcony that stretched the entire width of the house and overlooked the lush gardens below. There had been still more people crowding the wooden staircase and spilling out into a wide street that was crammed with coaches.

Quite a number of them spoke in English or accented Spanish—Paulina remembered her brother bragging about being friends with all the foreign mill owners, though she'd had the impression that they did not exactly treat him as an equal, having little money and no mill of his own.

Having found no familiar faces among them, Paulina

was nearing the musicians' platform when she saw Sebastian through a gap in the crowd. He had paused near the tall arch of the entrance, framed between two columns as he scanned the room with that tense watchfulness he had developed since his fight with the intruder.

He turned his head as if to show off his strong profile and chiseled jaw, the noble lines of his head displayed to best advantage by his close-cropped hair. In response to the sight, the ever-present ache in her chest flared into life.

It had been mere hours since she'd last seen him, but she was struck by the solid breadth of his shoulders and the way his long, lean legs echoed the columns at either side of him. It was almost as if she were seeing him for the first time, but better, because now she was familiar with the callused roughness of his fingertips and the hardness of his arms and thighs.

He was hers. Nothing that had happened in the past several weeks would support that conclusion, but Paulina knew it with a fierce intensity. Whatever had happened, and whatever *would* happen. Even if she never saw him again after the governor granted their annulment, Sebastian Linares belonged to her.

The cool breeze was still making its way through the ballroom, but Paulina was suddenly filled with the urge to snap open her painted fan and wave it at her warm face.

Then a woman dressed in black and dripping with jewels moved in front of Paulina; by the time she and her mustachioed companion had strolled past, Sebastian had disappeared from where he had been standing.

For a moment, Paulina thought that he was going to avoid her until it was time to speak with the governor.

But as disappointment crashed over her, the crowd parted again and there he was, standing in front of her.

He looked even better up close. Paulina's lips parted, but every word she'd ever known had vanished from her mind.

Luckily, Sebastian wasn't paying her any attention.

"Linares?" said someone to their right. "It is you. Funny, I don't think I've ever seen you in one of these events. I was beginning to think you were some sort of sugarcane hermit."

The voice belonged to a pale-skinned man with a handlebar mustache and light green eyes. He spoke Spanish perfectly, though his accent, Paulina noticed, was tinged with a Cuban lilt.

"Bass." Sebastian gave the other man a hearty handshake. "May I present to you my wife, Paulina."

"Oh, yes, I did hear you married recently. Enchanted to meet you," he said, greeting her in the American fashion, with a brush of his hands over her gloved knuckles.

"Paulina, this is William L. Bass. He's the proprietor of one of the largest sugar estates in the province. And quite a cartoonist, from what I hear."

"Oh?" Paulina asked as the older man roared with laughter.

"Just trying to keep the powers that be in line," Don William said. "But I'd hate to talk about business on such a nice evening. Ah, here comes Vicini's widow. Doña Laura, you are acquainted with Sebastian Linares and his splendid wife, are you not?"

The flurry of introductions was, in fact, followed by business talk. As it turned out, Doña Laura also owned a sugar mill, and all three of them had plenty to say about…well, Paulina wasn't entirely paying attention. She was taking advantage of the conversation to watch

Sebastian. Though older by at least a couple of decades, Don William and Doña Laura listened seriously to what he had to say, making it clear that they truly valued his opinion. As for Sebastian himself, he looked as at home among these wealthy landowners with their diamond tie-pins and blazing jewels as he had trying to solve a goat-related dispute in his shirtsleeves.

She was so absorbed in her examination of Sebastian's face that she didn't realize they were trying to include her in the conversation until Doña Laura had said her name two or three times.

"Oh, but we are taking too much of your time," she said when Paulina finally snapped to attention. "A young couple such as yourselves must be longing to dance. Come, William, let's stand aside and let them have their frolic."

Paulina licked her lips. To refuse would have been the height of rudeness. Surely Sebastian wouldn't…

"I believe my wife was just saying something about procuring refreshments—"

"Actually," Paulina said defiantly, "I would love to dance."

His gaze flicked toward her. Looking as if he was steeling himself, Sebastian bowed. "As you wish. Will you join me in a dance?"

Out of the corner of her eye, Paulina caught Doña Laura's beam. She could have hugged the older woman. Settling for a smile instead, Paulina took Sebastian's hand and allowed him to lead her to the dance floor as the first strains of a waltz began to play.

As he had when they'd danced on his terrace, Sebastian placed a hand at her waist and clasped her hand with the other. And as it had then, it felt extraordinarily intimate.

Or it would have, had Sebastian not looked furious.

"Your friends will wonder why the prospect of dancing with your own wife pains you so much," she remarked, though Sebastian's expression felt like it was scouring her from the inside out.

His shoulder flexed under her hand. "I don't give a damn what anyone thinks. I'm only here for the governor."

"I think he hasn't arrived yet," Paulina said. "So you might as well enjoy yourself. I may not be a Havana debutante, but I know how much you like dancing. Even with someone who treads on your toes."

For all that he was still in the grip of his foul mood, Sebastian was a pillar of grace and strength as he swept her along. He didn't seem to be troubled by her occasional misstep, and if she did injure his toes, he refrained from showing it, like a true gentleman.

"I didn't learn to dance in Havana," he said.

"Oh?"

"I learned by watching your mother's parties. I would climb up the mango tree outside the upstairs gallery and hide among the branches as I looked at the elegant couples swirling around."

"I was always watching, too," she said softly. "I hid under tables in my nightdress. Isn't it peculiar how we spent so much of our childhoods together, sometimes unknowingly? Only to end up here. Together, again."

"It was no coincidence that I ended up where I did," he told her. "Buying the mill from your brother, purchasing the only estate that neighbored your family's *quinta*... Those nights when I watched the parties from between the mangoes, I promised myself that I would have all of that someday—glittering friends, lavish tables bursting with flowers and all sorts of delicacies on silver platters, a laughing wife dripping with jewels."

He twirled her. "I dreamed about it when I was on the streets in Havana. A fine house, with great beds heaped with pillows and tables laden with everything I could eat. You want to know why I didn't tell you who I was at first? Because you only knew me as the little servant boy who came to play with you. You didn't know that when the games ended and the music stopped, I walked through the cane in the dark, to a wooden house with a cane-thatched roof that leaked and a floor made out of packed dirt that turned into mud at the slightest spill. I went home to an exhausted mother who had to rub lard on her hands to soothe the knuckles she had rubbed raw washing other people's clothes. We didn't spend our childhoods together, Paulina. We spent them near each other."

Her chest felt tight, even as she let him sweep her from one end of the ballroom to the other. He was right. Growing up, they had been separated by more than the cane fields. And yet. The achingly lonely little girl she'd once been still resided inside her, just as part of him was still a skinny boy with big eyes. Their pasts, and their losses, weren't something they had overcome, but what had made them into the people they were now.

People who were as irrevocably drawn to each other as if they'd spent their lives trying to find each other again.

The waltz was about to come to an end. Sebastian gave her one last twirl as the last strains of the song reverberated from the musicians' dais, and Paulina's gaze traveled around the room, over the matrons gathered in the sidelines.

When she returned to Sebastian's arms, it was with a pounding heart.

"He's here," she said. "Antonio's here."

* * *

In the deep ochre of her gown, sparkling in the oddly still electric lights, Paulina looked like she had been plucked from the midday sky. The fabric clung to her curves, glazing her in light.

It took a moment for Sebastian to register what she was saying, and still longer to respond. "I know," he said, "I saw him."

He'd given little thought to his own safety, because Despradel was a man who operated in the shadows—Sebastian couldn't fathom the man trying to cause him or anyone else any harm in this illustrious gathering.

Sebastian, on the other hand, was ready and willing to cause *him* grievous bodily harm, audience be damned.

His hand closed on Paulina's arm again, just above her elbow, but no matter how urgently he wanted to yank her out of the crowd and into safety, Sebastian knew that doing anything to attract the attention of the guests would draw her brother's as well, and he'd rather avoid that, at least until he had gotten Paulina safely out of the way.

Immediately grasping the situation, she raised a hand to his face and pulled him down as if to whisper something flirtatious. Sebastian couldn't hold back a shiver as her breath curled around his ear, even though her words were decidedly unromantic.

"Don't go after him. Please."

He was so tense, every single one of his muscles was screaming in protest. "I won't," he said. "Not until I get you out of here."

Her hand landed on his arm, squeezing with urgency. "We shouldn't leave until we've spoken with the governor. He hasn't arrived yet." Anticipating Sebastian's answer, she added, "It'll be better if we're both here to present our case."

"Fine. We'll wait on the balcony." Sebastian straight-ened and, telling himself it was mostly for the benefit of the people around them, offered her his arm.

She relaxed, but only fractionally, her hand light on his arm, as if she expected him to yank it away at any moment. Fair enough. He wasn't at ease touching her, either, or walking so close to her that the scent of her perfume overpowered all others.

Just outside the balcony, so close he was sure he'd be able to touch it if he stretched, was one of the new electric streetlamps. The unwavering light inside its glass globe was bright, dimming even the full moon that peeked out from behind the trees across the street. Two other streetlamps farther down the street shone like smaller, lesser moons.

Paulina, in that golden dress that shimmered with beads, was as resplendent as the sun.

Settling in an out-of-the way spot where they wouldn't easily be spotted, Sebastian turned away from her so as not to be dazzled.

With his back to the streetlamps, he would be able to see anyone who wandered onto the balcony before they had a chance to spot him. Paulina was also watchful. He knew it without having to look at her, the same way he knew that she was nervous about seeing her brother—and not only because of what Sebastian might do.

Whatever instinct he had developed where Paulina was concerned, it didn't extend to the other member of her family. Before either of them could break the silence growing between them, Despradel strode out onto the balcony, deep in conversation with another man.

Acting in unison, they shrank into the shadows of a potted palm. Sebastian turned to Paulina, leaning a hand against the wall behind her to obscure her face. He lowered his own in a gesture that might have looked amorous from the outside, with his expression concealed.

Paulina was tense in the circle of his arms. He couldn't stop himself from touching the sliver of bare skin at her shoulder with his free hand, meaning to be comforting but feeling as though sparks should be coming off the beaded band attached to her diaphanous sleeves.

Maybe it was himself he meant to comfort—regardless, all he'd done was make himself feel so unsteady on his feet, he was glad for the sturdiness of the wall under his right hand.

"It will take some time," Despradel was saying. He had lowered his voice somewhat but seemed to be trusting that his casual tone would dissuade potential eavesdroppers. "It's a delicate matter, after all, and one that needs to be handled with certain discretion. But it *will* get done."

Both men came to a stop in front of the wooden railing, less than a meter away from the dark corner where Sebastian and Paulina stood.

Despradel's companion made a low sound that Sebastian didn't know how to interpret. "And you're sure you can keep your hands clean?"

"It's easy enough to arrange all manner of accidents. I've a man who can do it quite inconspicuously. Don't you worry—I'll get rid of both of them by the end of month, and then we'll be free to toast our new venture."

Both of them. Sebastian's blood ran cold.

It wasn't just Sebastian that Antonio meant to have killed. It was Paulina, too.

Exploding into violence, Sebastian pushed off the wall and lunged for Despradel, grabbing him by the shoulder and hauling him around. Caught unaware, Despradel stumbled and didn't struggle as Sebastian wrenched a fistful of his shirt and used it to lift the shorter man to his face.

"You murderous little bastard," he hissed, pressing Despradel to the wooden railing that was now behind him.

Despradel's eyes, wide with surprise, narrowed into calculation. And then, with disconcerting ease, he rearranged his expression, affecting concern that looked so genuine it would have fooled Sebastian himself. "Sebastian Linares?" Despradel said, blinking. "Whatever's the matter?"

In response, Sebastian slammed him against the railing again, enjoying the flash of panic on Despradel's face when the wood shook beneath him. He was dimly aware of Paulina behind him, talking in an urgent voice, and of the fact that Despradel's companion had melted into the crowd that was beginning to gather in the balcony.

Despradel was much more cogent of his surroundings—and of the fact that he had a captive audience. "You may want to release me, Linares. This is the second time you have accosted me in public—completely unprovoked, I might add. If you're not careful, the good people of San Pedro will think you've something against me." Still smiling pleasantly, Despradel added softly, "And they won't be surprised if I find myself having to do something drastic to defend my life against your violent attacks."

His smile broadened when he saw the hesitation flickering in Sebastian's eyes. A rise in volume in the murmurs around them told Sebastian that this was indeed the case—anyone who was here tonight was a witness to the fact that Sebastian Linares had just tried to assault Antonio Despradel.

"You can't win against me, Linares," Antonio said,

just loud enough for Sebastian to hear the gloating in his voice. "It's pitiful that you even think you can try."

The truth of it slammed into Sebastian like a punch to the chest. He had just provided Despradel with an excuse for whatever the hell he was planning to do to him and Paulina.

So he did what he'd been wanting to do for weeks—he slammed his fist into Despradel's sneering face.

The other man's head snapped back violently, spraying blood. Sebastian felt it splattering the front of his starched shirt before two men seized him by the arms and hauled him back, away from Despradel, who was pressing a handkerchief to his streaming nose. Sebastian didn't bother to struggle but contented himself to look at Despradel's bloody face with satisfaction.

It was short-lived, vanishing the moment he saw Paulina's stricken expression. Then his gaze shifted over her shoulder, toward the man making his way through a gap in the crowd. No, not a gap. The people who had gathered to watch the altercation with eyes greedy for gossip were stepping aside to let him through.

He was glowering at them, eyes narrowed above his thick, dark mustache and beard. The medals pinned to the sleek black lapels of his jacket caught the light as he strode toward Sebastian, bristling with authority.

"What is the meaning of this?" he asked furiously. At a single stroke of his arm, the musicians stopped playing.

Sebastian didn't need an introduction to recognize him—it was the governor.

Chapter Seventeen

Antonio had wasted no time in ingratiating himself with the governor. He didn't simper or act injured—all he had to do was nobly absolve Sebastian of guilt while allowing the others guests to clamor on his behalf. Before Paulina could quite catch her breath—or meet Tío Ramon's troubled gaze—she and Sebastian had been summarily ejected from the governor's house.

As they left, escorted by one of the governor's man-servants, Paulina heard Antonio express what sounded like sincere concern over "the blackguard my sister saw fit to marry." The impulse to wheel around and tell the onlookers the truth about him was almost as strong as the sense of betrayal coursing through her.

It would have been useless.

Paulina wasn't quite sure how she managed it, but she held off the tears until Sebastian had helped her into his carriage. Only when they were speeding through the night in the direction of Villa Consuelo did her short, tremulous breaths dissolve into sobs.

She had never been close with her brother, nor particularly friendly. Shocking though it was to overhear him contemplating his own sister's murder—and to see how nonchalant he'd looked about it—it shouldn't have been so painful. And yet, her chest felt so tight with it, she was sure it would burst.

She'd always known he was despotic and petty and occasionally cruel, but capable of murdering her? For money, property and influence? She didn't want to believe it.

Her sobs echoed inside the small coach, and after a moment, she found herself being presented with a crisp white handkerchief. "Are you all right?"

"Would you be?" she snapped.

"No." Under her hand, his arm had been hard as steel—a marked contrast to the gentleness in his tone. "I don't suppose so."

"How could he? His own sister? His only one, for that matter. I know I've never been more than a pawn to him, but you'd think he'd have *some* consideration for my life."

Sebastian let out a slow breath, as though steeling himself to do something. Stooping to keep the top of his head from striking the bouncing carriage roof, he switched seats so that he was next to her rather than across and close enough to put an arm around her. "I haven't words foul enough to express what I feel about that *lacra*, so I won't even try. What I will tell you is that you have my word that I won't let anything happen to you," he said fiercely.

Her head fit perfectly against his shoulder. "What are we going to do?" Her voice, though still ragged with sobs, was starting to reflect the fury kindling in her chest. Her fingers clenched around Sebastian's handkerchief. "Would it be any help at all if I were to leave town— or even the country? Do you think he would continue to pursue you if he couldn't get the mill through me?"

"I wouldn't put anything past him. And I damn well

am not letting you go anywhere on your own. We'll go together."

Paulina twisted to look up at his face, though it was pitch black inside the coach. "But what about Dilia and Doña Josefa and the mill? You would leave them?"

"If it means ensuring their safety... I have to, don't I?" His voice sounded so bleak, it made Paulina put an impulsive hand on his.

Half expecting him to shake it off, Paulina was surprised when Sebastian turned his hand so that their palms touched. His fingers, strong and long and slightly rough with calluses, threaded through hers.

"I'm sorry," she said. "I know how fond you are of them, and how much you'll miss and worry for them."

She could hear his breathing above the rattle of the wheels. From experience, she knew that even if he felt them, he would never say the things she wanted him to say—*I'm fond of you, too. I would miss you if we were parted. I worry for you every day.*

He disengaged his hand from hers, as if he could hear her thoughts. But when he drew in another deep breath, what he said was, "Carlos didn't make me promise to look after his family. He said so to me, just before he died—that he didn't have to because he knew I would. And Josefa—I vowed to myself that I would look after her in her old age. Instead, all she's done is look after me. And now I'm just going to leave her, again."

Over the time they had shared, she had learned to read his expression, which she had once found inscrutable. She had come to understand the tones shading his words, too, enough to know that it was despair, not anger, that was making his voice rough.

"You feel like you're letting them all down," she murmured. "Just like you felt you failed everyone who looked after you when you stayed in Havana so long. And I think," she continued, too struck by her sudden insight into Sebastian's feelings to realize that he probably didn't appreciate her laying him bare, "though you haven't admitted it to yourself, that you feel that way because when Carlos died, he let *you* down."

The quality of his breathing next to her told her she had struck a nerve.

"You had so many plans together. With his help, you were going to put everything to rights. Then he left and left you shouldering all the burdens. And you've been so braced, waiting for everyone else to leave you, too, that—"

"Stop," Sebastian commanded, breathing harshly. Then, almost whispering, he echoed, "Stop."

Paulina gripped his arm. Under his jacket, his muscles were so tense it was like holding on to a tree branch. "They will be all right, even if you have to go away again. You've made every provision to ensure that."

Sebastian was silent for a long while. It wasn't until the carriage turned into the dirt road leading to Villa Consuelo that he spoke again, so low she almost missed it. "Everyone leaves. I was meant to be the one who stayed."

"We'll leave at first light." The front room, with its elegantly draped curtains and gleaming new furniture, came into view as Sebastian finished lighting the brass lamp on the table. Its paltry glow was no match to the abundance of light in the governor's ballroom, but Paulina still glimmered like a streak of gold in a dark mine as she hovered near the louvered door, which he'd pulled firmly closed behind them.

He should have sent her to her own bed, but even with

his hired guards stationed outside, Sebastian didn't want to risk leaving her alone. Grimly, he poured a glass of rum and handed it to her.

"I wouldn't leave if it were just myself in danger. But I'll be damned if I let that brother of yours harm a single hair on your head." He accepted the battered tin mug from her, pouring more rum into it before taking a deep sip and reaching up one-handed to undo the white bow tie at his throat. "We'll leave the country, both of us. I'll go at once to buy us passage on whatever steamer is sailing today—first I have to stop by the mill, though, to leave instructions for my foreman and take some money out of my safe. I need to make sure Dilia has enough for her family, and there's Leo and Josefa…"

"Will we stop in town to say our goodbyes to Dilia?"

Sebastian gave a hard shake of his head. "It's not safe. We have no way of knowing what your brother will do, or when he will strike. It's best for everyone if we leave as soon as possible."

"And after that?" One of the beads on her dress had come loose, and she plucked at it with her eyes lowered, her long eyelashes casting lacy shadows on her cheekbones.

"I suppose it's only sensible to make our way to Havana—I know plenty of people there, so it won't be too difficult to get ourselves situated."

From there, he would be able to hire a lawyer. He didn't know if putting the mill in Dilia's name would stop Antonio's pursuit of it, but the possibility certainly had to be explored. And, he thought reluctantly, he would also be able to hire someone to start annulment or even divorce proceedings. He wasn't familiar with the Cuban laws regarding such things, but surely it wasn't impossible.

Even if that were to happen immediately, though, they would probably have to remain in Havana for at least a year or two, until they could be damn sure that Despradel knew how futile it would be to go through with his plan—and that he wouldn't decide to carry it out anyway, out of sheer spite at having it thwarted.

He was startled to discover that it didn't feel like a terrible prospect. Not because he wouldn't miss his people, or because he was eager to escape his responsibilities, but because of the glow that ignited in his chest at the prospect of spending two years or more with Paulina.

The guardsman's violent intrusion into Villa Consuelo and Leo's resulting injury had shaken him, badly, when he realized just how close Paulina had come to being hurt herself. The strength of his reaction had led him to discover that his feelings for her went so far beyond friendship, or even mere attraction, that the notion that anything could have happened to her had made him put as much distance between them as he could.

He loved her.

And he wanted to keep her safe. And if that meant staying married to her instead of rushing to separate…

It was probably best not to mention any of that to Paulina, who looked troubled enough already. He touched her arm, briefly, and gestured toward the bed. "You might want to get some rest. It's only a few hours until we have to leave. I'll stay on guard, in the chair."

She nodded, but didn't move. "I hate that it's come to this. I can't help but feel that I should have said something—"

"It's my own damn fault, for losing my temper." And for not paying attention to the snakelike cunning in Despradel's eyes.

Swirling some water around the mug, he emptied it

into his shaving basin before filling it up with clean water and giving it to her to drink.

She shook her head, her brown fingers clasped tight around the dented tin. "I didn't mean only tonight. I've had years to do something about his cruelty. If I'd stood up to him…"

"You have stood up to him. I've seen you."

"Tiny, inconsequential acts of rebellion that in the end amounted to nothing."

"I'm sure—"

"Don't," she said. "I don't need to hear whatever placating thing you were about to say. All of this might have been avoided if I'd just stood up to my brother once or twice."

Sebastian leaned forward, seizing her hand from the handful of silk she was clutching. "This is not your fault," he said distinctly. "Whatever your brother does or fails to do is not on you. He and he alone is responsible for his actions and his decisions and his murderous intentions."

Despite the conviction in his tone, he could tell that his reassurance rang as hollow as hers had earlier. He touched a fingertip to the teardrop glistening in the corner of her eye like another bead. "Go lie down. Tomorrow will be a long day, and you'll need your strength."

She must have been tired, because she consented without much argument, following him through the inner door of his bedroom, where a straight-backed chair awaited him like a sentinel.

Turning away from the sight of her in his bed, he heard the soft thud of the glass being placed on the table, then the rustle of silk as she settled into the mattress.

Sebastian jerked off his bow tie, leaving it crumpled on the marble surface of his washstand, and headed for the chair. The sound of her voice followed him to the other side of the room.

"You can't stay in the chair all night." He glanced back, and damn if he shouldn't have been turned into a pillar of salt on the spot. She was propped up on one elbow, the folds of her dress spread out over the bedcovers. "You'll be terribly sore in the morning, and if anyone will need strength tomorrow..."

She had a point, but Sebastian shrugged it off. "I'll lie on the floor. I don't exactly mean to sleep tonight." He'd told Alfonso, the coachman, to watch the house along with the guards, but he'd feel much better if he remained alert himself.

"The bed is more than big enough for both of us." She sat all the way up and drew up her legs, wrapping her arms around the silk covering them. From across the room, she looked very small and very dark against the vastness of his bed. "I know you won't kiss me, and I won't ask you again. But will you...will you hold me?"

It would have taken a far better man than he to deny such an entreaty. It was her eyes, though, that broke his resolution. The exact color of the rum blazing a trail down his chest, they were filled with so much heartache that nothing could have stopped him from trying to ease it.

She watched him remove his polished shoes and dark socks. He had cast off his jacket inside the coach, and now he made quick work of his white waistcoat and the stiff white collar at his throat. He remained in his shirtsleeves and trousers, but the small act of partly undressing in front of her unwavering gaze felt breathtakingly intimate.

The mattress dipped beneath his knee, and the slight movement made the beads on her dress tremble and shimmer as if in welcome. When he gathered her to him, it was with the impression that he had taken a handful of candlelight into his hands—warm and necessary and potentially scorching.

Ignoring the danger, he tucked her against his side. He would burn, if he must.

"Sleep," he said against the curve of her neck. "You'll be safe here. I'll keep you safe."

"I know." She turned in the circle of his arms and regarded him seriously. "I should have recognized you as the little boy I used to know."

"Oh?"

"By your eyes if nothing else." Her fingers explored the ridge beneath his right eyebrow, which was now bisected with a thin line where the skin had split open during his fight with the guardsman. It was no longer painful, but his breath hitched regardless. "You've always made me feel safe. Even that young."

The back of her hand followed the contours of his face, not stopping when it reached his neck and the crest of his shoulder. The knife wound on his arm had broken open again earlier that day as he'd helped unload a cart at the mill, and he'd bound it quickly so that it wouldn't ruin his good shirt. She ran a hand over the thick bulk of the bandage and continued down his arm.

The marks the manacles had left around his wrist had mostly faded, but she touched those as well, looking grave. "You made me feel braver, too," she said.

Asking for his permission with a flicker of her eyes, she waited until he nodded before reaching for the buttons on his shirt. One by one, she eased them from their tight buttonholes. His shirt gaped, then parted, aided by her questing hand, and she swept it aside to reveal the discoloration over his ribs.

Her solemn accounting over, it was his turn to touch her. He hardly knew where to begin.

The air was thick with humidity, and her face was surrounded by a crown of ringlets. Paulina looked on with solemn eyes ringed by long lashes as Sebastian wound a single curl around his forefinger. Under the weight of her gaze, he felt himself become unmade.

She was the one who guided his face down to hers. He felt her breath first, sweeping over his lower lip in much the same way he had once swept his thumb over hers. They breathed in unison for the space of a heartbeat, then another—and then they closed the remaining distance between them and Sebastian was hard-pressed to keep from gasping out loud at the heat of her mouth. Her mouth opened beneath his, as pliant and warm as her body.

He'd been right. Sparks came off her when he touched her, sending an electric current rippling up and down his spine.

The bodice of her dress cradled the lush curves of her bosom, skimming over the tantalizing crevice between them. He traced the edge of the beaded band around the neckline, right where it met her amber-colored skin. When he lowered his lips to the spot his fingers had just vacated, he was rewarded by a soft, shuddering moan.

No—it wasn't sparks. It was lightning.

Rucking up her dress, Paulina caught his hand and pressed it to the heat between her legs. Their gazes locked, and the frayed remains of his resistance snapped.

And he gave in. To his desire, to Paulina's pleasure and to their future, whatever it held.

Paulina arched against Sebastian and was rewarded by something that sounded gratifyingly like a growl as he dragged his lips just below her jaw. Then his merciless mouth found the hollow of her throat.

She had seen enough glimpses of Sebastian's raw desire to know how much it must have cost him every time he chose restraint over indulging in passion. Selfishly, she wanted to see him lose every shred of self-discipline—and she wanted to be the one to drive him over the edge.

She reached for the waistband of his trousers and undid the first few buttons, using her thumb to explore the deep ridge pressing against them.

He hissed in a breath, and before either of them had time to take another, he had seized her wrist and was pinning it just above her head.

Hooking a finger into her bodice and dragging it down until he had exposed her nipple to the cool air, he nipped at the tight bud. She gasped at the sharp sensation, hardly able to draw breath enough to say, "Touch me, Sebastian. I want your hands all over my body."

He *had* promised to give her everything she wanted.

Each caress of his fingers on the sensitive skin of her thighs felt like raking coals. Like she should be bursting into flames—or fireworks.

His thumb traced gentle circles on the inside of her thighs, moving higher and higher until—

She bucked against his hand, biting her lip to hold in a gasp. The throbbing pleasure of his touch was more than she'd dared to dream of. It was almost more than she could bear.

She wrapped her legs around him, trapping his hand against her, and all of a sudden, he was the one gasping.

"I've wanted you from the moment I first met you," she told him, dragging his trousers down. "I want you, and I mean to have you. All of you."

"You already have me, Paulina." He sought her mouth again, exhaling kiss after kiss into it. Kisses that tasted of rum and sugar and the sweetest satisfaction. "You always have."

In the haze of her spiraling pleasure, she was barely aware that she was chanting, over and over again, "You're mine. You're mine. You're mine."

And all the while, her heart was thudding to the same rhythm, *I'm yours. I'm yours. I'm yours.*

Chapter Eighteen

Darkness still pressed against the louvered doors when Paulina heard a voice close to her ear. "It's time to go."

She hadn't slept much, but she had slept deeply. Even so, she didn't feel the least bit disoriented when her eyelashes fluttered open and she saw Sebastian sitting on the edge of the bed. The pillow under her cheek smelled faintly of him, just as she'd imagined it would. The scent was as comforting as the pleasant soreness between her legs—she hadn't imagined last night, nor had she dreamed it.

Sitting up, she reached for him, stroking the back of his neck as she brushed her lips against his.

The bristles on his jaw scraped against her skin, reigniting the glow of desire that pooled low in her belly as surely as if he had lit a lamp. Paulina would have liked to nuzzle against the delicious roughness, but he pulled away almost immediately.

"I fetched your clothes from your bedroom," he said, handing her the faded yellow dress. With a slight pang, Paulina thought of all the clothes they had ordered from Blanca—hopefully Dilia would be able to stop the dressmaker in time. "There's soap and tooth powder by the basin. We'll leave as soon as you're dressed."

Was it her imagination, or was he avoiding her gaze?

He certainly wasn't watching her as she slipped into her clothes, though his eyes had hungrily consumed every inch of exposed skin as she stepped out of her dress the night before.

Quickly, Paulina twisted her hair into a slightly haphazard knot at the back of her head, securing it with the pins he had placed on his bedside table after easing them from her hair. She didn't ask if anything was wrong—if he was having second thoughts about what they'd done, she didn't want to hear it. It had meant too much for her to hear it be called a mistake.

"I'm ready," she said past the lump in her throat. She hadn't any luggage—she would leave Villa Consuelo the way she had arrived, with empty hands and an aching heart. The only pang she felt was at the thought of her mother's portrait, secured within the plain locket that she had hid among her meager possessions in her family's *quinta*. It was the only thing she was sorry to leave behind.

They stepped out into the hush of very early morning. The frogs and crickets and other small creatures that came alive in the night were all quiet, and it was too early for birdsong. It was too early for sunlight, too. The carriage was a hulking shape in the gloom, the two horses at its head softly whickering shadows.

Paulina climbed inside without waiting for Sebastian's help; he remained outside for a moment to give instructions to the coachman, then followed her in and sat across from her, shifting so that his legs didn't touch hers.

The distance between their two seats could have been

kilometers. It welled up inside her chest until it felt tight enough to burst.

"Did you mean what you said last night?" she asked.

"You should know by now that I don't say things I don't mean."

"Then you've changed your mind. I don't regret it, you know," she told him, feeling infinitely tired. "Even if you do."

Those hours in bed with Sebastian had been more than stolen momentary happiness. Paulina knew it all the way down to her bones—the same way she knew that their coming together, as impossible as it had felt, had been inevitable.

"You're so willing to put your body on the line for the people you love," she said softly. "But not your heart. Is that how you truly want to live your life?"

He didn't answer. Out of the corner of her eye, she saw as Sebastian knocked a fist against the roof of the carriage, calling for the coachman to go faster.

The rattle of the wheels turned into a roar. Paulina's breath caught in her throat—not from the increased speed, but because there was something subtly wrong in the movement of the carriage, a certain reckless wobble. She met Sebastian's gaze, as wide as her own.

He had no time to shout a warning to the coachman.

There was a sickening sound of grinding metal, and the carriage swung suddenly to one side, as if it had been sideswiped by an unseen force. Paulina crashed into Sebastian with bone-jarring force.

One of the wheels must have caught on something, because the carriage came to a jarring stop and hung suspended for the longest second Paulina had ever experienced.

Then, slowly yet inexorably, it began to overturn.

* * *

Clouds were gathering.

It had smelled like rain all night. Lying next to Paulina, Sebastian had spent the hours between her drifting off to sleep and her eyes fluttering open feeling the humidity mount alongside something that felt like guilt.

It had taken him a long time to disentangle the snarl of thoughts and feelings that had taken residence in his chest. He had ruined their chances at an annulment, of course, but there was always divorce if she still wanted to head down that path.

Sometime in the very early hours of the morning, when the world outside his bedroom was still dark and quiet, it had come to him. Sebastian had always prided himself on being a protector of the innocent. He didn't take advantage of anyone in a precarious position—and he certainly didn't bed them.

If they hadn't done what they had the night before, she could have gotten her annulment and sailed straight into another marriage without having to provide any explanations or tell anyone about her misadventure at the hands of her brother.

She could have pretended that none of this had ever happened.

Would she have, given the opportunity? Sebastian didn't see why not. It didn't matter if there truly was love between them—ultimately, everyone left, whether on purpose or not. His parents had, and Carlos, and even her own parents. Why not Paulina as well?

He had opened his eyes to see the glint of the decanter Paulina had purchased for him, the new washstand topped with marble, with its shelf for his shaving implements that had replaced the mirror hanging from a single nail. She had put her imprint all over the house, and all over Sebastian's soul. If she did choose to leave... would he survive it?

The distant rumble of thunder made Sebastian wrench his eyes open. He was next to Paulina, but not in bed—they were jumbled up inside the carriage, like a brace of plantain that had been tossed into a sack and shaken. His temples were throbbing, and the stinging sensation on his upper arm told him the knife wound had reopened. Paulina groaned, and all of a sudden Sebastian jolted into awareness.

She lay on her back with one arm pinned beneath her. Crouching to avoid bumping his head on the padded seat above their heads, Sebastian helped her sit up.

"Are you hurt?" he demanded.

"My arm." Her face was creased with pain. "I wrenched it, I think—it hurts terribly."

Sebastian probed at it, his lips tightening at her wince. "I'll have to fashion a sling out of my jacket," he said, slipping out of the black garment and tying the sleeves around her neck. "We shouldn't linger here."

With his help, she managed to crawl out of the overturned coach. Her attention went immediately to the coachman.

"Alfonso!" she cried, lurching forward.

The young man had managed to jump out of his seat and was sitting in the brush several meters back, looking dazed. Blood streamed freely from a cut on his forehead. He blinked it away, looking up at Paulina and Sebastian. "The axle broke," he said, though neither of them had asked. With a shaking finger, Alfonso pointed at the wheel that hung at an improbable angle above the carriage, like a wounded limb. "It just...snapped."

"Cut, more likely," Sebastian muttered. His horses

looked fine, already scrambling to their feet. "We'll have to walk the rest of the way. Alfonso, can you stand?"

"I think my leg's broken, Don," Alfonso said with a grimace toward the stretched-out leg in front of him. "I don't think I can move."

Sebastian cast a glance up at the sky, which was growing pink with the incipient dawn above the storm clouds gathered on the horizon. "Stay with the horses, then. I'll send someone for you when we get to the mill. We haven't much time to waste."

Paulina made a small sound of protest.

"He'll be fine," Sebastian told her. "He's not the one your brother wants."

He started marching in the direction of the mill. A moment later, he heard Paulina scramble to catch up with him. "What in the world is *wrong* with you today?" she asked breathlessly.

"Nothing that wasn't wrong with me yesterday," he said without turning around.

"I'll have to agree—you've been out of sorts for days. I've had enough of your dark moods."

"Well, forgive me if I'm getting a little tired of fighting for my life. I wasn't bargaining on any of this—it's not like I had any choice in the matter."

"And I did?"

"No!" he exclaimed, whirling around to face her. "You hadn't a choice! That's precisely the problem! Neither of us had one, but if I'd held out long enough to get the annulment, we both would have. And then you'd have been free to seek out any sort of life you want."

"Oh?" she asked acidly. "And what sort of life am I supposed to want? I suppose you have it all figured out."

He spread his hands, sighing. "I don't know anything."

"She's good for you," Dilia had told him the day before in town, when he'd gone to fetch the invitation and Paulina's gown. "I know you're not in the mood to listen to what I've got to say, but I *have* to say it—I promised Carlos I would do my best to keep you from being too bullheaded, though we both know that's a losing proposition." Her lips had curled up with humor—not that Sebastian was inclined to admit there was any in the situation.

"Say it, then," he'd told her, taking pains to make his disinterest obvious.

"Paulina Despradel is good for you," Dilia had said with her usual bluntness. "The way you act around her... I haven't seen you this happy in years. I can't understand why, but you seem to be bent on ruining your chances with her. Whatever penance you think you need to pay, it's not worth it if it means you have to go through life alone."

"Are you finished?" he'd demanded, putting a foot on his carriage's mounting step to communicate his intent to be done with the conversation.

"No," she'd told him. "But I can see you're going to insist on being a fool." She gave a dramatic shake of her head. "Heaven spare me from stubborn men!"

The mill came into sight, the main building dark against the gray clouds that were beginning to cover the sunrise. By all rights, the mill should have been humming with activity—most planters kept their mills running day and night during cane season. Sebastian, however, had flatly refused to countenance such a thing, preferring to give his workers a decent night's rest even if it meant diminished profits. Beyond the mill, the wooden warehouse where the sacks of sugar destined for the refinery would be stacked also lay dark and empty.

It was as comforting as coming home, but Sebastian didn't dare draw a sigh of relief—not yet.

"Why are you trying to push me away?" Paulina asked as Sebastian dug into the pockets of his trousers for the key. "Why are you so afraid to let me in?"

Instead of answering, he unlocked the door and headed upstairs to his office. Over the sound of their footsteps on the rickety wooden steps, he could hear her snort of exasperation.

"You don't trust me, do you? You don't trust me to know my own mind."

"I have some rum around here," he said. He rummaged in one of his drawers until he had produced a bottle and a cup. "Have a drink while I get the money."

His safe was in a cupboard, shielded from prying eyes by towering piles of ledgers. Sebastian was in the process of clearing them away when she stepped into his path. "Is that it, then? Is that all you're going to say? Some nonsense about choices—after all we've been through? It's not enough to let me make my own decisions, Sebastian. You've got to respect them, too."

He tried to turn his face away, but she grasped it with her free hand.

"Even if I had a choice, I wouldn't want a different husband," she said fiercely. "Nothing has changed for me, Sebastian. I want you."

His breath rasped out into the warm room.

"I want a life with you," she said, digging her nails into his jaw to impress upon him the urgency of her words. "Even if it means..." Her voice wavered for a second, but she rallied. "Even if it means not having children."

"I would never ask that of you."

He kissed her. Not gently, like he had the night before, when he'd caressed her lips with his. This kiss was hard, and hot, and full of need. It made no promises and offered no peace.

Paulina pressed against him, pushing him against the edge of his desk. He sat, heedless of the papers and ledgers on its messy surface, and pulled her between his open legs to kiss her, again and again until they were both breathless.

Her fingers trailed down his neck to clench in the fabric of his shirt. "I want everything you can give me, Sebastian Linares—and so much more."

He could have gotten lost in the fire in her eyes. "Paulina, I…"

She pulled him down to her again, offering him as much as she took. Her lips were scorching on his, her little pants and gasps kindling. She scraped her teeth along his lower lip, then soothed the sting with the tip of her tongue, and if Sebastian had been undone the night before, now he was remade.

The door slammed open behind them.

"Well done, little sister," said a voice that sent chills of foreboding down Sebastian's spine. He pried himself away from Paulina to see Despradel lounging in the doorway, his cruel mouth twisted into a smirk. "I didn't think you had it in you to carry out orders, but you've played your part to perfection. Tell me, Linares, did you enjoy the line about her feeling safe with you? I thought it was a bit much, myself, but if it worked for you…"

"You unspeakably filthy liar," Sebastian said hoarsely. With a raw, animal roar, he launched himself over the desk, intent on wringing Despradel's sorry neck.

He didn't get within a meter of the doorway.

Calmly stepping aside, Paulina's brother raised the hand that had been concealed at the side of his leg. In it was a pistol, and its muzzle was pointed directly at Paulina.

Chapter Nineteen

It wasn't hesitation that made Sebastian draw to a sudden halt, but the certainty that Antonio Despradel wouldn't think twice about shooting his sister in cold blood.

"I didn't think you were the kind of man to do your own dirty work," Sebastian remarked in what he hoped was a sufficiently casual tone, leaning back against the wall with his arms loosely at his side to show Despradel that he meant to stay put.

It was a lie, of course, and seeing as there was nothing Sebastian wanted more than to slam his fists into the scoundrel, it was so damned difficult he could feel his muscles bunching with the effort of remaining motionless.

Despradel gave a nonchalant shrug. "Every great man has had to get his hands dirty now and then."

After their encounter with the guardsman, Sebastian was confident that Paulina would keep her cool, even as Antonio cautiously edged into the room and went around the desk to shove the pistol toward her head.

"Do you really mean to shoot us?" Paulina asked in a voice that was remarkably steady. "I thought you were going to try to make it look like an accident."

"Thanks to your beloved husband, I no longer have to—it didn't take much to convince the governor's guests that I was worried for my sister's life after her marriage to such a violent man." Despradel's eyes flashed with glee. "And it took even less to hint that they should be concerned for their own daughters, were he to require a new wife once he did away with my sister. I was so worried, in fact, that I went to see her as soon as it was light. Imagine my surprise when I walked in to find her husband standing over her with a loaded pistol."

It was chilling, the way Despradel spun his little narrative with the smug confidence of someone who thought he could alter reality. "Everyone in town will think me a hero."

"Everyone in town will know you for what you are," Paulina bit out. "A murderer."

Despradel laughed. "Dramatics don't suit you a bit," he told his sister. "You have done nothing to restore our family to its former glory. This is the very least you could do."

"Give you my life? That's unreasonable, even for you." There was genuine grief in her eyes, but there was nothing Sebastian could do for her but watch it grow. "Did it ever occur to you to work for it, like our ancestors did? They didn't sit around waiting to inherit the land, or kill anyone for it—they worked for it, and for everything they had. That, Antonio, is what made them worth admiring. Not the gold and silver they stuffed into their bank vaults."

"Still naive, I see. I had thought marriage would cure you of it, but I can see I was mistaken. I have no need to explain myself to you, but I will tell you this—no one who had any money worth remarking of ever got it by *working*." The disdainful emphasis on the last word was accompanied by a curl of his lip. "Anyone who's ever made a fortune has done it by seizing opportunities, and that's exactly what I'm doing. You can go ahead and call me a murderer if it will make you feel better, but everyone will know me for what I really am—a man of brilliance. A man of power. And, thanks to your husband over there, a man of extensive means. I'll buy their good opinion of me if I have to."

Sebastian let him talk. He felt himself go quiet as he tracked the other man's movements with the careful watchfulness of a hunter. His silence clearly unnerved Despradel, who had no way of knowing that Sebastian had never had a taste for pursuing innocent animals—and that Sebastian's limbs were burning with panic.

"Not that this conversation isn't terribly stimulating, but do hurry up and open the safe," Despradel commanded, carelessly knocking the barrel of his pistol against Paulina's head. "As long as I have you here, I might as well help myself."

She was very still, but only Sebastian recognized it for what it was—not the stillness of prey, but that of someone waiting for the perfect time to strike.

Paulina Despradel was no one's prey.

Sebastian let her see the admiration filling his own expression. Noticing that Sebastian was looking at his sister rather than the safe, Despradel glanced down at her. It was the barest distraction, but it was enough—Sebastian shouted at her, and she reared back, pushing Despradel away.

At the same instant, Sebastian vaulted over the desk and crashed into the other man's torso. The pistol went off, and Sebastian had only the sound of shattering glass and the absence of Paulina's scream to know that the shot had gone wide before he was grappling with the other man.

He managed to knock the pistol out of Despradel's hand before grabbing him by the collar and, much like he had done the night before, rushing him through the door and slamming him into the spindly wooden railing.

Wrenching himself out of Sebastian's arms, Despradel managed to shove Sebastian halfway down the stairs. Sebastian started to pick himself up, but a well-placed kick to his shoulder sent him rolling down to the main floor of the mill.

"Don't let him get the pistol!" he shouted up at Paulina, who had taken a heavy ledger from his desk. Despradel whirled around, but before he could touch Paulina, she struck out at him with the ledger. He took a step back to avoid it, clearly forgetting he was on the top step, and lost his footing.

Sebastian was waiting for him at the bottom of the stairs, battered and bruised but still standing.

With more agility than Sebastian would have given him credit for, Despradel flung himself over the side of the railing, landing in a crouch.

"Don't you understand by now?" he told Sebastian with a taunting smile as he walked backward into the shadows of the mill. "You will never get the best of me—either of you. You aren't clever enough, or strong enough. Your lives are mine to do as I see fit. Your so-called friends are mine to bribe and manipulate. I'd wager my family's entire fortune that you had no idea your coachman was in my employ—and all it took was a promise of twenty pesos for that scraggly goat of his grandmother's."

Alfonso? Sebastian's eyes narrowed. Damn the little bastard.

"Everywhere you go," Despradel continued, melting

farther into the shadows so that Sebastian was forced to rely only on the sound of his voice as he stalked after him, "everyone you think you trust…"

There was a sudden roar, like that of a great, metallic beast. The sudden scent of smoke and oil filled Sebastian's nostrils and he glanced back to see the milling machine coming to life.

Pistons churning and wheels turning, it was a sight to behold even while not in the middle of a fight with a murderous madman. To Sebastian, at the moment, they spelled out relief.

His foreman had arrived.

Heartened by the thought, though aware they wouldn't hear him call out over the machinery's noise, Sebastian started to turn.

Despradel took advantage of Sebastian's momentary distraction to charge him—the momentum of his running charge sent Sebastian falling backward, right toward the grinders used to crush sugarcane stalks into pulp. Sebastian thrust himself forward, but Despradel drove him back with a punch calculated to land on the cut above his eye. It hurt more than it should have, and it wasn't until Despradel wound his hand back that Sebastian caught the faint gleam of metal on his knuckles.

Clouds of steam were billowing from the machinery, clouding Sebastian's sight.

A second punch landed on his eye, and blood joined the sweat streaming from his face. Dazed, Sebastian struck out at the space in front of him, but Despradel dodged him nimbly, laughing.

The disembodied sound guided Sebastian's own fist.

He landed a glancing blow on Despradel, who answered it with an almost casual backhanded slap against the side of Sebastian's face. The brass knuckles cracked against his throbbing head, sending Sebastian reeling.

Suddenly, Despradel loomed out of the steam, his face contorted with concentration. He pushed Sebastian back, far enough that the backs of his thighs pressed against the iron railing around the rolling grinder. Sebastian struggled, but Antonio had the front of his shirt in a viselike grip and was reaching for Sebastian's arm with the other hand.

Most parts of the running machinery were dangerous in their own right—any number of accidents could befall the reckless and the unwary, which was why Sebastian had had the railings installed in the first place. The pistons could break a man's legs, the metal canisters where the sugarcane juice was boiled could get so hot they could sear a person's skin right down to the bone...

The grinder, with two metal rollers relentlessly crushing cane into pulp—it was singularly the most dangerous part of the entire mill.

And Despradel seemed determined to feed Sebastian's arm right into it.

Sebastian strained to break free, or at least pull his hand away, to no avail. Despradel was just too strong.

"Give up!" Despradel was shouting into Sebastian's face, spittle flying. "You will never win against me!"

It was the least tempting offer Sebastian had ever received, but he could feel his strength waning with each passing second. How much longer would he have to hold on? Any minute now, the rest of the men would arrive to start feeding cane into the grinder. They would surely come to his aid.

Any minute now...

His fingertips were so close to the grinder, he could

feel the whoosh of wind as the rollers reached their normal speed.

Out of the corner of his eye, he saw Paulina picking up one of the stalks of cane with her good hand. The length of a sword, and the general circumference of three broom handles tied together, it must have been heavy to wield. But wield it she did, hefting it in her arms.

Sebastian looked straight into Despradel's eyes. "Go straight to hell," he said and ducked.

The cane in Paulina's hand connected with the back of Antonio's head.

Despradel turned to her, screaming with rage. The blow he delivered to her sent her flying back—Antonio went after her, the hand with the brass knuckles raised to strike her again.

Summoning up the last of his strength, Sebastian dived for Antonio. He ripped him away from Paulina, noticing the long, angry scratch she had left on the side of her brother's face. Grabbing Despradel by his midsection, almost lifting him bodily off the floor, he hauled him away from Paulina and collapsed to his knees.

There was a scream behind him—a high, desperate, keening sound that sliced even through the powerful roar of the machinery. It was cut off abruptly. By the time Sebastian found the strength to turn around, Despradel was utterly silent.

A sudden flood of people rushed past Sebastian—the rest of the mill workers had arrived at last.

Paulina helped him up, and he turned, then wished he hadn't when he saw the mangled body they were laying on the floor.

"Call for the doctor," he croaked, but the grim look on the men's faces told him it would be no use.

Antonio was dead.

* * *

The skies had broken open and rain was gusting into the dirt clearing in front of the mill when Paulina stumbled out, followed by Sebastian. The mud had been churned by dozens of feet as the cane cutters and mill workers gathered for the start of their day, and Paulina felt equally churned up.

Someone helped her to a stool, and Paulina didn't so much as sit as crumple down onto its scarred wooden surface. The overhang of the roof prevented her from getting soaked, but the breeze blew welcome droplets into her overheated face.

Antonio was dead. Her brother, who had tried to murder her and Sebastian, who had pointed a pistol at her head with as little care as he would have pointed it at a sack full of beans...

He was dead. And this whole sorry business was finally over.

It wasn't relief that filled her, but an odd sense of numbness, as if the thunderclouds had taken residence inside her mind.

A handful of horses came galloping through the heavy rain, coming to a stop in front of Paulina's stool. Someone must have alerted Sebastian to their approach, because he was suddenly there at the entrance to the mill, a group of men in a semicircle around him.

Paulina got to her feet and slipped her hand into Sebastian's as two of the new arrivals came up to them. Their faces were mostly obscured by their hats and the relative darkness of the morning. It wasn't until she realized that one of the men was in uniform that she recognized them as the magistrate and one of the guardsmen from the prison.

Paulina could feel Sebastian drawing up stiffly, and

she realized that the rest of the men were also in uniform. She squeezed Sebastian's hand—and he responded by pulling his out of her grasp. It reminded Paulina that he hadn't said anything earlier when she'd told him she wanted a life with him.

Had it been due to Antonio's interruption, or had he never meant to say anything at all?

Was he reconsidering everything he had ever said now that he no longer had to contend with Antonio?

There was no time to worry about it just then.

"Are you Sebastian Linares?" the magistrate asked, pushing back his dripping hat with an air of distaste, looking annoyed to have been called out into the rain.

Sebastian nodded.

"We were summoned by your coachman," the magistrate said. "Something about his fearing for your wife's life. What seems to be the trouble?"

"Alfonso?" Paulina interrupted. The magistrate flicked a glance at her, noticing the arm that was still bound in Sebastian's jacket. "He was injured in a carriage accident—as were we. He was waiting by the side of the road until we could send for help."

"We came across the carriage on our way here, Doña," one of the guardsmen said. "There was no one there."

"Because he was in town, reporting the altercation." The magistrate shot the guardsman a quelling look before turning back to Sebastian. "Well?"

"As you can see," Sebastian said, with surprising equanimity given what he had just endured, "my wife is unharmed, save for the injury she sustained in the accident. As am I."

That was not altogether true—blood was coming down in ribbons from a cut on his temple, staining the shoulder of his shirt. Under the blood, his brown skin was ashen.

"My wife's brother, however, is not," Sebastian continued.

Paulina, who had been watching the guardsman's face, noticed the way his eyes bulged.

"Where is he?" the magistrate demanded grimly.

The crowd behind Paulina and Sebastian parted, and Paulina caught a spare glimpse of the sacks the cane workers had used to cover Antonio's figure. The magistrate ordered the guardsman to uncover Antonio, and Paulina turned her face away as the uniformed man twitched away the sacks.

The machinery must have been turned off. Over the clatter of rain, she heard the magistrate demand, "What the devil happened?"

A different voice, one Paulina hadn't heard before. "He fell into the grinders."

She glanced up at Sebastian, who looked briefly surprised.

"Linares?" The magistrate again. "Is that true?"

Sebastian was silent. He may have been too honorable to lie, but Paulina had no compunction in doing it for him.

"It's true," Paulina said, stepping forward and looking at the magistrate straight in the eye. "My brother fell."

Clearly unwilling to take the word of a woman, the magistrate turned furiously to the men gathered in clusters on the mill floor, his frown deepening when they all gazed impassively back. They all meant to stand by Sebastian, just as he had stood by them when it would have been easier, and far more profitable, to do what all other mill owners did. What Paulina's own brother had done.

The guardsman, she noticed, was giving Sebastian

a thoughtful look. Without Antonio to appease, or to defend himself against, he must have felt there was no need to pursue Sebastian any longer, because he came to a swift conclusion. "Señor Magistrado," he said, "I believe these people are speaking the truth. A most unfortunate matter, no doubt, but it does appear to have been no more than an accident. Is that not so, Don Sebastian?"

Sebastian jerked his head into a nod.

The magistrate threw up his hands, though Paulina noticed that he, too, looked relieved at being done with the whole business. "Death by misadventure it is, then," he pronounced. "I trust the deceased's family will see to the remains?"

He barely waited for Paulina's nod before stalking outside.

It was too bad that the stool wasn't nearby, because Paulina felt like crumpling again, only this time it was with relief. She reached for Sebastian, but he had turned away as someone called out for him.

Injured as he was, and likely shaken after such a close brush with dismemberment, he was still holding himself together in front of his staff as he answered their questions and issued commands. Tall and straight-backed, Sebastian moved through his people, patting a shoulder here and making a remark there, providing reassurance as well as instructions for how to proceed. It was clear, to Paulina and to the other people assembled inside the mill, that Sebastian was born to lead.

As for his marital responsibilities... It felt like centuries had passed, though it was surely no more than a handful of hours, since he had stood in the dirt of the road and talked about choices. Had he meant more by it than she'd understood in the moment? He had made no secret of the fact that he regretted being intimate the night before, after all.

Everyone's generosity had limits, and maybe she had come to the end of Sebastian's. With no threats to bind them together anymore, and no Antonio to put his family in danger, Paulina had to wonder if Sebastian wouldn't prefer to be done with her entirely.

She had told him she wanted to have a life with him. And he had said nothing in response.

Chapter Twenty

Villa Consuelo was dark by the time they got home, much later that day. It was silent, too, and still—for the first time since Sebastian had moved in, there was no one there to greet them when they arrived.

It made him feel a little hollow, but on its heels followed the realization that he needn't leave after all. He needn't leave the island, nor his home nor his people. He was free to do anything he wished—including getting the damn annulment.

A look at Paulina told him that she was, as usual, one step ahead of him. By unspoken but mutual agreement, they remained quiet as they gave their thanks to the cane cutter who had borne them home in his cart, through a half-denuded field dripping with the last of the day's rain.

Her hand in his, they strode through his property on their way to his bedroom, and Sebastian felt a tightening in his chest as he saw the marks of what they had been through. The blackened walls of the kitchen. The table with its matching chairs at one end of the terrace. The louvered doors to her bedroom with the new hinges that made them open without so much as a whisper. He wasn't the only one to bear scars—or to have been remade.

There was no question of Paulina sharing his bed.

First, however, they cast off their filthy clothes. Sebastian dipped a clean handkerchief in the few inches of water left in his bedroom jug.

"Come here," he said softly. Grasping Paulina's chin, he cleaned grime and tears and rainwater off her face. She tilted her head up, eyes closed, as he swept the rag over her collarbone and shoulders, outlining first one arm and then the other, and turning her to follow the long, elegant line of her spine.

Paulina leaned back against him, letting out a sigh when he encircled her with his arms. "I'm so tired," she said.

"Let's go to bed," he said against her neck. They still had plenty to talk about, and even more to decide, but that could wait for morning.

The sheets billowed above them like the sail of a ship they no longer needed to take. Before the thin cotton had settled over their bodies, they were both asleep.

Sebastian didn't fall so much as crash into unconsciousness. For the first time in weeks—months, really—he slept so hard, he was utterly unaware of the world beyond his bed. When he finally awoke, it was to the stifling heat of midday. He had given the workers the rest of the previous day off, but they must have already been at work for hours, and he would have to join them soon.

But first…

He kicked the light blanket aside, shifting to his side to slide an arm around Paulina—but there was no one on the crumpled sheets. Sitting up, he saw an envelope on her pillow.

His pulse was roaring in his ears, drowning out the birdsong and the sound of the breeze whistling through the trees. Ripping out the contents of the envelope, he skimmed the long letter that had been folded inside. Paulina wrote in a fair, neat hand, her letters looping into elegant twists that did not betray whatever it was she'd been thinking as she wrote. The letter itself wasn't addressed to Sebastian, but to Governor de los Santos. In it, she explained everything that had happened from the day of her birthday—avoiding, of course, the details of her brother's death—and ended with a plea to grant Sebastian the annulment he had sought.

His jaw was clenched so tightly, it was as painful as if someone had smashed it with a fist. But what was one more ache to Sebastian?

He lowered the letter and noticed a scrap of paper that must have fallen out of the envelope.

There is always a choice, it said in Paulina's hand.

He threw himself out of bed and into his trousers, heart pounding.

She couldn't have—she *wouldn't* have.

Slamming open the louvered doors, he burst out into the terrace, where he was arrested by the slight creaking of the rocking chair.

"Oh," he said, when he recognized its occupant, his heart in his mouth. "Dilia."

"Do try to contain your enthusiasm," she said wryly, then gestured at the large wicker basket sitting on the table. "I heard what happened yesterday and thought I had better bring food."

He glanced at the basket and gave it a dismissive wave. "Have you seen Paulina?"

She looked startled. "I thought she'd be with you."

"She was."

The patter of raindrops, which had slowed down considerably since the day before, started up again. Sebastian went to the railing, to the unfinished section he had been working on for months, and braced himself against the stripped wood.

"Should I take the disconsolate droop of your shoulders to mean you think she won't be coming back?" Dilia asked behind him.

"I don't know." The rain had gone on so long that it had saturated the ground of the kitchen yard, forming puddles that quivered as they were struck by raindrops.

"Will you go after her, then?"

"I don't know," he said again.

"I don't know whether to scold you or comfort you." Dilia let out a sigh. "After everything the two of you have been through, will you really let your pride get in the way of everything you could have together?"

"It's not pride." With a flex of his forearms, Sebastian pushed himself upright and turned to face Dilia. "I'm not sure how much you know about Paulina's life. Her parents died when she was young, and she was raised—if you could call it that—by her brother. He never allowed her to have a say in her own life. She wasn't allowed to make any decisions."

Dilia nodded as she grasped his meaning. "And with her brother gone, now she can."

"She wrote a letter detailing her brother's plot against us. She means for me to take it to the governor and annul the marriage. The first thing she did after gaining her freedom, Dilia, was seek to be separated from me."

Dilia cocked her head. "Does she know that you love her?"

"It wouldn't make any difference."

"Wouldn't it?" Dilia shook her head. "How can you not see it, Sebastian? Paulina is so obviously in love with you, I would be surprised if she meant anything by that letter other than to give you a way out. The only reason she left is because you can't seem to let her in."

"Let her in?" he asked indignantly. "I brought her into my home!"

"Let her into your heart, you absolute dolt," Dilia said, with an exasperated roll of her eyes. "You've kept her at arm's length far past the time when you realized she wasn't guilty of trying to trap you. And you have made every excuse you can think of to continue doing so even though anyone can see that you would die for her—and almost did."

Sebastian stared at Dilia, wanting to deny her assertions even as the truth of them tumbled over him. "I... But..."

"Quite," Dilia said dryly. "It's natural to be scared. She's your first love, isn't she?"

"My only love," Sebastian replied.

Dilia nodded. "Well, what are you going to do about it?"

The first thing Paulina did upon arriving at her family's *quinta* was go directly into her bedroom, where she found the locket with her mother's portrait. She flicked the catch with her fingernail, easing the enamel face open to reveal her mother's image in miniature.

She was laughing in the photograph, as she was in Paulina's memories. Life had been easy for her in a way it hadn't been for Paulina. And yet, Paulina didn't harbor any resentment for her.

Her mother had had the world. She'd lived her life, and she'd enjoyed it. It was up to Paulina to find a way to do the same.

The trembling in her hands made it difficult to clasp it around her neck, but she managed it.

It felt unnerving to be in the house—not only because she half expected Antonio to come stomping in and demand what she was doing, but because she felt so far removed from the person who had once lived within these walls. In a fearsomely short time, Villa Consuelo had become more of a home than the *quinta* ever had.

And Sebastian...

He was more than home to her. Her protector, her heart, the man who had given her things she never knew she could want. She'd awoken with his muscular arm around her waist, his long-limbed body tucked protectively around her, like she had longed to the first night she'd arrived at Villa Consuelo.

So much had happened since the night she had arranged her hair on her pillow in the hopes that Sebastian would visit her in the night. And yet, how much had really changed?

He had refused to believe her when she told him that he was what she wanted. That given every choice in the world, she would choose him, over and over again.

But that only went so far. At some point, he had to choose her, too.

If Paulina was certain of anything, it was that she wasn't willing to settle for anything less than true, unreserved love. Sebastian could keep his doubts and his mistrust. He could push everyone away if it made him feel safer.

Paulina touched the locket resting against her chest, feeling comforted by its solid weight. And then she fashioned a sling for her arm out of an old shawl and began to pack up the house.

Chapter Twenty-One

Sebastian was soaked to the skin before he made it out onto the road that stretched between Villa Consuelo and the Despradels' *quinta*. His horse had never minded the rain, and neither did he—in fact, it felt fitting that the same kind of weather that had delivered Paulina to his doorstep would accompany him to hers.

The lantern by the front door was lit, though it was blowing in the wind, the flame hissing at the raindrops that managed to evade its protective cover. Sebastian struck the old iron knocker against the wood of the door, once, twice, and was about to lift it for a third time when the door opened.

She was in the yellow dress, her hair bound back with a kerchief and a long streak of dust on the prominent curve of her cheekbone. She looked, momentarily, as if she'd had the wind knocked out of her. Then she straightened her back, lifted her chin and said as gracefully as a society matron, "How nice it is to see you here. I'm afraid the house is not fit for company at the moment—"

He let out a bark of laughter, though what he wanted was to howl.

"You needn't let me in if you don't want to," he told her. "I only came to tell you something."

The glimmer of curiosity was obvious even through her polite, "Oh?"

"I do trust you. The one I haven't been able to trust is myself. Not because I didn't love you, but because I knew what would happen if I did. I…" Sebastian rubbed a hand over the back of his head. "If you had asked me as much as a day ago, I would have told you that I'm not a man who has ever lived in fear. And yet, that's what I've been doing for years."

"Fear?" she asked softly.

"Of losing more than I already had. Of being left by yet another loved one. I realize now how selfish that was—keeping you at arm's length so that I wouldn't have to risk the pain of your leaving me. But if you have the courage to choose me, of all people, I should have the courage to love you regardless of what may happen." He let out a breath. "Of course, if you've changed your mind and you really do want to be done with all this, I will take your letter to the governor."

"Sebastian," she said, in an altogether different tone than she had used earlier. She reached up, her fingertips featherlight on his dripping jaw. "I didn't want to leave you. I thought it was what *you* wanted."

A sharp, bright ray of hope lanced through him.

"In that case…" His aching fingers released the door frame. "I never gave you a wedding present."

She frowned at the sudden change in subject. "That hardly…"

Sebastian didn't mean to let her finish. Thrusting his hand into his pocket, he held out a small box. It wasn't covered in velvet, nor bound with a silk ribbon, but its contents were no less precious for that. "Please. Just look at it."

Her frown didn't budge even as she unwound the twine holding the box closed—in fact, it only grew deeper when she plucked out what Sebastian had laid inside. "A scrap of newspaper?"

"A promise," Sebastian said softly. The square he had neatly clipped out of that day's paper contained a listing of all the houses for sale in town. "And a question. I can't give you the world, but I can give you a family. Paulina Despradel, would you like to make a home with me?"

The frown faltered. "Sebastian, I…"

"You're the light of my life. And it wouldn't be much of one if I couldn't spend it beside you. I should have told you so weeks ago, the moment I realized I had fallen in love with you. I want you," he said in a ragged whisper. "And the opportunity to give you the world. All of it. A house in town, and a dozen children to fill it up and to have frolics with. All the dresses and candlesticks and tablecloths your heart could wish for. Everything you have longed for, and everything you deserve."

Her hand drifted to his shoulder, which she used as leverage as she rose on her tiptoes and sought the side of his neck with her lips. "I do love you, you know."

Her mouth found his, and she melted against him, as if her body no longer had the will or the reason to offer any resistance to their melding into one. Sebastian pressed her against the ancient wooden door, feeling her dress absorb the rainwater from his clothes until she was as soaked as he was. Beyond the wooden porch, the rain continued to pour down, faster now, and the thunder rumbling in the distance was as loud as Sebastian's pounding heart.

"I could curse at the fates for the way they brought us

together," he told her, spanning his hands over her narrow, uncorseted waist and letting them trail down the swell of her hips. He laid a delicate kiss on the corner of her lips, smiling when she tilted her face up for another. "But I will never regret the fact that they did."

Chapter Twenty-Two

Two years later

The pale yellow house at the end of Calle de la Restauración was fairly ringing with noise on the day of Paulina's twenty-third birthday.

Paulina had sold the Despradel *quinta* to Sebastian's foreman, but they still owned Villa Consuelo. The handsome old house welcomed them and their friends on the occasional weekend jaunt to the country. Most of their time, however, was spent in town, in the house they had built on San Pedro's busiest street.

With its balcony that overlooked the plaza where the town's residents promenaded on the weekends, and two long galleries shaded by cascades of white bougainvillea that Paulina used as a ballroom whenever the occasion arose, it was everything Paulina had imagined it would be when she saw the land being advertised for sale in the newspaper.

The parlor was as large and airy as she had once dreamed, its tall windows hung with delicate lace drapery that filtered the light and cast intricate shadows on the plush upholstered armchairs and shapely tables. Brass electric lamps with shades like miniature moons were dotted around the room—all the better, Sebastian said laughingly, to complement Paulina's luminosity.

Best of all, the house was equipped with modern plumbing and a great claw-footed bathtub next to which Sebastian kept a stool, so that he could keep her company while she bathed…and kiss the droplets that trailed down her back when she rose out of the water.

Her good taste in furnishings had been a source of intense conversation among all the friends she had made in town, who flocked to her for help in decorating their own homes. Devouring many a book on the subject, she had smugly informed Sebastian that the blue-and-white candlesticks she had chosen at Don Enrique's store were actually jasperware, and likely designed by Mr. Wedgwood himself.

Her favorite part of the house, however, was the wall where the portrait of her parents hung next to a daguerreotype of Carlos that Dilia had given them and a framed painting of Villa Consuelo that Sebastian had commissioned. In a prominent place beside them was a photograph of what Paulina called their *true* wedding—the one they'd held in Villa Consuelo, four months after the one that had been forced on them by Antonio.

Once the thunderclouds left behind by his death had receded, Paulina had allowed herself to mourn. Not so much his person, but what could have been. The brother she could've had if he had cared for her half as much as he'd cared about maintaining his wealth and influence. The scars he had left behind would take a long time to heal, but she was well on her way.

Paulina was up on a stool, nailing a garland of greenery above the frames, when the mouthwatering scent of *lambí empanadas* preceded Sebastian into the room. He almost dropped the platter he was holding when he saw her aloft. Setting it hastily on a side table, he hurried to her side, arms outstretched.

"I won't fall, you know," she said with amusement, staying on her perch as he wrapped his arms around her hips. "I fixed this stool myself."

"I know," he said, looking up at her. "But you won't deny me the pleasure of helping you down, will you?"

She held the back of his head, stroking his close-cropped hair as he laid a kiss on the barely perceptible swell beneath the waistband of her skirt. "I can't seem to deny you much of anything these days."

"Isn't that the truth!" Doña Josefa bustled in from the hallway, a vase full of flowers in one hand. She frowned when she saw the precariously placed platter of *empanadas* and went immediately to its rescue, nudging it farther onto the table. "You're getting to be quite spoiled these days, my boy. Along with someone I won't name."

That someone toddled in at her heels, managing to grab an *empanada* and shove it into his mouth before any of the adults could react.

Paulina felt Sebastian's laugh vibrating against her stomach. "All right," she told her husband, "get me down from here so I can help Josefa defend the *empanadas* from ravishment."

"Oh, let Carlitos eat," Sebastian said comfortably. "I can always go and get more."

"You're not going anywhere," Paulina told him. "There's a lot to do before the party tonight. And like my mother used to say, the preparations are half the fun."

"Before we get started on the fun," Sebastian said, helping Paulina down and extracting a small velvet box from his pocket. "Carlitos, will you help me give Mama her birthday present?"

Obligingly, their son toddled away from the *empanadas* on his chubby little legs. Paulina and Sebastian both crouched to receive him, and he nestled comfortably into Sebastian's arms as Paulina opened the velvet box.

Inside lay a length of red ribbon. Paulina misted over, more touched than if the box had contained a handful of diamonds and pearls. She unwound the ribbon, meaning to tie it immediately into her hair even though it clashed with her leaf-green skirt...and gasped out loud when she caught a glimpse of the bracelet nestled beneath it. Caught between twining bands of gold were diamonds, pearls and tiny beads of amber that looked as if they had been carved into roses to match the earrings he'd given her almost two years before.

"Do you like it?" Sebastian perched his chin on Carlitos's curls and regarded her with his intense brown eyes. Paulina knew he meant more than the ribbon, or even the bracelet.

"It's all I ever wanted," she said and kissed him.

* * * * *

ALLIANCE WITH HIS
STOLEN HEIRESS

To G.G.T., who would have been tickled at having a romance heroine named after her.

And to my little sister, who is forever rescuing me.

Chapter One

San Pedro de Macorís, 1905

The sky was a pristine, unblemished blue, but something about the clouds hovering in the horizon made Amalia Troncoso think of rain as she alighted from her family's carriage.

It could not rain—not today of all days. Not after all the trouble she had gone to in planning this outing.

The patch of grass she landed on was still slightly slick with morning dew, so she turned back to offer her younger sister a hand.

"You can stop glaring at the sky," Lucía said, looking at Amalia with amusement as she grasped her hand. "It won't rain, you know."

Amalia cast another threatening look at the clouds in the horizon. "It had better not."

"As convinced as I generally am of your ability to take control of every situation, I think we'll have to draw the line at the weather." Lucía's giggles were hard to come by these days, and all the more precious for it. Amalia couldn't help giving the seventeen-year-old's fingers a brief, fond squeeze as she helped her down from her perch on the upholstered seat.

"That's what *you* think," Amalia answered her sister with a carefree chuckle that was not altogether genuine. For Lucía's sake, she would do far more daring things than attempt to glare rainclouds into submission.

Lucía joined the other young ladies gathered beneath an ancient *anacahuita* tree, to a chorus of eager greetings. A dozen lightweight wicker chairs had been arranged in the shade. The young ladies had likewise arranged themselves as picturesquely as if they were expecting their portrait to be taken. Bedecked in white and ivory frocks edged with delicate bands of lace, they looked like flowers among the lush tropical greenery.

Amalia smoothed down her own ivory-colored skirt. The slim column was paired with a square-necked blouse in the same shade, pale brown leather pumps and a straw hat ringed with silk flowers. It was not the ensemble she would have selected for a day spent traipsing around the countryside, but Lucía had been firm on the matter. The Troncoso sisters were not only fabulously wealthy, they were *always* fashionable, as well.

Given any choice in the matter, though, Amalia would have rather been pragmatic.

She'd also have preferred a nice wander through the narrow dirt paths that led to various sugarcane fields, or even a poke around the crumbling ruins of an eighteenth- or seventeenth-century estate that sprawled behind the tree. Unfortunately, there was no time for any of that today.

The maid that had accompanied them, riding alongside the coachman, was unloading the baskets containing their midday meal. Tucked into buckets filled with rapidly melting ice, the sparkling wine would have to be served quickly, before it grew warm. Amalia gave the young woman her instructions, then went to greet her sister's guests.

She went around the semicircle of chairs, bending to press her cheek against each of the guests, as was only polite. Though Amalia had been acquainted with them all for years, they really were mostly Lucía's friends. By the time Amalia dropped into the empty chair next to Paulina de Linares, Lucía had been drawn into the conversation and was chattering away animatedly.

The chairs had been arranged with their backs to the morning sun; the small amber earrings Paulina wore caught the light, looking like live embers. "It's good to see you, Amalia," she said. "I thought you would be joining us at yesterday's garden party, but Lucía said you were under the weather."

Amalia went blank for a second as she tried to remember the excuse she'd given for not attending. "Oh, yes," she said after a small pause. "I was so sorry to miss it."

Paulina smiled. "I hope you've recovered enough to attend the dinner I'm hosting tonight."

Amalia didn't squirm, but it was a near thing. Paulina had been trying to deepen their acquaintanceship into something more like friendship for weeks now, and though Amalia thought the young mother was very nice, she couldn't help the little flare of panic that sprang to life in her chest at the thought of getting too close to anyone.

Hoping that her smile didn't feel too forced, she said, "I was actually—"

The rest of her sentence was cut short by the thunder of approaching hoofbeats. The tangle of vegetation behind them quivered, then parted violently as a horse and rider burst through.

The horse was ordinary enough, brown and sleek with perspiration. Its rider, however...

Amalia stared up at the masked man in the saddle. Bristling with weapons, his sleeves rolled up to exhibit a pair of gleaming, sunbaked arms corded with muscle, he looked like—

"A bandit!" shrieked one of the young ladies.

The man in question inclined his head in acknowledgment, raising his pistol in the direction of the coachman standing on the other side of the clearing.

"A pleasure to make your acquaintance," he drawled, the cockiness in his tone turning the pleasantry into something slightly mocking. Swinging a long leg over his saddle, he dropped easily to the ground, contriving to keep his pistol pointed toward the coachman. "As loath as I am to break up your little party here, I've some business to conduct. I should very much appreciate your assistance."

Amalia's nerves might have failed her at that moment, if Lucía hadn't made a frightened whimper.

Brushing off Paulina's restraining hand, Amalia rose from her seat and took a step that put her between the bandit and the young ladies. "What is it that you want?" she demanded in strident tones.

Over the kerchief covering the bottom half of his face, the bandit directed a look at Amalia that made her knees quiver. "You."

Something more powerful than a shiver racked Amalia's body at the simple syllable. Almost without thought, she took a step forward, as if her body was responding to his command. Lucía let out another noise.

Amalia cast a quick look toward her sister. "I'll be all right, Lu," she called, making her voice as firm as she could. "Don't you dare worry about me."

Out of the corner of her eye, Amalia saw a wild-eyed Paulina reach for a tree branch. Did she really think she could fight off a pistol-wielding bandit with a *branch*?

"I wouldn't do that if I were you," the bandit drawled, lifting his other hand to point a second pistol at Paulina. Even in the dappled shade of the *anacahuita* tree, the sunlight glinted threateningly off the muzzle.

Amalia's pulse quickened. "Please don't. I don't want any of them hurt."

Keeping his pistols trained on their targets, the bandit sauntered toward Amalia with infuriating cockiness. He closed the distance between them with two strides of his powerful legs.

A shockingly hard arm came around her midsection, and Amalia almost gasped at the touch as he drew her against an equally solid chest. For the space of several breaths, all Amalia was aware of was the sensation of her body pressed tightly against his—she had never stood this way with a man, not even while dancing. That she couldn't see his expression made it all the more…

Her brain supplied her with the word *exciting*, but Amalia refused to consider it. There was nothing exciting about *this*. She should have been nervous, or at the very least annoyed at this abrupt and unsolicited embrace.

The bandit lowered his head to hers, and Amalia almost shivered as the edge of his kerchief brushed the curve of her ear. "Aren't you going to struggle?" he asked, his voice rich with amusement.

Surprise followed by irritation swept over Amalia. Before she could give him a swift kick in the knee, the moment was broken in a sudden explosion of violence.

Caught in the frisson running through her, Amalia wasn't quite sure what had happened. All she knew was that the muscles bulging against her tensed, and suddenly he was whipping around, barely pausing to take aim before he released a shot that sliced through the bottles of champagne her maid had laid out on a table.

Shrieks, screams and the sound of shattering glass pierced the air. The Troncosos' coachman, who had clearly been attempting to edge toward the spot where Amalia was being held by the bandit, threw up his arms to shield his face from the flying shards.

The bandit took advantage of the commotion to burst into action. Within moments Amalia was on his saddle and he was swinging himself behind her, his thighs and arms making an inescapable cage around her. She couldn't have gotten away if she wanted to and, well...

She didn't want to.

It wasn't only because the bandit had turned his horse toward a path too narrow for the coachman to pursue in their cumbersome carriage—in the time it would take him to unhitch a horse and give chase, Amalia and her captor would be long gone. They were racing at a speed that left Amalia breathless, the path so narrow that branches and vines tugged at Amalia's hair and clothes. Only the bandit's unyielding—and not altogether unwelcome—grip around her prevented her from tumbling into the tangle of vegetation.

Amalia supposed she should have found it terrifying, but in truth, it was actually rather…exhilarating.

It was—

Amalia didn't so much hear as feel the bandit's roar, gusting at her ear. She glanced back, uncomprehending, and caught a glimpse of a pair of flashing dark eyes before he threw his torso on top of her, making a sheltering cage of his body.

A moment later she felt the overhanging branch they had just narrowly avoided, scraping off her hat. Amalia's gasp was swallowed by the wind, but she could hear his breathless laughter in her ear as they rushed on, even faster than before.

The thundering of hooves grew more frantic, and Amalia's heart was galloping to match. Neither slowed until they reached the end of the path and burst out into a clearing. Amalia hardly had time to notice the small wooden shack nestled among the trees before she found herself being unceremoniously dumped from the saddle.

To the detriment of her already damaged ensemble, she landed on her bottom on a patch of dirt. The bandit dismounted with considerably more grace—and without sparing her a glance.

Indignation propelled Amalia to her feet, though her knees felt like they had been replaced with rice pudding.

The wind—not to mention the loss of her hat—had pulled long tendrils of hair out of the confines of her hairpins. Making an ineffective attempt to smooth them back, Amalia drew herself up to her fullest height.

"What the devil was that?" she asked the bandit furiously. "No one pursued us. There was no need to—to imperil our lives in such a way."

"I thought you would appreciate a little excitement, Your Highness," the bandit said, flicking a look at her as he finished hitching his horse to a nearby post. With more delicacy than she would have thought him capable of, he plucked a single leaf off her shoulder and let it flutter gently to the ground. "Isn't that why you hired me?"

Julián Fuentes had made a lot of mistakes in his wretched lifetime, but this surely had to be the worst.

His pulse was roaring in his ears when he removed the kerchief covering the black bristles on his chin and jaw, and used it to mop up the perspiration trickling down his brow.

The ride itself, and even the little interlude in the clearing, had been exciting enough. It had cleared the cobwebs, in any case.

This woman, however...

Barely ten minutes in her presence and already he was certain that he was no match for her.

Her lacy white clothes were littered with leaves and broken twigs, and thanks to his ungentlemanly removal from the saddle—necessary before she realized that it wasn't in fact his pistol that was digging into the small of her back—she also sported a long smear of dirt down her skirt. Coupled with the glistening flush on her cheeks, and the wild curls tumbling from their pins, she was quite possibly the most striking woman Julián had ever seen.

"In any case, you were supposed to wait until I was away from the group," she huffed, trying and failing to brush the dirt and grass clinging to her once-pristine skirt. "I wanted witnesses, not potential victims!"

Julián raised an eyebrow. "Victims? No one came to any harm."

"No thanks to you," she snapped. "What did you mean by flinging that pistol around? The last thing I wanted was for anyone to get hurt."

"Someone would have if I hadn't done what I did— your uncle's coachman looked like he was about to do something incredibly foolish. Now, when he faces your uncle, he'll say truthfully that he did try to rescue you from my clutches. That will keep him from getting into trouble, just as my shooting the bottles kept him from getting seriously hurt."

"I— Oh." She gave him a grudging nod. "I suppose that was quick thinking on your part."

"Mmm…" Giving his horse a final scratch between the ears, Julián made sure there was enough water in the trough before marching toward the shack.

It wasn't home by any stretch of the imagination, but for the past couple of nights, the dilapidated wooden structure had provided him with shelter. Which was more than he could say for his own family.

He had cast off his shirt and had plunged both hands into the full basin before realizing that she had followed him inside. Unbothered by her presence, Julián splashed the lukewarm water on his face, feeling rivulets run down his bare chest when he turned back to her.

He couldn't help but notice how she tracked them with her gaze, all the way down to where the water pooled on the waistband of his trousers, before biting her lip and flicking her eyes toward his face.

"I'm afraid I don't think much of your hospitality," she said, lifting her chin.

"You hired me for a *rapto*, Your Highness, not hospitality."

Julián had burst out laughing when she'd approached him with her idea. He'd been lurking in the street outside the large house where she lived with her uncle, wearing borrowed clothing he thought would help hide his identity, when she'd stormed out the front door, almost stumbling over him in her haste. Julián hadn't said a word, but she'd caught him crouching behind the family carriage and gotten entirely the wrong idea about who he was, and he'd only had a split second to decide whether or not to go along with it.

Julián reached for the tin mug on the shelf above his table and lightly tossed it in her direction, half expecting her to fumble. She caught it neatly, however, and held it out in that imperious way that Julián was still trying to decide was charming or irritating.

Either way, something about the way she seemed so determined to hold on to her composure made him burn to knock her ever so slightly off balance. That may have been why, instead of pouring her water from the clay jug, he unstoppered one of the bottles on the shelf.

She sputtered at the first sip. "What in the world is this?"

"Aguardiente," he said, hiding a smirk.

"Ardiente is right," she muttered, before adding with exacting politeness, "Might I trouble you for some *agua* of the nonburning variety? If it wouldn't be too much trouble, of course. I wouldn't want to inconvenience you in any way."

Thriftily disposing of the remains of the alcoholic beverage by knocking back the contents of her cup,

Julián grinned at her. "I think I've made it clear by now that I am completely at your disposal, *señorita*."

She had positioned herself in such a way that he had to reach past her to get anything off the shelf. Her lips parted when his arm brushed the frills on her blouse, a soft intake of breath stirring the heavy, warm air between them.

Although only a moment before, Julián was enjoying teasing her, the sudden, fierce wave of desire that swept over him was disconcerting enough that he almost dropped the water jug. It didn't break, merely struck the table with a solid *thunk*.

Forget knocking her off balance—he was making *himself* unsteady.

"Water," he said, swirling some around the mug and tossing it out the hole that served as a window before refilling the vessel. He held it out to her with a gentlemanly bow, adding mockingly, "With my compliments to Your Highness."

Her eyes narrowed, though Julián caught the gleam of humor within them. "That's Your Majesty to you," she said, and Julián had to admit that there *was* something majestic in her bearing, even in her disheveled state.

He obliged her with a booming laugh, which served to dispel some of the tension crowding thickly between them.

She flashed him a smile, then turned to look out the window hole, holding herself slightly less tautly.

"It will probably be a few hours until your uncle receives the ransom note and gathers the money," Julián pointed out. Belatedly remembering his half-naked state, he pulled his one clean shirt off the nail it hung from and slid it over his shoulders. "You might want to occupy yourself with something more entertaining than looking out the window."

Why in hell did everything he say today sound so lascivious? Or did it just sound that way to his ears because he was still not quite recovered from the sensation of her lithe body pressed against his, the sweet scent of her hair threatening to overpower all his senses? The temptation to draw her close again and bury his face in the soft skin of her neck was almost more than he could bear.

If Julián knew how to read people—and he did—Miss Amalia Troncoso, eldest niece of Francisco Troncoso and heiress to a fortune so vast it made him dizzy, was also burning with desire.

Before she had a chance to remark on his less than felicitous turn of phrase, Julián elaborated. "Seeing as how I'm fairly new to banditry, I hadn't really realized how much of an appetite one could work up by snatching maidens. Am I mistaken in thinking that you must be hungry, too?"

"Famished," she admitted, and Julián would *not* mistake the faint flutter of her lashes for anything more than a simple change in expression.

"An early lunch it is, then. I think I have some crackers around here…"

Most of the coffee he'd brewed that morning was still in the percolator. Julián peered dubiously into its inky depths, then poured it out anyway, and plucked a large, round cracker from a covered plate.

And then he turned around.

For lack of a better seat, she had perched on the edge of his cot and was removing the few pins that still remained lodged at awkward angles in her dark hair. Julián watched her long, lustrous curls tumble down her shoulders, grasping, for the first time, just what it would mean to share these extremely close quarters with her until her uncle turned up with the ransom.

It had been a long, long time since he'd seen a woman at her toilette. Long enough that the sight of her fingers dragging slowly through her thick locks was doing unspeakable things to his self-control. He didn't just want to tangle his own fingers through her hair, tugging lightly until he dragged a gasp out of her. He wanted to spread it over her bare shoulders, tracing the soft whorls with his fingertips and—

Julián's heart was pounding. There was no way he was going to be able to keep from disgracing himself. His only course of action, unbefitting his status as a fearless bandit though it was, was to flee far, far away.

Thrusting the coffee and cracker in her general direction, Julián muttered something and strode to the door, meaning to find a less hazardous occupation outdoors—like standing on his saddle while his horse leaped over fallen logs.

Even before he reached the opening, however, he could see the first few droplets that had begun to darken the patch of dirt in front of the shack. Julián swore under his breath. Two more strides, and the light patter had turned into a proper tropical deluge, trapping the two of them inside.

Together.

Chapter Two

What in the world had Amalia gotten herself into?

She had heard dozens of stories about *raptos*. It was always evil scoundrels snatching innocent young women from their homes and taking them deep into the wilderness, or two lovers getting around their families' disapproval by pretending that one of them had kidnapped the other when in reality they had run off together.

She'd never heard of someone organizing her own *rapto*, but there was always a first time for everything, and Amalia Troncoso never left anything to chance.

She sat on the bandit's bed, her hairpins in a little heap on his shabby blanket, watching as he rummaged through the various cans and lidded jars on the table that seemed to serve as his washstand and makeshift kitchen.

From the relative barrenness of the shack, she could only assume that it wasn't his permanent residence. If the scatter of food on the table was any indication, though, he had spent at least one night here. Amalia couldn't help the tendril of curiosity unfurling inside

her. Where *did* he live? And if it was true that he was
new to banditry, unlikely as that seemed after his little
display with the pistols, what profession had he been
engaged in before turning to a life of crime?

The man may have looked every inch a bandit, but
he was very well spoken and clearly educated. She tried
to picture him sitting behind a desk, wearing spectacles
like her uncle's bookkeeper, and almost laughed out
loud. Not an accountant, then, nor yet a lawyer. Amalia gazed thoughtfully at his back. It was respectably
covered by a clean shirt, but the sight of his sunburned
chest was engraved in her mind. A man of property,
perhaps, one accustomed to galloping the length of his
lands under the punishing sun. Maybe he was trying
to outrun some sort of tragedy. A dark loss.

Much to her annoyance, Amalia *was* hungry. Nibbling at the slightly stale cracker, she thought long-
ingly about the baskets crowded with delicacies that her
maid had packed for the outing and wished she'd had
the presence of mind to pack a little basket for herself
and stash it somewhere. Though of course, it wouldn't
be too long before Tio Francisco sent someone with
the money. Once she had it, she'd not only be able to
buy herself as lavish a meal as she wanted, she'd also
be able to afford something she and Lucía had longed
for for years—security.

Then again, Tio Francisco was ever wary of thieves
and didn't keep much money around the house. The
amount Amalia had instructed the bandit to ask for in
his ransom note would require her uncle to visit the
bank. The rain would probably delay him even further.

She must have sighed, or made some sort of sound,
because the bandit cast a glance at her.

As soon as it began to rain, he had retreated toward a stool in the corner with his own mug of tepid coffee. He had been staring deeply into its depths, his earlier cockiness faded into a less brash thoughtfulness.

"Everything all right?" he asked. His black hair was long enough to curl around his ears, and he seemed to have a habit of raking it back with his fingers. Without the benefit of a comb and pomade, that was only a temporary measure—within moments a rakish lock would flop back over his forehead, and the entire thing would begin again.

It was almost as distracting as the sight of his bare chest, and considering the latter's extremely chiseled quality, that was saying something.

"Oh, yes," she answered lightly, if a few seconds too late. "Just…thinking."

"About all the frocks you'll buy with your share of the ransom?"

"Frocks?" Amalia frowned. She had far more important things to put that money toward than frocks—her and Lucía's freedom, for one. Tío Francisco had taken over their care when their father died, almost fifteen years before. He had made sure the sisters never lacked for anything, but he had kept them both on a tight leash.

"I'm assuming it's not food or shelter you need," the bandit went on. "And unless you've some very serious gambling debts—"

"I don't gamble," she told him censoriously. "And women have more uses for money than adding to the contents of their wardrobe. You don't know anything about me, or my life—"

"So tell me."

"I beg your pardon?"

He leaned forward in his seat, his empty mug dangling from one strong finger. "What trouble could a pampered miss like you have possibly gotten into to justify staging abductions and consorting with scoundrels like myself?"

A pampered miss, was she?

"I'm not in any sort of trouble," she said tightly. "Before my father died, he made his brother, my uncle Francisco, the custodian of my sister's and my inheritance. I'd always thought it was only until we reached our majority, but it appears I was mistaken. Several weeks ago I was informed by my uncle that my father was so apprehensive of my sister and I being taken in by fortune hunters, that he wrote it into his will that my uncle should have control of our holdings and properties in perpetuity."

Julián's eyes gleamed in the dimness of the hut. "And he doesn't intend to relinquish that control?"

Amalia shook her head. "For years, I thought he was just really concerned with carrying out his late brother's orders. He's made everybody believe that he's this selfless, altruistic paragon of virtue whose only preoccupation is to keep Lucía and me safe from people who want to use us for our money. But the truth is, he just wants an excuse to keep his greedy paws on what's rightfully ours—and the only way he can do that is to shackle us to him. Or to whichever suitor makes him the best offer."

Her hands clenched around the dented tin mug, so hard her fingertips felt bruised. "My father was so busy protecting us from fortune hunters, he didn't realize his brother was the worst one of all. Sometimes I wonder if he would have done the same thing had my mother been around to talk reason into him. Or if he would have trampled over her opinion, too."

As wonderful as her father had been to her and Lucía, Amalia had always known him to be the sort of man who had a deep need to be right at all times.

Amalia hadn't realized how loud her voice had gotten until she reached the end of her speech and heard the raindrops thudding against the shack's cane thatch roof. It was desperately unfair that she had to resort to schemes like this one just to have some measure of independence. She and Lucía had all the frocks they could ever want. But that wasn't *all* they wanted.

"Lucía wants to study music abroad," Amalia said, past the sudden raspiness in her throat. "And I should love nothing better than to take her."

"I just want frocks, myself," the bandit said so offhandedly that Amalia gaped at him for a moment, before she dissolved into laughter.

In the process, she upset the mug she'd been holding, dribbling the dark dregs of her coffee over her much-abused skirt. With a raised eyebrow, the bandit offered her the kerchief he had discarded, which she used to blot at the stained fabric.

"I may have to purchase one or two myself, after all this," she said when she had recovered. "Seeing as I have completely destroyed this ensemble."

His tanned, calloused hand landed on her arm, and Amalia looked down in surprise to see that he had crossed the dirt floor to crouch in front of her. "Count on me to do whatever it takes to get your money back from your uncle," he said with quiet intensity, his eyes gleaming in the dim room.

As close as she'd been pressed against him earlier, she'd had her back to him. It was only now that she saw the thin scar running through one of his eyebrows.

She'd thought him a man of property? No—he was a bandit through and through.

And she had placed her trust in him, at least temporarily.

Trust was not something Amalia gave easily. In her experience, people were rarely worthy of it. She wasn't certain if this man was, at least not yet. But the sincerity shining in his eyes made her want to believe in him like she hadn't any other man.

It felt...dangerous. Trust Amalia to run full tilt toward it, foolhardy though it may be.

His fingers closed around the thin, delicate skin of her wrist, and Amalia almost gasped at the startling intimacy of being touched on the exact spot where her pulse was thrumming.

"I— You—"

All thought seemed to have vanished from Amalia's head. All, save for one—she didn't want him to let go.

Boldly, she placed her hand over his. He couldn't have known what she was longing for, but something compelled him to brush a kiss over her knuckles. He must not have shaved in days, and the bristles that lent him a roguish air scraped delightfully against her skin.

Her breath caught, her fingers reflexively squeezing his. And then Amalia did something she had never even contemplated doing before.

She lowered her face and pressed her lips against

his, feeling almost like this was part of the adventure she had embarked on.

She had expected his kisses to be as rough as his hands. She had expected…any number of things, but certainly not the exquisite, delicate gentleness with which he parted her lips with his own.

Amalia shouldn't have been surprised by her own boldness. After all, it had taken a great deal of it to even think of this scheme. Amalia was nothing if not filled with grit and valor. This wasn't even the first kiss she had ever shared with a man, just the first she had initiated…and the first that left her aching for more.

Until now, this moment, she had never allowed herself to stop thinking and scheming and let herself be carried aloft by pure sensation. Her body rocked with shivers as he followed the kiss with another, and then another and then…

He laid a ring of kisses around the base of her neck, right where the necklace she usually wore would rest if she hadn't removed it that morning. Amalia congratulated herself on her foresight, though it had been nothing more than prudence that had prompted her to put away her jewelry before haring off into the countryside with a bandit.

On the whole, it had not been a bad idea—the removal of the jewelry nor the haring-off part. Nor the bandit.

There had probably been an easier way to go about this whole business. But Amalia had to concede there was one distinct benefit to this particular plan, and it was currently pressing a kiss just below her ear.

Amalia had been a favorite at balls. She had kissed a man or two. But those kisses were nothing like these—

and those other lips couldn't come close to comparing to the rightness of his. There was something truly wicked about his lips when they curled into a smile. But when they were pressed against hers? It was nothing short of thrilling.

Julián was playing with fire. He knew it, and what was worse, he didn't care.

He was no stranger to wanting what he couldn't have—sometimes it seemed like he'd spent half his life surrounded by all kinds of riches and finding little interest or enjoyment in any of it. Amalia was just one more item on that long list.

Her skin tasted as sweet as it had smelled when he'd held her against him earlier. He reveled in it, his lips ranging over her neck, then her eager, welcoming mouth, then back again.

If Julián had been able to draw a breath long enough to speak, he would have cursed the current fashions for making skirts so slender. Kneeling in front of her, pressed against her legs, he would have done anything to have her open them wide enough to accommodate him.

That thought, more than anything, was what made him pull away.

As well as the crashing realization that she didn't really know who he was, or what he was after, or why he had been so willing to agree to her request.

Julián had never intended to pass himself off as a bandit—but when Amalia had unknowingly provided him with the perfect cover to investigate his father's shady business dealings, he had seized it. It had been an impulse, and a poorly thought out one at that. Even now Julián wasn't all that sure what he thought he'd accomplish by it.

All he knew was that her uncle was also embroiled in the situation, and that the whole thing was linked to the end of his last relationship, a messy split that Julián now knew had been engineered by his father. It was doubtful that Amalia even knew what was happening, but it occurred to Julián that when her uncle came with the ransom, maybe Julián could extract something besides money from him—information.

He knew what his family had done, but not why.

Julián would find out what had led his father to destroy his relationship with Concepción. And then he would make things right with her—if that was even possible anymore. It was certainly too late for him. His heart had shattered the moment she'd sent him away from her doorstep, and even though almost a year had passed since then, his chest still ached with the emptiness of those first weeks without her. The memory of it surged over him now, overwhelming in its intensity.

"We should stop," he told Amalia now.

She murmured something incomprehensible against his mouth, holding his face between her hands. Her lips had been rubbed red by his beard, and Julián couldn't resist soothing the scrape with the ball of his thumb as he stepped away.

"Must we?" she asked.

Her having concocted this scheme was already proof enough that she didn't have much of a care for her reputation. Though to the other people at the gathering she had ostensibly been an unwilling participant, Julián knew that everyone would assume he'd had his way with her. Especially if the truth of who Julián really was ever came out.

All that considered, perhaps it shouldn't have been surprising that she'd be not just willing, but eager, to pursue the dangerous path they were on. If she was about to return home to find her reputation ruined, why not actually do what she would be accused of having done? Had he been in her position, he would have thrown caution to the wind and himself into bed.

Maybe it was just Julián being his usual contrary self, but if anyone was going to be throwing herself into *his* bed, he would have rather it be because she wanted him, not because he was merely convenient.

As the notion came into his mind, Julián was uncomfortably reminded of all the women he had bedded precisely for that reason. He had never been in love and as far as he knew, none of his dalliances had ever been in love with him. That was how he'd preferred it.

So why did the prospect of doing the same with Amalia ring so hollow?

Julián laid a final kiss on the corner of her mouth. "We do," he said, and all his saintly self-denial earned him was a frown.

Disengaging himself, he retreated to the stool in the corner. Outside, the rain continued to pummel the shack's thatched roof. Julián was grateful for the sound, if only because it drowned out his ragged breaths.

What the hell had come over him? Sitting there panting like he'd tried to outrun a locomotive, from nothing more than a series of kisses.

Hearing about her uncle had moved him into offering his protection—not something he'd ever done before. But he felt it roaring over him at the thought of her trying so valiantly, and so desperately, to look after her sister. Julián hadn't met Amalia until the day she'd approached him with her plan, but he'd been vaguely aware of the Troncoso sisters, heiresses to one of San Pedro's largest fortunes.

He could never have imagined that they had been dealing with a tyrant of their own. Just as he had.

"You've got a lot of principles, for a bandit," Amalia told him, rubbing her thumb over her lips. "Have you ever stolen anything?"

"Do hearts count?" He raised a sardonic eyebrow, feeling his mouth twitch when she laughed. "Principled or not, you're not scared of being alone in the wilderness with a bandit?"

"I'm not scared of anything," she replied swiftly. "And besides…" The considering gaze she dragged over him made Julián's pulse race. She gave a minute shrug. "I'm match enough for you."

"Are you?" he asked, letting her see his amusement.

As much as he ached to prove her wrong, Julián thought he had better be prudent for once in his life.

"I don't want any trouble when your uncle comes with the ransom," he offered by way of explanation. "If someone were to think that I took advantage of you…"

Amalia couldn't hide her disappointment, and seeing how much she wanted him almost made him kiss her again.

"Why would you care what San Pedro society thinks about you?" she asked.

"I don't," Julián returned. "I care about the Civil Guard and their pesky little habit of tossing delinquents into prison. Which is where I'll be headed if anyone thinks I've touched a single hair on your virginal head."

"I thought you were an outlaw."

"I might be, after today."

"In any case, they're all bound to think the worst." She gestured at her torn, dirty clothing, then began scooping up her hair once again, returning it to its former orderly state.

"I'd just as soon not prove them right." *Them* in this instance being not the townspeople, but his father and cousin. Not that he was inclined to elaborate. Before she could open her mouth to ask him any more questions he'd rather not answer, he beat her to it. "Why are *you* so unconcerned about everyone thinking you've been…liberal with your affections?"

She made a noise that sounded distinctly like a snort. "Keeping my virtue intact doesn't serve my plans," she said. "In fact, the only person it serves is my uncle and whichever dolt from a wealthy family he's scheming to marry me off to. I am hoping that being abducted will do enough damage to my reputation to keep him from getting any more ideas, at least long enough for me to leave town, but if it's not enough of a deterrent…"

Julián had never heard a woman speak so frankly and with such pragmatism about so delicate a subject, but as shocking as it was, he had to admit that Amalia wasn't wrong. "Are you saying that you would willingly trade your virtue to keep your uncle from attempting to arrange a marriage? What if you meet someone and want to marry *him*?"

"Oh, I'm never getting married." Her tone was as final as the metallic snap of a key turning inside a lock. "Not willingly. And not for anything foolish, like love. After all, my father loved us. My uncle claims to. And that didn't stop either of them from locking Lucía and me in gilded cages. What would stop a husband, even a loving one, from doing the same? And besides, a husband would expect to be obeyed," she said scornfully. "Marriage would only make him think he had the right to control me, and I've had quite enough of that."

Julián could not bring himself to believe that was even possible. Whoever tried to control Amalia Troncoso would surely find it as easy as trying to control a bolt of lightning.

"What if you married a man with so much property of his own that he would never have any need of yours?" he asked.

"That would only be exchanging one captor for another." Amalia was full of conviction, her face mobile as she explained the reason for this belief. "My father settled a very large sum on my mother when they married. In theory, she was to have complete control over her own expenses, and to manage it as she saw fit. In practice... He was always questioning her decisions. Did the household really use up that many pounds of flour a week, and couldn't she find a less expensive brand of chocolate for breakfast? She would pore over her account books, anxious that she had made a mistake or not noticed that someone was overcharging her. I'd hate to live that way for the rest of my life."

"Not everyone's like that, you know," Julián said. "Some of us are shockingly neglectful with our money."

Amalia shrugged. "Why take the chance?"

Julián shifted in his stool, wincing slightly as he stretched out his cramped legs.

"Are you uncomfortable? There's plenty of room on the bed if you want to sit here," she said, patting the empty stretch of mattress next to her. "I promise I won't take advantage of you."

"Oh, no, Your Highness. I intend to stay far, far away from those sweet lips of yours." Julián leaned back against the wooden wall, crossing his arms and regarding her with mingled regret and amusement. "I'm not about to let you seduce me."

"Oh?" She cocked her head, a small smile playing right where he'd laid his last kiss. "I thought I already had."

Julián felt his lips spreading into a grin. She really was like no other woman he had ever met.

Chapter Three

Night was falling.

Amalia and Julián had managed to keep their hands off each other. Mostly because he had gone outside as soon as the rain eased, and Amalia had taken a long, lonely and unsatisfying nap on the cot that smelled faintly of him.

And still, her uncle hadn't come.

Of all the potential downfalls in her plan, it hadn't occurred to Amalia that he might refuse to pay the ransom, or to rescue her at all.

Standing in the doorway to the shack, Amalia watched the shadows lengthen as light leeched from the sky. Julián was mostly in shadow, cursing under his breath as he tried to light a fire beneath the brick cooking ring with wood that had to be soaked. Amalia's lips twitched at the sight, but the apprehension sweeping over her in a cold wave did not allow a smile to bloom.

Julián gave the crumbling bricks a swift kick, then, looking mulish, seized the pot from the ring and began hauling it inside.

Amalia moved aside to let him pass, but he paused

in the doorway, seemingly unperturbed by the weight of the iron pot. He cocked his head, his dark eyes raking over her.

"Everything all right?"

It was the second time he'd asked her that today—twice more than any of the men in her family ever had. Amalia started to nod as she always did, but it must not have been all that convincing. Julián set the pot down on the floor and placed a finger beneath her chin, lifting it until she was looking into his eyes.

"What's wrong?" he asked softly.

The concern in his expression was breathtaking. Amalia couldn't remember the last time someone had looked at her like this. She'd grown so used to being the strong one, the clever one, the one who found a solution for every problem. No one ever looked at her as though trying to determine whether or not they should offer comfort, or even help.

"I shouldn't have done this." Under the warmth of his concern, the words spilled out faster than they would have otherwise. "I shouldn't have tested my uncle's affection and risked my reputation and—"

"Amalia," Julián said. "The day isn't over. There's still time for him to comply with our demands. And let's not forget that he's a busy man—he might not have even seen the note yet. Maybe he's in the middle of some important deal. Has he mentioned something of the kind to you?"

Amalia frowned. "I wouldn't know. Tío Francisco isn't exactly forthcoming when it comes to all that. He doesn't even entertain his business acquaintances at home."

"That is curious," Julián said softly, adding when

Amalia's brow furrowed tighter, "You don't know that he's given up on you. In fact, for all you know he might be gathering an entire troop's worth of soldiers and preparing to storm our impenetrable fortress."

He gestured at the wooden walls around them, which Amalia would call neither impenetrable nor a fortress. She couldn't help but laugh.

For a ruthless bandit, Julián could be extraordinarily kind.

"All right," she conceded. "I'll try not to worry just yet. Although it looks like I may have cause to, seeing as you seem determined to burn our impenetrable fortress to the ground."

"I'm hungry," he explained. "It's been hours since the coffee and crackers and I did explain that banditry works up an appetite."

"I suppose I had better help you, then. Wouldn't want our fortress to go up in flames just because you don't know how to roast a *batata*."

As it turned out, neither of them were very adept at cookery. Amalia was used to meals appearing on the table, or on a tray in her bedroom, then whisked away as soon as she was finished by one of half a dozen people her uncle employed in the *quinta* that used to belong to her parents. Lavish meals in restaurants were also the norm, as well as vast arrays of delicacies at the house parties she and Lucía frequented.

All right, so maybe Julián hadn't been completely wrong when he'd called her a pampered miss.

Peeling a plantain left her hands as sticky as if she had dipped them into a pot of paste, but eventually the two of them managed to cobble together something that vaguely resembled a soup. Leaving it to simmer in the pot, Amalia retreated toward the basin, where she tried to scrub her hands to no avail.

"Let me try," Julián said. He dipped his kerchief into the water and rubbed the rough fabric over her palms, standing so close to her that his shoulders brushed hers.

His nearness was as overwhelming as it was intoxicating. It was shocking how Amalia had known this man for less than a day and already she craved his touch. Already, his hands on hers weren't enough. She longed to lay her head on his sculpted shoulder and tilt up her face until he could capture her lips with a dozen kisses.

When she caught sight of a smear of dirt on his forearm, it was only polite for her to return his ministrations. After taking the damp kerchief from him, she smoothed it over his muscles, sweeping along his corded forearm until she reached the edge of his rolled-up sleeve. She was raising the kerchief toward his face when he caught her by the wrist.

"I know I need a proper bath, but let's not get carried away," he murmured.

Amalia lifted her chin a fraction of an inch. "I'll have you know I am on my very best behavior."

"You had better be, Your Highness. I refuse to have *my* virtue compromised."

With a crooked grin, Julián slid away, going over to the pot to poke at the liquid bubbling within with a long, dented ladle. "I think it's edible," he reported.

"You don't sound terribly sure." Amalia took a moment to spread his kerchief on the table, though in this dampness it wouldn't dry any time soon.

"There's only one way to find out," Julián said and

scooped out a ladleful, which he presented to Amalia with a flourish.

"Coward," she said, laughing. She took the ladle from him and brought it up to her lips. A rich, salty, warm broth flooded her mouth. "Oh! It's not bad." She took another sip. "It's actually very good. A trifle garlicky, maybe, but good."

"Garlicky, hmm? All the better to avoid temptation. Maybe I should drop another few cloves in there."

"Don't you dare ruin it," she told him, tugging him away from the pot. "Go fetch the bowls—I don't think I can wait a second longer."

"Me, either," he said, and Amalia knew he wasn't just talking about the *caldo*.

Each holding a bowl, they retreated to their spots— Amalia on the cot and Julián on the stool with his long legs stretched so far into the room, his boots were almost inside the fire.

"Your uncle wouldn't have gone out of town, would he?" he asked, his pewter spoon flashing in the flickering light. "Maybe he was called away on business and that's why he hasn't received the note."

Amalia felt a flicker of surprise at his return to their earlier conversation. "It's possible, I suppose."

"Does he often have business outside of San Pedro?"

The surprise turned to suspicion. There was nothing subtle about Julián's interest in her uncle and his business dealings. She hoped it wasn't out of a desire to do Tio Francisco mischief when all this was over. She and Julián had settled on what she thought was a fair payment, but what would stop him from trying to extort more out of them at a later date?

"Why do you want to know?" she asked, unable to keep her eyes from narrowing.

"Just making conversation," he said easily. "If only to distract myself from the fact that I'm not eating roast pork and *moro de guandules*."

He laughed when Amalia wrinkled her nose. "What's the matter?" he asked. "You don't like *moro*?"

"I don't like *guandules*," she said.

"Not even with coconut?"

She shook her head. "Not at all. I like beans better—stewed ones over rice, not mixed in with it. Our housekeeper makes the creamiest beans."

"I'll have to get the recipe," Julián said, quirking an eyebrow. "What about dessert? What would you have?"

"Dulce de naranja," she said promptly. When made right, the sweet made out of oranges had just enough tartness and bitterness to make the flavor really complex while still being light and fresh. More often than not, Lucía ended up choosing dessert, and she always opted for something rich and overly sweet. "I don't suppose they make *dulce de naranja* in Europe, though."

"Maybe you can learn to make it," Julián remarked. "Are you as musical as your sister?"

"Heavens, no." Amalia made a face as she scooped a piece of plantain from the broth. "I can scarcely follow a tune. And I never learned to read music."

"Then what do you intend to do with yourself while she's studying music?"

"Buy pretty frocks," Amalia answered, and they both smiled reflexively. "I think there will be plenty to occupy me, wherever we end up. But honestly, that's the least of my worries. I just want her to be happy." She felt her mouth turning down at the corners as she contemplated Lucía. "She hasn't been, lately, and my heart breaks for her. Do you have any sisters of your own?"

"No siblings at all," Julián said, his mouth compressing into a tight line. "But my father did raise one of my cousins. I suppose you could say we grew up like brothers, but we're not particularly close. He and my father are," he added, almost offhandedly, then gave her a wolfish grin that didn't quite cover the pain in his eyes. "I'm the black sheep of the family, as is only befitting for a bandit."

"Don't tell me you took up banditry just to be contrary."

He laughed. "Something like that."

He didn't seem to be inclined to add much more, and they ate the rest of their meal in companionable silence. Afterward, Amalia braved another few sips of the *aguardiente* and felt her limbs grow languorous as the alcohol traveled down her chest. Giving up what little remained of her sense of propriety, she stretched out on the cot again, hardly noticing when Julián quietly removed the plate and spoon from her hand.

A low noise startled her awake sometime later. She rose up onto her elbow, peering intently into the gloom. The sound came again, and her stomach sank when she recognized it. Birdsong.

When she sat up, she could see the sky burning with the first glow of sunrise through the opening in the shack's wall. The night had gone by, and it was almost morning, and judging from the way Julián sat slumped on his stool, no one had taken advantage of the cover of night to storm their defenseless fortress.

Amalia's gaze met his, and even in the dimness, she saw the truth written all over his face. "My uncle's not coming, is he?"

* * *

Julián awoke with a foul crick in his neck and an even fouler disposition, directed toward the men in Amalia's family—namely, her late father and her uncle, who was just as late if in a different way.

He didn't know much about Francisco Troncoso, but what little he had been able to glean about him left a bad taste in his mouth. What kind of scoundrel could be this unfeeling—or careless—toward the very people he was supposed to look after? Amalia was no more a defenseless miss than she was a pampered one, but all her tenacity wouldn't have kept her safe if Julián truly had been a bandit and bent on getting more from her than information.

Nobody had ever depended on Julián, and he'd always been inclined to see that as a good thing. He could barely look after his own interests, let alone that of anyone else. As his father and cousin relished in telling him, Julián was a dissolute, irresponsible scoundrel with little regard for other people. And that may have been true, but if there was one thing he knew about himself, it was that he could never be this callous when it came to the safety of anyone under his care.

Anger started to build inside his chest, propelling him to his feet. Though he had expected Amalia to be likewise livid, or even indignant, she only looked worried.

"Something must have happened," she said and gnawed briefly on her lower lip. Julián could have done without the sight of her sitting up in bed, unbound hair tumbling every which way as she blinked sleep out of her eyes. Now that he had been witness to it, he was sure he'd be seeing it in his dreams. "Do you think it's possible that the ransom note went astray? Or maybe Lucía took sick."

"Is she sickly?" Julián asked. "Prone to sudden ailments?"

"No, but…" She shook her head. "I should go home. I could never forgive myself if something had happened and I wasn't there for her."

Her teeth sank onto her lower lip again. Julián grasped her by the chin. "You'll injure yourself," he said roughly, and her luscious lips parted with surprise. "It's a long way to walk. I'll take you home, if you really feel you need to go."

And if it turned out that her uncle wasn't the kind of rascal that would let his charge be snatched and this was merely his plan to ambush Julián on the road, well, Julián had gotten himself out of trickier situations.

Of course, most of those had involved slighted women, not guardsmen with pistols. The way some of them wielded their parasols, though—and, in one memorable case, a very old and valuable tome of poetry—Julián would rather take his chances with the Civil Guard.

"Are you certain?" Amalia asked, pushing a lock of hair off her face. "I wouldn't want you to get into trouble after all you've done to help me."

"I'll be fine."

He always was. For the most part.

Pushing away any more thoughts of ambushes, he poured a clean stream of water into the basin and left Amalia to make her morning ablutions while he went to saddle the horse. He was down to his last clean shirt, which would in any case have required him to visit the set of rooms he'd rented on the outskirts of town. His landlady had not only a genius for laundry, she was also discretion itself and never thought to question his erratic comings and goings.

Tending to his horse and readying him for the long trek into town didn't take as long as Amalia did to pull her hair and clothes into a semblance of order. The sun had begun to chase away the bluish shadows of early morning by the time she emerged from the hut. Her tumbling mane had been coerced into submission, probably with the aid of those half a million pins she'd extracted from it the day before, and the brown skin over her cheekbones looked scrubbed and faintly pink.

"Are you ready?" she asked, and Julián realized with a start that he had been staring.

"I've been ready for hours, Your Highness. Here, let me help you up."

But before he had finished cupping his hands into a makeshift foothold, she had hauled herself onto the saddle. "What are you waiting for?" Even her teasing smile couldn't erase the worried line between her brows.

He couldn't blame her. If he'd had a sister, he wouldn't have been able to breathe for the worrying. When younger, Julián had felt keenly his lack of siblings, but maybe it was for the best. Twenty-seven years of looking after only himself had been difficult enough.

A little too aware that he was showing off for her benefit, Julián pulled himself behind her with a single athletic bound. He began reaching around her for the reins, then realized she was already holding them in her small, finely articulated hands. She brushed him away, indicating that she didn't mean to let go, which was just fine with Julián, who had always been content enough to sit back and let someone else take the reins.

A light pressure from her knees and a soft murmur of encouragement was all it took for his horse to set off down the path. Julián wrapped his arms around her waist to keep them both steady.

Without the prospect of being chased by overzealous coachmen, riding pressed up against Amalia was an altogether different proposition than it had been the day before. This time he was able to notice that her head fitted just under his chin, her body tucked into his like they had been molded as a pair. This time there was no escaping her soft curves, or the talcum-sweet scent rising from the folds of her blouse.

Her back was perfectly straight, her muscles rigid, as she strove to keep the precarious sideways perch required by her slim skirts.

An image flashed into his mind—Amalia riding astride in one of those split skirts he had seen caricatured in a magazine once, the kind it was said American women wore for riding bicycles. The notion made him wobble atop the saddle, and he found himself gripping her tighter to keep from toppling over.

She cast a quick look over her shoulder. "Is everything all right back there?"

"Perfectly fine," Julián gasped.

It wasn't long before they burst out of the path, shady with overhanging branches, and into the main road. The morning sun was golden on the tall stalks of sugarcane as they passed through fields that were already bristling with cane cutters. Not too far in the distance, a black cloud issued from one of the great smokestacks that signaled the presence of a sugar mill.

There were far more of those in the region than Julián cared to count. San Pedro was sugar country these days, though plenty of the old cattle ranches still remained. There was the town, too, large and growing every day, with its bustling port and thriving commercial district. As far as he had been able to determine in a couple of weeks of sleuthing, the Troncosos' fortune lay mostly in shipping and imports, though there was also a great deal of land and some property in town.

Had he wasted his brief time with Amalia? He should have been able to glean more information from her instead of letting himself get swept up into the melodrama of her worries and smiles and kisses.

Then again, who would have been able to help it?

The kisses in particular, or at least reliving the memory of them, would be enough to carry him through this endeavor. Julián's father had made sure he learned his lesson about entanglements—the hard way. After the heartbreak of the past year, Julián would hardly welcome another love affair, no matter how tempting it proved. No matter how inflamed he was by the very thought of Amalia's luscious, generous, eager—

"This isn't an admission of defeat. My returning home, I mean." Amalia's voice broke through his reverie, making Julián realize that he'd been stroking her side with his thumb.

Luckily, it didn't seem like she could feel it through the boning of her corset.

"I wouldn't dare think so," he reassured her.

"It's only a temporary setback. A detour, if you will. I have only to think of another plan. So you needn't be worried about your payment."

Julián didn't care a fig about the money she'd promised him. But it *was* one way to keep her tethered to him until he could find what he was looking for.

"I'm not worried. I trust you to deliver it when you're able."

She twisted around. "Are all bandits this accommodating?"

"I'm not your average bandit," he told her.

"So it seems." A thoughtful pause stretched between them. "Do you think it might have anything to do with how new you are to the profession? Or is it your upbringing that makes you so unusual?"

Julián let out a laugh. "Have you been wondering about me, Your Highness?"

"I don't know if you noticed, but I haven't exactly had much to occupy me in the past twenty-four hours."

It was too bad she couldn't see his expression. Julián made up for that by lowering his head so that his breath ghosted over the back of her exposed neck. "What a short memory you have."

She may not have been able to feel his thumb stroking her side, but he was all too aware of the shiver that traveled over her body. As a distraction technique, his whisper had been all too effective.

The only problem was, she wasn't the only one affected by it.

Julián contemplated the damp little curl plastered to the back of her neck and thought about what would happen if he dragged his lips up and down the graceful column, all the while keeping her tight against him. Would she let out one of those shuddery little breaths like when he'd kissed her the day before? Or would she be as delightfully vocal as he suspected she could be, and intersperse a string of words with moans? Would she allow her eyes to flutter closed, or would she turn to fix him with her direct gaze?

Julián straightened up. He was *not* going to discuss his upbringing with this woman, but neither was he willing to work himself into a state to avoid it. "You're not exactly a regular sort of heiress, you know. At least, I've never heard of a debutante who consorts with bandits."

"Maybe they should start. I can speak highly of my experience so far."

"I'll remember that if I ever need a reference for my services," Julián said.

In the course of the next hour, the sugarcane fields gave way to the series of ramshackle buildings that announced they would be soon arriving in town. Before long Amalia was guiding the horse onto the road that wound alongside the Higuamo River. Over the roofs of the elegant masonry houses, Julián could see the smokestack of the Porvenir sugar mill jutting into the blazing blue sky, as well as the very top of the red-and-white firehouse at the center of town.

Had it been taller than a single story, the Troncosos' *quinta* would have had a lovely view of the river. Surrounded by a wrought iron fence and *coralillo* bushes in full bloom, the elegant white house was set back from the street. Graceful steps led up to a central front door, from which two wings extended, each bearing a porch ringed with Corinthian columns and crowned with the kind of ornate plasterwork that proliferated on San Pedro's newer buildings.

Unfamiliar as he was with the Troncosos' home, Julián was nevertheless immediately assailed by the strange stillness that hung over it. There were no housemaids sweeping the porch, no coachmen—or a coach, for that matter—idling out front. The shutters covering the many doors and windows that faced the street were all tightly closed, though they'd been hospitably propped open in every other house they had passed.

"Something *is* wrong," Amalia said tightly, giving voice to his thoughts. Barely waiting for the horse to stop, she leaped down lightly and took off running around the side of the house, disappearing from his sight in mere moments.

Julián swore as he scrambled to hitch his horse. Giving the reins an experimental tug to make sure his knot was tight, he sprinted after Amalia.

Chapter Four

Unused to being out in the sun without her hat and parasol, Amalia felt the heat in her face as she dashed through the front gate and around the side of the house. Her heart was hammering wildly inside her chest as, even in her haste, she noticed all the little things that alone would have been merely unusual, but together added up to a domestic catastrophe—the dirty front steps, the closed doors and windows, the fallen leaves littering the garden. The last might have been the most alarming, as her uncle employed a small army's worth of gardeners to keep the property looking perfectly manicured at all times. Those leaves would have never been allowed to remain scattered on the lush grass if Tio Francisco were around to see it.

She flung open the second gate that led to the kitchen yard, almost skidding to a stop when she saw one of the new housemaids, Ana. The young woman, evidently not expecting to be burst upon in such a fashion, dropped the pail she'd been carrying, and Amalia had to take a hopping step back to avoid the tidal wave of dirty water splashing her way.

"Where's my sister?" Amalia demanded, shaking water from the tan leather of her shoes. "Is she ill? Has there been an accident?"

"Your—no, miss. Not to my knowledge."

Amalia barely had a moment to feel relief as the slap of footsteps on the paving stones alerted her to Julián's presence. That, and the widening of the maid's eyes as she took in the sight of Julián and Amalia's disheveled appearance.

"He said you eloped," she blurted out, her gaze flitting from Amalia to Julián. "Don Francisco did, I mean. I was dusting in the parlor when a messenger came with a note. He said you had run away with a lover and was sending word that you were never coming back."

An incredulous snort popped out of Amalia before she had a chance to stop it. "A lover, me? When would I have had the time to find one?"

Julián made a discreet noise behind her, as if to remind Amalia of her attempt to do just that the day before. She flashed him an irritable glance, then turned back to Ana. "Where is everybody? I had a terrible fright when I saw the house all closed up."

Something like surprise flickered over Ana's expression. "Why, they've all left."

"Left...?" Amalia echoed, feeling as suddenly breathless as if the pail of water had been upended over her head instead of the ground.

Her tone must have been sharper than she'd intended, because Ana took a half step backward. "When your uncle got the note, he asked the housekeeper to pack up the house and—and your sister's things. By the time she arrived from her outing, we had packed all the trunks and were bringing them outside. I... I hope you don't mind my saying so, but your sister did not look at all happy at being made to leave."

"He kidnapped her?" Julián asked bluntly.

The maid looked suddenly frightened. "I wouldn't say that, exactly..."

"Why not?"

"Because he's her guardian," Amalia snapped, "and allowed to do whatever he wants without it being considered a crime. Did he say where he meant to go?"

"Not to me, miss." Ana hesitated for a moment. "But I did hear the coachman say something about taking them to the port."

The port. Amalia's head was spinning. That could mean any number of destinations, any number of countries or continents...

What the devil had happened while she'd been gone?

There was only one reason why Tio Francisco would spirit Lucía away with such haste—he must have found her someone to marry. Someone he knew Amalia would disapprove of. He had as much as admitted it the week before, when Amalia had accused him of trying to sell her off to the highest bidder. He'd said, in that wretched patronizing tone of his, "I'm afraid you wouldn't fetch a very high price, dear." But Lucía would. Sweet, biddable, seventeen-year-old Lucía, who wanted nothing more than to practice her music and giggle with her friends.

Julián caught Amalia by the shoulder before she could stumble. Firmly, he guided her toward the wood and rush chair that stood just outside the back door. The fibers creaked in protest when Amalia sank onto the rough seat, her face in her hands.

Her brilliant plan hadn't just failed—it had *backfired*. Tio Francisco, who was shrewd enough when it came to business, had known to use Amalia's absence to his advantage. For all her scheming and planning, that was one thing she hadn't counted on.

In trying to improve her sister's life, had she actually ruined it?

Dimly, she realized that Julián had crouched in front of her and was tugging on her wrists. She raised her head and allowed him to grasp her hands firmly in his larger ones. "Everything is going to be all right," he was saying. His searching gaze found hers, and she squeezed his hands reflexively as she saw the concern and strength in his dark eyes. "We will find your sister, and we will make sure she comes to no harm."

Amalia jerked her head into a nod.

"Does your uncle have a study?"

Another nod, this one fractionally less dazed. "There's a small room off the parlor that he uses as an office."

Ana, who had vanished without Amalia realizing it, came forth now, bearing two glasses of water. "The house is locked up," she said, looking wary.

"That won't be a problem for me," Julián said, releasing Amalia's hands as he stood up to take one of the glasses from Ana.

As the haze of panic receded, Amalia realized that the girl had probably been entrusted with the care of the house and was rightly nervous that she would be reprimanded for the intrusion. She accepted the water and touched Ana's hand gently. "Please don't worry. I'll make sure you don't get into trouble with the housekeeper or my uncle."

Ana nodded. "Much appreciated, miss."

"Thank you for all your help." Amalia drained the glass, noticing for the first time how thirsty she was after the long, hot ride into town. Passing the glass back to Ana, she stood up and looked at Julián. "Let's go inside."

Under Julián's skillful hands, locked door after locked door fell open as he and Amalia traversed through the darkened house until they came to her uncle's office. The high-ceilinged room with its tile floors and whitewashed walls was lined with glass-fronted bookcases and a series of framed maps. The aroma of his cologne was still heavy in the air, as if Tío Francisco had merely stepped away for a moment and was sure to return and catch Amalia rifling through his desk.

Not that there was much to rifle through. A quick perusal of the desktop showed Amalia that the vast expanse of its leather blotter was empty, and so was the correspondence tray. Only a folded newspaper lay discarded in a corner.

"He must have put his papers in the drawers," she told Julián, tugging on a brass handle to confirm it was also locked. "Or taken it all with him."

He stepped up beside her. "Let's find out."

Sinking into Tío Francisco's heavy leather chair, Amalia sat back while Julián worked. Even through her anxiety, Ana's words kept replaying in her mind. *He said you were never coming back.*

So her uncle really had given up on her. He'd threatened it often enough, but Amalia hadn't really thought him capable of it.

She didn't know how effective his lie about her had been—the other girls at the outing had seen her being stolen away by a bandit, after all. The other girls and Lucía, who didn't know the truth of what Amalia had been plotting.

Something sour and bitter welled up inside her. Amalia's relationship with her uncle had always been rocky—that couldn't be denied. But for all the arguments they'd had, and all the times she'd stormed away to the sound of his long-suffering sighs, she had somehow, inexplicably, believed that he truly did have their best interests at heart. That his paternal act wasn't a complete lie.

How wrong she'd been.

Dwelling on it would get her nowhere. Amalia forced her thoughts back to the matter at hand.

"I wonder…" she said musingly, not realizing she had spoken out loud until Julián's gaze flicked up from the drawer he was attempting to open. "If Lucía had even a moment to come inside the house, she might have tried to leave me some hint of where they were going."

She sprang up from the chair and began to make her way to the front room. The pair of bergère chairs by the window that had once been her mother's had been covered with white bedsheets, turning them into hulking ghosts. The sight of them assuaged some of Amalia's turmoil—Tío Francisco would have taken all the furniture and decorations if he never meant to return.

Reflecting the chairs was an oversize mirror, toward which Amalia headed.

"We used to leave secret notes to each other behind the mirror," she said, running her fingertips around the heavy gilt frame.

Out of the corner of her eye, she saw Julián leaning

against the door frame, taking in the luxurious room with his usual inscrutable expression. Heaven knew what he made of it all—the cloisonné vases that were empty now, but which usually held massive arrangements of cut flowers, the lace drapery, the oil paintings her family had collected over generations, the burled wood secretary where Amalia sat in the mornings to answer invitations to all kinds of frolics. It was a far cry from the shack where they'd spent the night.

True to Julián's unflappable nature, even in his muddy boots and shirtsleeves, he looked at home among the trappings of elegance that provided the background for Amalia's life. He picked up a silver frame from one of the side tables, his lips curling up slightly as he looked down at a portrait of Amalia. The photograph had been taken two or three years before, when she'd dressed up as Spring for one of the many dances held by her and Lucía's social club. Her unbound hair had been painstakingly decorated with tiny silk flowers, dozens of them, and in gauzy white classical robes, she looked as ethereal as a nymph. Julián seemed to think so, too, judging by his smile.

Or maybe he was inwardly laughing at all the silly things society people did to pass the time.

Amalia's covert examination of him came to a swift end when her fingertips met with the crackling of paper. Holding her breath, she teased out the scrap, hoping against hope that it wasn't some leftover note from their childhood.

"You found something?" Julián asked, coming closer. "Want me to move the mirror?"

"I don't think that'll be necessary." Amalia crowed triumphantly as she pulled out a scrap of paper. It looked like it had been torn from an envelope, and there were only two words hastily scribbled on one side—Puerto Plata.

Amalia was almost weak-kneed with relief. Not another continent, then, or even another country.

"That's your sister's handwriting?" Julián asked, glancing down at the paper.

Amalia nodded. "I have to go after them," she said, and began to pace as she worked through another plan.

Puerto Plata was on the northern coast of the island, only a few days' travel from San Pedro on the southern coast. But traveling overland had always been a chancy proposition, even with the new railroad.

One thing was immediately apparent—there was no way she could do this alone. She had never left San Pedro and she knew next to nothing about arranging a voyage, in particular one that would most certainly end in a confrontation.

"I think our best chance is to get on the next ship headed there," she said out loud. Puerto Plata was a port city, much busier than San Pedro, so it would take a while to track down Tío Francisco. "Once we're there, we— Oh." Whirling to face Julián, she gave him an apologetic look for having assumed that he would abandon all his bandit-related pursuits to run off after her sister with her. "I know I have no right to ask you for anything else, particularly as I haven't the means to compensate you for everything you've already done— yet. So I will understand if you refuse."

Before she could get any further into her request, Julián swept into a flourishing bow. "Your Highness, I would be delighted to escort you to Puerto Plata."

The smile that broke through Amalia's inner turmoil

may have been tremulous, but it was genuine. "Keep being this gallant, and you'll find yourself pressed into service as an escort the next time the governor of the province has a ball."

His expression at the prospect made Amalia burst into outright laughter. "I'd take you to the ends of the earth, but I draw the line at wearing a set of tails."

"Well, lucky for you, Puerto Plata is only on the opposite side of the island," Amalia said, hoping her matter-of-fact tone was enough to hide the frisson that had gone through her at the first part of his sentence.

She started to turn away, saying something about looking up departure schedules in the newspaper she had seen on Tío Francisco's desk. Julián halted her with a soft touch to her arm.

He was an entire head taller than she was, but he captured her face between his hands and tilted it up so that she could look into his eyes and see that his jesting tone had vanished.

Framed by his long, calloused fingers, her face felt as hot as it had out in the sun. As hot as the desire curling through her. Her lips parted, but he didn't kiss her.

"I am at your service, Amalia," he said with such blazing intensity that she found herself burning to believe him.

The logical part of her brain won out in the end. Likely, all he wanted was a bigger share of the payment she had promised him.

"Your offer is much appreciated," she said briskly, drawing back, away from his warm fingers. "And please, be assured that I will compensate you for this as soon as I can manage it."

"Yes," he said after a moment's pause. "Compensation. That's exactly what I want."

She stood, eager to put enough distance between them to quell the irrational flutters in her chest. If she had any hope of finding her sister, she couldn't let herself be distracted by this man's words, however pretty they might sound. She wouldn't be at all shocked if he was trying to flirt in the hopes of getting more money out of her.

Her mouth firmed. This was a business arrangement, not a love affair, and Amalia could not let herself forget it.

Julián strode out of the Troncosos' house as fast as if he expected someone to chase after him. *I am at your service.* The devil was wrong with him? He'd known Amalia Troncoso for all of five minutes and already he was making a fool of himself, spouting declarations of allegiance as if he were one of the medieval knights in the storybooks he'd read as a child.

Julián was the furthest thing from a storybook knight, and Amalia must have known it.

To his bemusement, she had gone to a spindly legged secretary and fished out a necklace from a tiny wooden box. "It's not extraordinarily valuable, but it should be worth enough to exchange for two cabins on the next steamer."

A simple gold chain studded with amber and ending in a delicate pendant, it, in fact, was not all that impressive as jewels went. Only the slight tremble of her lips betrayed the fact that it must have held some sentimental value.

He'd tried to refuse, forgetting for a second that he

was supposed to be a ruthless bandit. But she'd insisted. "It's all I have," she'd said, squaring her jaw. "Tio Francisco put all of the valuables we inherited from our mother into some sort of safety deposit box at the bank that we can't access. And we've already established than when it comes to actual money, I'm as penniless as an urchin."

Sighing, Julián had held out his hand. "All right, then, I'll see if I can get a good price for it."

Pulling back slightly, she frowned. "I'd really rather do it myself."

"You're a suspicious little soul, aren't you? I won't run off with your necklace, if that's what you're worried about," he'd told her, then added, smirking, "It's not really worth my while."

It was the truth, too, though she couldn't begin to know the reason why. Hopefully, she'd take it to mean that he had stolen much more valuable things.

There wasn't much time to argue and Amalia knew it, though that didn't keep her from looking annoyed as she reluctantly handed over the necklace and watched as he tucked it into the pocket of his trousers.

"I'll try to be back in less than an hour," he had said. "With passage on the next ship and whatever money's left over after I hock the necklace."

Julián would be damned if he'd do such a thing. Unlike her, he had plenty of cash—the spoils that came from being the son of a railroad tycoon. All he needed was to go fetch it.

San Pedro may have been growing into a prosperous town, but it still wasn't all that big. It didn't take too long for him to reach his rented rooms. His landlady's small house was unfashionable, but he had the whole of the second story to himself, and a private entrance via a set of wooden stairs built into the side of the house.

He thundered upstairs, and within minutes had stuffed his shaving kit and several changes of clothing into an old carpetbag. Only when his bag was packed did he unbutton his shirt, exposing his perspiring chest to the balmy breeze filtering through the shutters—and the sheaf of documents he had pilfered from her uncle's study.

He had just eased open the drawer he'd been trying to unlock when she'd rushed off to check the mirror for notes. She hadn't noticed him glancing through the papers inside. He hadn't planned on taking anything, but when he'd spotted his father's name on one of the letters, he had shoved the whole bundle inside his shirt, tightly folded and tucked securely into the waistband of his trousers.

There was no time to go through them now, but Julián meant to scour them as soon as he had a free moment. He was starting to get the distinct feeling that there was more to the situation than he'd previously thought. For her uncle to have whisked her sister away to Puerto Plata, the city of Julián's birth and where his father still lived…

Julián wasn't sure what it meant, but he knew it couldn't be good.

Wrapping the bundle of letters in one of his shirts, he buried the bundle in the bottom of his bag. And then, after extracting a stack of bank notes from his hiding place in the rafters and tossing it in with his clothes, Julián set about transforming himself into a respectable gentleman—he might not have been a real bandit, but neither was he anything resembling respectable.

The worst part of the whole thing was that he'd meant it when he'd told her he was at her service, and not just because, at the moment, her interests aligned so closely with his. She wanted to get her fortune back from her uncle, and he wanted to interfere with his father's business just as his father had interfered in his relationship.

Julián had taken one look at the pain and determination in Amalia's eyes and he'd forgotten his promise to himself to avoid new entanglements. Because as dangerous as it was to do so, she made him want to forget. That should have been alarming enough to make him abandon this entire pursuit and refuse to give another thought to anything beyond dancing with pretty women and growing a mustache.

And yet…

Julián had been a good-for-nothing all his life. He had never done anyone a scrap of good. No one had ever needed him. Until now.

Chapter Five

They were in luck. A steamer bound for New York, with a brief stop in Puerto Plata, was scheduled to leave in precisely two hours. The harried clerk had almost laughed Julián out of the ticket office when he'd asked for two cabins, and it had taken a great deal of Julián's money and charm to secure the last remaining one. No matter. He was used enough to rough living—it would be no bother to let Amalia have the cabin while he found an empty spot on deck for himself.

The Julián who returned to the Troncosos' *quinta* was a different person than the bandit who had left that morning. In an exceptionally respectable black suit, and with his hair pomaded into submission, he looked...

Well, he still looked like a rakish scoundrel, thoroughly disreputable under the black-banded Panama hat, but in this ensemble, his proximity to Amalia would cause no suspicion.

He was not only in possession of two steamer tickets; after leaving the ticket office, he had managed to acquire a gleaming black carriage that was as genteel and respectable as his suit. As the coachman rolled to a stop in front of Amalia's house, Julián hopped down and tipped his hat.

"Buenas tardes, señorita," he said, stifling a laugh as Amalia, clearly startled at being addressed by this well-dressed stranger, returned his greeting with an automatically polite one of her own.

Then she recognized his face under the shadow of his hat's brim. Her lips parted in surprise. *"Julián?"*

"In the freshly bathed flesh."

She took a step toward him as hesitantly as if he had truly been a stranger. His breath caught as her fingers fluttered up to graze his jaw, which suddenly felt far more naked than the absence of a few bristles could account for. "You shaved," she said softly.

Why was his mouth dry all of a sudden? "I did," he said in a raspy voice. Julián cleared his throat. "Couldn't let you board the steamer on the arm of an unkempt ruffian."

Her eyes were shaded by her own hat brim, and by the long sweep of her lashes. "I liked the unkempt ruffian," she said, and her lips moved into a sudden curve. "And I find I also quite like this schoolteacher ensemble. All that's missing is a pair of spectacles."

"Yes, well, you don't look half bad yourself. Nary a streak of mud to be seen."

There was nothing practical about her traveling costume. The short-sleeved suit was a delicate pale pink, trimmed with braids and frills and buttons. From the neckline of the jacket peeked out a scrap of gossamer that Julián supposed was meant to be a blouse. Simple pearl earrings frosted the tips of her ears, behind which danced enticing little curls. Even her hat looked like something that had been made in a confectionary shop, decorated as it was with pink satin and miniature flowers.

Julián's compliment was by no means inspired, but she met it with a gracious nod. "Shall we go? It's a long ride to the docks."

Evidently, she hadn't realized that the carriage waiting less than a meter away was to convey them to their destination. "Do you really think I'd make you ride a horse in that getup?" Julián asked. He signaled to the coachman to take the valises at Amalia's feet, which the other man did promptly. "May I ask why you packed as though you're going on a pleasure cruise instead of a rescue mission?"

"We have no idea what the rescue mission will entail. Better to be prepared for all eventualities," she said, shrugging.

"Looks like you're prepared for a second great flood."

"I am nothing if not thorough." The smile she flashed him belied her haughty tone.

Julián offered her his hand, and she took it with the air of someone who had never gotten into a carriage without being helped up.

It was an open carriage, with a short canopy to keep the sun from broiling the tops of their heads. Julián asked the coachman to return them to the docks, then went around to the other side and leaped inside in a single bound to find Amalia frowning suspiciously as she examined the plush upholstery.

"Julián," she said, "why are we riding on the Gonzalezes' carriage?" At his uncomprehending look, she elaborated. "I recognized it by that little stain over there. The boys are fond of port and they have a dreadful habit of bringing their wineglasses along when we go on drives after dinner. There's a matching stain on my favorite evening gown," she added, looking aggrieved.

Julián hid a smile of amusement. "Oh, I borrowed it," he said airily.

"Borrowed?" She narrowed her eyes. "Are you using that word in the traditional sense?"

He shrugged. "If by that you mean that I convinced their coachman that I was the visiting Frenchman he'd been sent to pick up. But it should be all right. We're headed directly back to the docks, after all. By the time they discover my deception, we'll have boarded the ship."

"I can't say I approve of your methods, but I am grateful at not having to walk all the way there."

"I should think so, considering the five tons you're carrying in those valises of yours." Julián sat back, listening to the clatter of the wheels as they set off at a brisk pace. The Gonzalezes' carriage was a roomy one, intended for a family, which left plenty of space between him and Amalia.

Or that would have been the case, had she not been battling with the wind as it tugged artfully arranged ringlets out from under her hat. Well armed with hairpins, she held her elbows extended like a set of wings that grazed Julián with every bump and jolt of the carriage. Until a particular hard jolt sent her careening toward him, and the word *grazed* was no longer applicable.

"I'm so sorry," she said, pulling herself upright. "The

Gonzalezes' carriage has a lot to recommend it, but I don't think I can say the same for their coachman."

Julián didn't laugh so much as wheeze, rubbing the spot on his chest where her elbow had dug in. "It's fine," he said when he had regained his breath. "Here. Let me help you."

She hesitated for a second, peering out at the street they were speeding through. This close to lunchtime, there were no passersby to be seen. "I— All right."

Unpinning her hat and holding it on her lap, she turned slightly so that her back was to Julián. He disposed of her hairpins by easing them out and dropping them on her upturned palm, then raked a hand through brown locks that were as unruly and willful as she was. The sensation of them slipping against his rough palm was almost more intimate than the kiss they had shared the day before. A deep longing to caress those silky curls until they reached their destination almost overwhelmed Julián—but he knew better than to surrender to it. Grimly pushing it down, he made himself focus on the matter at hand.

Taking care to smooth back the shorter curls in the front that had most plagued her, he wound the long mass of her hair into an efficient twist at the nape of her neck and secured it with the pins he had removed. It wasn't a work of art by any means, but at least it would keep her hair out of her eyes.

"What do you think? Can I list hairdressing among my many accomplishments?"

"Well, you certainly can't add modesty to the list," she said, laughing as she returned her hat to its rightful place.

"I've never been partial to it," Julián admitted.

"Modesty, I mean. It's always struck me as insincere. If I'm good at something, why not take pride in it?" He was veering into perilously earnest territory, which required as sharp a left turn as the coachman had just made. Lounging back against the seat, he folded his arms behind his head. "Take my extraordinary talents in the art of dressing ladies' hairs."

He snuck a peek at Amalia and came away with the distinct impression that she was seeing clear through him and wasn't at all impressed.

"Why do you do that?" she inquired.

Julián was the picture of innocence as he looked down at himself. "Do what? I can assure you, Your Highness, I spend most days striving to do nothing at all."

She gave an impatient wave of her hand. "Act like a rascal when you and I both know you're not."

"On the contrary," he said softly, feeling the smirk slide from his lips. "I'm the worst kind of rascal you could ever meet. The sooner you realize that, the better it'll be for you."

If she had any sort of response to that, it was lost as the carriage reached San Pedro's bustling port. The rattle of carts heavy with barrels and crates and the din of men hurrying back and forth as they loaded freight into one ship's cargo hold and out of another was familiar to Julián's ears.

He would have never predicted that he'd be boarding another steamship so soon after his return from Puerto Rico, where he'd spent much of the past year. This time, at least, he wasn't running off with his tail between his legs and bitterness swirling in his heart.

This time he was on his way to seek all the answers he hadn't realized he needed.

This time he was going home.

The port was crowded with great merchant ships flying French, American, German and Haitian flags, their masts rising into the clear blue sky in a way that reminded Amalia of the mills past which she and Julián had ridden that morning. Instead of burnt sugar, though, the air around her was redolent with the scent of salt. The Caribbean Sea, undulating gently behind the steamer, reflected the intense blue of the sky.

Amalia's knees felt oddly liquefied as she walked up the gangplank, her fingers so tight around Julián's forearm that she would have worried about bruising him if all her attention hadn't been on the possibility of stumbling in her heeled pumps and plummeting to the water below. She hadn't normally a fear of heights, and was tempted to attribute this sudden lack of stability to Julián's having unnerved her with his gentleness in the carriage. She could still feel his fingers sliding through her hair, brushing her scalp and the back of her neck and sending tingles all down her body.

It was almost more than she could bear. And then to turn around just to witness his little display of unfeeling insouciance…

It reminded Amalia of why she refused to trust most men, but especially the young, handsome kind. Bandit or not, he was just like all the others.

Amalia shouldn't have cared. She *didn't*.

She stepped off the gangplank and onto the steamship, and the relative steadiness of the boards under her feet firmed up her knees as well as her resolve.

Disentangling herself from Julián's arm, she marched up to the uniformed officer who was checking off passengers against the list cradled in the crook of his arm.

When she gave him her name, he responded with a courteous, "Your checks, *señora*?"

Checks? Amalia stared at him, so nonplussed that she forgot to correct him. A woman had to be married to be called *señora*—though perhaps he'd mistaken Julián for her husband.

"Here are your luggage, berth and meal checks," Julián said smoothly, pressing several rectangles into her hand. "I'm sorry. I should have given them to you earlier."

It only took a few moments for the officer to confirm their tickets against his list. Then he beckoned to one of the men who stood to one side like porters or stewards.

"I'll show you to your cabin, *señora*, *señor*," the steward said. Clyde-Mallory was an American line, but the men who crewed the steamers on the southern route seemed to speak proficient Spanish.

"Cabin?" Amalia asked, turning to Julián.

"There was only one left," Julián murmured into her ear. "It's all right. I'll find accommodations elsewhere."

Amalia frowned, but said nothing as she followed the steward down a narrow hallway. Her bedroom for the single night it would take to go around the eastern coast of the island was about the size of the dressing room she and Lucía shared at home; it was, however, far better appointed than she'd expected. Paneled walls, a double bed covered in a gleaming satin coverlet and even a polished mahogany-and-marble washstand with an oval mirror.

"Your luggage will be up shortly," the steward said and withdrew, looking pleased at the sizable tip Julián had discreetly tucked into his palm.

Julián himself lingered by the door, his hands in his pockets. "I'll leave you to get settled in. I'll be out on the deck if you need me."

"The deck? Is that where you're planning to sleep?"

Julián shrugged. "Or in the lounge. There's bound to be one on a ship this big. It won't be the first time I've slept on a chair."

"Sounds comfortable," Amalia replied with studied blandness.

There it was, that infamous smirk of his. "You're sure you don't want to offer me a corner of that big bed?"

Placing a hand on his shoulder, Amalia maneuvered him to just outside the doorway. "Not if you were the last bandit left on earth," she said sweetly and closed the door in his face.

It wasn't long before her luggage was brought up by yet another crisply uniformed man. As he stacked the valises along one wall, she dug furtively into her handbag for a tip and, to her embarrassment, was only able to come up with a handful of copper *cheles*. The low-denomination coins must have been left over from the last time she and Lucía had convinced the housekeeper to part with a fraction of the marketing money for them to buy sweets for the household—a necessary ruse when their uncle generally refused to let the sisters handle money, and kept close track of everything they charged to his account at the various stores in town. Both Lucía and the housekeeper had an insatiable sweet tooth, so the arrangement worked to both their benefit.

To Amalia, there was no benefit at all in the whole thing. She'd have much rather earned those coins herself than have to scrabble or beg her uncle for them. In fact, she had been seriously considering abandoning her plan in its entirety and seeking employment in Europe when she managed to spirit Lucía there.

But of course, she would need money to do *that*. What an infuriating world this was.

There was also the matter of Julián's payment—the reason he had agreed to take her halfway around the island. Another man would have cut his losses and made do with the sum fetched by her mother's necklace. The fact that he hadn't must mean that he expected far greater recompense from Amalia. After all the trouble he'd gone to to help her, she would be damned if she didn't deliver it.

Dropping the few paltry coins into the porter's hand with a murmured apology, she closed the door behind him.

The shortness of their time aboard meant that there was no real need to unpack, save for her nightdress and something to wear at dinner. After laying out a fresh dress for the next day and putting her little wood-and-velvet toiletries case in the adjoining lavatory, Amalia ventured out to the deck.

The wind was blowing in earnest here. Amalia patted the back of her head to assure herself that all was in order, and found that Julián had done as good a job on securing her hair as he'd done undoing every lock in his path that morning. There seemed to be nothing his quick, clever fingers couldn't do.

Before Amalia could pursue that singularly intriguing line of thought, the man in question came into view, lounging against the railing as if it were the bar of some disreputable tavern.

Even in his sober black suit, Julián stood out from the respectable crowd strolling on the deck. A wolf in sheep's clothing was still a wolf, after all. What he wore didn't matter—his true nature was written on the long, powerful lines of his body and the rakishness of his smile as he turned to look at Amalia crossing the deck to where he stood.

Her step didn't falter, but it felt as though her heart did. With the exception of her younger sister, had anyone ever watched her approach with such unbridled welcome in their smile? Another pang went through her at the sudden realization that sometime in the next few days, whenever she finally found Lucía, she and Julián would probably part ways. And when they did... who would look at her with this much joy? With such wicked humor sparkling in his eyes? Who would caress her hair like it was made out of silk or spun gold?

She'd get used to doing without it, as she had all her life. Julián had only been in it for two days, after all.

"I knew you would change your mind about letting me into your bed," he remarked when she reached him, low enough to avoid being overheard by the other passengers.

"As I recall it, you were the one who declined the honor yesterday. Did no one ever tell you that life rarely gives second chances?"

A gull soared overhead, its shadow flickering in Julián's dark eyes. "No," he said. "No one ever did."

The shadow was gone before she could tell if it had been real or not. Mildly disconcerted, Amalia tried not to show it. "Well, even gently reared young ladies get tired of extending the same invitation multiple times."

The easy grin was back, though Amalia could tell it wasn't altogether genuine. "I'll have you know no one ever gets tired of inviting me into their bed."

She was not the most practiced flirt, and her heart jumped inside her chest when she stepped closer to Julián and trailed a fingertip over the line of buttons on his waistcoat. "And what exactly would you do if you were in mine?"

"Are you really sure you want to know?" he asked, capturing her hand like it was some sort of prey and keeping it captive in his.

The murmur of the crowd receded and for a long moment, all Amalia could hear was Julián's harsh breaths, underlaid by the restless rolling of the waves and the purr of the steam engines beneath their feet.

The tip of her tongue stole out and swept over her lower lip. His gaze dropped to track its progress with such scorching intensity, it was almost as if she was being kissed by him again. Her body remembered all too well how it had felt to be in his arms. As her heartbeat quickened and her limbs flooded with a warmth that had nothing to do with the sunlight bearing down on them, it was all Amalia could do to keep herself from straining toward him.

He seemed to be having the same problem.

His fingers grew tighter around hers. Not enough to cause her pain, but enough for her to know that he was as reluctant to let go as she was.

With his free hand, he brushed the curve of her jaw, following its contour all the way to the hollow behind her ear. Suppressing a shiver, Amalia leaned into his touch. It was almost worrying, this hunger she felt around Julián, this desperate craving for his hands, his mouth. She wanted to seize fistfuls of his shirt, or his hair, and pull her to him until there wasn't a breath of space left between them.

If he was a wolf, she wanted to be devoured.

"Sleep," Julián said, his voice rough. It took a second for Amalia to remember the question he was answering. Then his eyebrow quirked up, and he released her hand to scrape back his hair, and the tension that had been mounting between them was suddenly broken. "I haven't slept in a proper bed in days."

"Fair enough." She stepped back, feeling flushed from the sun and the laughter and the provocative turn of the conversation. "I could use a little rest myself. It's been…a most interesting couple of days."

And there were many more to go. Whatever Amalia had started by orchestrating the *rapto*, it was only just beginning.

She turned to look out into the port and the city beyond it. The familiar sights of San Pedro were rendered strange from this vantage point. Strange and beautiful. The oddly elegant lines of the port, the lines of houses trailing along the edge of the river and unfurling into two- and three-story buildings farther inland, the great smokestacks jutting into the sky…

The deck lurched beneath her, making Amalia stumble gracelessly against Julián.

He caught her by the elbow, his long fingers firm on the bare skin below the cuff of her short-sleeved jacket. "Steady there. You'll get your sea legs soon enough."

"Will I? I've never been on a ship before," she admitted.

"Never?" he asked, sounding surprised. "I thought society people spent their lives flitting off to Paris to order new frocks and up to New York for, I don't know, shoelaces."

"Not us. Tio Francisco always claimed to be too busy with work."

Skepticism was written all over the arch of his eyebrow. "But surely you have plenty of friends who plan house parties at their country homes or excursions to the seaside."

Amalia shook her head. "My uncle won't hear of us accepting any invitations that take us out of town, no matter how many respectable matrons are to be in attendance. He has a horror of letting us out of his sight—or among people who might have ulterior motives for befriending us." She frowned. "Or at least, that's what he claims. To hear him speak, half the people in San Pedro are after our money. In any case, I haven't been…anywhere."

"Did you want to?"

"It would have been nice to see the world. It *will* be."

The shudder of engines beneath their feet intensified and, within minutes, the ship started to move. Amalia's fingers tightened reflexively on the white railing, even though the metal was uncomfortably warm from the sun.

Julián glanced over, but remained where he was standing. "Well, you're going somewhere now."

"I am, aren't I?"

Keeping the sun from shining would have been easier than keeping her anxiety at bay. The city of her birth was receding into the distance, far quicker than she'd expected. Amalia found herself leaning forward, as if she could make the ship move faster through sheer force of will. Before long all she could see of shore were white beaches and palm trees rising out of great tangles of vegetation.

A sidelong glance at Julián, who had fallen silent, revealed that he was leaning against the railing with his eyes closed, his straight, longish hair buffeting in the wind. For a fleeting moment Amalia wondered what it would be like to unpin her own hair and join him. The other passengers around her would find it scandalous, certainly. Julián would get a kick out of it. And Amalia herself?

To her, it would feel like freedom.

Julián's eyes opened slowly and he turned to meet her gaze, the corners of his lips already curling into a smile in response to whatever he saw on her face.

And though she was fully aware of all the reasons why she shouldn't, Amalia tilted up her head and kissed him.

Julián sank into the kiss like his body had known it was just a matter of time until it happened again.

Like it had been inevitable.

His arm settled around Amalia's waist. She had risen to her tiptoes in order to reach his mouth, and with the engines rumbling underfoot, steadying her was only the polite thing to do. Mindful of the crowd around them, he didn't crush her against his chest or plunge his fingers into her firmly coiled hair. As for bending her over the railing and having his wicked way with her...

His arm tightened around her as he considered the possibility. Amalia replied with an encouraging little moan against his lips, and Julián applied himself to the task of making her do it again. Very lightly, he nibbled on her lower lip. Her hands, which had been cradling his face, slid down to clench on his lapels.

Even in a lifetime of being scandalous and improper, Julián had never done anything this self-indulgent. It felt damn good—then again, indulging always did. That was why he did it so often. Not to besmirch his family's name, as some of them liked to claim.

Amalia was an enthusiastic kisser, and a skilled one. Julián, who had made sport of every willing widow who'd crossed his path, had no patience for fumblers. Her mouth on his was hot and sure, and it tasted like the salt-tinged breeze whipping around his head and—

"Amalia Troncoso! Is it really you?"

Julián very nearly swore out loud as a tremulous feminine voice intruded into the kiss. In fact, he wasn't altogether sure he hadn't.

The gray-haired woman standing before them wore a smile that flickered on and off like a faultily wired electric lamp as she shifted her gaze from Amalia to Julián. Amalia composed herself enough for a polite greeting, but all Julián could manage was a baring of his teeth that made the woman blink uncertainly.

"And this must be your new husband," she said. At Amalia's look of surprise, she elaborated. "I hope I'm not speaking out of turn, but your uncle mentioned something yesterday about your having…eloped."

Amalia looked close to panic in the face of the older woman's scrutiny. Julián couldn't blame her—from his own experience, he knew how unpleasant it was to find out just how easily your own relations could cast you aside. And Amalia's uncle hadn't just failed to rescue her from a presumed bandit, he'd also thrown her reputation into the garbage pail.

"Oh, Doña María, I..." Amalia licked her lips, which Julián was pleased to notice were dusky from the pressure of his own mouth. "Well..."

Briefly compressing his own lips in a silent plea for patience, Julián extended his hand. "Julián Fuentes, Doña María," he said, echoing the name Amalia had just used. "Enchanting to meet you."

A flash of motion at the corner of his eye made him glance toward Amalia. Ah, of course. He'd never told her his last name. She didn't appear to recognize it as belonging to one of her uncle's business connections, though of course there was no real reason why she should. With each moment that passed, it was becoming more and more evident to Julián that Amalia had been completely shut out of her uncle's business affairs.

It didn't necessarily mean that this whole pretense had been in vain. If not for her, he would have never gotten access to her uncle's desk and the correspondence he had stolen from it. Hopefully, the contents of those letters would be enough for him to start piecing together his father's business with Amalia's uncle. And hopefully, *that* would give Julián some insight on why his father had destroyed Julián's relationship with Concepción.

Mollified by the civility of his greeting, the older lady seemed to gather impulse. She stepped closer and laid a confiding hand on Amalia's arm. "I told my sister yesterday—you remember my dear sister Carmen, don't you? Well, I told her yesterday that I didn't see how it could be at all possible that such a well-brought-up girl like yourself could have done something so scandalous. After all your dear uncle sacrificed to raise you girls."

Julián almost snorted out loud. "An elopement? There must be some confusion, Doña María," he said with scrupulous politeness, giving her one of the boyish grins that made older women fall into puddles at his feet. He took Amalia's hand. "Amalia and I have been engaged for a year. Only I've been in Puerto Rico on business for almost as long. It wasn't until several days ago that I was able to return and I'm sure you will understand, as did Don Francisco, that I simply couldn't wait a moment longer to be wed to my beloved."

He was laying it on a little too thickly, but the gray-haired woman was lapping it all up. "I did tell my sister that I was sure there was not even a hint of impropriety to the whole thing." She turned to Amalia, who was looking decidedly less delighted with Julián's prevarications. "My dear, you must be delirious with happiness. Won't you let me see the ring?" As an aside to Julián, she added, "I have yet to meet a newlywed who isn't excited to show off her wedding ring."

Amalia's fingers clenched around Julián's. "Oh, I'm afraid I—"

Watching her flounder was too painful to his inner bandit. Julián stepped in smoothly, reaching into the inner pocket of his jacket. "I have it right here, *mi cielo*. I put it away earlier—for safekeeping, you know. One can never be too careful when traveling," he explained to Doña María, who gave a vigorous nod in agreement.

The diamond ring he extracted from his pocket would have been impressive in the dull light of a single candle. On the deck of a steamer, with the faceted stones catching the sunlight and not a scrap of a shadow to dull its brilliance, it was…

"Astonishing," gasped Doña María, inching closer for a good gawk.

Ignoring her, Julián slipped the slender gold band onto Amalia's finger. She was very quiet as he did it, and when he lifted her hand for an impulsive kiss that wasn't entirely for the older woman's benefit, her eyes gleamed out at him from under the brim of her hat. She didn't look gleeful or even relieved. She looked troubled.

Julián lowered her hand, though he kept their fingers lightly linked.

The speculative gleam that had come into Doña María's eye at the appearance of the ring didn't fade as she lingered over their conversation, obviously trying to find out more about Julián and his business in Puerto Rico. As he really *had* spent most of the past year in Ponce, he found it no trouble to answer her many questions. Her many, *many* questions.

It was no use resisting the older woman's inquisitiveness. And in any case, from the dark looks emanating out from under Amalia's hat brim, Julián was fairly certain that they would not be returning to their earlier occupation.

Something about the ring had clearly troubled her, and Julián had no idea why. It was only a bauble—albeit an enormously expensive one. No matter. She'd talk when she was ready. In the short time Julián had known her, Amalia hadn't struck him as someone who would hold back on anything that was bothering her.

Sure enough, the moment Doña María was beckoned by her traveling companions and she was forced to abandon her line of inquiry, Amalia turned to Julián. "You got me a ring?"

Never had Julián's shoulder risen into a more casual shrug. "I had it lying around and I figured it might come in handy."

"I should give it back to you," she said, twisting it off her slender finger. "I would have liked to think that I'd prepared for all eventualities, but this was not something I imagined happening."

He held his hand up. "You can keep that for now," he said offhandedly. "In case we run into her again."

"I don't… I shouldn't feel comfortable wearing the spoils of banditry." She gave a little shake of her head, then said, "I know it's silly for me to object to it now, after I've spent all day benefiting from your, ah, skills, but I can't in good conscience wear what is most likely stolen property. Whichever poor woman you took this from—"

Julián's lips twisted into a smile. "The ring was my mother's, Your Highness. But you could say that procuring it was my first attempt at banditry, so you're not entirely wrong. And the least we say about how she came by it, the better."

That made it sound like his mother was an outlaw who rode around robbing people on moonlit roads. At least it made for a better story than the truth—the ring had been a wedding present from his father, who was so bloodthirsty in business that he put real bandits to shame.

Julián watched Amalia's eyes widen.

"You haven't said much about your family," she ventured.

"And I don't mean to. My father and cousin are both

scoundrels—and so am I. My mother deserved better. She was...happiness itself. The kind of person who could find fun in the dreariest of days." And the only person who could coax laughs out of his father. Julián couldn't remember the last time he'd heard his father express any kind of joy. "She loved taking me on all kinds of outings, always somewhere different. Except on Friday afternoons, when we always went to her favorite hotel for lunch. We would sit in the courtyard and compete over who could come up with the silliest jokes or the worst riddles."

The entire household had lost its color when she died. Julián's father, never the warmest of men, grew more absorbed in his work than ever, leaving Julián to deal with his cousin on his own.

"Has she been gone long?" Amalia asked, looking sympathetic.

"She died when I was six. Railroad accident," he added curtly. Before she had any brilliant ideas about trying to comfort him, he turned from her and folded his arms over the railing. "It was a long time ago. I don't remember much."

A few minutes passed before Amalia spoke up again. "I lost my mother to a fever. I was older, though—twelve."

Old enough to have gotten to know her. Julián didn't know which was worse. The few memories he had of his own mother were bad enough—how much worse would it be if he could remember her better?

"I'm sorry," he said, softening his tone.

Julián had spent enough time batting away inconvenient swells of feeling that he was fairly accomplished at it by now. He'd built an entire fortress to keep them out. But as hard as he tried to shore up his walls, something about Amalia knocked down all his defenses.

He wasn't used to feeling so off balance, at least not where women were concerned. Amalia was not the only one to probe into corners of his life that he'd rather not even think about, but whereas he'd been able to satisfy the others with shallow explanations or distractions, he had a feeling that this tenacious heiress would not be put off so easily.

Julián kept his gaze on the waves cresting in the distance. He didn't have to look to know that Amalia was giving him one of her piercing looks.

"Will you kindly stop scrutinizing me and just ask whatever it is you want to ask?"

If she was surprised by his bluntness, she didn't show it. As if she'd only been waiting for an invitation, she promptly said, "If you've never broken the law, and you don't go around stealing exquisite jewelry from women, what is it that you actually do?"

Julián turned to look at her; at her dark eyes, ringed by impossibly long lashes; at the well-formed lips that fit so well against his own. He was as drawn to her as she so clearly was to him, but he'd be damned if he'd let her break through what remained of his walls.

With a gesture that bordered on impudent, he chucked her under the chin and wasn't surprised when she pulled away, her back rigid. "That, Your Highness," he said with a smirk, "is none of your business."

Chapter Six

Amalia returned to her cabin to freshen up before dinner. The second the door closed behind her, she divested herself of her jacket, hat and shoes, and cast a longing glance at the neatly made bed. Surely, she had plenty of time to lie down for a few minutes. Unused to being on horseback for so long, her thighs ached from the long ride into town that morning. All the muscles in her upper back, too, seemed to have clenched tightly in response to the day's stress.

The water in the lavatory's basin was as refreshing on her face as the thin layer of cold cream she applied to her nose and cheeks. After undoing the buttons of her blouse, she loosened her corset and shuffled barefoot back into the bedroom.

She let out a sigh of pure, contented bliss as she lay on top of the quilted satin bedcovers and stretched out her bare feet. The mattress was almost as good as the one she had back home, and the down pillows were fluffier than the pink-tinged clouds outside her cabin's tiny window. Curling up onto her side with one of the delightful pillows tucked into the crook of her neck, Amalia fell into a deep sleep.

When her eyelashes finally fluttered open, the blazing sky had turned black and her pillow was awash in moonlight. Groggily, she propped herself up on her elbow. A glance at the clock on the paneled wall told her that she'd slept clear through dinner. It was so close to midnight that she might as well finish undressing and try to fall back to sleep—heaven knew she needed the rest. But she was so hollow with hunger, she was sure it would keep her awake for hours.

Amalia put herself back together, making sure to add a dab of violet-scented toilette water behind her ears before venturing out of her cabin in search of a steward or someone who might be able to find her something to eat.

It was galling. Amalia never left anything to chance and she hated to rely on anyone else. If she'd been thinking clearly, she would have asked Ana to pack her some *cazabe* before leaving. That it hadn't occurred to her made Amalia wonder what else she had missed in her haste.

Brass sconces placed at intervals down the quiet, empty hallway shone their weak light on the carpet as Amalia made her way to the grand staircase. At its foot were the social areas—namely, the lounge and dining room—that she and Julián had explored earlier that afternoon, after their kiss had been interrupted by Doña María and he'd rebuffed her attempt to satisfy her growing curiosity about him.

It served her right—however intriguing she found Julián, she knew better than to probe into his private life. Just because she'd invited him into her business didn't mean she had to go poking into his. And in any case, as she had to keep reminding herself, it wasn't like she would ever see him again when this was all over.

A good thing, too, because merely being around him made her act as flighty as a leaf dancing in the wind.

Amalia didn't know what had come over her earlier. It was one thing to kiss a man, even a bandit, in a secluded shack where there was no chance of being spotted. Doing so on the deck of a ship, in full view of all the other passengers *and* one of the biggest gossips in San Pedro? Even with all those people around them, she had been a hair's breadth away from losing her head entirely.

It wasn't just bold; it was reckless. And that was something Amalia couldn't afford to be, not with so much on the line.

Still, she was finding it hard to muster up sufficient repentance for her impulsive gesture. The searing memory of his lips on hers was cause alone, never mind the way he'd held her, steadying her as if he knew that feeling his mouth on hers made her limbs quiver as if they'd been turned to flan.

Even now, as she traipsed through the steamer's darkened interior, she was aware of a slight tremble in her knees.

The dining room's double wooden doors were locked, but there was a lamp burning in the lounge opposite, so Amalia changed courses. Through the panes of glass set into its doors, she could see the richly appointed room, paneled like her cabin, and filled with sumptuously upholstered armchairs and gleaming lamps with fringed silk shades.

Julián lay in an elegant sprawl in one of the armchairs, his head pillowed on his folded jacket, unaware of the steward striding toward him.

"Excuse me, *señor*," the steward said, shaking Julián's shoulder. "I'm afraid you can't sleep here."

Julián's head jerked up, and he was halfway off his seat before Amalia could draw in a breath. From where she stood, it looked like it took him a moment to recognize the other man as a steward. When he did, a blink was all it took for him to shed his bellicose expression for an apologetic smile.

"I'm sorry," he told the steward, running a hand through his messy hair. "I'm afraid my wife and I had a little disagreement and she was adamant about my not returning to the cabin. You must be used to such things, I imagine. Is there a place for exiled husbands to pass the night?"

"There isn't one. You'll have to return to your own cabin," the steward said firmly.

"It's all right, darling," Amalia said, striding into the light. "I have come to forgive you."

Relief flickered over both the men's faces, but not for long. Facing the steward, Amalia said, "I hate to bother you, *caballero*, but I was wondering if there was a way for me to get a bite to eat."

"Not until breakfast, *señora*. The galley is closed this time of night."

She'd been afraid of just that. Amalia's hollow stomach sank. "And there's no way..."

The steward started shaking his head before she had even finished talking. "They lock the doors when the dinner service is over. I could bring you a pitcher of water, if you like, but..."

Amalia glanced at Julián, who was busily folding his jacket over his arm. She had no doubt that he could have charmed or wheedled the gray-haired steward into finding her something to eat, but Julián didn't offer so much as a pleading look. It was the suspiciously bright glint in his eyes that made her tell the steward, "That's all right. Thank you, anyway."

He replied with a polite murmur, stepping away but not leaving the lounge. Evidently, he wasn't about to risk having anyone else fall asleep there. Under the steward's watchful gaze, Amalia took the arm Julián held out to her and followed him to the staircase.

They were almost out of sight of the lounge's glass-and-wood doors when Julián jerked his head to one side. "Come this way. I know a shortcut."

It turned out to be a plain service door leading to an even plainer set of metal stairs. Their footsteps echoed in the enclosed space.

Amalia peered down, feeling a rush of excitement. "We're going to sneak into the kitchen, aren't we? The galley, I mean."

"What makes you think that?" he asked, raising his eyebrows in mock outrage at her suggestion.

"Because you're an expert at unlocking things and I'm *famished*. Did you go in to dinner?"

He nodded. "I knocked at your door twice, but you didn't answer. I should have saved you a roll or something. This way."

They turned into a nondescript hallway, narrower than the ones above and much plainer, save for the visible rivets and pipes running along the closed doors. One more turn and they reached a set of double doors with round windows like portholes set into each side.

"This is it, I think," Julián said in a low voice, reaching into his jacket as he bent over the lock. "I did a little exploring of my own after we parted."

In the dim lamplight, his wink was a mere flicker. It was enough, however, to make Amalia's chest fizz and pop with champagne bubbles. To quell it, she tapped her foot soundlessly against the floor in imitation of one of the lively tunes her sister enjoyed composing.

He glanced at her over his shoulder. "Are you having second thoughts?"

Amalia shook her head. "Wondering how you learned to pick locks."

"As with all my skills, it's the product of a misspent youth," he answered, flashing her a smile.

"You spent your youth breaking into locked rooms?"

"Breaking out of them, actually. For a handful of years, my cousin Victor found it great fun to lock me in my father's office, which we were prohibited from entering. My father would find me hours later and roar at the intrusion." He shrugged. "Eventually, I learned how to let myself out. Victor tried to lock me out of the house on more than one occasion, but I could climb trees before I learned to read, so that was never a problem." He paused. "Except for the time a branch snapped and I broke my arm."

Julián had said so little about himself that Amalia was tempted to hold her breath, lest the sound remind him that she was still there. Still, she couldn't help but ask, "How old were you?"

"Seven or eight or so." He must have read the horror in Amalia's expression, because he shrugged. "Little boys are beastly like that. Ahh, here we go."

After another second of careful maneuvering, the

mechanisms holding the door shut sprang free. As it swung open, Amalia reflected that she'd have undoubtedly done the same if she'd been the one receiving such attention from his skillful hands.

The thought flooded her with heat as she crossed the threshold. It was soon replaced by a more prosaic sort of hunger as she took in the gleaming moonlit surfaces. If she had expected the remains of the dinner banquet, she was sorely mistaken. There wasn't so much as a grain of salt to be seen.

The ghost of every onion and bulb of garlic that had ever been chopped in the cramped galley hung in the air in a thick, savory miasma that made her stomach rumble in earnest.

Julián didn't seem fazed by the cupboards, which had been fastened shut with metal latches. Amalia peered over his shoulder as he swung open one door and studied the neat metal canisters lining the shelves.

"There's nothing to eat," she said in dismay.

"There will be," he said with a confidence Amalia found unwarranted, given his struggles with the plantain soup the night before. "Take a seat, Your Highness, and leave the cooking to me."

"A seat?" Amalia echoed, looking doubtfully at the stoves and cupboards.

Strong fingers grasped her waist and she found herself being swung atop the pristine work surface.

"How's that for a throne?" Julián flashed her a wicked grin before turning around to continue rooting through the canisters. "How does a Spanish *tortilla* sound? I think I can manage that."

She raised an eyebrow. "Can you?"

Julián's arms were laden when he stepped away

from the cupboard, kicking the door shut behind him. He'd found a covered plate crammed with rolls, several eggs, a green pepper and a potato. Amalia seized a roll and began nibbling at it.

He reached behind her for a bowl and began cracking the eggs with surprising proficiency. "As it happens, I was taught by a beautiful girl from Sevilla I used to…be acquainted with. Here," he added, handing her the bowl and a fork. "Beat the eggs while I chop the potatoes."

Amalia set the roll aside and dipped the tines into one of the yolks, swirling it around. "I suppose you're acquainted with a great many beautiful girls from Sevilla," she remarked.

"Quite a few."

"Oh? Are they aware of each other's existence?"

He made quick work of the pepper, chopping it into thin strips. "All my paramours know what they're getting into. I have dalliances, Amalia. A great many of them. It's fun for both parties, and when it stops being fun…" He shrugged. "We both move on. I've never cared to form attachments."

"I didn't realize it was possible," she said. "To be intimate with someone without growing attached, I mean. Somehow, I'd imagined…"

He grunted. "Yes, well, plenty of people can manage it. Some even prefer it."

Amalia thought she might. To let herself succumb to temptation without the fear that her heart would betray her and she would find herself trapped. It sounded like the sort of pragmatic arrangement that would suit her just fine.

The dull thud of the knife striking against the wooden

cutting board ceased for a moment as he cast a sideways glance at her and frowned at her lackluster egg beating. "You'll have to put more energy than that into it, Your Highness. Like this."

Instead of taking the bowl, his fingers closed around hers, warm and strong and sure as he guided her hand into a brisk pace. His touch was as intoxicating as a second glass of Veuve Clicquot. Or a third or a fourth.

Heat bloomed in Amalia's cheeks. She could feel it rising from where their hands touched, all along her arm, curling over her shoulder and neck like the ghost of a touch. She had left off her hat and jacket, and the delicate silk organza of her blouse felt like too flimsy a barrier.

Then again, she would have felt the same if she'd worn a suit of armor. She didn't know what it was about Julián that made all her barriers feel as thin as her blouse.

His mother's ring—if that was what it truly was—still glinted on her finger. The large diamond at its center, and the two smaller ones flanking it, flashed in the low light as their tangled hands moved faster and faster, until his fingers tightened suddenly around hers.

"Devil take me, but I should really like to kiss you again," Julián said roughly.

With trembling fingers, Amalia set the beaten eggs aside. Her heart started to pound. "Why don't you?"

His lips found the hollow behind her ear. It was yearning, she realized. The curling warmth that flared to life whenever Julián was near. Sometime in the past two days her body had begun longing for his touch, and the few embraces they had shared were not enough to satisfy that craving. She wanted more.

She needed more.

Amalia found Julián's lips, thinking that he kissed like he moved—with deliberation, with confidence that bordered on arrogance and with a great deal of grace. He was holding her lightly by the waist, as he had earlier, only now his hands were proving more adventurous as they roamed to the small of her back and explored the hard edges of her corset.

The questing touch thrilled her. She could have no more asked him to stop touching her than she could have asked the waves to stop their ceaseless rolling or her heart to stop beating.

Dimly, she realized that her own fingers were gripping the edge of the work surface. She loosened her grip and wound her arms around his neck instead. This time she was the one who was pulling him close, desperate to feel the hard, lean lines of his body against her.

Looking at Amalia felt like falling.

Julián had tumbled from his perch on a high branch once. For a bare handful of seconds, falling had been as exhilarating as he'd imagined flying would be.

Then he'd struck the ground. As the sickening pain spread from the arm he'd broken and through the rest of his body, he'd dazedly promised himself that he would climb every tree in the grounds until he was good enough at it that he would never fall again. And he had. He'd become so damn good at climbing he'd spent half his boyhood escaping his cousin Victor's torments by shimmying up the slim trunks of palm trees.

Maybe swearing off women had been a wrong idea.

Maybe what he needed was to treat them like palm trees—make a game of how many he could climb.

Indulge in their bodies without letting his treacherous heart get involved in the matter.

He had a feeling that Amalia, with all her talk of never wanting any part in the farce that was love and marriage, would agree. If nothing else, she seemed to like the indulgent part just fine.

Three kisses—four now, maybe five, who the devil could keep count?—and they had already found a rhythm to it, ravenous and urgent and no less thorough for all that.

He could feel the lushness of her curves even through her corset's stiff boning. Julián's hands roamed over her hips, her rib cage, right up to the spot where her corset gave way to yielding skin. The scrap of a blouse she wore was thin enough that he could feel her warmth as well as the slight shudder in her breath when he pressed a kiss to the hollow of her throat, just above the prim little ruffle that ringed her collar.

If their earlier encounters had been driven by reckless impulse, this time Julián was scrupulously deliberate. A proper seduction—and one he could control.

He pulled away, just enough to look into her eyes. Even in the galley's dim light, their brown depths seemed to dance with laughter and glints of gold. The curves of her lips, as generous as those beneath his hands, stilled as he caught her gaze and held it, letting his own fill with the desire coursing inside him.

"I want to unwrap that blouse like the bow on a present," he murmured, dragging the tip of his finger over the delicate fabric covering her collarbone. "Open it wide and sink into you like you're something rare and expensive that's been saved just for me." He outlined the swell of her breasts with the back of his hand. "I want, Your Highness, to make you feel like the gift that you are."

The shudder in her breath wasn't slight anymore. Julián let his lips curl into a smile as he took in the effect his words had on her. Yes, Amalia was enjoying the indulgent part just fine.

"Do you want me to keep going?" he asked, returning his hand to her waist.

"You had better," she commanded raggedly and licked her lips.

"In deed, or in words?"

In response, she fisted her hand in his shirt and dragged him down. Her mouth opened beneath his. When his tongue delved into its warmth, she kissed him back just as deeply. And when he reached for the tiny, cloth-covered buttons marching down the back of her blouse, she helped him undo them. The blouse fluttered to the floor, as ethereal as a cloud, and Julián was finally free to revel in her breasts. They pressed against the thin cotton of her chemise as if straining toward him. What could he do but ease the slender straps off her shoulder and bare her skin to the balmy air—and to his merciless mouth?

Quite a few hours had passed since he'd shaved that morning, and he made sure to scrape his bristles over her tender skin. With something that sounded like a breathless curse, she parted her legs as far as her skirts allowed her and pulled him even closer.

Yes, this was more like it. No tender murmurs, no declarations of love, no telling her that he was at her service. Just seduction, and an eager and willing response.

She leaned back, all the better to expose her chest and the long column of her throat. Julián devoured her, his mouth ranging over her silky skin, tasting salt and brine and the underlying sweetness of her and feeling her body shudder with each ragged exhalation.

Julián didn't intend to let her catch her breath.

"Pull up your skirt," he said, tracing light circles on her tight nipple with his thumb.

He should have known that she wouldn't care to give in to commands, no matter who issued them and why.

"Pull it up yourself," she managed to retort through something that sounded like a cross between a gasp and a moan.

"Are you always this contrary?"

"I try," she started to say, but her words were swallowed by another gasp as his fingers closed gently around her other nipple.

"You are a maddening woman, you know that?" He nipped softly at her smooth shoulder. "Maddening and beautiful and fearless. I've wanted to do this from the moment I saw you."

She opened her mouth, likely to make another smart remark. As much as he wanted to hear it, he wanted her mouth more. He covered it with his, skimming his hand up the silk stockings covering her shapely calf and feeling her skirt rise in its wake. And then, unable to resist, he pulled back enough to watch as the velvet ribbons at the top of her stockings were revealed.

Placing a kiss on the slice of bare skin between the ribbons and her drawers, he grasped a length of pink velvet and pulled. It did feel like unwrapping a present, the anticipation of it building in his chest as he uncovered her inch by inch.

Call him impatient, but he had never been one to bask in anticipation. Julián, if nothing else, had always been a man of action.

He started by kissing the crook of one knee, then the other. Her thighs were warm and firm and obligingly pliant as he stroked his way higher and higher. His questing fingers found the edge of her drawers and he lifted an eyebrow in inquiry.

Her eyes widened at the intimate touch. "What...are you proposing to do?" she asked breathlessly.

Julián straightened up. "I should like to touch you. Kiss you, too. Would you like that?"

Whatever scrap of doubt there had been in her eyes vanished at his question and was replaced by that defiant look he was beginning to recognize as one that appeared whenever she was contemplating doing something society would consider improper. "I won't know until you try it, will I?"

She nudged him with her knee, looking regal enough to suit his name for her. He didn't need more urging. Hiding a smile, he found her wet heat again. He knew just how to touch her to make her squirm—his fingertips light but sure, stroking up and down the seam of her drawers.

Amalia's breath hitched, and her hand shot out to grasp Julián by the forearm.

He stilled immediately. "I can stop if you want me to."

"Don't you dare," she all but growled. "You mentioned something about kissing?"

He had indeed. "Lift your hips so that I can pull down your underthings."

Bracing his palms on the work surface on either side

of her, Julián applied himself to his task. Her fingers twined in his hair, and the pleasant tugging in his scalp reminded him why he'd never liked cutting it shorter.

He couldn't see her face, but he didn't have to. He could feel her pleasure in the quivering of her thighs, the unsteady breaths gusting from her mouth, the tightening of her fingers on his hair. He could feel it when she began to move against him, cautiously at first, then with more and more abandon, until her legs were clenching around him.

It wasn't anything he hadn't done with at least a dozen other women. There was no reason for why it should feel so different this time, only it did. And whether that was due to Amalia herself, or to this past year wreaking some sort of change in his character, he wasn't altogether sure.

All he knew was that he didn't like it.

Feeling dazed, Julián gripped her thighs until the shuddering stopped.

"That…" she started, and then stopped to let out a low moan as her body shook with another tremor. Her knees were parted, her breasts bare above her corset, and he was filled with the sudden urge to take her back into the circle of his arms and brush her trembling lips with his own and—

Devil take him, he had to get a hold on himself.

Julián straightened up, flicking her a practiced grin. "I take that to mean you liked it?"

She made a noise in her throat that sounded distinctly enthusiastic. It took her a moment to regain her breath long enough to ask, "What about you?"

"I liked it, too, Your Highness."

"No, I meant—do you want me to return the favor?"

She was looking at him with those frank brown eyes, with none of the blushing or stammering he'd have expected from a pampered heiress.

"I'm fine," he lied, turning away. His own arousal was straining painfully against his trousers, and though he would have liked nothing better than to plunge inside her, he was no longer as confident in his ability to keep a safe distance.

He left her to put herself to rights and went back to the cupboard for the bottle of cooking sherry he'd noticed earlier. He pulled out the cork and took a steadying swig—and then another, until he'd drained nearly half the contents. Only then was he able to smooth out his expression and turn around.

Looking markedly more rumpled than when they'd wandered into the galley, Amalia was nonetheless fully covered and biting down on a roll. Julián ignored the pang of disappointment and went straight to the eggs they had abandoned.

"Have some sherry," he said, reaching for the sliced green pepper that had gotten knocked halfway down the work surface. "It'll dull the hunger until the food is ready."

She put a hand over his with enough pressure that he glanced at her with surprise. "Everything all right?" he asked.

"Is it? You look remarkably unenthused for someone who claimed to enjoy what we just did. If you're having second thoughts…"

Her gaze was sharp on his. Of all the heiresses he could have gotten embroiled with, he had to go and choose the only one who could lay him bare with a single look.

She would see through any of his practiced smiles, too, so he opted for something that was close enough to the truth. "I'm not. I just didn't expect to enjoy myself quite so much." He let go of the pepper and went to press himself against her legs to convince himself as much as her that he hadn't been as affected by their encounter as his racing heart wanted him to believe.

Her arms slipped around his neck. "So you're not wishing I was a beautiful woman from Sevilla?"

"There was only ever one of those, and she's long gone from my life." Julián let out a careful breath and was surprised to feel that the pain he'd carried for the past year had faded from a knife wound to a thorn in his side. "I wouldn't trade you for the Queen of Spain, Your Highness." It was the kind of line he might have employed on any number of casual acquaintances, but it had a ring of truth when he said it to Amalia.

Maybe the shock of it was wearing off, but he didn't feel as overwhelmed as he had a handful of minutes ago. "I know we've known each other for a very short time. But when all this is done—"

She pressed her lips against his. "Don't make me any promises. Just…kiss me again."

He was only too happy to oblige. Somewhere in the back of his head, he was aware that he'd promised her dinner; that they were at risk of being discovered; that he had a bundle of letters hidden in the small of his back that he had taken from her uncle's house.

He had retrieved it from his carpetbag earlier, and had read through most of them in the lounge while Amalia napped. From experience he knew that his father couched important details regarding his business in what to an outside observer would look like personal correspondence. Julián knew how to read between the lines, though, and he thought he had a good idea of what his father and her uncle were trying to do.

He would tell Amalia the truth of who he was soon enough. When there weren't so many sharp things close at hand.

Julián teased her lower lip with the tip of his tongue, unsurprised but definitely pleased by the unrestrained fervor with which she responded.

A brief noise made him pull away abruptly.

Amalia's small sound of protest was overlaid by the sound of the fork clattering to the floor.

"Wait…" Julián murmured, putting out a hand to stop her as she hopped down from her perch to retrieve it. "Do you hear something?"

Amalia stiffened. "I don't—" she began, but was interrupted by a heavy tread outside the galley doors.

A moment later an authoritative voice pierced the silence. "Is there anyone there?"

Putting a finger to his lips, Julián seized the sherry and the rolls and beckoned for her to follow him to a second door set at the opposite end of the galley. As it closed behind them, he glanced back and saw the steward from the lounge peering into the darkened galley and frowning when he saw the scattered remains of their would-be dinner on the work surface. Then his gaze shifted, and he caught sight of them creeping out. "You, there! What are you doing here?"

Amalia's hand closed around Julián's arm. "Run!"

Chapter Seven

Julián hadn't been well behaved a single day in his life, but getting into trouble had never been this much fun.

He pelted after Amalia as she raced up a different service staircase than the one they'd descended earlier. She was running as fast as if there was an entire legion chasing after them rather than an elderly steward who, Julián suspected, had given up pursuit halfway up the stairs.

"Did you see his face?" she panted, flashing him a grin as she slowed down. "Oh, I haven't run this fast in years. Haven't run at all, as a matter of fact. Being a proper young lady can be so boring."

"I wouldn't know," Julián replied breathlessly. "I haven't been proper a day in my life."

"I can't say I object to that," she said, turning a corner and pausing to smile up at him. He was suddenly breathless again, for an entirely different reason. "I've never had much use for propriety myself."

They were almost at her cabin, and she was clearly as loath as he was to part for the night. A more prudent man would have insisted she go to sleep, mindful that the following day was bound to be a strenuous one as they arrived in Puerto Plata and started the search for her sister. Julián was even less prudent than he was proper, and he was prepared to linger in this corridor until daybreak if it meant getting his fill of her hungry mouth and luscious curves.

Julián took a swig from the bottle of sherry he'd swiped from the kitchen. "Ever been improper in the corridor of a steamship?" He dipped his head lower to speak into her ear and found himself unable to resist brushing the delicate curve with his lips.

"Someone might see," she murmured, but she didn't pull away.

"Or they might not. It's dark and everyone's asleep."

"Except for the steward."

"Mmm…" He found the hollow behind her ear. "He's had enough shocks for one night, hasn't he?"

He slid his free arm around her and she let out a soft noise as she nestled deeper into his embrace, tilting her head up so that he could kiss his way down her neck. He was so busy savoring the taste of her skin that he almost didn't notice when she stiffened.

He glanced up sharply to see what had alarmed her and immediately tensed as he spotted a man in a brown suit leaning against the wall, several paces from her door.

The man had been making a pretense of leisurely perusing the newspaper he was now folding, but his hard, darting eyes gave him away. That, and the fact that it was well after midnight and the steamer held far more comfortable places for an insomniac to pass the time.

"Evening, *señor*," the man said, and it sounded mild enough.

Too bad his tone didn't match the coiled menace in his limbs.

Julián had spent too much time in taverns and gaming halls to not recognize the other man for the ruffian that he was. The only question was—what the devil did he want with them? Robbery? Wouldn't surprise him, not after the way Julián had foolishly flashed his mother's ring for all to see.

Or did the ruffian have something more sinister in mind? Heaven only knew Julián was embroiled in enough intrigue to make the latter a more likely proposition.

He strove to keep the wariness out of his voice as he returned the man's greeting. *"Saludos."*

Julián was still holding the bottle of sherry by its neck. He forced himself to relax his grip, though every instinct screamed at him to wrap his fingers around the bottle as if it were a club, in case he had to wield it as one. From experience he knew all too well that wielding a bottle as a club should be left for a last resort— there wasn't much a person could do with broken glass save for seriously injuring someone else, and the last thing he wanted was to put Amalia in the middle of a nasty brawl.

He'd much rather put her inside her cabin, where she'd be moderately safe, or at least behind a locked door, but they'd have to go past the ruffian. Julián might have tried it, had the man not unpeeled himself off the wall and sauntered their way, too casually to be anything but suspicious.

Julián considered reaching behind him for Amalia's hand. That would tie up his free hand, though, and under the circumstances it would be better for her to remain out of bottle-swinging range. Maybe he could maneuver her around—

He didn't sense the other man at his back until pain was blazing between his shoulder blades. He staggered, reeling, and another blow caught the back of his head, hard enough that he saw stars. Julián whirled, or tried to, but the first ruffian had reached him and was pummeling him with large, grimy fists.

Julián swung back and missed. It was laughable how he'd thought that a lifetime of brawling in taverns—and quite a few elegant hotels—had prepared him for the rigors of banditry. This man was a true professional, landing one vicious punch after another, each calculated to inflict the most damage. Julián's second attempt to punch back was deflected with a flick of the other man's arm, like someone swatting an annoying mosquito.

Between blows, Julián caught a glimpse of Amalia trapped in the grip of the man who'd struck his back. Her face was ashen, her brows twisted with pain.

"Let her go," Julián croaked, throwing up an arm to deflect one of the fists barreling unerringly toward his jaw. The sherry bottle, he noticed dimly, had fallen to the carpet and rolled just beyond his reach. "Whatever you might want with me, just—"

Don't hurt her, he wanted to say. But it was too late—they already had, and it was his fault.

He should have known this would happen. Nobody

got to be around him without getting hurt—in every sense of the word.

"Take her in there," the ruffian said to the man who was holding Amalia, nodding at the door to her cabin. "No use waking up half the ship."

Amalia didn't hesitate to show her displeasure with that decision. As Julián fended off another blow, she let out a furious cry and did her best to yank herself out of the scoundrel's grip. He only laughed and gripped her tighter, in a horrible mockery of the embrace she and Julián had just shared.

Julián's blood boiled. Bellowing out his rage, he rushed at the scoundrel—and stopped abruptly at the sound of breaking glass. A glance behind him confirmed that the man who'd been striking him had gotten hold of the sherry bottle and he apparently had no compunction over using it on Julián.

"No heroics," he said. "Or Miss Troncoso gets a nice new carving on the side of her face."

At the sound of Amalia's name, realization crashed upon Julián. They hadn't come for him at all—it was her they were after.

Fury at his own helplessness rushed over his limbs, but he forced himself to remain still as the ruffian shoved him against the corridor's striped wallpaper. "What do you want with her?"

"Nothing that concerns you." The man turned to his associate, jerking his head. "Into the cabin, quickly."

He had a key out, which Julián realized opened the cabin next to Amalia's. How the devil had they arranged it? How had they *known*?

The man who'd grabbed Amalia started to drag

her inside. Julián tensed, willing for their attention to waver for even a second. There wasn't time to formulate any sort of plan—the most he could hope for was a moment's distraction during which he could launch himself at them and give Amalia a window in which she could run and hide or fetch the steward...

Amalia must have seen his determination, because she stopped struggling. "They won't hurt me," she said calmly from the doorway of the cabin. He met her gaze, frowning, and almost missed the slight widening of her eyes. "Not if they've been sent by my uncle. They might hurt you, though, so please—"

The rest of her words were drowned out as the henchman holding her let out an unearthly howl and yanked his arms from around her to grab at his side. Julián didn't waste any time in swinging around to slam his fist into the other ruffian's eye. He had a moment to drive his foot into the man's knee and watch in satisfaction as he went down, yelling, before Julián was following him to the floor, grabbing for the sherry bottle.

Holding the jagged remains by the neck, Julián pressed them into the side of the bastard's neck, his other forearm pressing down hard on the man's collarbone.

"Maybe you'd like to reconsider telling me what you want with Miss Troncoso," Julián said, more politely than the ruffian deserved.

Spitting out curses, the man jerked his head to one side. All that did was make the sharp glass slide against his skin, shallowly enough that blood didn't spurt, only trickled down over Julián's fingers.

There was no time for more. All down the corridor,

the doors to the other cabins were popping open and passengers, befuddled and irate at having their night's rest interrupted by a brawl, were beginning to venture out of their cabins.

It wasn't long before the startled passengers were joined by a handful of stewards trying to find out what had happened while simultaneously attempting to usher those not involved back into their cabins, to little effect. The two ruffians, now injured and unable to flee, seemed prepared to try and brazen it out.

And apparently, so was Julián.

"What happened?" Julián snapped at the crew, as haughty as an aristocrat not just in his manner, but in the way he squared his shoulders to take up more space in the narrow corridor. "My wife and I have just been assaulted. That's what happened."

Amalia, who had long since tucked the eggy fork she'd used to stab the ruffian into her skirt's pocket, clung to Julián's arm. It wasn't a pretense, or at least not entirely—she was more shaken than she would have cared to admit, and her legs were undecided as to whether they would continue to hold her up. It was damned infuriating. Amalia had never been the swooning type and she didn't intend to start now.

Straightening her spine, she started to step away but was forestalled as Julián briefly pressed her hand against where it was trapped between his biceps and rib cage. Amalia's first instinct at this silent command was to yank her hand out of his grasp and tell him in no uncertain terms that she didn't need his help. But she did need it, didn't she? She might have been able to make her way to Puerto Plata alone, but she would have never been able to overpower those brutes without his help.

It had been brutal having to stand there motionless, watching the ruffian deal him blow after blow as Amalia waited for the right moment to strike. And yet, had it not been for him, she would have been locked up in some cabin, entirely at their mercy.

Next to her, Julián was spinning a tale about taking a midnight stroll around the deck. "When we realized how late it was, we decided to return to our cabin—and that's when we were set upon by these scoundrels. They didn't bother to hide their evil intent, so I was forced to defend my wife and myself."

Amalia didn't try to conceal the revulsion in her expression at the memory of those rough arms wrapped around her waist. Safe against Julián, she glared at the ruffian, then switched her gaze to his companion, who was once again wearing that vaguely smug smile as he raised his hands as if attempting to look harmless.

"My associate and I were hired by the girl's uncle to rescue her from this brigand," he said. "Who abducted her from the family home and is attempting to—"

"That's a damned lie," Julián said furiously.

The man extracted something from his pocket. "Then you would say you aren't the author of this ransom note?"

Amalia had to struggle to control her expression as she felt Julián freeze beside her. She'd only caught a glimpse of the note, but even at a distance, it looked very much like the one her uncle must have received the day before. She'd asked Julián to write it in case her uncle recognized her handwriting, though she was the one who'd dictated its contents.

"I have a note from her uncle, too, in which he asks me to do whatever necessary to return the young lady," the ruffian said, waving another folded piece of paper.

The chief steward turned to look at Amalia and Julián, eyes narrowing suspiciously.

Amalia stepped forward.

"I have most certainly not been kidnapped," she began with as much scorn as she could muster.

"I should say not!" A diminutive figure wriggling its way through the crowd was revealed a second later to be Doña María, in a wrapper and braided hair. "How dare you impugn this man's character?" she demanded, bristling with indignation. "He happens to be the son of one of the most prominent families on the island and my dear Amalia's beloved husband."

Amalia very carefully did not look at Julián. He must have made quite an impression on the elderly woman for her to mount such a vigorous defense on his behalf.

Looking apologetic, the chief steward tried to get a word in edgewise, but Doña María talked him into submission until he was forced to promise that he would have the ruffians confined to their cabins.

"Considering what I've seen of your security measures, I'd feel much safer if you tossed them overboard." Julián exchanged a glance with one of the men in the crowd. "When I booked our passage, I was under the impression that the Clyde-Mallory lines valued the safety of its passengers."

A rumble of agreement among the other passengers made the chief steward hasten to appease them all. He did his best but the commotion didn't show any signs of subsiding, and a select few were beginning to complain loudly about interrupted sleep. Finally, the chief steward held up his hands.

"I can offer you all my assurances that this matter will be dealt with by the proper authorities as soon as we make port. In the meantime, these gentlemen will be escorted into one of the crew cabins downstairs."

"Post a steward to stand guard at each end of this corridor and I might be persuaded to believe you. At the very least, it will make everyone in this section of the ship sleep easier."

The crowd voiced their vehement agreement, and the chief steward had very little option but to concede to Julián's demand. So assuaged, the passengers dispersed as the ruffians were hauled away.

Amalia felt the tension leave Julián's biceps, though when she glanced up, his expression remained unchanged from the impassive mask he had worn for the past quarter of an hour. The mask stayed in place as he guided her toward her cabin, waiting as she reached into her pocket for the keys.

Stepping inside after her, he inspected every corner of the cabin and the adjoining lavatory, going so far as to get on his hands and knees to look under the bed. When he was satisfied that there was no one lurking under the dust ruffle, he turned the lock on the thick cabin door. The slim piece of metal seemed awfully fragile to Amalia, who would have considered asking him to pile all the furniture in front of the door if most of it hadn't been fastened in place.

"You're staying?" she asked him.

"If it's all right with you. I'd rather not leave you alone with those two still on board and with the key to the cabin next door." He nodded toward the bed. "And

I don't much relish spending another night in a chair, however little there's left of it."

Amalia grasped him by the collar. "I wouldn't have let you leave even if you'd wanted to. You're hurt, and tired and I'm—"

She cut herself off swiftly. Amalia had never admitted to being scared out loud, and she wasn't about to start now.

Julián seemed to understand. He ignored the last part of her sentence and smiled, wincing slightly as the gesture pulled at the cut on his lower lip. "You know me, Your Highness. Always at your command."

He said it lightly and Amalia, already overwhelmed by the tangle of feelings inside her, answered in kind.

"Well, then, I command you to sit down and let me clean those cuts." He sank into the armchair. Gently, she pressed her fingertip to the corner of his mouth. "You'll have another scar, I think."

He shrugged and put his hands on her hips. "It'll only make me handsomer."

She ought to have found it irritating, the remark and the practiced smile that accompanied it. Only this time it didn't sound as insincere as it had in the carriage, mostly because she was beginning to see beyond his flippant tone to the pain and worry shading his dark eyes.

That he didn't care to let her see it didn't mean it wasn't there.

She cupped his face in both her hands, turning it to both sides to get a full look at the damage. A split lip, a wicked bruise beginning to spread over his temple and around his eye, a swollen nose…all incurred in her defense.

"I think I've seen him before," she said, releasing his face and going into the lavatory. She dampened a towel with water from the jug and returned to find him pulling off his necktie and undoing the button at his throat. "The first man, the one with the newspaper. On the deck, but also— I think he's an associate of my uncle's. The kind that deals with unpleasant matters."

Julián nodded grimly. "I wouldn't put it past him to have left word for you to be restrained if you turned up."

"He knows I would go after Lucía. Whatever his plans for her, they must be important enough that he was willing to go this far to keep me away."

"You don't think he'll—"

"He won't have me hurt, if that's what you mean. Not physically, in any case. I have no illusions about the strength of my uncle's feelings toward me, but he's never been inclined to violence."

Julián grunted as Amalia pressed the dampened cloth to his lip. "Depends on how you define *violence*. I'd argue that ruining your reputation by telling everyone you ran off with some man could be considered as violent."

She felt her lips twisting with wry amusement. "It was vindictive of him, yes. He's always hated that I'm not some pliant, impressionable girl he can mold to his will." Amalia refolded the bloodstained cloth and patted Julián's temple with a clean corner. "Honestly, having everyone think I'm married is not the worst that could have happened. It'll mean more freedom. And it means he won't find it as easy to marry me off to one of his business associates. It's the last thing he intended, but I think he might have done me a favor."

"Favor or not, I'd still like to strike the bastard when we find him."

His use of the word *we* sent a dart of relief through her. It wasn't that she thought he would back out of their agreement, but surely any rational person would think twice about getting embroiled in a situation after being pummeled like he had.

"Oh, he's done plenty to deserve it," she assured him, brushing back his hair to wipe the cloth over his forehead. "Though I did aspire for a little more subtlety." She sighed. "I just hate knowing that I worried Lucía as much as I did over a scheme that didn't work."

"You didn't consider telling her the truth?"

Amalia shook her head. "I didn't want to risk it, in case the plan failed and my uncle suspected she was involved."

He grazed her wrist with his fingertips. "We'll get to your sister soon, and she'll be able to see with her own eyes that you're fine."

"We will," Amalia said, trying as always not to let the smallest scraps of fear and doubt cloud her certainty. It was either that or carry her anger like a heavy mantle over her shoulders and let the weight of her uncle's greediness make her bitter.

She ran the damp towel over the back of Julián's neck. His eyes fluttered closed and he lowered his forehead to press it against Amalia's midsection. "That feels good. Nice and cool."

The back of his neck was dark from the sun and oddly vulnerable. Amalia rubbed the cloth over his overheated skin, watching his hair curl with the damp. How was it that this felt so much more intimate than what they'd done in the galley? She rested a cautious hand on top of his warm head.

She could feel each individual beat of her own heart, echoing through her body. Surely, Julián heard it as well. Could he tell how it quickened every time he was near? She'd been inclined to think that it was merely a response to the thrill of adventure and the relief of finally doing something to better her and Lucía's situation. But maybe…

Maybe it was something more.

The thought should have terrified her. It might have, if it didn't feel so right.

Chapter Eight

Julián lay on his back, watching the sky grow lighter by degrees.

Amalia was on her side with her back to him, her long curls flung over the pillow and his chest. Just before she'd fallen asleep, he had plunged his hands into her hair as he'd wanted to do in the carriage and released it from its pins just to watch her tight curls cascade down to the small of her back.

He picked up one of the strands and pulled it lightly, watching as the curl straightened, then bounced back into its original coil as soon as he let go. Would he be able to spring back, too, whenever he and Amalia parted? Or had the past two days changed his shape for good?

As much as Julián wanted to pretend otherwise, there was no doubt in his mind that they *would* eventually part. Maybe she'd agree to a dalliance, for a time. But eager as she seemed to further their acquaintance, there would come a time when her interest in him would fizzle and go out like a sputtering candle. Just as it always did.

He would find someone else, in time. There were plenty of women in the world who would be willing, even eager, for their turn in Julián's bed.

The only trouble was none of them would be Amalia Troncoso.

Amalia stirred beside him, and Julián realized she hadn't been as deeply asleep as he'd thought.

"Did you get any sleep?" she asked drowsily.

"An hour or so, maybe. It's early still—it'll be a few hours yet till we dock. You should try to get some more rest."

"I'm all right." Her sleeve was a pale flutter in the gloom as she raised a hand to cover a yawn. Julián could feel her legs flexing against his, even though he'd been prudent enough to wear his trousers to bed.

Prudent, Julián. What a laugh.

Julián tightened the arm she lay on, pulling her close enough for him to place a row of kisses on the nape of her neck. Her squeak of surprise was thoroughly enjoyable, as was the irritated little huff she let out when he stopped.

For a while they lay in silence as the sun inched its way up the sky. Amalia's body was a solid weight at his side, firm in some places and pleasantly yielding in others.

"You fit well in my arms."

It must have been the blaze of exhaustion that made Julián say such a thing out loud. Amalia must have been as surprised as he was by the sudden break in the silence, because she stiffened suddenly.

He forced out a low laugh, loosening his hold on her. "You needn't worry about being ravished, Your Highness. I'm too exhausted to have my wicked way with you."

Not that he wasn't burning to. But first, there were precautions he had to take and secrets that needed to come out into the light.

"I wasn't worried," she felt the need to point out. "In case you hadn't noticed, I very much enjoyed your earlier attempt at ravishing."

He'd noticed all right, and the memory of it was making his body reconsider his statement. "Then what's the matter?"

"Earlier, when you said you never form attachments. Does that mean you've never been in love?"

"Love? Never heard of it, Your Highness," he said lightly. "Why do you ask? Are you thinking you might want to give it a try?"

"Never," she replied promptly. "I don't want any part in that sort of thing. But we're not talking about me right now."

Julián had never been the sort to bare his heart. It wasn't pleasant, or even productive, and his few attempts at sincerity had always been met with uncomprehending coldness from his father and sneering from his cousin. Here in the near dark, however, with Amalia curled against him, her cheek pillowed on his arm...

"I thought I loved someone once," he found himself saying, unable to muster up another deflective, lighthearted reply. "And I was foolish enough to think she loved me back. Maybe she might have, if circumstances had been different—I have reason to believe that she and I were both lied to, in a deliberate attempt to break us apart."

For a long moment Julián listened to the sound of Amalia's even breaths.

"Then again," he said, even more softly than before,

"I wouldn't blame her if love was the last thing on her mind. I'm not…" He paused and breathed through the shame and grief blooming in his chest. "I'm not the kind of man who's easy to love."

There was a rustle of starched sheets as she turned over to face him. The jaunty little curtains at the cabin's window did little to block the faint sunshine beginning to press against the panes. The pale glow of dawn touched her features as gently as he would have if he'd been able to unclench his hands from the crisp sheets.

"Do you really believe that?"

"I'm not a good man," he said, more harshly than he'd intended. "I'm a damned blackguard, a scoundrel, and everyone who gets close to me ends up getting hurt."

"Yes, yes, I remember. The worst kind of person, right? Well, let me tell you something." She leaned closer until the tip of her nose was almost brushing his, her breath trailing over his lips like a sultry breeze. "I don't think you're as bad as you like to pretend you are."

"And you don't know me as well as you think you do."

A year ago—maybe even a week ago—he would have found it necessary to avoid those eyes that seemed to pierce him through even in the faint light. Now, however, he met them with matching intensity.

"Don't I?" she asked.

He didn't back down from the challenge in her gaze. "You don't know me at all, Your Highness."

"I know that you came all this way here with me when you didn't have to."

"What makes you think I'm not just interested in the money?"

She raised her shoulder in a slight shrug that made her prim little nightdress slip off her shoulder. Julián couldn't resist pressing his lips to the smooth skin it revealed. "What does it matter if you are?" she asked. "I doubt bandits do a lot of things out of the goodness of their hearts. That's not all you care about, though. If it were, I don't think you would have put yourself at risk defending me from those two men."

"I may have just been protecting my investment," he pointed out. "I've wasted a lot of time and effort on you not to see this through to the end."

"You had every opportunity to pilfer valuables from the house when you were there," Amalia said. "And the knowledge that not only was it unattended save for a single maid, but that none of the locks are a match for you. You could have stayed behind and burgled its entire contents." She stroked the patch of hair at the center of his chest, her fingernails pleasantly sharp as they scraped his skin.

"You make a good case for me," he said softly.

"And yet, I can see you don't believe me."

He wanted to, with such a swift and fierce desperation that he found it hard to keep from swearing out loud. "I've always been a worthless, reckless scoundrel. My own family hasn't much use for me—why would anyone else?"

"I have use for you." Amalia lifted herself up on her elbow as if to emphasize her point. "But that's not why I— Why I don't believe you're a scoundrel. You don't have to be useful in order to be a good person— or worthy of love."

Julián's throat felt tight. "I thought we both agreed that we want nothing to do with love."

"I don't," she said quietly. "What I'm trying to say is that maybe your girl from Seville had more affection for you than you realized. You aren't difficult to love, Julián. Not for those who partake in such things."

Amalia may have been bold and fearless, but she had led a very sheltered life and knew so little of the world. Still, she spoke with such conviction that Julián was almost convinced. Almost. Twenty-eight years of hearing his father listing, in unsparing detail, all the ways in which Julián had failed as a son and as a man and as a businessman were not that easy to overcome.

Her hand was venturing lower, and Julián was finding it hard to remember why he shouldn't flip her over and repeat everything he'd done to make her pant the night before. Reluctantly, he captured her hand in his and held it tight.

"You're not the only one who has family troubles, Your Highness. I—"

There was a loud rap at the door, too demanding to have come from a steward. Julián was instantly on alert, springing to his feet and reaching the door in a couple of long strides.

"Yes?" he asked sharply.

"Good morning, my dears," came Doña María's voice through the thick wood. "Will you be coming in to breakfast? They opened the dining room early, on account of no one being able to rest with those two ruffians on board. I sent my nephew down to save us all seats at the same table, but I'm afraid there's a rush and—"

"We'll be there in a few minutes, Doña María," Julián called, deciding it was better to appear a little rude than to open the door and scandalize the elderly lady with the sight of his bare chest.

There was a muted creak behind him and then Amalia was pressing herself against his back, her breasts round and soft through the thin fabric of her nightgown. "Minutes?" she murmured, nuzzling his shoulder.

He turned. "Wouldn't want to disappoint the nice lady."

"Then we'd better hurry," Amalia said and dashed into the lavatory.

There was nothing Julián wanted more than to give chase, but a man needed to know his limitations. Following her into the lavatory would only result in his insisting on brushing the nightgown off her shoulders to watch it glide down her body. He wouldn't be able to resist reveling in her skin, licking droplets of water off her curves as she bathed, diving into the deep cleft between her breasts and refusing to resurface for hours.

Forget breakfast—they would probably miss their chance to disembark in Puerto Plata and find themselves halfway to New York before he found the strength to pry his lips away from Amalia's.

There would be time enough for all that later.

Thanks to Julián's noble restraint, they made it into the dining room only forty minutes after Doña María had knocked on their door. The space was more beautiful flooded in morning light than it had been the afternoon before. The intense rose glow of the sky was reflected in the copper pots that held fishtail palms, and on the cut-crystal vases from which sprouted tall sprays of pink and red ginger flowers, hardy blooms that would withstand the days until the ship reached its final destination. Damask drapes and silk-shaded sconces reminded Julián of some of the higher-end hotels he had visited on the European continent.

The walls here were paneled, too, only these were carved so intricately they were a match for Amalia's frilly shirtwaist. She had unearthed another thoroughly impractical ensemble from one of her valises, this one consisting of a shirtwaist laden with lace and a pale green skirt that was saved from looking dull by the lustrousness of the fabric. A darker green sash threaded through with a buckle cinched her in at the waist and made Julián crave to measure the tight circumference against the span of his hands.

After greeting Doña María and her young nephew, Julián pulled out a chair for Amalia. The soft, clear glow of early morning suited her as well as moonlight had. It made her curls gleam and her rich brown eyes sparkle, and it made the gold ring she still wore shine like a beacon, guiding him home.

The devil take him. This was more than mere infatuation. This was—

He caught Doña María's eye as he sat, and the knowing look would have made him blush if he was capable of such a thing.

Instead, he gave her a shrug and the kind of faintly sheepish smile he imagined would come naturally to a newlywed.

"You're smitten, aren't you, *mijo*?" she asked from across the table.

"And happy to be," he replied airily, unfolding the linen napkin and spreading it over her lap. Beside him Amalia was exchanging pleasantries with the nephew, a boy who couldn't have been older than fifteen or sixteen. "Doña María, I haven't had the opportunity to thank you for coming to my defense last night. We—"

She dismissed his gratefulness with a wave of her heavily ringed hand. "I should have hated to see your honeymoon ruined over such a thing. My dear sister had a terrible time of it on *her* honeymoon and she's every bit as upset over it twenty years later as she was that day. I don't believe I asked yesterday—are you on your way to New York as well?"

"I'm afraid we're disembarking later this morning, once we make port in Puerto Plata."

"Of course, of course," the older woman said. "That's where your people are from, aren't they?"

Julián was spared having to answer by the appearance of a waiter with a coffeepot in one gloved hand and a carafe of ice water in the other. He poured them each coffee from the silver pot, which Julián noticed was etched with the same Clyde-Mallory symbol printed on their tickets and the breakfast menu. Julián made a production out of adding cream and sugar to Amalia's coffee before attending to his own and remarking, as he did, upon the extensive list of jams and marmalades printed on the crisp menu.

He kept the table entertained until the waiter returned with their eggs and sausages and another acquaintance of Doña María's joined them at the table and seized the older woman's attention with a very long and involved story about a mutual friend of theirs. The nephew was drawn into the conversation, too, leaving Amalia free to turn to Julián.

"Were your eggs all right?" he asked, nodding to her plate, which she had cleared with impressive speed. "You can have my toast if you want. And look, they have orange marmalade—it's no *dulce de naranja*, but I think you'll like it."

She shook her head. "Thank you, but I couldn't eat another bite." Leaning a little closer to Julián, she said, "I keep looking around as if I expect to find those men from last night lurking in the corners. I think I'd rather return to the cabin and get our things together—it won't be long before we make port and I'd like to be ready to go as soon as possible."

Julián seized the linen napkin on his lap and laid it beside his plate. "Let's go and pack."

There was barely an hour left until Amalia would cease to be Julián's new, if fictional, bride, and she intended to take advantage of every single minute of it.

Unfortunately for her, the chief steward found Julián before they reached the cabin. With an apologetic smile and a squeeze of her hand, Julián walked her to the cabin and made sure she had locked herself in safely before going with the older man.

He had placed his things neatly back into the old carpetbag he'd brought, but the clothes Amalia had worn the day before were strewn around the small cabin. She picked them up, folding them into inexpert bundles that she stuffed back into one of the open valises.

As she shook out the white organza blouse and tried to work out how to put it away without crumpling it beyond ruin, she couldn't help but think of the delicate ease with which Julián had removed it the night before. He'd clearly had plenty of practice. He also hadn't seemed to think much of their sharing a bed, though of course they'd both been too tired to do much other than sleep and talk.

Maybe that was normal to the kind of life he led, but it had been the first time that Amalia had ever lain next to a man. The awareness of his proximity had burned through her all night, even in her dreams, the cotton of her nightdress so thin it might have been made out of spun clouds.

And then waking up with her body still snug against his, sharing confidences as the day brightened around them...

She had always expected such intimacy to rob her of something—instead, being with Julián gave her strength. It made her feel powerful. Like the sort of person who galloped through narrow country roads, dodging branches and defending herself from ruffians and chasing maidens in distress halfway around an island.

Like the kind of person strong enough to create an entire new future for herself and for her sister.

The thought of Lucía was like a little shock of ice water against sun-warmed skin. Whatever her feelings for Julián, she couldn't let herself forget the real purpose for this journey. Her sister's safety came first.

But once that was assured...

Then Amalia could let herself dream about what might come later, and who she would share those moments with.

When Amalia had finished packing and Julián still hadn't returned, she went out onto the deck and stood looking past the railing, as she had upon their departure. During the night they had left behind the bright, placid waters of the Caribbean Sea and crossed into the fiercer, darker Atlantic Ocean. She was just in time to watch as the steamer made its way into the intense blue waters of the Puerto Plata bay. At the entrance to the half circle, to Amalia's left, were the sturdy brown walls of what looked like a colonial-era fort, topped with crenellations and surrounded with palm trees.

"That's the customs building."

The scent of Julián's shaving soap was faint enough in the overpowering salt tinging the air that Amalia wouldn't have perceived it had he not stepped in close to her. Even though they'd been parted for less than an hour, the desire to seek out his skin with hers flared as intensely as if they had been separated for weeks. Amalia gave in to it after a slight pause, and twined their fingers together.

Pressing his shoulder to hers, he extended his free hand to point at something in the distance. "And over there, behind those trees, is a pretty little park with a two-story gazebo right in its center. Just the place to while away a lazy afternoon."

"You've been here before," she said, twisting around in surprise.

"I was born here, Your Highness."

At some point along the way the nickname had stopped sounding faintly mocking and had become almost affectionate.

"We should get ready to leave as soon as the gang-plank's lowered," Julián continued, before she could react to the scrap of information he had volunteered.

Julián raked a hand through his hair, and Amalia realized he wasn't wearing a hat. The bridge of his nose was already reddened by the sun. "The chief steward and the captain both gave me their reassurances that the ruffians will be taken into custody by the Civil Guard as soon as I make a formal complaint against them. But there's every chance that your uncle is having this port watched as well, and I'd just as soon not get pummeled again."

"No argument from me there," Amalia said and smiled as Julián pretended to be astonished. "My things are packed—I'm ready to go."

But not quite ready to leave him, though now that they were so much closer to reaching Lucía, Amalia could feel herself growing impatient to get her search started. Julián seemed to share her mood—he was restless, almost twitching with impatience as he gathered their luggage and waited by the door to the gangplank.

He exploded into motion the minute their feet struck solid ground. He'd asked a steward to run down ahead of them to fetch a carriage, tipping him handsomely. This allowed Amalia and Julián to lose themselves in the crowd descending from the ship before quickly getting into the waiting carriage. If there were any more ruffians waiting for them, Amalia was moderately sure they had avoided them.

"Where will we start?" Amalia asked as the coachman guided them away from the bustle of the port.

"We'll leave your things at a hotel I'm acquainted with." Julián took her hand to stroke the back of it with his thumb. The movement made the faceted stone on Amalia's finger glitter in the sunlight.

He hadn't asked for the ring back. Amalia knew she should say something about it. She didn't understand what was holding her back. She wasn't interested in marriage—of that much she was still certain. When Julián had told her that he found it easy to engage in physical affection without being ensnared in feelings, she'd been intrigued. As far as she could tell, their interlude in the galley hadn't sparked any inconvenient feelings or emptied her head of important thoughts. She hadn't simpered or giggled or heaved any dreamy sighs. If anything, she felt more powerful and sure of herself.

So why this reluctance, then?

Impatiently, Amalia twisted the ring off her finger and thrust it toward Julián, noticing immediately how weightless her finger felt without it. "Before I forget, here's your mother's ring. There's no need for it anymore."

Julián hesitated. "Keep it for now," he said. "Just in case we find ourselves needing to continue the ruse."

Amalia slipped the ring back on. And there was no denying it—it did feel right.

Chapter Nine

The coachman took them straight to the Hotel Europa, a three-story building with wrought iron balconies and shuttered windows twice Julián's height.

"Will you wait for me here?" he asked Amalia as the coach rolled to a stop beneath the striped awning at the hotel's entrance. "Just for a few minutes—I cabled ahead before leaving San Pedro and I want to make sure everything has been arranged as I asked."

If it hadn't been for the urgency to find her sister, Julián would've been tempted to act like a true bandit and steal away with Amalia—tell the coachman to turn right around back to the port and whisk her into the next ship headed for Europe, where they could both forget their names and responsibilities and devote themselves solely to the pursuit of losing themselves in each other's bodies.

Sometime during the previous night, in between listening to her soft exhalations as waves of pleasure rocked her body and whispering confidences in the half dark, the world he used to know had shattered around him and been remade. And at the center of this new world was Amalia, as bold and fearless as he had always longed to be. His mission, which had seemed so important a few days ago, more than paled in comparison.

Julián waited for Amalia's nod before reaching for her. Softly, he ran the pad of his thumb over the sweet curves of her upper lip, wondering why those slopes and valleys made his chest ache with longing. He dove into its depths for one kiss, and then another, but that did nothing to quell the deep well of need yawning inside him.

So he flashed her a crooked, breathless smile and said, "I'll come back for you in a minute or two."

He leaped lightly out of the carriage and he strolled inside with a friendly nod to the crisply uniformed bellhop standing in the rectangle of shade cast by the awning.

The strength of his desire for Amalia didn't make him panic—not quite yet, at any rate. He was well aware that he was a little too infatuated. That *infatuated* wasn't even the right word, because the thing that had been building between them was too large to be contained by the words in his insufficient vocabulary.

Only the knowledge that Amalia didn't want to be bothered by love or commitments kept Julián from fully losing his head.

A good thing, too, because he needed his wits about him, especially now that he was back in Puerto Plata. He wasn't sure what they would find when they tracked down her sister, but he had a good idea of what awaited them. And of Amalia's reaction when he confessed the truth of why he had come all the way here with her.

The sooner he explained, the better. Maybe she'd

agree to come upstairs with him for a few minutes of uninterrupted conversation so that—

Halfway to the front desk, Julián collided against an elderly gentleman who all but struck Julián upside the head with his silver-tipped cane as he yelled something about brigands.

"My apologies, *señor*," he murmured, steadying the man with a quick grip of his elbows.

It wasn't until Julián heard his own name being spoken out loud that he recognized the older man as an acquaintance of his father's. Instead of a simple greeting, the older man launched at once into an anecdote about the time when he was set upon by bandits.

Julián would have found it interesting at any other time, but the last thing he needed at the moment was to get drawn into a long and involved conversation. He was trying to think of a polite way to extricate himself from it when the older man said, "Oh, but I shouldn't keep you. I'm sure you're eager to get back to your father." He gave Julián's shoulder a kindly pat. "Go on. I know how much Reynaldo dislikes being kept waiting."

Dread as cold as ice swirled through Julián. "He's waiting for me?" Puerto Plata was large as towns went, but gossip spread with astonishing speed and his father had a network of informants to rival any emperor's. He'd figured everyone would know soon enough that he'd returned—he just hadn't expected it to be this fast.

"In the courtyard. Isn't that why you're here? For the party?"

Julián let out a word that made the man's mouth drop open. Without pausing to apologize, he bolted back the way he'd come from.

He had to get Amalia out of here. Immediately, before

anyone in his family saw her and guessed that she was there with him.

Before she herself stumbled into the truth of all he'd been keeping from her.

The coachman was leaning against the carriage's back wheel, legs crossed as he touched a match to a crude wooden pipe. He glanced up wildly when Julián came barging toward the carriage.

"Don Julián? Is something wrong?"

Julián didn't stop to answer him. He wrenched the carriage door open and stared frantically into the plush—and empty—interior.

Amalia was gone.

No more than a minute or two after Julián left, Amalia was tumbling out of the carriage and into the hotel's lobby. She had never been able to bear being told to sit and wait quietly, and she had no intention of ever complying with such requests, however well intended they might be.

The lobby was spacious and more luxurious than she'd anticipated. A stretch of terra-cotta tiles gleamed unbroken from the entrance to a wooden counter equipped with a brass bell and mahogany-and-brass pigeonholes that Amalia assumed were for mail or keys. Birds of paradise in glazed pots, stained-glass sidelights on the doors and graceful fretwork arches so intricately carved they looked like the lace edging on Amalia's shirtwaist, provided a background to the bellhops in their sharply tailored uniforms and dark blue waistcoats.

A seating area to the right held a grouping of love seats and armchairs. Amalia's gaze flitted from a trio of little boys setting up a game of marbles beside a side table to an older gentleman who seemed to be waving his silver-tipped cane at Julián. She couldn't see Julián's face, but the conversation seemed to be taking an intense turn.

Curiosity would have prompted her to sidle closer, had Amalia not caught a glimpse of a figure that looked curiously familiar, disappearing through an arched colonnade that surrounded some sort of outdoor space.

Was that—? Surely, that couldn't be her sister.

Her heart suddenly hammering wildly inside her rib cage, Amalia didn't hesitate in bounding after the girl.

It wasn't until she had gone through that she realized that the large, brick-paved courtyard had been set up for a party. The white bougainvillea spilling from the second- and third-floor balconies, twined with trailing vines, looked festive enough on its own without all the added decorations. The half a dozen trees in the courtyard, all of which were ringed with the same red brick of the floors, were as strung with garlands as the female guests were with ropes of pearls and amber.

At the far end a tiled fountain was flanked by two long tables that appeared to be blooming with Castilian roses and lacy ferns in silver vases. More silver gleamed on the white damask tablecloth—trays and salvers piled high with imported apples and grapes and all kinds of party food.

Amalia glanced away from the *pastelitos* and ham *croquetas* and the delicately frosted cakes. To the right, on a small stage underneath one of the balconies, musicians in evening wear played a lively waltz. None of the elegantly clad couples were dancing, though. They stood in loose clusters around the courtyard, holding champagne flutes as they chatted. The figure Amalia had followed to the courtyard didn't seem to be among them.

And even though it was more than likely that the girl hadn't been Lucía after all, merely a product of Amalia's wishful thinking, and though Amalia was aware that finding her sister wouldn't have been so easy, she could feel disappointment flooding through her at the notion that she had lost her sister yet again. It was an irrational thought, but one Amalia couldn't seem to shake off.

Lucía wouldn't have been involved in any of this if it hadn't been for Amalia. She couldn't help but think that if she hadn't tried so hard to defy her uncle's authority, he wouldn't have seen Lucía's docility as a reason to use her for his plans instead of Amalia.

Swallowing back her guilt, Amalia turned to make her way back to Julián and begin the search in earnest. That was when she saw her.

Lucía, dressed in an ivory cotton voile frock with a high neck of floral lace that made her swan-like neck look fragile. Two men stood at either side of her—Tio Francisco to her right, expansive as he held court over a small group, and a younger man to her left, who contributed the occasional aside to the gathering. He must have been as charming as his smile indicated, because the group obliged him with frequent laughs.

When Amalia had pictured this moment, she had seen herself charging in like a knight on a white horse and wrestling her sister away from a wicked villain, not a party.

Then again, Amalia knew how oppressive some parties could be.

Lacking the armor and the white horse, Amalia opted to glide toward the shadows behind one of the columns where she could avoid being spotted until she was able to capture Lucía's attention.

It didn't take long before Lucía's attention wandered in the direction of Amalia's hiding place, which showed how engaging the conversation must have been.

Her eyes widened, though she stopped short of gasping. Quickly composing herself, she made her excuses to the group and began walking toward Amalia. Instead of stopping when she reached her sister, though, Lucía continued straight through the arched colonnade.

Amalia waited a beat, then followed her sister into what turned out to be the hotel's dining room. Breakfast evidently over, the ample space was empty and dark. It had already been set up for the midday service, with fresh linen tablecloths and polished silver cutlery. Amalia had just enough time to catch a glimpse of the carnations in the small silver vases at the center of each table before Lucía had launched herself at her, sweeping her into a long, tight hug.

"Are you all right?" Amalia demanded when she was finally able to pull away, holding her taller sister by the shoulders.

"Me? Are *you*? The last time I saw you, you were getting ki—kid—"

Lucía dissolved into tears and Amalia gathered her close again, murmuring soothing things into her ear. But Lucía was no longer a child with a scraped knee, and when her sobs subsided she had plenty of questions for Amalia.

There wasn't much of a chance for Amalia to answer them, though, because the door to the hotel's dining room swung open and their uncle strode inside, followed by the younger man who'd been standing with them.

"Lucía, there you are," Tio Francisco said irritably. "What do you mean by abandoning your guests? We—"

The astonishment in his face when he caught sight of Amalia was almost comical. He stopped so abruptly, the other man narrowly missed walking into his back.

Amalia had to stifle the impish urge to wave hello. "Tio Francisco," she said as neutrally as she could manage.

Her uncle stopped, licking his lips and darting a look at the man next to him. "Amalia. I'm so glad that you've made your way back to us," he blustered. Though he'd had a few moments to compose himself, he couldn't quite conceal the virulent glower flickering beneath his bonhomie. "And just in time to join in the celebration."

Amalia's arm was threaded through Lucía's; it was impossible to miss the sudden tension in her sister's body at the word.

"Celebration?" Amalia asked sharply.

"Surely, that's not an unfamiliar concept," the stranger said.

Above the starched white collar was a face that Amalia would have called handsome if she hadn't taken an instant dislike to the sardonic tilt of his eyebrow. He had ruddy skin and pomaded black hair that had been combed back so carefully, she could see the ridges where the comb had passed through.

Something in his demeanor reminded Amalia faintly of how Julián had looked when he was demanding to the chief steward that the men who'd attacked them be hauled away.

"Who the devil are you?" Amalia snapped. She knew she was being unforgivably rude, but she didn't much care. Whoever this man was, he was clearly in cahoots with her uncle.

Something like amusement flashed over his face. "I'm Lucía's fiancé."

The word clanged unpleasantly through Amalia, as if someone had rung a bell directly over her head. It was exactly what she'd feared—Tío Francisco was trying to marry off Lucía and he'd taken advantage of Amalia's absence to hasten it along. She'd known he was planning something, but upon this confirmation, scalding anger welled up in her chest.

Before it had a chance to come pouring out, the outline of a man filled the open doorway.

"Victor."

She almost didn't recognize Julián's voice, filled as it was with barely restrained loathing. Then her brain registered what he'd said. "You know this man?"

"Know me?" The man's sardonic tones matched the expression on his face when he raised an eyebrow and drawled, "He's my cousin."

Chapter Ten

Julián didn't deny it, and why would he? It was clear from a single glance that the man he'd called Victor was telling the truth.

Beside her, Amalia heard Lucía gasp. "You're the bandit!"

Amalia herself couldn't say a word. Shock waves were reverberating through her as her gaze traveled from one man to the other, cataloging the similarities in their appearance. Both were devastatingly handsome, with angular noses and firm jaws. She could see it. Take away Julián's bristles, substitute the rusty black suit for a more sharply cut one... In Victor, though, the sharp humor that made Julián's dark eyes warm translated into something that made her blood run cold.

"All this time..." Amalia said slowly, pausing to gather her thoughts. "You knew I was trying to save Lucía and you were working with them all along?"

"No. *No*, Amalia."

"Were you planning on delivering me back to my uncle? Or to your father? Or—" Amalia thought back at all the subtle questions he had asked her about her uncle's business. "Or was it information you were after? Some juicy tidbit you could bring back to your father to finally make him notice you?"

Her words must have cut close to the truth because Julián looked suddenly and carefully blank.

"You have no idea what you're saying," he said, looking every inch the aristocrat.

Amalia's stomach—or maybe her heart—sank as she recognized the snobbish tones as the accent he had used while trying to get the ship's chief steward to lock away the ruffians who'd assaulted them.

Doña María had been right when she'd called him the son of a prominent family. She'd known all along who Julián truly was. Only Amalia, absolute fool that she was, had been in the dark.

She swallowed past the knot in her throat, willing for it to turn into anger.

All the little things Julián had let slip about his family were notching into place. His mother's outrageously expensive ring, which still encircled her finger. What he'd said about his father's office, which had made Amalia assume his father to be some sort of book-keeper or clerk.

And then there was the cousin, who used to lock him in it. Whatever Julián had claimed about little boys being wild, she had privately thought that the cousin must have been unspeakably cruel to do such a thing. As she looked into Victor's face, she found it easy to match her mental image of that awful boy with the man standing in front of her, his smile intact even as his gaze raked over her and took in her shock—and the ring on her finger—with something like calculation.

Amalia would have rather expired on the spot than

give him the upper hand by being the first one to turn away, but her attention was drawn to the door as yet another person made his unexpected way into the dining room.

"The return of the wayward son." The crisp voice belonged to someone accustomed not only to issuing commands, but also of being heeded without question. It belonged to a barrel-chested man, whose neat gray mustache and thick eyebrows did little to hide the cold assessment in his eyes as he took in Lucía's tearstained face as well as Julián and Amalia.

Amalia would have known this was Julián's father just from the way Julián's jaw tensed, so hard she was sure it must be aching. Her own jaw firmed as she made herself look away, unwilling to catch his eye even for the most fleeting of seconds. Not until she could properly vent her fury at his deception. He must have known that she was reeling with shock, but he wasn't trying to apologize, or even explain. Knowing him, he was probably congratulating himself on a successful performance.

Half the things to come from his mouth had probably been lies, but Julián had been honest about one thing—he was most definitely a scoundrel.

"I'd apologize for whatever he's done, Francisco, but I'm afraid that taking up that particular habit would use up all my time," Julián's father continued. Not so much as a greeting passed between the eldest Fuentes and his son.

Tio Francisco responded with an unconvincing chuckle. "Not at all, Reynaldo. As it happens, we were just making introductions. It appears that my dear niece has become acquainted with your son."

"Ah, yes," Don Reynaldo said. "My son does have a most unfortunate habit of making acquaintances with every pretty young woman in the vicinity."

The reprimand in his voice was obvious, but all it did was make Julián smirk. "I wouldn't call it a habit so much as a talent," he said.

Forcing herself to look as if she hadn't just been shattered, Amalia looked past Julián to his father. "Actually, I was just being introduced to your nephew. Victor, was it? I can't say it's a pleasure to meet you."

Victor laughed with as much delight as if she'd offered him a compliment instead of a rude comment. "I was warned that you were spirited."

"Did they tell you I was curious, too?" she shot back. "Mostly about how my sister found herself whisked off to a new city and in possession of a fiancé in the space of two days."

A cold look from Don Reynaldo was apparently Tio Francisco's cue. "What I'd like to know is where *you* have been for that time," Tio Francisco said with a creditable attempt at a fatherly scolding. "Your claim to care about Lucía would be much more believable if you hadn't abandoned her to run off into the *monte* with a man. A fine example you're setting for her."

It was nothing that Amalia hadn't spent the past day telling herself, but she tried not to let any of them see the wave of guilt washing over her. "Anything I've done has been for Lucía's sake, which is more than I can say about you, Tio. Tell me, how much is Victor here paying you for her?"

Victor's faintly amused expression didn't so much as waver, but her uncle reacted as if she'd thrown lamp oil at a fire. "How dare you suggest such a thing?" he hissed, rounding on her. "As if I haven't given up my entire life to raise you ungrateful—"

Don Reynaldo cleared his throat, and the sound doused Tio Francisco's temper almost immediately. Visibly pulling the shreds of his self-control around himself, Tio Francisco tightened his mouth briefly before saying, in a much more measured tone, "I was hoping you'd decided to do the right thing and step aside so that your sister could make a decent match. The Fuenteses are a respectable family and if anyone stands to gain from the alliance, it's Lucía."

Amalia knew how much Lucía hated confrontation, and how much it must have cost her to say, "I don't want to marry Victor. I just met him last night."

"You're very young. You don't know what you want yet," Tio Francisco said dismissively. "You'll thank me someday."

"Ah, now that's a familiar tune." Julián half sat on one of the sturdy tables, crossing his arms over his chest as he looked at Lucía. "Far be it from a rascal like me to offer anyone advice, but being intimately acquainted with that particular song and dance, it's my displeasure to tell you that future thankfulness rarely materializes."

"Your opinion is as unwanted as it is unsolicited," his father told him shortly. "This affair is none of your concern."

"Isn't it?" There was a challenge in Julián's gaze that Amalia didn't quite understand. His relationship with his father and cousin was clearly adversarial, and had been since he was much younger. But there was something else at work here, and it clearly had something to do with the Troncosos.

"Why *are* you here?" Victor asked.

"I've always liked the Europa," Julián replied lazily. "The food's good and the wine's even better."

"In town," Victor clarified. "You've been carousing your way through Puerto Rico for the better part of a year. Why return now? And why feel the need to intrude in what is clearly a private family matter? After all, I seem to remember you renouncing this family and all it stood for just before you stomped away in a huff."

Cold dread was starting to rise in Amalia's stomach. More and more things were falling into place, because Julián was not the enigma she'd made him out to be; just a very good liar.

"You knew, didn't you?" This was the first time she'd addressed Julián directly since the truth of his identity had come out, and she couldn't miss the way he blanched when her accusing gaze landed on his. "About the engagement. That's why you did all this. That's why you pretended—"

Fury choked off the rest of her words. She'd been grateful—*grateful!*—that he'd agreed to accompany her all the way to Puerto Plata.

The enormity of his deception was crashing over her in waves, as the whole thing was too much for her mind and her heart to comprehend at once. He hadn't just lied to her about who he was. He'd let her believe that he was helping—that he was at her service.

Even worse than that, he'd let her believe that he cared.

The breeze filtering in through the half-closed shutters was heavily scented with flowers and perfume. It turned Amalia's stomach.

Victor's sharp gaze scraped over her like knives. "Don't worry. You aren't, by far, the first woman to fall for Julián's lies. And if I were a wagering sort of man, I'd say you won't be the last."

Don Reynaldo looked at his son with disgust. "Have you a single shred of decency left?"

"That would imply he had any to begin with," Victor put in.

Amalia didn't have to be endowed with superior powers of perception to notice the gleeful twist to Victor's smile. It made her sick to look at it, and not entirely for Julián's sake—this man who seemed to delight in cruelty was who her uncle expected sweet, innocent Lucía to marry? Did he even care how it would ruin her life?

His arrangement with the Fuentes family must have been very profitable indeed.

She turned to glare at Tio Francisco, only to be met with a triumphant expression. "You see, Amalia," he said, trying to sound like the kindly uncle he had never been, "this is why I ask for your obedience. All I have ever tried to do is keep you and Lucía safe from those who would use you for your fortune."

Julián scoffed. "I have no need for Amalia's money."

"Perhaps not," Tio Francisco said, "but you used her all the same."

His words fell into the thick silence with the force of a cannonball. Already uncomfortably aware of all the eyes on her, Amalia did her best to stifle a loud gasp—or was it a sob?—as she felt the inescapable truth of it drive itself into her seizing heart.

Julián hadn't just lied to her. He'd used her.

Julián had long since given up hoping for any shred of approval from Don Reynaldo Fuentes. But from the moment he'd walked into the hotel's dining room to see Amalia face-to-face with Victor, he'd been holding himself in such rigid control that even his father would have been proud.

All it took to crack it was one remark from her uncle.

No—that wasn't right. It was the look on Amalia's face when she came to the realization that Don Francisco was right. Julián *had* used her. Not for the reasons they all thought, and his interest in her wasn't entirely mercenary, but well, there it was.

Amalia didn't just look hurt. She had that dazed look of someone who'd just had the floor pulled out from under her. He couldn't have hurt her more if he'd deliberately set out to do it.

Julián's heart—if he had such a thing, and if it hadn't already shriveled beyond recognition—felt like it was splintering.

And there would be no putting it back together. He had already seen Victor glance down at the ring Amalia still wore. The sharp narrowing of his eyes when he recognized it made Julián's stomach sink. He knew what was coming. He'd seen Victor do it once before, almost a year ago now, and he wasn't about to give his cousin the chance to do it again.

Shielding Amalia from Victor's machinations was going to be impossible now. But at least Julián could soften the blow. Unfortunately, the only way to do that was to make Victor and his father believe that he had little interest for her beyond what he could get out of her. So instead of throwing himself at Amalia's feet and showering her with apologies, Julián was going to do his best to break her heart.

And the remains of his with it.

It was for the better. He'd vowed to himself that he

would never put himself in a situation where someone he cared for could be used against him. Not again. Never again.

Julián summoned up one of the insolent smiles he knew irritated his father beyond all reason. "*Used* is such an ugly word," he said lightly, forcing himself to look directly at Amalia. "Especially when our journey from San Pedro proved so pleasurable. Dare I say mutually so?"

There was a split second in which Amalia's eyes were wide and unguarded and raw with the shock of his betrayal. Then they shuttered, and grim determination hardened her generous mouth.

Less than an hour ago Julián had laid claim to those lips. He had reveled in the dips and hollows of that sumptuous mouth, thinking that it would be his— maybe not forever, because he knew better than to aspire to that much happiness, but for a little while at least. Long enough for him to commit her taste to memory.

"I doubt she would describe any time spent in your presence as *pleasurable*," Victor said.

Amalia didn't bother to hide her irritation. "I can speak for myself," she told Victor, before turning to Julián. "Whatever it is you're trying to imply—"

"I'm not implying anything," Julián said, knowing how much the interruption would annoy her. He felt a bitter sense of satisfaction. Whatever his father believed, Julián was good for one thing at least. "I'm saying it outright—we had our fun on the ship, but I thought you knew better than to expect anything else from me. I was perfectly clear when I told you that my dalliances never last long if I can help it."

"Trust me when I say I don't expect anything from you," Amalia said with chilly politeness, and Julián found that much more gut-wrenching than if she'd given in to her anger.

He shrugged. "Then we can dispense with the re-criminations and the questioning about what I may or may not have known, or who I may or may not have used. That's bound to get tiresome, and I have better things to do with my time."

Don Francisco was making a halfhearted attempt to sputter out something about his niece's honor, as if he hadn't gone and ruined her reputation by telling half of San Pedro that she'd run away with a stranger.

"I think we've had enough of your contemptible behavior, Julián," Victor announced over the older man's bluster. "Clearly, you've only returned to embarrass us, as you've always done. Or because you think that ruining my future happiness will somehow make up for the mistakes you yourself have made in the past."

Future happiness? Victor hadn't so much as glanced at his fiancée since Julián had joined them. The girl was still clinging to Amalia's arm, looking anxious. Julián felt a dart of pity—she was entirely too young to be caught up in his family's schemes, much less find herself tied for life to someone like Victor.

Less than a month ago Julián had returned from Puerto Rico with no other purpose than to get to the bottom of his family's involvement in his relationship with Concepción. There was something more important to be done now—keeping Amalia's sister away from them at all costs.

"Go back to your life of debauchery," Victor added,

his eyes glittering in the low light. "Nobody wants you here."

The corners of Julián's mouth lifted into something that wasn't quite a smile. "What's the matter, Victor? Don't tell me you're still jealous that women like me over you. Or are you worried that you'll never be able to find a woman who wants to marry you without being paid by my father?"

"Only you would put women and payment in the same sentence," Victor snapped.

"I've been gone a whole year and you still haven't developed a sense of humor." Julián pretended to sigh. "What a shame."

Amalia made an impatient gesture with her hand. "If the two of you are done with your little squabble, there are more important matters at hand." She shifted her gaze to Victor. "I don't know what my uncle promised you, but if you'd care to renegotiate your arrangement, I can offer you better terms."

Devil take him, but Julián relished the note of defiance in her voice.

He saw the flicker in Victor's eyes a fraction of a second too late. "Would those be the same terms you offered my cousin?" he said nastily.

Julián's muscles bunched with the urge to pummel the sneer off his cousin's face. Only the knowledge that he couldn't show his hand, not now, kept him still.

Victor's lip curled. "I'm afraid I don't have his taste for—"

"Victor," Julián's father said sharply, before Julián could give in to the violent impulse coursing through him.

He realized with a start that his fingers had closed

around one of the knives on the table next to him. With difficulty, and hoping that no one had seen his instinctive gesture, he loosened his fingers and laid his hand flat on the tablecloth.

Heeding the rebuke like the obedient little boy he'd always been, Victor wiped the sneer off his face and addressed Amalia with scrupulous politeness. "There's nothing you can offer me. You have no control over your and your sister's property, and no ability to dispose of any of it. You may be an heiress, but you have nothing." He glanced at Julián. "Not even my cousin's friendship, if that was what he offered you."

Don Reynaldo's voice was like the crack of a whip. "That's enough. Might I remind you all that we've guests just outside?" He nodded at the dining room's half-closed shutters. Through the slats, Julián could see glimpses of the milling crowd, interspersed by the waiters' more purposeful movements as they navigated their way around the courtyard bearing salvers crowded with champagne flutes.

Even if no one had told him the party was being held by his father, Julián would have guessed, purely from the lavish display. However much of a sham Victor's marriage to Amalia's sister might be, Don Reynaldo never missed an opportunity to make a social splash and have his name in the papers—or to display his wealth.

"You will leave," Don Reynaldo continued, pointing at Julián, "without a single word to any of our guests. I don't know what you were hoping to accomplish by coming here today, but I will not let you ruin the young lady's happy day."

"You're ruining her life and you haven't bothered

to learn her name?" Once upon a time Julián would have paid dearly for the impudent remark. His father had never been violent, but his cold silence was punishment enough when all Julián wanted was a little paternal comfort.

His father looked profoundly weary. "I will have you dragged out if you don't leave immediately, Julián. This affair is none of your concern. As for everyone else... I have to ask that you rejoin our guests."

Evidently thinking there was nothing more to be said, Don Reynaldo began to turn away.

"Wait," Amalia said.

She twisted the ring off and held it out to Julián, jerking her hand away when it brushed his palm. The look in her eyes would have killed him, if he hadn't already felt like he was beyond even death. But it was still not as bad as when she turned to his father, asking, "Has the engagement been announced?"

"Not yet," Don Reynaldo said warily.

"Then I will ask you one thing. Spare Lucía," Amalia said, her voice clear and her gaze fierce. "Spare her, and I'll marry Victor instead."

Chapter Eleven

Julián went home.

Not to the sprawling estate where he'd once lived with his father and cousin, but to the light blue house he had bought when he realized that he'd rather become a wastrel than keep trying and failing to meet his father's expectations. Both its stories were so luxuriously appointed as to make the Troncosos' home look like a pauper's den, especially the set of rooms on the second floor where Julián romanced all of his conquests.

His own bedroom was markedly plainer, if no less comfortable—a feather mattress in a handsome wooden frame, an upholstered armchair by the window and no fussy drapes to block out the sunlight. At the foot of the bed was the leather trunk full of things that had once belonged to his mother. Next to the armchair, a small round table with a lamp and a decanter that he usually kept filled with French brandy. A mahogany armoire and a matching chest of drawers contained his expansive wardrobe, mostly made up of Italian leather shoes and bespoke suits and shirts he'd had tailored during his travels around Spain.

The whole house was modern and bright with electric lights, and with the exception of the married couple he employed to see to the interior and grounds, utterly deserted.

He lost two days to his smoldering resentment. He could feel it festering inside him, as well as the old urge to drown it in drink and women. But his usual pursuits no longer held much appeal. Playing the dissolute rake had been his way of getting his father's attention, at least at first. When it became clear that there was little he could do to satisfy Don Reynaldo's exacting demands, Julián opted for distraction instead.

Now there seemed little point to continue inquiring into the damned mess with Concepción. His charade was over, and so was his investigation. There seemed little point to it now.

Julián should have known that Amalia would volunteer to marry Victor in her sister's stead. She would throw herself into a flaming pyre if it meant keeping Lucía out of it. Nor was he surprised that Victor had accepted her impulsive proposal. His cousin had never had any scruples, and he would think nothing of what it would mean for Amalia's or his own future if it meant taking something away from Julián.

Once again, Julián's life was crumbling to pieces and there was little he could do to shore it back together.

When Concepción left him, Julián had been crushed, as breathless with his pain as if his house had fallen around him and he was trapped under the rubble. It was nothing compared to what he felt now, knowing that Amalia not only despised him, but that she was days away from marrying his cousin, as well.

It was the work of an hour to find out what he'd

suspected—his father had put the Troncosos up at the Hotel Europa, which he had purchased while Julián was away. Why not? He owned practically everything else in town.

Julián didn't waste time in wondering what would have happened if he'd taken Amalia somewhere more circumspect. He'd thought about it—a humble set of rooms like the ones he'd occupied in San Pedro, paid for discreetly in cash. The Europa was one of the few places in Puerto Plata where Julián had halfway pleasant memories, and sentimental fool that he was, he'd wanted what little comfort could be scrounged from them.

The hotel was where his mother used to take him every Friday for lunch. Contrary to what he'd told Amalia, he remembered those afternoons with painful clarity. Victor, who was two years older than Julián, had his French lessons on Fridays, and Don Reynaldo was often working, so it was always just Julián and his mother. He could close his eyes and picture her as she'd looked sitting at a table in the courtyard, bathed in golden light as she laughed and teased him.

Julián remembered them as some of the few moments when he'd felt unreserved joy. When he'd felt safe from his demanding father; safe from Victor's little cruelties...

And then she'd died and he hadn't visited the Europa again until he was old enough to continue the tradition on his own. Julián, who spent most of his days and evenings in the company of his cronies and whatever woman was currently tolerating him, had always gone to the Europa alone. Until now—until Amalia—there hadn't been anyone he'd wanted to share it with.

In any case, she and her sister and her uncle would be at the Europa for the foreseeable future, and Julián was finding it damn difficult to stay away.

In the handful of days that followed the absolute disaster of their arrival in Puerto Plata, Julián walked halfway there three times and turned back each time.

Amalia wouldn't want to see him. He'd made sure of that. As for Julián… He obviously hadn't learned his lesson. Even after seeing the speculation in Victor's eyes, that little glint of triumph when he'd worked out that Amalia and Julián had been more than simple travel companions—even after all that, Julián was still considering lurking in the lobby behind a newspaper, if only for a quick glimpse of her.

He should have been used to this howling loneliness. He'd never stopped feeling it, even when he surrounded himself with the loudest, wittiest, most amusing people. It had all but dissolved in the two days he'd shared with Amalia. Now it was clinging to him again, more unbearable than the suffocating heat.

Every once in a while he would take the necklace Amalia had given him to pawn out of the pocket where he kept it, and the sight of it would remind him of all the strength and courage that ran through her small frame. Thinking about all she had gone through made his own loneliness less desperately unbearable.

It wasn't until the fourth or fifth day that Julián realized that he had one valid excuse for paying the Troncosos a visit—he'd left his carpetbag with Amalia's luggage. He didn't care about the clothes in it, but there was some money there as well as the documents he'd taken from her uncle's desk. Julián snagged his hat from the stand by his front door, and set off for the Europa.

He asked for the Troncosos' rooms at the front desk and was unsurprised when he was told that the family was out for the day.

"I'll wait," Julián said and marched over to the seating area before anyone could tell him he wasn't welcome.

According to the clock set behind the front desk, barely ten minutes had passed before Amalia's uncle strode into the lobby. Julián was up like a shot, intercepting Don Francisco before he could reach the staircase toward which he was heading.

The older man's glance of irritation changed into a scowl when he recognized Julián.

"I was under the impression that you would not be troubling us again, young man." Don Francisco's side whiskers, liberally streaked with gray, were almost quivering with outrage. "Your father assured me—"

"My father has no say in what I do," Julián said as evenly as he possibly could. "He doesn't keep me caged, as you do Amalia and her sister."

Don Francisco's expression remained twisted with obvious dislike. "I would ask you what you want, but it's painfully clear. My niece does not want to see you. Now that your shameless dishonesty has been revealed, I sincerely doubt that she ever will. So if you will kindly step aside…"

Julián had no intention of doing anything of the sort. He stood his ground and said, "She has something of mine and I want it back."

"You ought to have considered that before you inveigled her into doing whatever it is you had her do on your journey here."

"You and I both know that Amalia does exactly what she wants and nothing more. It's a nuisance for you, I expect. What with your flagrant attempts to rob from her and her sister. But I happen to think it's glorious." Julián watched the other man flinch and smiled. "Whatever you tell yourself—or society—about your dealings being all for the benefit of your wards, I hope you're aware that I know the truth. You're robbing them of everything they've got, including their youth and freedom."

Don Francisco remembered his indignation. "How dare you accost me with such lies? The hotel's manager has been instructed by your father to have you hauled away if you so much as stepped inside. I need only call for help."

Julián may not have been a true bandit, but he certainly knew how to behave like one. Lowering his voice into a silky whisper, he said, "My father and cousin are not the only powerful Fuenteses in town. You do anything to hurt Amalia or her sister, and I will make you regret it, Don Francisco. I can promise you that."

Then he spun on his heel and walked away.

The sky was a pure, uninterrupted blue, and Amalia was wishing for rain.

Her limbs were twitching with inaction. She'd done nothing but rest for the three days she and Lucía had been confined to the suite while Tio Francisco and the Fuenteses hammered out the details of her marriage to Victor. Nothing, that was, but desperately try to think of a way out of it.

She and Lucía were sitting in the long, narrow balcony that stretched along their four-room suite. It was a well-appointed set of rooms with upholstered armchairs and costly Tiffany lamps. Lace curtains framed the windows, and the round, marble-topped table by the entrance held an ostentatious bouquet bearing a note from Victor.

To my spirited new fiancée. Looking forward to the wedding.

Amalia wanted to knock it over.

The sound of carriage wheels traveled up from the street below, loud enough that she almost missed Lucía's words when she spoke.

"I hate to think that you've made yourself miserable for my sake."

Lucía was the one who looked miserable, huddled in her chair with a small booklet of sheet music on her lap. Amalia had twined Lucía's hair into a braid that morning, since they had no plans to leave the suite, and the hairstyle made her sister look even younger than her seventeen years.

Amalia leaped up from her own seat, flinging aside the newspaper she had been staring at with sightless eyes.

"I would commit crimes for your sake," she said fiercely. "Move mountains. Glare the sky into submission if thwarting a storm would make you happy."

Lucía bit her lip. "I wish you could. You've had thunderclouds hanging over your head since you got here, and I don't blame you. The very prospect of having to marry that Victor..." She shuddered.

Amalia wanted to swear out loud. The thing hanging above her head wasn't thunderclouds—it was a tempest. And Amalia wanted to rage with it. At her uncle, at the Fuenteses and even at herself, for not having figured out what was happening sooner.

"I can't help but think it's not just marrying Victor that's got you all twisted up, bad enough as that would be," Lucía ventured. "What happened between you and his cousin? I know you said that he escorted you here, and he implied some shocking things, but…"

Shocking. That was one word for what Amalia and Julián had done—not just aboard the ship, but in the two days they'd shared. Amalia was half inclined to call her lack of sense shocking, too.

It had been so easy to let herself get swept away by the thrill of being around him and doing things she'd never imagined she'd be able to. That, Amalia decided, had been Julián's main allure. Her rebellious nature couldn't entirely be chalked up to her circumstances— she'd always gotten a kick out of doing the forbidden. That was the only reason she'd let her guard down around Julián. Not because she'd felt anything for him.

Amalia waved away the thought with a flick of her wrist as she went to lean against the wrought iron railing and peer at the goings-on below. Puerto Plata, or what little she had seen of it, seemed as busy as San Pedro, and the Hotel Europa was clearly a favorite with both the travelers conveyed into town by the great steamships and those from the interior of the island who came for weekend jaunts on the express trains.

Watching people stream in and out was one of the few ways to pass the time, since Tio Francisco would rather she and Lucía not wander around an unfamiliar city, and Amalia was trying hard to appease him by feigning obedience until she worked out her next move.

It had nothing to do with being on the lookout for a dark-haired man.

Amalia frowned. "Julián Fuentes is a liar. And he was just a means to an end." Turning toward Lucía, she explained her reasoning behind the fake kidnapping. "I'm sorry I didn't tell you. It was damn heartless of me to make you worry, but I didn't want you to be in trouble with Tio Francisco if he found out. If I'd known he would be glad to have me out of the way—"

"You didn't know," Lucía said quickly. "You couldn't have. To be honest, I don't think it would have made a difference—he would have found a way to keep you in the dark about what he was planning. He's scared of you, you know. Of what you might do or say."

"Good," Amalia said grimly. "I hope he's terrified. What he's doing to us isn't right, no matter what Papá's will says. We're not his pawns to do whatever he wants with and even if we were, he's terrible at chess. I won't let him ruin both our lives to satisfy his greed."

"It didn't look like Julián was happy about it, either," Lucía pointed out. "If you ask me, I think he almost went into apoplexy when you said you would marry Victor. I saw your face when you looked at him, too. Whatever Julián is to you, you need him more than you think."

"I don't need *anyone*," Amalia said fiercely. "Except for you."

"And I think you liked him more than you care to admit," Lucía continued, with more determination than Amalia thought her sweet, quiet sister had in her. "If he hurt you in some way—"

"He couldn't have," Amalia said, raising her chin. "You have to care for, or about, someone for them to hurt you and I wouldn't give three whistles for Julián Fuentes."

Lucía was giving her a scrutinizing look. "Sometimes I think that the more you like someone, the harder you try to push them away. You do know, Amalia, that everything Tio Francisco says about people only liking us for our money isn't really true. I'd say that especially applies to Julián."

It had taken very little effort—and a couple of conversations with the maids who'd come in to tidy the suite—for Amalia to find out that the Fuenteses were railroad tycoons, with a fortune to rival Mr. Vanderbilt's in America. They didn't just own the hotel, they owned land and businesses all through the island, and their influence extended just as far. The gold-and-diamond ring Julián carried around with him, valuable though it clearly was, must have been a trinket compared to the jewels that must have hung around his mother's neck.

"He may not have tried to get close to me for my money, but he still used me," Amalia said tightly, adding, before Lucía could remark on the sudden brightness of Amalia's eyes, "In any case, Julián doesn't matter. I don't plan on ever seeing him again." At Lucía's puzzled look, she elaborated. "I'm not going to marry Victor. I'm going to get my hands on some money, even if I have to rifle through Tio Francisco's pockets or pawn his watch and its gaudy chain. And then you and I are going to get as far away from here as we possibly can."

Lucía looked as if she didn't dare to hope such a thing was possible. Then she glanced over Amalia's shoulder, her eyes widening. Amalia followed her gaze and saw her uncle striding toward them.

Heart racing, Amalia moved back into her chair. He couldn't have heard her speak all the way from the doorway, could he? His expression held nothing more than his usual dourness, though, and Amalia forced herself to relax.

"How were the negotiations?" she asked airily. "Did you trade me for pigs or for sheep? No, wait, I forgot—you're much too business savvy to accept anything less than a herd of cows."

There it was, the furrow that tended to appear between his brows whenever he and Amalia had any kind of exchange. "If you're asking after the health of your betrothed," he said pointedly, "I'm pleased to tell you that he's very well—and that he has extended an invitation for the three of us to join him and Don Reynaldo for dinner at their home."

Amalia immediately resolved to cut the evening short by feigning a headache. "He wouldn't have if he knew what I could do with a fork," she muttered, ignoring the puzzled glance that earned her.

Tío Francisco eased himself into an armchair. "I really hope you'll be sensible on this matter, Amalia—none of your contrariness. I wouldn't have had to go to the lengths I did if you had acted right from the beginning."

"I could say the same," she told him. "If you ask me, I'm getting tired of this little waltz."

As usual, her uncle mistook her meaning. "I'm glad to hear that. Cooperation is all I've ever asked. All I do is for your sakes, you know."

He said it often enough, but Amalia had wondered more than once if he truly believed it.

Knowing that he was five seconds away from a lecture on docility and gratitude, and knowing just as well that in her current mood it would only end in her doing something wildly inadvisable, Amalia rose from her seat. "If you'll excuse me, I'm going to look through my clothes to see if I can find something suitable for dinner. Lu, will you help me?"

Looking happy to abandon their uncle to his own company, Lucía hastened after Amalia. "You're already trying to work out how to skip the dinner, aren't you?" she asked when the door to the bedroom they were sharing closed behind them.

Amalia grinned. "I would, but I wouldn't want to leave you alone with all those snakes."

Her luggage had been unpacked by the hotel's maids, who had folded and hung up her clothing in the large wardrobe in a corner of the room. Neatly stacked below her gowns were her valises and hatboxes—and Julián's ratty old carpetbag, which was a testament to how accomplished a liar he had turned out to be. He hadn't missed a single detail.

As Lucía perched on the bed and continued to peruse her sheet music, humming under her breath, Amalia yanked out the carpetbag and set it on the bed. Ordinarily, she would have never dreamed of going through someone else's things. Under the circumstances, however, she felt justified.

Unsnapping the old clasp, Amalia opened the bag to see that Julián hadn't packed a great deal of clothing. At the time Amalia had imagined he hadn't had more. She knew better now—Julián probably had wardrobes upon wardrobes full of bespoke suits from the best tailors in the country, if not the world.

There were only a couple of neatly pressed shirts in the bag, and some folded linen garments that she set aside hastily, heat rising to her face.

Amalia's embarrassment faded almost immediately as her gaze fell on two stacks of banknotes as thick as a brick, bound together with twine and a paper band stamped with an insignia that she recognized as that of the National Bank.

The money gave her pause. There was enough in there for her and Lucía to live comfortably on for a year or more in a nice little garret in Vienna. Those stacks of bills would solve all their problems. Or if not all, then certainly the most important ones.

But Amalia wasn't a thief.

Pushing the money out of the way, she continued her exploration until she found a sheaf of papers nestled at the bottom of the bag. She would have thought nothing of it, save that the first few lines of handwritten text bore her uncle's name. Amalia pulled out the papers, going through them slowly. They were all letters, and all addressed to Tío Francisco. Julián must have pilfered them from his desk when she'd been distracted looking for Lucía's note.

It only served to remind her that at every step of the way, whether he was proclaiming that he was at her service or kissing her senseless on the steamer's deck, his little errand had always been on his mind. He had used her—Tío Francisco had been quick enough to point that out the day before. He'd also lied. But the most unforgivable thing Julián had done was that he had made her trust him.

And he'd made her forget that nothing good ever came from trusting men.

Her hands were shaking slightly as she put everything back into the carpetbag. *Seek and you shall find.* Wasn't that what they always said? If there was an equally apt saying about throwing your lot in with bandits, Amalia didn't know it.

Her resolve hardened as she stared down at the papers. She was going to confront him—and she was going to make him tell her what these papers were all about. She wanted answers, and she wanted them now.

With a decisive snap, she closed the carpetbag and seized the handle. Sneaking out of the suite wouldn't be easy with her uncle just outside, but she'd done it at home plenty of times. "Lu, will you tell Tío that I've got a headache and will lie down for the rest of the afternoon?"

Lucía looked up from her music, her brows drawing together in apprehension when she saw Amalia holding the bag. "You're going out?"

"Yes, but don't worry, I'll be back in time to dress for dinner."

"Where are you going?"

Amalia gave her sister a grim smile. "To pay a bandit a visit."

Chapter Twelve

It had been far too easy for Julián to slip into his old habit of rising well past noon and sitting down to eat hours after most people had enjoyed their midday meal. He couldn't remember the last time he'd sat in front of a plate of beefsteak with only the ticking of the clock for company. He'd briefly thought about going to one of his usual restaurants, but he couldn't stomach the thought of sitting at a table full of fashionable people and listening to their gossip and stories and jokes and having to pretend to find it all amusing.

A sudden banging at the front door propelled Julián out of the dining room. He reached the entrance before his housekeeper could so much as peek out of the kitchen, which was located at the very back of the house.

Julián was grateful for that when he opened the door and found an heiress on his doorstep.

"Amalia?"

"Were you expecting someone else?" she asked tartly.

She was breathtaking in a dark olive skirt with black

squiggles made out of some sort of braided material and jet beads that matched the trim on her white shirt-waist. Beneath the brim of her straw hat, her gaze was so dispassionate as to be almost cold.

Julián rarely lost his composure, but a smooth greeting was beyond him at the moment. "How the devil did you find out where I live?"

"I followed the scent of *eau-du-liar*," she snapped, and Julián couldn't hold back a grin.

Amalia was beautiful at the best of times. Anger made her resplendent. Part of him wanted to tease her just for the fun of it, but Julián was more aware than ever that he still needed to put distance between them.

"I went to the Europa earlier," he said over his shoulder as he led her to the front room. "Had a nice chat with your uncle. Did he tell you I stopped by?"

Instead of answering, or sitting, Amalia dropped something heavy onto one of the side tables. His carpetbag. Stomach sinking, Julián threw himself on a cane-backed chair. It was too stiff for a proper lounge, but Julián tried his best to strike up the proper insouciant attitude.

Not that Amalia was paying him any attention. She reached inside the bag and flung a stack of papers onto the table with enough force that half of them skidded on the polished wooden surface and cascaded to the floor. "Is this why you came to the hotel? To look for these?"

"In part, yes," he said with a calm he knew she would find maddening. "Much obliged to you, Your Highness. Anything else I can do for you, or would you rather rifle through my wardrobe?"

She placed her hands on her hips. "I'm tired of being lied to. Far be it from me to demand honesty from *you*, but I want you to explain to me exactly what's going on. I tried to read the letters, but there doesn't seem to be anything about business in them. So I'm asking you to tell me—why are our families so determined to see this marriage take place? What do they have to gain by it?"

The shell of anger around her cracked at the last question, letting Julián see past it and into the despair that had been driving her from the moment he had pulled her into his saddle and pretended to abduct her.

Julián wasn't the reason that Amalia and her sister had gotten involved in this mess, but nonetheless he felt like he owed her an explanation. After all, it wasn't like anyone else was going to offer her one.

"It's a very long story, and I've just now begun to piece it together." Julián cocked his head. "Do you think you can stand being around me long enough for me to tell it?"

Amalia crossed her arms. "I'll manage."

Julián, on the other hand, had serious doubts about his ability to be this close to Amalia without letting all the things he shouldn't say tumble out into the space between them. To quell the urge, he went to the decanters set out on a sideboard and poured himself a double whiskey. He thought about the *aguardiente* in the tin mug from the shack, wishing he and Amalia were still there and that the past few days hadn't happened.

"I joined my father's company as soon as I turned seventeen," he began, flattening the long-seated anger out of his tone. "Victor already had, a few years earlier, and he was acquitting himself excellently in my father's eyes by the time I came along. I didn't think I was doing too badly myself—I was never very studious, but I did have a head for figures."

Julián drained the last of his drink with a second deep swallow and immediately poured himself another glass, walking with it over to the window for the simple reason that he needed something as sturdy as the frame around it to prop him up. "I had this absurd notion of making my father proud. But I quickly found out that I didn't have the stomach for the way he and Victor do business. They're ruthless to the point of bloodthirstiness and they think nothing about destroying the life of whoever stands between them and their profit. Victor especially seems to get a thrill from it."

"Just the kind of people my uncle loves to associate with," Amalia said tightly.

"My father's company was awarded the contract to lay the railroad track between Puerto Plata and Santiago around ten years before I started working with him. He made a fortune importing steel, even with import duties being so high, but it didn't take him long to realize that the real money was in the lands the government was purchasing. After President Heureaux was killed in ninety-nine, my father began trying to use his influence with the new government to extend the railroad all the way to San Pedro. He hadn't been successful—until now."

"That must be why he wants our lands so badly," Amalia said, guessing in instants what it had taken Julián days to work out.

"And they'll stop at nothing to get them, not after all they've already done. They have ruined lives for this railroad deal. Including mine. Last year…" Julián's throat was suddenly so tight it took him a few seconds to get the rest of his words out. "I was courting a woman."

Something, perhaps recognition, flickered in Amalia's gaze. "Your young lady from Seville?"

Julián nodded. "She inherited a great deal of land from her grandfather—land that my father knew would be bisected by the new railroad. He wanted to buy it, but the price was more than he could afford."

It flared up again, the rage and the grief that had driven him for the past several weeks. And yearning. There was yearning, too. Not for Concepción, not anymore, but for the life Julián might have led had her affection for him not been stolen away.

A series of thoughts always came on the heels of that one. That maybe nothing had been stolen from him. That he'd never had Concepción's affection. That the affair was always going to end with Julián alone and brokenhearted, because Julián had never done anything to deserve more than that.

If his own father couldn't bring himself to love him, why would anyone else?

As he'd done so often over the past year, Julián tried to drown out his feelings with another sip of whiskey.

"Victor used my proximity to Concepción to get information about the other offers she and her mother were entertaining. And then he and my father hatched a plan to drive the value of her lands down and offer to buy them for a pittance. My father has never been able to countenance having his wishes thwarted, and he knew I would do anything in my power to keep them from cheating Concepción—I'd been a thorn in their side for years by then. Victor arranged it so that my father walked in on me and Concepción in bed. My father pretended not to have known about the affair—and that he was irate that I had seduced a young woman from a good family."

That particular wound was no longer as raw as it had once been, but Julián still recalled the sting of it. "I had been drinking and carousing a little too heavily, and it provided him with another excuse to send me away. Honestly, I was half convinced that someone like Concepción could never truly love a rascal like me, and I was relieved at the excuse to leave before she came to her senses." Julián lifted his shoulder into a shrug, though he knew that Amalia would see past his attempt at appearing unconcerned. "They had to make sure I didn't realize what they were doing because they knew I would try to stop them. So I wasn't there to keep them from driving Concepción and her mother to ruin."

"Why return, then? Why didn't you stay in Puerto Rico?"

"An acquaintance of mine told me that Concepción and her mother had been forced to leave the country and stay with relations in Seville. I wrote to her, and when she didn't answer, I wrote to one of her friends. That's when I found out that Victor had used my departure to turn her against me—to make her believe that I had never cared for her and was only working on my father's behalf."

"Only you did care for her," Amalia said. "She was the only woman you've ever loved."

Her words hung heavily in the air between them. Julián found himself unable to dispel them with one of his smart remarks. It was true, after all... Wasn't it?

With something of a start, he realized that he didn't think about Concepción as often as he once did. Hadn't thought about her, in fact, beyond his speculation of what his father and Victor had done.

Julián had held on to the pain of losing Concepción for close to a year. He hadn't just let it drive him. He had been well on his way to letting it consume him. And maybe it was just that the events of the past few weeks had offered him a distraction as much as a purpose, but he was a little disconcerted to find that the resentment he had harbored for so long had...maybe not faded, exactly, because he still felt strongly about the injustice that had been done to them both. It had changed.

And so had he.

"Right," Julián responded after a lapse of several moments.

It wasn't until he saw Amalia's mouth drawing into a tight line that he realized that she'd been looking for an entirely different answer. And even though he hadn't meant to hurt her—not this time, at least—it was just a matter of time before it happened. No one who got close to him escaped from getting hurt, after all, and why should Amalia be any different?

And in any case, if she really was going to be forced to marry Victor, the more she despised Julián, the less ammunition Victor would have to use against her.

He made himself cock his head. "Oh, Amalia," he said softly. "I thought I had made myself clear. I'm not looking for love, or for marriage, or for anything more meaningful than a night's pleasure."

For a moment Amalia looked like she was contemplating striking him. But all she did was toss her head back, her voice crackling with fury as she said, "Surely, you're not referring to what happened on the ship? That was nothing more than a dalliance. Not even that. It was—" she waved her hand in the air "—nothing more than a momentary lapse of judgment."

A lapse of judgment. Well, she wasn't the only woman to tell him that. And she very likely would not be the last.

"And yet, you're angry with me," Julián said, quirking up his lips into a suggestion of a smirk.

"I'm not," she said. Her upper lip was shaped like an archer's bow and in Julián's opinion it was just about as lethal. When it curled, it was like an arrow flying into his midsection. "If I'm angry at anyone, it's at myself— for believing that I could count on you, and for expecting that you would be any different than every man I've ever known. You're not a good man. You told me so yourself, Julián. You said it over and over again and I refused to listen. But you were right, weren't you?"

Slowly and deliberately, mostly so that she wouldn't notice the slight shaking in his fingers, Julián drained the last of the whiskey from his glass and set it aside. "I hope that made you feel better," he said casually. "It's nothing I didn't already know, though—you'll have to do better than that if you really want to hurt me."

Beneath her frilly blouse, Amalia's breasts were heaving up and down with shallow breaths. A handful of steps put Julián so close to her that she couldn't fail to notice his insolent gaze on her shirtfront.

Her expression shifted, and he curled his lips into a smirk. "If you have nothing more to say, may I suggest that you go back to your hotel? Unless you were hoping I would take you upstairs, in which case I would be more than happy to oblige."

She gazed at him and he knew she felt it, too...the

desire spanning between them that made the air crackle with heat.

The moment stretched, tension mounting between them until Julián had almost convinced himself that she was a second away from falling into his arms. The thought was followed by a rush of anticipation that he had difficulty quelling, though he knew that she would never give him the satisfaction. Not after everything he had just said to her.

And sure enough, Amalia broke the moment not with a kiss, but by giving him a look that by all rights should have withered him on the spot.

"You're despicable," she said, and with one last furious glance at him, turned on her heel and left.

Maybe it was a good thing that every single second they had spent together was engraved in Julián's mind, in luxurious detail, as there was no chance that Amalia Troncoso would ever willingly touch him again.

Enraging. Julián Fuentes was the most enraging man Amalia had ever met.

Now that he had gotten what he could out of her, he had abandoned all pretense of politeness. In fact, it almost seemed like he was doing his best to push her away. If he was, he was clearly doing it to be insufferable—one had only to see Julián around his father and uncle to notice how much pleasure he derived from being contrary.

Of course, anyone could say the same about her and her uncle. But she didn't care to find any common ground with a scoundrel like Julián.

She'd told him the truth when she said she wasn't angry with him. She wasn't even disappointed. If she had been thinking clearly at any point during the past several weeks, she would have seen past the rage and worry and exhaustion filling her and realized that she was breaking one of her cardinal rules.

Don't trust men.

Then again, knowing that he was a liar hadn't kept her from feeling like she would give anything for the pleasure of burrowing into his arms. She had grown too used to relying on him for everything, including comfort. Another minute and she might have found herself giving in to the urge.

Standing outside Julián's door, Amalia took a moment to gain control of the emotions raging inside her chest. A fortnight ago Julián had been nothing to her. Another couple of weeks, and anything she felt toward him now would have dissipated like wisps of smoke.

She didn't need Julián. What was more, she didn't even want him.

In a few hours she would sit at the table with his father and cousin and sip their wine and smile at their jokes. Then, while her uncle slept, she would comb through his luggage for anything of value. By the time the sun rose the next morning, she and Lucía would be on their way elsewhere. Maybe not Europe, as they had dreamed, but even a shack in a mountain somewhere would be preferable to being maneuvered and controlled by Tío Francisco and the Fuenteses.

Having a plan made her feel better. Squaring her shoulders, Amalia finished going down the steps.

She unlatched the iron gate at the front of Julián's house and paused when the sleeve of her shirtwaist caught on one of the twigs protruding from the hedge growing inside the fence. Cursing under her breath, she turned to free the fabric—and realized it wasn't a twig, but a man, and a familiar one at that.

She had just enough time to see the thin red line above his collar where Julián had sliced him with the broken bottle. Then the ruffian from the ship grabbed her by the waist, pinning her arms to her sides.

A rough, heavy hand that smelled vaguely of stewed cod clamped around her mouth before she could let out so much as a breath. Amalia swallowed back her scream, wishing for a fork or a knife or any kind of eating implement, even a spoon, as she tried and failed to drive the heel of her shoe into his instep.

The ruffian lifted her bodily off the ground and swung her toward one of the carriages lining the street. Amalia bucked wildly, kicking out ineffectually as she was stuffed into the carriage and the door slammed shut.

Her heart was pounding as she shakily hauled herself onto the seat. She ran her hand over the carriage door to find that the inner handle had been pried off, and the truth of what had just happened shuddered through her.

She was being kidnapped—this time in truth.

Chapter Thirteen

"Amalia, wait!"

The slam of his front door drowned out his words. Julián's body tensed with the need to run after her, but what was the use? He needed to make her hate him and judging by the look in her eyes, he had clearly succeeded.

If there was one thing Julián had always been able to do well, it was making himself disagreeable to everyone around him.

Julián stayed by the window, gripping the frame until his fingertips hurt as he tried to will himself not to care. Not about Amalia, not about the fact that she and her sister were about to be cheated out of their inheritance, and most decidedly not about the giant tear in his chest.

He almost didn't hear a muffled cry coming from the direction of his front gate. Sharply, Julián glanced outside in time to see Amalia being seized by a man in a brown suit.

A string of curses rolled out of his mouth as he vaulted out the window and pelted to the swinging gate. By the time he had shoved it open and thrust himself through it, though, Amalia had been bundled into a waiting carriage. One snap of the reins and the two horses at its head were galloping away.

Julián swore again, though a great deal more breathlessly than he had a moment before.

The carriage was plain black with no distinguishing marks, the horse pulling it, ordinary. He hadn't gotten a good look at the man who'd grabbed her, but he would be willing to bet a large portion of his fortune that it had been the ruffian from the ship. They'd assumed the man had been sent by Amalia's uncle, but now that he knew just how deeply Victor was involved in this whole business, Julián was damned sure who was behind this.

He didn't bother with his hat and jacket. Mounting his sleek, dark horse, which was hitched in front of his house, he galloped to the commercial property that housed his father's offices.

The three-story building occupied one of the busiest corners in town. Above one of its doors, which had been set at a forty-five-degree angle from the two on either side, a painted sign bore the name *Reynaldo Fuentes & Hijo*. The latter part had always twinged unpleasantly through Julián whenever he happened to look at it, as it served as one more reminder that he had never been the kind of son his father wanted. It must have affected Victor a similar way, though Julián had never asked.

Now, though, as Julián flung himself off the saddle and stormed inside, he hardly spared it a glance.

The front room was lined neatly with desks and bookcases stuffed with ledgers; bypassing these without a word for any of the clerks who voiced their protests to his intrusion before they recognized him, Julián thundered upstairs and to the glass-paned door at the end of the second-floor hallway.

"Where did they take her?" he demanded as he shoved open the door.

But it wasn't Victor sitting behind the massive mahogany desk, it was his father.

Looking neither startled nor alarmed at the intrusion, Don Reynaldo flicked his fingers in dismissal and the young clerk who had been taking notes on the other side of the vast desk hastily gathered his things and exited, closing the door softly behind him.

For a long moment the only sound in the room was the *snick* of the latch as it caught. Then Julián's father lifted an eyebrow. "Am I to guess what you mean by bursting into my office, or did you intend to offer an explanation?"

The two wooden chairs in front of the desk were now vacant, but Julián remained where he was. "Amalia Troncoso was just kidnapped exiting my house," he said, shaping each word around the gaping wound left behind by the sight of Amalia being hauled into that carriage like a sack of plantains. "There's no doubt in my mind that Victor is behind it."

"So you came here demanding to know her whereabouts. I wish I could say I was surprised, but you have always been transparent as glass."

And Don Reynaldo was as hard and unmoving as a boulder.

Outside his father's office, Julián could hear the clatter of typewriters, interrupted now and then by the clerks' hushed voices as they went about their business.

Because the world hadn't stopped when Amalia was taken; only Julián's heart.

He had paused to marshal his thoughts into some semblance of order, but now he took a moment to consider his father's expression. It was something Julián had done for as long as he'd had reason—for years he had studied his father with more scrutiny than his schoolbooks, intent on finding the secret to pleasing him. Don Reynaldo was reserved, but Julián had learned to read every slight twitch of his eyebrows and minuscule tightening of his mouth.

"It wasn't Victor," Julián said slowly. "It was you who gave the order."

Only a jerk of his fingers on the leather blotter betrayed the fact that his father was not, in fact, a boulder. "I'm sure I don't have to tell you that this deal with the girl's uncle is as delicate as it is important. Whatever you may feel for the girl—"

"I don't feel anything for her," Julián said, and knowing his protest sounded hollow, added, "but she does for me. She's headstrong and stubborn and will keep making trouble for you as long as her sister is involved. I can assure you that whatever you've asked that ruffian to do isn't enough to hold her back."

Don Reynaldo's eyes narrowed ever so slightly.

"Amalia isn't easily manipulated, but she has grown to trust me, and she dislikes Francisco. If I marry her, I will be better positioned legally to get rid of him. Bypass him altogether and you won't just have the lands you need—you'll have her entire fortune. Which, as I understand, includes plenty of property for development. I'd want seventy percent, of course," he added offhandedly, knowing his father could never resist a negotiation.

"Thirty," Don Reynaldo said automatically, and Julián held back a triumphant smile, "as I'd have to put up the capital."

The elder man sat back in his chair, fingers steepled together in thought. Julián knew he shouldn't push, or seem too eager, but every second that ticked by was one more second in which Amalia was alone in the company of that brute.

"It's not a bad scheme," Don Reynaldo said, and his eyes seemed to bore into Julián's. "Though I'm not altogether convinced that your reasons are purely mercenary. She is a very attractive girl, after all."

Everything in Julián revolted at the implication. He would have liked to slam out of that room—maybe he would have, if he hadn't been so worried for Amalia. This time, however, he was going to play his father's game. And he was going to win.

"The journey from San Pedro wasn't a chaste one, if that's what you're referring to," he made himself say casually. "I wouldn't object to sharing her bed in the long term." Sauntering to the desk, he laid both palms against its gleaming surface. "I can carry this off far better than Victor, and you know it. Force is effective in its own crude way, but it *is* a risk. Do things his way, and you open yourself up to speculation, at the very least, or a social outrage—Amalia will make sure of it. Make her believe I'm working on her behalf, and we have her full cooperation."

Don Reynaldo gave a thoughtful nod. "Victor is obedient and moldable. But he's not nearly the asset you would be if you weren't so softhearted. Triumph in business, as well as in life, requires a certain ruthlessness. You've never had it, Julián. What makes you think you have what it takes now?"

Julián gave his father a slight, humorless smile, glad that he had waited to confront him over Concepción. "I lost my head over Concepción, and paid for it by spending almost a year in exile. I like to think I've grown up since then. I know what it is to stand in your path now, and I'm not fool enough to think that a woman is worth the consequences."

His father didn't say anything, just looked at him. Julián had been on the receiving end of those looks long enough that he knew not to try to fill the silence with exhortations, promises or explanations. He emptied his body of all thoughts and simply gazed back.

"I had hoped you'd learned a thing or two," Don Reynaldo said finally. "It seems like perhaps you have."

Julián jerked his head into a nod. "I do have conditions, of course. If I've learned anything else over the past year, it's to never give anything for nothing. The first is that you sell me the Europa. In its entirety. I want to be the sole proprietor. The second..." He hardened his voice. "Get rid of Victor."

A slight twitch of his father's lips that could have been the beginnings of a smile made Julián turn around. It was only then that he realized that at some point during the conversation, the door behind him had opened. It wasn't a clerk at the doorway, but Victor, standing still as a snake that hadn't decided how to strike.

Julián turned back to his father, who had a clear view of them both. Don Reynaldo had always played them against each other, perhaps believing that would make them stronger. Julián, who had seen the way

Amalia cared about her sister, couldn't help but think that his father had been deeply mistaken. Maybe, under different circumstances, he and Victor might have been able to be friends.

"Is that your way of saying that you agree to my terms?" Julián asked his father, who looked faintly amused.

"Show me that you're serious about it," Don Reynaldo answered. "And I'll consider it."

Julián couldn't fail to notice that Victor hadn't said a word. "Where is she?"

To his surprise, his father answered. "The train station."

That was all he needed.

Victor didn't step aside as Julián exited, so he shouldered past him, walking out with his stride unbroken.

For once in her life Amalia was doing exactly what she was told.

Granted, it was only because of the knife being pressed against her lower back, but she still felt like she deserved some credit.

"You do know," she told the ruffian who'd abducted her, in as conversational a tone as she could muster when her heart was racing inside her chest, "that the boning in my corset will probably bend that cheap knife of yours if you tried to stab me with it."

There was nothing cheap about the heavy blade and the ruffian must have been clear on that point, because all he did was grunt.

He had been about as gregarious on the carriage ride to the train station where they stood. She had seen the single-story building from the carriage when she and Julián first arrived in Puerto Plata. It was hard to believe only a scant few days had passed since then when so much had changed. She'd lost Julián, or the person she had believed him to be, and now she was on the verge of losing what little hope she'd had of getting away with Lucía.

The station was crowded with families in a flurry of departure and uniformed porters rushing to and fro with carts laden with luggage. Quite a few people had already boarded the train, and the open windows of each car were full of travelers waving goodbye to those they were leaving behind.

All save for the car toward which the ruffian was guiding her. Dark blue curtains with tassels shielded its interior from prying eyes, so it wasn't until Amalia stepped inside, past a man standing to one side like a guard and through a narrow, carpeted corridor, that she saw that instead of a row of seats, it contained an opulent parlor.

Paneled in gleaming mahogany, with brass fittings and tasseled curtains at the window, it held an imposing desk on one side below a large oil painting in an ostentatious gold frame, and a seating area in the other. The furniture was finely crafted, the upholstered seats plush and comfortable.

The man sitting stiffly on one of the armchairs, on the other hand, looked out of place and ill at ease.

"So it's true," Tio Francisco said heavily as Amalia was pushed the rest of the way into the car. "You defied my orders about staying in the suite—and to go to Julián Fuentes, of all people. I didn't want to believe it, but I've learned to be cautious when it comes to you."

Amalia heard the *snick* of the door shutting behind

her, and she felt her shoulders relax at the relief of no longer having a knife against her back. "You didn't tell me he'd come to the hotel."

The air inside the car was stale and smelled vaguely of cigar smoke. There were plenty of places for Amalia to sit, but she felt better standing. A small part of her wanted to take a page out of Julián's book and lounge insolently against the paneled walls, just to see if it would get a rise out of Tio Francisco.

"He didn't come for you," her uncle said curtly. "He doesn't care for you, and if you think he's going to look out for you instead of himself—"

"I don't," Amalia said crisply, but she could tell that he didn't believe her.

"Amalia," he began, and she tensed at the patient, reasonable tone that he employed when he wanted to imply that she was being the exact opposite. "I'm not an unfeeling sort of man. I remember what it was like to be young. And I understand that my efforts to shelter you and Lucía from the ravages of fortune hunters and other opportunists have been so zealous that neither of you has had the opportunity to learn much about human nature. Julián Fuentes is not a good man. His own father despairs of him. He's trying to sow discord within his family and he's using you to do that. Whatever he may have said to put you up to this—"

Amalia's eyes narrowed. "If by this you mean saving Lucía from an unwanted marriage, I can assure you that Julián had no part in it."

Tio Francisco gave her a brief, infuriating smile. "I'm sure that's what he's led you to believe. You needn't feel embarrassed about falling for his manipulations. Men like him always know to target naive young—"

"What is this about?" Amalia demanded impatiently, noting in satisfaction her uncle's irritation at being interrupted yet again. "Did you have me kidnapped and forced aboard a train just to give me a lecture? You could have saved yourself the trouble—I was on my way back to the hotel to get ready for the blasted dinner with your new friends. I'm doing everything you've asked of me—"

"You've been planning to abscond with your sister," Tio Francisco snapped. "I heard the two of you plotting earlier. You had no intention of marrying Victor, and I would appreciate if you stopped lying about it." He took a deep breath, as if to gather his patience. "Women like you and Lucía have a responsibility to your families. I have tried my hardest to raise you to consider more than just yourselves—it would be the height of selfishness for you both to insist on a love match."

For a long moment Amalia couldn't do anything but stare at her uncle. Selfish? He thought they were selfish for not wanting to submit quietly to a life they hadn't chosen? She couldn't tell if he truly believed that, or was only saying so for her benefit.

Maybe it didn't matter. Both were bad enough.

And in any case, he hadn't raised her—her parents had. When her father died, a year after her mother, Amalia had been thirteen and more than old enough to look after her sister. All Tio Francisco had looked after was their money, which he clearly prized more than his nieces.

"A union between us and the Fuenteses is mutually beneficial," he continued, firm under her incredulous gaze. "This arrangement will make you and Lucía very rich women indeed. You'll be able to do anything you like...buy anything you want."

"*You* certainly will," Amalia bit out, finally finding her voice. Tío Francisco didn't understand—he never had. More money didn't always mean more freedom. It meant more obligations and never knowing if someone liked you for yourself. "I hope you're being paid well for this. I hope you're getting everything you ever wanted. Because we're not your property to sell or trade as you see fit, and one day I will give you cause to regret having ever treated us as such."

Amalia half expected her uncle to launch into his usual performance designed to show her that she was being unreasonable—he stifled sighs, pinched the bridge of his nose, massaged his temples as if to ward off incipient headaches and, something she found supremely annoying, he injected a hint of scorn into his tone to convey just how absurd he found her.

He didn't do any of those things. If anything, he just looked furious. "I've given you girls *everything* and that's never been enough for you. And now you're doing your best to poison your sister's mind."

"Lucía has a mind of her own," Amalia snapped. "She's been very clear about not wanting to marry Victor, or anyone else. If you go through with this, I'll do what I should have done from the start. I'll go to the gossip papers. I'll tell everyone I know—everyone *you* know—that you put your greed above your nieces' happiness."

Tío Francisco's face, normally a pale brown lighter than Amalia's own, reddened until he looked like he was going to burst.

Amalia had never seen her uncle like this. Irritated beyond reason at one or another of her exploits, yes. Even angry. But he had never glowered at her with such virulent dislike. He leaned forward, his eyes on Amalia's, his voice low and hard.

"And who would believe you? I have been nothing but devoted to the two of you, and all of San Pedro society would attest to that fact. Whereas you have only done what pleases you, with little regard for how it reflects on your family. Are you willing to damage your sister's reputation as well as your own, just for the sake of getting your own way? Will she thank you for that? When she's cast out of good society, starving in some garret and forced to play her violin on street corners for crusts of bread, will she be grateful or will she resent you for ruining her life?"

Amalia reared back, feeling as though she'd been slapped.

Her uncle wasn't finished. "I'm done trying to reason with you, Amalia. You have tried to undermine me and my plans from the moment your father left me in charge and it's clear you're never going to stop. I spoke with Reynaldo and Victor earlier, and they have agreed to release you from your engagement. I'm sure you understand why I can't allow you to return to the hotel."

Amalia clenched her fists so hard her nails left bloody half circles on her palm. "Will you at least tell me where I'm being taken?"

"This is the express train to Santiago. The journey won't be long, and you will be made comfortable once you're there." Tio Francisco stood. "I'd instructed my men to keep you there until the wedding is over—but if living by my rules is so intolerable, then I should probably consider finding you permanent living arrangements elsewhere. You did say something about Europe this afternoon, if I recall correctly."

"You can't do this." She struggled to sound defiant through the anger and frustration coalescing inside her. Amalia Troncoso didn't cry. She *never* cried. "I won't let you."

"I regret the necessity of doing this, Amalia, but you have forced my hand. The men won't harm you—unless you give them cause."

With those ominous parting words, Amalia's uncle let himself out of the compartment, closing the door firmly behind him. Amalia didn't bother to try it. Even if it wasn't locked, she knew that the ruffians would be waiting on the other side.

A few moments later the train began to roll away from the station, taking Amalia far away from her sister and any hope of getting her out of this mess.

Chapter Fourteen

If the hardy horse Julián had bought in San Pedro had been fit for a bandit, the thoroughbred he kept in Puerto Plata was perfect for the son of a railroad tycoon. Sleek and beautiful and expensive, it was also fast.

And Julián was desperate.

The train whistled just as he arrived at the station. Julián looked wildly at the windows, hardly daring to hope—

There. He caught a glimpse of her a fraction of a second before the air between them was filled with steam. She was in the third car from the end, which had long ago been designated as his father's private car. Through the window's filmy glass, Amalia looked as he had never seen her—utterly discouraged.

Julián's heart lurched. And in a split second, he made his decision.

He never wore spurs, out of principle, and he had no need of them now. A single nudge to the racehorse's flank was enough to make him explode into motion. He bent down low over the saddle as they leaped nimbly over a low fence and galloped after the train as it started to slowly pull out of the station.

It was much smaller than some of the great locomotives he'd seen in other parts of the world. The last couple of cars were made out of wood, and probably held luggage and some sort of cargo.

The roar of the train had become the roar of his own heart. As its engine belched coal into the blazing sky, Julián's entire world narrowed to one of the two iron poles jutting out from the back of the car. He had a single attempt and only a few moments to do it—once the locomotive reached its full speed, there wasn't a scrap of chance that he'd be able to overtake it.

Fail, and he'd break an arm or a leg or both and be of no use to Amalia or himself.

Another nudge and his horse put on a burst of speed, unflappable even as they neared the locomotive's chugging wheels. Julián stood up on the stirrups, holding the reins in one hand and reaching for the pole with the other. His fingers brushed the iron, a mere centimeter too far for him to grasp it.

Just a little farther—

The moment the palm of his hand connected with the pole, Julián flung himself off his saddle and onto the small platform at the back of the cargo car.

He slammed hard against the sun-warmed wood. The impact, or the leap, or the utter foolishness of what he'd just done, snatched his breath away, and he had to lean back against the car for a few minutes until his worry for Amalia forced him back into action.

As quickly as he could, Julián clambered to the top of the car and made his way past the hair-raising gap between each car to where Amalia was being held. Julián hadn't traveled with his father in years, but he remembered the layout of the car well enough, as well as his father's preference for keeping his staff separate from himself so that he could conduct business in private.

He also remembered the accident that had led to his father installing a hatch on the roof of his car.

The late-afternoon sun was beating down on his bare head, sending rivulets of sweat streaming down his temples in spite of the warm breeze that buffeted the damp hair around his face. The desperation and audacity that had allowed him to leap aboard a moving train was quickly fading away, and memories were rushing like waves over the sand to fill in the space they had left behind.

The sickening jolt. The weightless sensation of being flung into the air. And—worst of all—the sound of crunching metal, underlaid by the screams of agony he still heard in his dreams.

Julián sagged to his knees. The locomotive was no longer a roar in his ears, but a live beast charging beneath his braced hands, ready to buck him off at any moment.

With fingers that had grown suddenly clumsy, he scrabbled for the hatch—the hinges had been set so that it could be pushed or kicked open from the inside. He grasped the latch, yanked it to one side and then he was sliding through the opening and dropping onto the compartment's thick carpeting.

He landed on his feet, but the jostling of the train cost him his balance and he found himself pitching right into Amalia.

Her curves provided him a cushioned landing. He slid down her body until he was kneeling between her thighs in a position that was quickly becoming a familiar one.

The devil himself knew there was nowhere else he would rather be.

He took one look at her wide, panicked eyes and covered her mouth with his palm to silence the scream that would bring her captors running. And then he made himself grin, because it was either that or let out his own howl.

"Missed me, Your Highness?"

Above his hand, Amalia's face was a study in shock. Her breath was quick and hot against his palm as he released her mouth and skimmed her cheekbone and the line of her jaw, telling himself he was only making sure that she was unharmed. Her creamy brown skin was unblemished and unbroken, as perfect as it had been on the day he'd met her. But her eyes were rimmed with red, and that proof of her distress was enough to make him vow to rain down vengeance on Victor, his father, her uncle and everyone who'd ever wronged her.

Reaching down, Amalia twined her graceful fingers in the fabric of his shirt and used it to pull him toward her. For the space of a breath, maybe two, they stared at each other, swaying slightly along with the train as it raced on.

"I'm sorry," she said in a rush. "I'm so sorry for what I said. I didn't mean it—and I thought I'd never see you again to tell you so."

And then their mouths were meeting with violent desperation. Greedily, Julián drank in the taste of her lips, the soft plushness of her thighs beneath his spread hands.

Amalia was clinging to him like he was one of the life preservers he'd seen hanging on the deck of the

S.S. New York. And Julián was holding on just as tightly, half-afraid that he would drown in the waves of desire as he stole kiss after kiss from her.

But it wasn't stealing, was it, when it was so freely given?

Julián's heart seized with a pleasure that felt almost like pain. He'd never expected her to direct another word at him, much less for something like this to happen. Another man might have taken it as his due, especially after what he'd just done, but Julián knew that kissing Amalia Troncoso was a privilege—and that he would do much more than jump into a moving train for the right to do it again and again.

Amalia made a little sound in her throat. Her grip on his shirt tightened for one long moment. Then she flattened her palms against his chest and pushed him away.

She did it lightly enough, but Julián responded at once to the repudiating touch and cast himself backward, forgetting about the armchair behind him. All the furniture had been nailed to the floor, so it didn't budge, but he did crack the back of his head against its wooden frame.

He swallowed back a curse at the sudden pain flaring through his head, then remembered it was Amalia in front of him and went ahead and cursed out loud. Another woman would have probably shot him a disapproving glare, but Amalia merely looked interested at this evidence of his prodigious vocabulary.

His hair was already so disheveled that rubbing his head made little difference. "My apologies," he said, even though he hadn't been the one to initiate the kiss. "I was overcome with emotion."

He hauled himself into the leather armchair, feeling

every muscle in his body protest the slight effort—he led a more active life than most, but even his body had its limits. "For what it's worth, I'm the one who should be sorry. I was trying to hurt you. And I—"

"Succeeded," she said and clamped her lips together, casting a glance toward the door.

Julián answered her unspoken question. "They won't hear us over the sound of the train. My father had the compartment soundproofed so that he could conduct business in here without worry of being overheard."

Amalia acknowledged it with a nod. "How in the world did you get up there?"

He shrugged. "Did some acrobatics—isn't that how all the fashionable people board trains these days?"

Her frown made it clear that she didn't appreciate his attempt at humor. "How did you find me? How did you know where I was?"

"A bandit has his ways," Julián said. He tried to punctuate his flippant remark with an equally offhand smile and failed miserably. He was so tired of dissembling and pretending and turning everything into a joke. "I went to my father. He told me where you were in exchange for me saying everything he's always wanted to hear—that I was finally ready to stop being such a wretched disappointment and pull my own weight in the company."

"Did you mean it?"

Julián shook his head. "I was lying through my teeth the whole time. I'm very good at that, as I'm sure you'll remember."

That earned him—not a smile, exactly, but something approximating one.

"Well," she said a little grudgingly. "You may be a lying scoundrel, but you are brave."

"Brave?" Julián's head ached. For that matter, his thighs and biceps were also in agony. The motion of the train—or maybe just the knowledge that he was in one—was making him want to pitch himself out the window. The hell with trying to pretend that he didn't want her. "I'm a wretched coward, Amalia. If I'd truly been brave, I would have let you walk out of my life. I would have stayed away from your hotel and refused to let you inside when you came to my house this morning. Or even better—I would have turned around when I saw Victor follow you and your sister into the hotel's dining room instead of bursting in there and making everything worse. Everything I've done, from the moment you glared at me when I gave you that glass of *aguardiente* when you'd asked for water, has been out of fear of losing you."

She'd been staring at him as he spoke. With a little hitch of her breath, as if she'd realized she was staring, she looked away. "That was a very nice speech," she said in a tone chilly enough to fuel an entire ice factory. "Pardon me for not swooning."

"I didn't expect you to. And I don't expect you to forgive me." Julián scraped his hair back. "I know I went about it all the wrong way. I should have told you everything from the beginning and I should have never hidden my identity from you."

She cocked her head and let another arrow fly from those bow-shaped lips of hers. "That would imply there's ever a time when you're truly yourself. Do you have any idea of who the real Julián Fuentes is?"

This wasn't the first time she had laid him utterly

and uncomfortably bare with a single look. "I don't know," he said after a moment. "But I do know that whoever that person is, the closest I've ever come to being him has been when I'm around you."

Amalia didn't know what to say. Was he being manipulative, or had he actually decided to try honesty for once?

Even now, after everything that had happened, she longed to experience what she had on the night they'd spent together—that surge of power and strength that had come from surrendering herself to his embrace.

But for every bit of her that wanted to throw herself into Julián's arms, there was a much larger part screaming at her to hold back.

As warm as it was inside the compartment, the temperature had risen noticeably with his presence. He had literally dropped in, windblown and dashing and looking every inch the bandit in his shirtsleeves, without a hat or even a necktie. Amalia's surprise at the sudden—and not altogether unwelcome—intrusion had gone to her head. That was the only reason she'd kissed him.

That, and the hot, undeniable, inescapable desire that had flooded her as soon as his body had come into contact with hers.

She took a steadying breath, trying not to notice how the scent of Julián's cologne, underlaid by faint traces of his exertion, cut through the stale, cigar-tinged air of the compartment. Then, instead of trying to find a way to answer his declaration, she opted to change the subject.

If he was a coward, then so was she.

"Any ideas on how we're going to get out of here?"

"I'm not going to jump out of a moving train with you in tow, if that's what you're asking," Julián returned, looking like an arrogant young aristocrat as he sprawled back on the leather upholstery. The man could do many things, but sitting upright did not seem to be one of them. "It'll be dark when we get to Santiago—it won't be too hard to slip away then."

"There are two men outside the compartment," she said. "They—"

"Have pistols, yes. I expected as much," Julián said. "I'm entirely unarmed, save for my dashing smile, and somehow I don't think that'll be enough to keep them from shooting at me."

Amalia stared at him, feeling disconcerted. "You're unarmed, and yet risked your life coming in here."

"I couldn't let them take you away," he said simply. "I would have done much more than that for you."

"Why?" she burst out. She could understand it when he'd been a bandit waiting for his payment. But surely, he had gotten everything he wanted from her.

"Because I would rather die than be one more in the long list of men in your life that have done you wrong. Because I—"

"Don't, Julián," she said quickly, tamping down the champagne-bubble flutters rising into her chest. "Don't say another word. I don't want to know how you feel—I don't *care*. I have things to do, and I can't afford to let you distract me more than you already have. This would have never happened if I hadn't gone to your house today."

"None of this is your fault, Amalia," he said, looking flinty.

Amalia had gotten so used to his calling her *Your*

Highness that her heart gave a little jump at the sound of her name as it tumbled from his lips. Her eyes lingered on them for a brief moment, watching them tighten.

"But it is my fault," she said. "I convinced them that I was willing to marry Victor, though I never planned to go through with it. I had it all worked out—I was going to sneak money out of my uncle's wallet and spirit Lucía away. But I *had* to go to your house instead of sending a messenger. I told myself there was no other way to find out the truth, but what difference does knowing what they wanted make? And now I've ruined the last chance I had of preventing them from carrying out their damned plan."

Amalia realized she was trembling. Taking a slow, deliberate breath, she pressed her palms onto the seat on either side of her skirt.

Julián was shaking his head. "My father had no intention of letting you marry Victor—he thinks you're too difficult to control. They only pretended to accept as a ploy to keep you quiet while they worked out how to get you out of the way. And now that they suspect how much you mean to me…" He leaned forward in his seat. "I'm not sure you understand quite how powerful my father is, or how far his reach extends. Or how ruthless he can be when he really wants something."

Amalia tilted up her chin. "My uncle said I won't be hurt."

"That may be what he thinks. But don't you see? It's my father who's in charge here and he wouldn't hesitate to do anything to get you out of the way. And he knows it won't be enough to keep you out of town for a day or two, not when you've proven that you're willing to make trouble for them at every step of the way. You're just as much a thorn in their sides as I ever was," he added.

"You really have a way with compliments," Amalia muttered.

But Julián didn't seem to have heard her.

"My father won't stop," he continued intently. "He will never stop. And I can assure you that he is prepared—even willing—to flatten any obstacles in his way. As for Victor..." His lips compressed into a thin line. "He wouldn't hesitate to compromise your sister ahead of the wedding if it would ensure that no one would object to it."

Amalia recoiled. "You really don't think he would do such a despicable thing."

"He's done worse," Julián said flatly. "Victor is the kind of person who reads *The Prince* a couple of times and fancies himself as cunning as Machiavelli. He likes to think he's a great strategist and a manipulator, but he's just a nasty little *lacra* who has grown too used to trampling over everybody."

His words filled her with a dawning horror. Suddenly, Amalia couldn't keep still. Leaping to her feet, she began to pace on the dark green carpet. "I have to get out of here. We have to get out of here."

She had already roamed around the compartment, poking into corners and opening the desk drawers, and had found nothing but an old newspaper, a half-empty box of matches and a withered cigar. She went through it all again, though what she was hoping to find, she didn't know.

"He never keeps anything important in here," was Julián's contribution from the other side of the compartment. "Though he and Victor are the only ones who ever use this car."

"I'm really not looking for anything. I just—"

Feeling suddenly stifled, Amalia yanked at the tasseled curtains until they parted enough to let her open the window. Letting the warm breeze tug her hair into disorder, she leaned her palms on the window frame and looked up. It must have been later in the afternoon than she thought, because shades of orange and crimson were starting to stain the pure blue of the sky.

The rolling landscape was bright in the golden light, save for the dark outlines made by the clusters of palms jutting out from fields of crops that Amalia would have probably recognized if they were on her plate as opposed to hidden behind leaves.

"You're not going to hurl yourself out the window, are you?" Julián asked behind her.

"I'm considering it," Amalia said curtly.

She pulled the curtain open farther, letting in a wash of brightness, and turned in irritation as Julián made a small noise.

It was only as her gaze fell on him that she noticed his shallow breaths. He had crossed his legs, but his grip on the armrest was tight and his chiseled jaw was clenched so hard, it was a wonder it hadn't snapped.

She had noticed the strain in his eyes earlier, and had assumed it had something to do with the conversation. But it was evident now that what she had taken for annoyance was actually something closer to panic.

It came to her as suddenly as a crack of lightning— on the deck of the ship, he'd told her that his mother had died in a railroad accident. "You were there," she blurted out. "When your mother was—"

Julián's face went blank—the expression of a man who'd trained himself not to reveal any weaknesses. Then his head jerked into a nod. "I was there. And I didn't—I wasn't able to—"

Amalia felt her heart constrict as she guessed at the words Julián didn't seem able to say out loud. Could it be that he felt guilty—or had been made to feel guilty—for not having done more to save his mother, even though he'd been so young when the accident happened? Having met his father, she didn't find it difficult to believe that he'd been capable of blaming his six-year-old son for whatever had happened then.

"I'm sorry," she said instead of giving voice to her thoughts. "I wouldn't have opened the curtains if I'd known." She gave the curtains a hasty yank to close them and was dismayed when the fabric tore away from the brass rings, leaving half a windowpane uncovered.

Julián's jaw tightened as he averted his gaze from the landscape speeding by. "I'll be fine. I just…need a little distraction."

The thoughts that went through Amalia's mind at the word *distraction* made heat rush immediately to her face. Her skin was too dark to show it—she hoped—but Julián had an irritating aptitude for reading the most minuscule changes in her expression.

Abruptly, she stood up again, holding out a hand. He glanced at it, clearly puzzled.

"You won't feel the motion as much if you're also moving," she explained and gave her hand an impatient shake. "I'm not asking you to waltz, Julián—pacing up and down will be enough."

His hand slid into hers. His fingers were long and elegant, but she could feel the roughness of the calluses that had formed where reins rubbed against his palm. It may not have been the hand of a bandit, scored with evidence of a hard life, but neither did it belong to an arrogant young aristocrat.

Maybe his real self was somewhere in between.

After tucking his hand into the crook of her elbow, Amalia towed him along as she resumed her earlier pacing. He walked with his usual leonine grace, but his grip on her was tight.

"I never told you why I decided to pretend to be a bandit," he said suddenly.

She made a noise that sounded suspiciously like a snort. "You never told me a lot of things."

"Fair enough." Julián raised an eyebrow. "I used to climb a lot of trees when I was a boy—mostly to get away from Victor. I was so small for my age I used to be able to shimmy up to the very tops of the palm trees in our estate. It helped, for a while, until Victor decided to throw stones at me one day. I fell and broke my arm and couldn't climb until it had healed."

Looking at him now, with his head almost brushing the compartment's upholstered ceiling, Amalia found it hard to believe. Her own head didn't reach much higher than the distracting curls that brushed the top of his collar—which meant, she couldn't help but notice, that the hollow at the base of his throat was exactly at her eye level.

"Is that where you got…?" Amalia's fingers fluttered near Julián's temple as she gestured to his scar.

He shook his head. "I didn't get that until a few years later, and that was mostly due to my trying to show off in front of a girl." He gave her a rueful smile. "Beautiful women have always been my downfall."

Amalia harrumphed, and Julián's smile widened.

"In any case, back then Victor was much bigger than me, and had longer legs, so I couldn't outrun him. One day it got so bad I ran into the horse paddock and climbed up on one of my father's racehorses, determined to get as far away from Victor as I could."

"Did you?"

"Almost fell and broke my other arm," Julián replied. "I would have, if it hadn't been for the head groom. Miguel had seen Victor tormenting me, and had been wanting to intercede on my behalf but hadn't known how to do it without reprimanding Victor—he had a nasty habit of making trouble for anyone who dared reprimand him."

"Typical," Amalia remarked.

"I could ride well enough, but Miguel had fought in the War of Restoration, back in sixty-three, and he knew all kinds of wild tricks. Soon, I was rushing out to the horse paddock once the tutor released Victor and me from our lessons and spending entire afternoons with the grooms, goading each other into performing one outlandish stunt after another. I'd never experienced that sort of camaraderie, and before long my visits to the horse paddock ceased to be about escaping Victor and more about enjoying their company."

They reached the end of the compartment for a second time and turned back to retrace their steps. Talking did seem to be getting Julián's mind off his discomfort, though Amalia knew that talking about his past always seemed to cause its own distress. Having met Victor and Don Reynaldo, Amalia could certainly understand why.

"How nice," Amalia said softly.

"It was—for a time. Victor told my father, of course,

and it went just about how you'd imagine it. Miguel was sent away, and the others had their pay docked for wasted time. My father made sure I knew that I wasn't their friend, just a nuisance they tolerated to keep from losing their jobs. And then he told me it was my fault he'd had to dismiss Miguel—that if I had behaved as I'd ought to, he wouldn't have been forced to take away the man's livelihood. I was nine years old," he said without a trace of bitterness in his tone, only sorrow, "and I knew that to have a friend, or to care for anyone, was to condemn them to certain misfortune."

There was a long pause in which Amalia tried and failed to find something to say that could provide Julián with just a fraction of the comfort he'd needed as a boy. Don Reynaldo wasn't just cold and distant—he was as cruel as Victor in his own way.

Then Julián said, hardening his tone, "That's the kind of man my father is, Amalia. He takes anything that's good in your life and turns it against you."

"That's what he did to you and Concepción, isn't it?"

Julián nodded. "And what I was afraid he would do to you if he knew…"

Hardly knowing whether or not she wanted him to complete his sentence, she caught her breath and held it.

"I know you don't want me to talk about my feelings for you," he said. "And I mean to respect that. I just need you to know that I meant it when I said I was at your service. Not because I want to thwart Victor and my father, though I do, or even because I feel like I owe it to you after I involved myself so callously in your affairs. I want to do everything I can to get you and Lucía out of this because it's the right thing to do. I'm not asking you to like me, or to forgive and forget everything I've done. I just ask that you accept my help."

Her desire to believe him was so strong, it gave Amalia pause. "You're not just asking me to trust you with my life. You're asking me to trust you with Lucía's."

"I'm not asking you to trust me at all, Amalia. I'm asking you to trust yourself to make the right decision."

Julián paused and Amalia, whose arm was still linked with his, was forced to stop as well, shifting so that she was facing him.

"I've never believed I had much to offer a woman by way of a relationship or a future," he said. "But I do have something to offer *you*—an alliance. Let's band together to rescue your sister." His other arm rose to grip her shoulder. "And when that's done, we can go our separate ways if that's what you truly want."

"You would do that for me?" she asked softly.

He tucked a strand of her hair behind her ear. "I would do so much for you, Amalia. But this… This is what I should have done from the moment I met you, instead of hiding the truth about myself."

Amalia felt herself teetering on the edge of a choice. To trust Julián again and risk being hurt a second time. Or to return to relying only on herself and chance failing her sister—and falling back into a loneliness she hadn't known she felt before meeting Julián.

She opened her mouth to speak, but was interrupted by a noise from the entrance of the compartment as the sliding door was jerked to the side and the large, bulky ruffian who abducted her appeared in the opening.

Chapter Fifteen

There were two men—the large one he'd cut on the ship and behind him, a younger, wide-eyed man with a pistol. In Julián's opinion, there were very few things more alarming than a pistol being wielded by someone too young and too scared to keep themselves from doing anything reckless.

Subtly edging in front of Amalia, Julián addressed the large ruffian. "What the devil do you mean, interrupting our conversation?"

The other man seemed unimpressed by Julián's bluff. "Seize him," he told his companion.

To Julián's luck, the younger man only licked his lips. "Don Francisco said we weren't to harm them."

"Her," the ruffian corrected. "We weren't to harm her. He said nothing about him."

Julián lifted his chin, infusing his voice with cold arrogance. "You do know who my father is, don't you?"

A glint came into the ruffian's eyes. "You mean the man who told me that I shouldn't hesitate to use force on his worthless son? He knew you'd be showing up, though how you managed it, I'll never know. I searched every nook of this train before it left the station."

Something cold and bitter washed over Julián. He should have known that fooling his father wouldn't be so easy. Reynaldo Fuentes hadn't built up the largest fortune on the island by being a fool, much less where his son was concerned.

He twisted his lips into a smirk. "It's a special talent. Second only to my flair for hairdressing."

Julián's arm was still around Amalia. Without releasing her, trying to look as if he was guiding her to safety, he moved them over to the window. He was completely unarmed, and there was nothing in the carriage he could use as a weapon—save for the curtain rod.

"What in the world do you think you're doing?" Amalia said loudly after a sidelong glance at him that made it clear that her words were more a ploy for distraction than real anger. "I've seen you do a lot of low things, Julián, but using me as a shield?"

"If you hadn't noticed, Your Highness," Julián ground out, playing along, "I'm trying to protect you."

"You heard what the man said—I won't be harmed. So let go of me this instant, you wretched coward."

"Have it your way," Julián snarled, and released her.

In the instant that Amalia wrenched herself away from him—and directly toward the ruffian—Julián reached for the curtain rod and ripped it off its brackets. He flung the curtain itself at the man with the pistol, startling him long enough to get in a good blow.

For her part, Amalia was whisking herself away from the enraged ruffian, as lightly as an heiress in a ballroom.

Julián grinned at her as he used the brass rod to knock the pistol clear to the other side of the compartment. If it was discharged in the compartment, a bullet could pierce the walls and strike someone in the next car—which on Sundays was usually full of families returning home from their weekend holidays. Julián's blood ran cold. "Get the pistol," he told Amalia. "Throw it out the window."

"Don't you tell me what to do," Amalia replied at once, but she did put on a burst of speed.

Julián used his makeshift weapon to keep both ruffians occupied long enough for her to dispose of the pistol. He felt marginally more at ease when it was gone, but only for a second—ducking suddenly as Julián swung the rod, the younger man got around him and shoved him from the back.

There wasn't much room to maneuver with the furniture fixed to the floor getting in the way. Julián twisted as his shoulder struck the paneling and grappled with the men to keep the rod from being wrenched out of his grip. Sweat streamed down Julián's face as he slowly lost his hold on his one weapon.

A muffled shriek from the other side of the compartment made Julián's blood curdle. Grunting as one of the men's fists connected with his chest, he cast a wild glance over his shoulder.

There was a third man.

He had gotten hold of Amalia and had lifted her a few inches off the floor as she kicked at him. The heel of her shoe connected with his kneecap with a sound that was audible even over the locomotive's chugging wheels, but his grip on her didn't loosen. Julián saw Amalia's eyes go wide, and it took him a second to realize it wasn't in reaction to her captor.

"Julián!" she screamed raggedly, and he turned his attention to the other two ruffians just in time to catch the glint of a knife slicing down in the direction of his chest. He dropped to the floor at once, avoiding the knife but not the men, one of whom stomped a booted foot on Julián's back as he tried to dive toward Amalia. They pinned him down like an insect, Julián's cheek pressed against the plush carpet so that he could feel the miserable, nauseating motion of the train as it sped on and on.

Julián was no match for three men, much less ones accustomed to this kind of violence. What the hell made him think he could protect Amalia from them? Or from her uncle or his father or anyone else for that matter? Abject defeat coursed over him, heavier than the boot planted in the middle of his back.

Raising his eyes from the patterned carpet, he watched as the newcomer flung Amalia at one of the other ruffians and reached into his pocket. With heavy strides that made the floor shudder under Julián's face, he approached Julián and knelt, saying, "With compliments from your cousin."

A starburst of pain bloomed in the side of his head as the man struck him with something hard and metallic. Julián inhaled sharply, feeling the acrid scent of gunpowder settle in the back of his throat.

Amalia swore out loud, making Julián's lips twitch into the ghost of a smirk.

"He told me to make it hurt," the man said as he struck Julián on the opposite side, making his vision go black in spots.

Julián tried to toss his head to the side to avoid another blow, but the boot grinding just below his shoulder blade made it almost impossible to move. "Whatever he promised you," he said through a groan, "I can give you double."

The man gave him a nasty smile. "Before I toss your carcass off the train, I'm to make sure you know that you have never had what it takes. You'll never be half the man he is." The man bent even closer, lowering his voice as if he was about to confide a deep secret. "And he said to tell you that the girl will never be safe—and there's nothing you'll be able to do about it."

It was as if someone had tossed an entire bottle of liquor into a flickering fire.

Letting out a roar of pain and anger and frustration and denial, Julián bucked hard enough to make the man stepping on him lose his balance. He tried to stagger to his feet, and rose just enough to knock his head against the underside of the third man's chin, hard enough to make his teeth rattle.

A howl came from the other side of the compartment, where Amalia had just freed herself. She rushed toward Julián, swinging the curtain rod at Victor's henchman. It connected with the back of his head and bounced clean out of her hands, thudding harmlessly on the carpet and rolling under the love seat.

Julián knocked him aside with his elbow and made himself get up from the carpet, grasping Amalia to keep his balance as dark spots danced in front of his vision.

"Go," he gasped out, following her through the open door of the compartment. Yanking it closed, he plunged a hand into her curls for a hairpin, which he jammed into the locking mechanism.

"That won't hold them long," she said as the men reached the door.

"I know," Julián replied grimly, shaking his head to clear it.

Taking her hand, he pulled her toward their only

hope—the door at the end of the short corridor. He unlatched it, and as he pulled it open to reveal the landscape rushing by, he turned to look at her.

"I won't let anything happen to you." He had to shout to be heard over the roaring of the train and the rushing wind.

She shook her head, clinging to the open doorway. "Surely, you don't mean for us to jump. We can't jump, Julián!"

"There's no other way."

Stubbornly, she held on to the doorway. "We'll be killed."

There was a loud, sharp retort behind them—a pistol being fired. It was followed by the unmistakable sound of splintering wood.

"It has to be now. Trust me, Amalia," he said, softening his tone so that his words sounded less like a command and more of a plea.

Her hesitation was written all over her face. He knew how much it would cost her to put her trust in yet another man, especially one who had already disappointed her.

Especially when he was asking her to do something as dangerous as jumping out of a moving train.

The three men were barreling toward them. Amalia didn't glance back at them—she didn't take her gaze off Julián as she put her hand in his and gave him one hard, decisive nod.

Together, they took the leap.

Amalia found only breathless exhilaration in the brief moments when she and Julián were suspended in the air, as light as birds.

Then reality—and the ground—rushed to meet them.

It wasn't the cushiest landing. Amalia's left shoulder and hip were throbbing, though Julián had curled around her to absorb most of the impact.

Her pulse roaring almost as loudly as the locomotive that was receding into the distance, she ran her hands over his chest and biceps and down to his hips to reassure herself that he was whole. When her searching, anxious gaze met his, she was stunned to discover his remarkable self-possession crumbled away, leaving only a worry so profound, it made tears spring into her eyes.

"Are you all right? Amalia, are you hurt?"

Impatiently, she blinked away the sting and pressed her lips fiercely to his. Julián took her face into his hands and returned her kiss with exquisite tenderness, tracing the outline of her upper lips with his own and lingering in the deep indentation there.

It was a kiss that demanded nothing and gave everything.

It was a reassurance—that they were alive and whole and for the next several moments at least, no longer in danger.

And it was a promise—that they would continue to survive together.

Amalia couldn't resist letting her hands roam over his body again, this time in leisurely exploration. The muscles of his chest were so defined she could feel them through the fabric of his shirt, his thighs so hard they could have been molded from steel.

Then her knuckles brushed the placket of his trousers and he started.

Breaking the kiss, Julián pressed his forehead to hers. "Please tell me you're not injured."

"I— No." She licked her lips and tried again. "I'm fine. Just a little bruised and scratched. I think the boning in my corset must have protected me from most of the damage. And you, of course."

The reassurance seemed to bolster him. He squeezed his eyes shut then nodded, sitting up. "If anything had happened to you…" Julián let out a careful breath, then Amalia watched as he forced his lips into a crooked grin for his benefit. "I would've had to become a bandit *and* an outlaw after I chased down the men on that train and made them jump off a very steep cliff. Can you walk?"

Her legs felt fine, if a trifle shaky, though Amalia suspected that was entirely due to the kiss. "I think so."

"In that case, we ought to get moving. It'll be night soon, and I'd just as soon not get caught out here in the dark," he said grimly.

"Where would we go?" she asked, looking around at the greenery surrounding them. In one direction the fields ended in what looked like an impenetrable tangle of vegetation. In the other stretched the mountain range that separated Puerto Plata and Santiago. There was very little blue left in the sky above its peaks, and Amalia felt a shiver at the prospect of being out here once the last of the light had fled from the sky.

There were no wild beasts or poisonous creatures on the island, but Amalia was all too aware that the dangers she and Julián faced were all human.

"Whoever tends to these crops must live nearby," Julián said.

He offered her a hand—Amalia was about to take it

when she noticed first the long scrape along the right side of his face and then the slight wince when he moved his right arm. The sleeve covering that arm, she was aghast to realize, was shredded.

"You're hurt," she exclaimed, scrambling to her feet under her own power.

"It's not too bad," he said quickly. "Just my shoulder. I think it's just a sprain."

"And I think you're lying to yourself," Amalia said and started to unbutton her blouse.

It was a shame that old-fashioned petticoats with their many ruffles were no longer in fashion. Fortunately, her formerly white blouse was made so sheer by the lace panels inset into its front that she'd worn a plain white linen cover over her corset.

"What are you doing?" Julián asked, staring.

"Making you a sling out of my undergarments."

She handed him the blouse, which might as well have been a rag for how filthy and torn it was, then wriggled out of the sleeveless corset cover.

It was almost mortifying to note how often Julián had seen her in dishabille, especially taking into consideration that they really hadn't known each other all that long.

Julián, who must have gazed upon dozens of half-dressed women, looked distinctly dazed. "Amalia…"

"Are you shocked?" Amalia raised an eyebrow. "I was under the impression that you've seen dozens of women in all states of undress."

"None of them were you," he said flatly. "I'll turn away if you want me to."

She cast him a teasing glance. "Could you?"

"I'd try if I had to," he said. "I've done all sorts of

difficult things in my life, Your Highness, but voluntarily looking away from such a sight is beyond me."

Under his devouring gaze, Amalia found herself arching her back just the tiniest bit, angling herself to show the contents of her chemise to better advantage. She felt shameless, in the best possible way, liberated from the embarrassment she would have felt with anyone else. She wanted to strip off every layer, and revel in his appreciation.

The thought of undressing for him, here in the full sunshine, filled her with so much heat, she was surprised that the garment in her hands hadn't ignited.

The thin cotton tore with a satisfying rending sound. Amalia tied the two ends together and started binding Julián's arm to his side. It should have been a swift process, but the filmy fabric kept slipping from her fingers as the combined sensation of the warm breeze on her bare shoulders and her awareness of Julián's body conspired to make her fingers clumsy.

As she finished tying the last knot, the fingers on his uninjured side rose to graze the naked skin of her shoulder. Amalia's breath caught and her eyes fluttered shut as he followed the lace edging on the neckline of the chemise she wore under her corset.

"Your skin is the loveliest shade of brown." His fingers reached the green velvet ribbon whose ends trailed between her breasts. "It has a luster to it, as if you were an oil painting come to life."

Amalia held her breath as she felt the warmth of a fingertip playing over the knot at the center of the bow the ribbon was tied in. With her eyes closed, and with the last of the day's sunlight beaming down upon them, Julián and the fields were replaced with a crimson haze. His finger hooked over the knot and he tugged it lightly before dropping away.

Reluctantly, Amalia opened her eyes.

"We should get going," he said and turned away, though not before she saw her own disappointment mirrored in his face.

Amalia made quick work of her buttons. As soon as she was as neatly dressed as her ruined blouse allowed, they set off through the fields, toward the thick cluster of vegetation.

Amalia had never been good at reining in her impatience, and even though she knew that getting back to Puerto Plata before the next morning was close to impossible, what with the state of the roads and the darkness that was about to fall, she couldn't quiet the sense of urgency that almost made her groan out loud when Julián stopped at the edge of the path.

She had barely spared a glance at the banana and plantain grove that was at the edge of the field, but Julián headed directly toward one of the short palms. With a quick wrench of his wrist, he separated a couple of bananas from a hanging bunch.

He passed her one and kept one for himself. "You must be hungry by now."

"Aren't they a little green?" she asked doubtfully, looking down at the curiously small thing in her hand. "I like them when they're speckled."

"They're plenty ripe," Julián said, pulling down another one, having already eaten the first in two bites. "Go ahead and give it a try—you won't be sorry."

Amalia bit her lip. If she trusted Julián enough to go along with him when he asked her to jump out of a moving train, what harm could there be in eating one of these tiny bananas?

She peeled it slowly, then took the top edge between her teeth and bit down.

"Oh!"

The sweetness that burst into her tongue was as intense as it was unexpected. The rest of the small banana was gone in two bites and she was reaching for another.

"Ready to admit that I was right?" Julián was watching her, his lips curled into a smile so smug, she wanted to stroke her tongue over its insolent curve.

"I'd rather eat dirt," she said swiftly, mostly out of habit.

He smirked. "Pairs well with fruit. Here. Have another one."

Amalia nibbled the top of another banana, and she was surprised anew by how its exterior had belied its richness of flavor. It reminded her of Julián, actually. Not because he had an unassuming exterior—even standing in a plantain grove with his shirt shredded to pieces and streaks of dirt up and down his body, he looked every inch the powerful man that he was.

But because she would never have believed in the sweetness of his interior if she hadn't sampled it for herself.

"Your Highness?"

Amalia glanced up to see Julián looking at her with concern. Their traipse through the fields had darkened his nose and cheekbones into a light bronze tinged with red. Against it, his brown eyes looked as soft and warm as wax from a lit candle.

"Are you sure you weren't injured?"

She shook her head. "Just thinking." As happened

all too often around Julián, she could feel the previously solid ground shifting beneath her, and reforming into something different.

Heedless of the sticky dirt clinging to it, Julián leaned against the palm's short trunk and looked at her as if he had all the time in the world to listen to her half-formed thoughts.

She started slowly, struggling to articulate what was going through her mind. "I was thirteen when my father died and Tio Francisco came to live with us. Lucía and I had lived charmed lives until then, even though we'd lost our mother. Then all of a sudden, there he was, telling us to be careful about who we spoke with and forbidding us to so much as go out into the garden without someone to accompany us. He made it seem like people were lining up to take advantage of us—and that the only reason anyone would want to get close to us, or even offer us friendship, was to use us in some way."

"If it's any consolation, I'm interested in you for your body, not your fortune," Julián remarked impertinently.

Amalia smiled and flicked the peel at his uninjured arm. "I know you are, you scoundrel. I can't help but think that if my uncle had really been interested in keeping us safe, he would have taught us how to recognize and deal with those situations instead of driving away anyone who showed the least bit of interest in us."

Briefly, she caught her lower lip between her teeth. "I have spent so much of the last twelve years rebelling against my uncle, in all ways but one—I've been as distrustful as he has taught me to be. I look back at all the moments when I held myself back, or away from someone who could have been a friend, and I feel so much regret. I had even begun to think that you had proven him right." Julián opened his mouth to say something, and Amalia held up a hand. "Don't you dare apologize again. I think what I'm trying to say is…yes. I accept your offer. I want you as an ally. Just…please don't disappoint me again."

"Unfortunately, Your Highness," Julián said with one of his crooked smiles, which Amalia was starting to realize hid a wealth of pain, "disappointing people is all I ever do."

She frowned at him. "I know that's what your father believes—or what he wants you to think. But you and I both know that's not true. You could be capable of so much good, Julián, if you only allowed yourself to believe that you are the decent, honorable person I know you can be."

Julián let out a hollow laugh. "No one's ever accused me of being decent and honorable before."

"Maybe it's time they started."

Amalia held out her hand for Julián's banana peels and piled them neatly with hers beneath the palm. Then she started walking again, her pace fast and purposeful.

"My uncle has given me plenty of causes to dislike him," she said.

"I have a number of things to add to the list," Julián remarked.

"But the worst by far is how he acts as though he should be showered with accolades for agreeing to be guardian to his brother's children. It always irritated me, but it wasn't until a few years ago that I realized it was his way of making us feel like we should be grateful for what he's done, and to keep us from questioning his decisions. I think that your father does something very similar to you. The more he starves you of affection, and the more unworthy he makes you believe you are, the more likely it is that you'll do anything to please him."

At her side, Julián was silent and thoughtful.

"The worst part," she said, "is that he's made you think that love is something you have to earn. But it's not, you know. Love that isn't freely given, that comes bound with obligations and requirements and conditions—I don't believe that's love at all."

"I don't think he knows that, Your Highness. He's... I won't make excuses for my father, but he had a hard time when he married my mother. She was the coddled youngest girl of a very wealthy family and her relations made it clear to my father that he didn't deserve her. I think he's spent the past thirty years trying to prove them wrong—and to earn her love, not knowing that all he had to do was make time for her. Her death didn't stop him and I doubt his own will." Julián snorted. "He had a monstrously expensive mausoleum brought over from Italy—made out of Carrara marble and crafted by some celebrated sculptor or another. Had it placed right across from theirs so that he could lord it over them even in the afterlife."

"That's no way to live your life," Amalia remarked. "Certainly not the way I'd want to live mine."

"How would you? What will you do when all of this is over?"

"I hadn't thought that far," she admitted, then broke out into an impish smile. "Now that I've gotten a taste for jumping out of trains, I can hardly go back to needlework and garden parties. I don't have a vocation, like Lucía and her music, but I'm determined to find something that thrills and interests me, if I have to search the entire world for it."

"I have no doubt that you'll find it," he said softly.

"And you? How will you live your life?"

As the question fell from her lips, Amalia experienced a sudden tug of wistfulness as it occurred to her that she might not be there to see it.

Julián pushed aside a thin strand of vines dangling from an overhead branch. "Maybe I'll give up banditry and try piracy instead," he said lightly, then sighed. "I really don't know. Returning to my old life doesn't seem all that appealing to me, either. Maybe I'll travel."

Or maybe he would marry. Why wouldn't he?

The thought suffused Amalia with an irrational sense of panic. She kicked a fallen palm frond out of her way.

"What are you thinking that's making you huff like a little locomotive?" Julián asked.

She glanced up at him. "Marriage," she blurted out, then added, "Or rather, the wedding. Do you think they're hauling Lucía into the registry office as we speak?"

Julián looked thoughtful. "It's possible, but I don't think they will. Knowing my father, he'll want the wedding to be a lavish affair with plenty of guests. Partly because he delights in any opportunity to show off his wealth, and partly because that would make it harder for you or anyone else to contest the legitimacy of the marriage. You can hardly accuse them of a secret conspiracy to defraud you when it's all being done in front of hundreds of people, after all."

Julián reached out with his good hand and tangled his fingers through her hair. "We'll get there in time.

And when we do, will you allow me to loan you the funds to take Lucía to Europe? I have plenty of money, and little use for most of it. The two of you could be on your way to Vienna as early as tomorrow evening."

"We will," she said with far more confidence than she felt. "Once we get her away, though, there's still the matter of my father's will."

"I could have my lawyers look it over and see if there's anything to be done. Or..." His lips spread into a grin.

Amalia raised an eyebrow as little shoots of excitement began to unfurl in her stomach at the sight of Julián's expression. "Or?"

"We could perform one more act of banditry."

Chapter Sixteen

Night was starting to fall when they reached a large hacienda. Its occupants proved more than happy to put them up for the night when Julián explained that he and his wife had been en route to Santiago when they were set upon by bandits who had robbed them of their carriage, luggage and even his necktie and hat.

With no one of Amalia's acquaintance here, Julián knew they could have very well dispensed with the pretense they'd been forced to use on the ship. But after the day they'd just had, he'd be damned if he'd risk her sleeping alone in an unfamiliar house with strangers. Amalia had agreed—more than that, she had reached for his hand and kept hold of it as their hosts, a planter and his family, clucked over their ill fortune.

He watched her fidget all through dinner, obviously anxious about her sister's fate. When the family retreated to the porch after dinner with tiny glasses of liqueur, Amalia excused herself, claiming that her head ached after the day's events.

After a few minutes' wait, Julián went after her.

They'd been put into the bedroom that belonged to

the planter's daughters, who had been relocated for the night. A wooden armoire and a four-poster bed spread with a crocheted coverlet took up most of the space, but a little dressing table with a flowered skirt had been tucked into a corner. Amalia sat in front of the oval mirror in her borrowed nightdress, yanking a comb through her wet hair, her frustration evident in each short stroke.

They were too far from any town for the hacienda to be reached by any of the electrical grids that had recently been installed throughout the island. In the dancing glow cast by the oil lamp on the table, she looked even more like someone out of an oil painting. The warm light painted her profile, highlighting her stubborn chin and the glint of determination that always shone in her eyes.

It wasn't just that he was drawn to her. It was that he felt as though he would expire on that spot if he didn't touch her, or kiss her, or contrive a way to feel the warmth of her skin beneath his palm.

"We could borrow a horse," she blurted out when she met his eyes in the mirror. "And a lantern. And—"

"And we'd be set upon by bandits—real ones—long before we got back to town." Between the bad roads and the roving bands of men ready to cause mayhem at the slightest provocation, few people of Julián's acquaintance would venture out into the wilderness after dark, even with guards at their side. Julián gave her shoulders what he hoped was a comforting squeeze. "I know you're worried about your sister. I promise you I'll get you to her as soon as possible. But risking your life isn't going to do her any good."

As if to further underscore his point, raindrops began

to beat a tattoo against the wooden shutters. Within seconds the light patter turned into a roar that muffled the faint sounds coming from beyond their door.

"I know," Amalia muttered, rubbing her face. "And I'm sorry for being so impatient."

"There's no need to apologize for being anxious."

Amalia gave a fretful nod and once again began attacking her curls with the comb.

Unable to hold back a wince, Julián held out his hand. "Here, let me help. My hairdressing skills are celebrated and unparalleled, as you might remember."

"I'd settle for plain competency at the moment," she said, surrendering the comb and sighing as she stretched her shoulders. "My arms are beginning to ache. Lucía always does this at home. It's such tedious work—my hair tangles something fierce and it's far too long."

Julián was of the opinion that her hair was, in fact, perfect, but he resisted the urge to say so out loud.

The hair at the nape of her neck had tangled into vicious little knots. Julián, who would have never described himself as a patient man, took his time teasing out the snarls while Amalia offered suggestions on how to get back to Puerto Plata that very night, each more outlandish than the last.

Julián could tell that she wasn't serious, though; just talking through her nerves. Figuring she could use the distraction, he encouraged her by adding impractical suggestions of his own and trying not to laugh when she came up with a convoluted plan involving a submarine, a hot water balloon and a contraption he suspected she had read about in a Jules Verne novel.

Almost a quarter of an hour later, Julián set aside

the comb. Her hair was beginning to dry in the balmy air, the heavy strands shrinking and curling into a riot of light-touched waves. Lightly, he threaded his fingers through the strands, then dove through them to rub her scalp with gentle pressure.

Letting out a contented little noise that went straight into Julián's rib cage like an arrow, she leaned her head back into his touch. He was amused to see her toes curling under the hem of her nightdress.

"I've been wanting to do this ever since that time in the carriage," he said softly as he stroked the short little curls at the nape of her neck. "Your hair is like the sea."

"Blue and wet?" she asked with an arched eyebrow.

He laughed, lifting a strand to admire the way it coiled. "Beautiful. Full of movement. I could drown in it."

Their eyes met in the mirror again, and Julián knew he wasn't the only one who was feeling the thrum of possibility charging the atmosphere until it felt like standing outside a second before a strike of lightning.

She rose from the small chair in a single fluid motion, like a sea goddess rising from the water, and moved the spindly legged chair aside with a slow thrust of her hip that sent a sudden rush of heat over Julián.

"Were you planning on dancing around the subject all evening, or will we talk about it before daybreak?" she asked.

"Talk about what, Your Highness?"

"Your sharing my bed."

She cocked her head, and the challenge in her eyes kindled a slow smile on Julián's lips. "Been thinking about it, have you?"

"From the moment you told the planter we were husband and wife," she said, taking a step that made the front of her billowing nightdress brush against him. "I was hoping you'd done it because you intended to sleep next to me."

"I said it because I want you safe—and the only way I can make sure that you haven't been snatched in the night is to keep you with me."

"Is that the only reason?" she asked, reaching up to fiddle with the buttons on his borrowed shirt.

Maybe Julián wasn't as much of a scoundrel as he considered himself. He pressed his hand to hers, trapping it against his chest. "It is if you want it to be."

In answer, she rose up onto her tiptoes and brushed her lips to his throat, just above his collar. That slight touch seared him.

"I know that we'll part soon," she said. "But we still have tonight."

As if that was enough. As if that could ever be enough.

He had to bend to touch his forehead to hers, breathing out her name. "I used to live my life as if pleasure was one thing and emotion another wholly separate thing, and the pursuit of one did not really require the other. I spent years having one meaningless dalliance after another. It has been so long since I was satisfied by those shallow affairs because it wasn't affection or even companionship that I found with them. It was oblivion—a distraction from all the things I felt I could never have, or even be. I don't want oblivion anymore, Amalia. I don't want a night's worth of amusement when I could have a lifetime."

"What *do* you want?" she whispered.

Julián inhaled the floral scent of hair oil rising from

the top of her head and felt her respond to his tightening grip by shifting closer into his embrace. "You."

The sound of her breathing filled the space between
them. Amalia didn't say a word. So he spoke for them
both.

"I want more of you than I have any right to. I want
to have an endless string of nights in your bed and at
your side, because the very thought of being without
you drives me to my knees."

"I don't love you." Her voice broke, and her next
words came as a whisper. "I can't love you."

Julián rubbed the pad of his thumb over her enticing lower lip. "There is nothing you can't do, Amalia. You've proven that twenty times over in the short
time I've known you. Time after time you have done
the impossible."

He had always believed that it *was* impossible for
anyone to love a worthless wreck like himself. But
Amalia was the kind of person who was undaunted by
the impossible. If there was anyone in the world who
could love him, it was this wild, headstrong, fierce
heiress.

Here it came again. That heady, breathless moment
when the possibility of a kiss hung suspended between
them, as bright and shining as gold. He knew better
than most not to take it for granted—possibilities often
turned to ashes, and a next kiss was never assured.
There was every chance that Amalia would turn around
and leave the room.

She was the first one to move, surging up onto her
tiptoes to reach him. Their mouths collided and all the
passion and need that Julián had ever felt coalesced into

that one kiss. And he thought that maybe he *would* expire from the terrible joy of loving this woman.

Her skin was the rich, warm brown of molasses and honey, and just about as sweet. He drank in her taste and her scent, the way her body felt against his. He could have stood there forever, just holding her, relishing in her.

But time, tide and daylight waited for no man, not even him.

Releasing her reluctantly, he went to the spindly chair she had vacated.

"All right, Your Highness. Have your way with me. Use me for your pleasure."

Sitting back, he folded his uninjured arm behind his head and watched her through slitted eyes. If he'd thought that Amalia would grow uncertain, he was wrong. A determined look that was quickly becoming familiar to him came into her eyes and she went to him at once, stepping between his parted legs as she reached for his braces.

After washing earlier, he had replaced her makeshift bandage with one provided by the planter's wife. He hadn't had the heart to throw away the remnants of her chemise, though, and had tucked it into his pocket.

She unwound the bandage and eased his shirt over his injured shoulder. When she pulled the sleeve down his arm, Julián was struck by a thought—no one had ever treated him with such care. Not any of the dozen women who had shared his bed, and certainly not his family. It staggered him that this rebellious, strong-willed woman should be the one to offer him tenderness.

Amalia undressed him with as much confidence as

if she'd done it dozens of times before. As each article of clothing fell away, collecting into an untidy pile on the tiles, Julián felt his skin break out into gooseflesh that had nothing to do with the sultry breeze stealing through the open shutters. He had never seen a more heart-stopping sight than the clearly visible outline of her body as lamplight shined through the fabric of her nightdress, turning the long garment into the robes of a temptress.

She hitched up her hem and placed her folded leg on his thigh. The gathered fabric floated over the bare skin of his abdomen as delicately as the fingertips she was pressing to his jaw. Even sitting while she stood, he was taller than Amalia by two or three centimeters, but he enjoyed the novelty of not having to stoop to reach her lips.

Her kiss was as bold as a bandit's, stealing his breath away as she thoroughly plundered his mouth. The hand she had braced on his good shoulder slid around him and all of a sudden, the light touch of fabric was replaced with a heavier weight as she leaned against him, head inclined so that her glorious, fragrant hair fell like a curtain around them. The world beyond the open shutters faded away as the soft strands grazed his shoulder.

The tight buds of her nipples were hard against his chest. He clasped her by the waist and held her close, following the curve of her hip with one hand. His lips hadn't left hers—he dragged them down her throat, coaxing breathy little moans out of her.

The soft sounds reverberated through him like thunder.

If there was any resistance left in his body to the

idea that he was utterly and deeply in love with Amalia, it vanished when he reached the hollow of her throat. Her hands were resting on his shoulders, her leg on his thigh, her hair all around them—she was entirely in control and he was all too happy to surrender himself to her.

"Your Highness," he murmured. "I'm not just at your service—I am entirely at your mercy."

Amalia reached for the placket of Julián's trousers, remembering what he'd said on the ship about wanting her to feel like a present being unwrapped. Undressing him was like unwrapping a present, too—an all too brief moment brimming with the anticipation of pleasure.

She'd always been the kind to impatiently tear at ribbons and colored paper, but she meant to take her time with Julián.

The top button of his trousers slid out of its place with a twist of her fingers. Before she could reach for the next, Julián's hand shot out and seized her wrist. His grip wasn't painful, but it was firm.

Amalia's gaze flew up to meet his. "What's wrong?"

"I changed my mind, Your Highness."

For a heart-pounding moment, Amalia thought he meant to leave. Then, in a single swift movement, he rose and lifted her by the waist with his good arm. She hardly had time to wrap her arms around his neck before he was walking her to the bed and sweeping aside the mosquito netting to lower her onto the intricately crocheted coverlet.

Then his hot mouth was on her neck and on the swells of her breasts, still covered by the cotton nightdress, and it was overwhelming in the best way possible.

Turning her gently so that she lay on her side, he curled his long body behind hers and continued exploring the delicate skin of her shoulders with his mouth. The jaw that had been perfectly smooth when he'd found her on the train had sprouted bristles in the course of the evening. Amalia couldn't help letting out a moan when Julián rubbed his rough chin against her neck.

"I will never stop craving you," he murmured and her body trembled in sync with the vibration of his voice.

His questing hand found her fabric-covered breasts. She arched her back in a silent plea for more, though her movement had the added benefit of putting her lower back in contact with that interesting bulge in his trousers.

It was a singular sensation, being pressed against a man's body with so few layers between them. Too much and not enough, all at once.

Grasping the ribbon that held the neckline of her nightdress gathered into a drawstring, she pulled it open with a single jerk, exposing her skin to the warm night air and his relentless touch. Heat washed over her breasts as he thumbed the stiff points, flooding her until she felt incandescent.

I don't love you. She'd said that to Julián, willing it to be true. Love had never served her. The things done to her in its name had only brought her grief. But just like she had decided to reassess her mistrust of people, knowing Julián was making her want to reconsider everything she had always believed of love. The thought was terrifying, and she had to bite down on her lip to keep her impulsive self from blurting out something she might regret later.

In any case, Julián was doing a very good job of distracting her from her thoughts. He had raised her nightgown and his warm mouth trailed scratchy kisses down her spine, blazed a path over the curve of her hips—and then, when he turned her gently on her back, did unspeakable things to the thin skin of her inner thighs.

Under his encouragement, Amalia let her legs sprawl open, her pulse quickening as he dipped the tip of his tongue into the crease of her thighs. Liquid heat pooled between her legs, spreading up her midsection in languid waves.

Amalia had never been a very patient person at the best of times, but this slow teasing was nothing short of agonizing. She writhed into the bedsheets, pleading for release through breathless pants. Julián only laughed.

"Was it Napoleon who said, *'Dress me slowly, I'm in a hurry'*?" he asked, shaping the words against her skin in a way that made her stop writhing and start trembling.

"Who the devil knows?" Amalia snapped. "And who the devil cares?"

Julián chuckled again. "We have so little time together… I intend to go as slow as possible and savor every second."

"I can appreciate that—in theory. In practice, though…" Amalia gave him a subtle nudge with her hips, loving how wanton she could let herself act around him. "I need you."

Dipping his head, he captured one of her nipples in

his mouth, tonguing it until it grew tight and hard, then retreated just enough to blow cool air over it.

When he had her breathing unsteadily again, he raised himself up to bring his mouth to hers. His lips tasted like the mint liqueur they'd had after dinner, and the cool fire of it filled her, racing along her limbs. She had once compared kissing him to champagne bubbles, little knowing that spirits were much more exciting than the pale fizz.

But Julián wasn't like genteel liqueur, either, or at least not entirely—he was *aguardiente*, as searing as liquid fire. And he was hers, if only for one more night.

Amalia never wanted it to end.

And she didn't want to think, or make any more plans, or do anything but sink into this heady rush of sensation. She was going to fall apart at any moment, and she wanted to enjoy every second of her dissolution.

Then Julián sank into her, slowly and gently and rolling his hips in a way that had Amalia muffling her cries against his shoulder. And she realized that she had gotten it wrong.

This wasn't falling apart. It was coming together.

The warm glow from the lamp kissed Amalia's bare curves as she lay on her side. Stripped of her lace and frills and velvet ribbons and pearl earrings, clad only in lamplight and plain cotton sheets, with her long, dark lashes fluttering as sleep tugged on her eyelids, she was beauty itself.

Julián had always thought that it wasn't fair to compare women to each other, much less those who had been kind enough to share his bed. Even if he was to disregard his rule, it would be impossible to compare Amalia to anyone else, purely because she was beyond comparison. She reminded him of something his mother used to say, about big surprises coming in small packages. Or was it big gifts? Amalia was both those things.

Julián was exhausted, and his shoulder bothered him more than he wanted to admit, but he couldn't seem to stop running his hands over the deep indentation of her waist long enough to drift into sleep. They were both slightly sticky with sweat, and the humidity in the room had given her curls volume and a life of their own. They tumbled wildly over her shoulders and the crisp white pillow, sticking to her skin in places. Gently, Julián gathered it all in a bunch and twisted it away from her neck.

She murmured something incomprehensible, giving a little sigh of relief when he blew cool air toward her nape.

"Where are you going?" she asked drowsily when he stood up.

"Nowhere, Your Highness."

He went as far as the washstand in the corner. Dribbling some water onto the towel she had used earlier, he returned to the bed to wipe her down with care, rubbing the fabric over her body as if he was polishing a bronze statue.

"That's lovely and cool," she said, voicing her pleasure with a breathy moan.

Turning onto her stomach, she slid her arms under the pillow and hugged it to her chest.

Julián pressed a kiss to the small of her back, and then another one on the nape of her neck, for good measure. He tugged the crumpled blanket out from under her hip and covered her up, tucking it securely around her. The coverlet was heaped on the floor at the foot of the bed, and Julián left it there—the night was too hot and humid for another layer.

"Get some rest," he said, though she was more than halfway into sleep. "Tomorrow's going to be a long day."

He went over to the chair to spread the towel over its back so that it would dry by morning. Then he blew out the lamp and got into bed next to Amalia.

She rolled over to face him, eyelids at half-mast and lips curled into a lazy curve that was barely visible in the moonlight streaming through the shutters. Even in the faint light, her eyes sparkled as she asked, "No midnight secrets tonight?"

"I have no secrets left, Your Highness," he told her, smoothing back one of the curls springing over her forehead and bending his face down to hers. "And nothing to confess. Not anymore. I think you've seen all the way into my soul."

She kissed his throat, hitching up a leg and tucking it between his thighs. "If I have, I've liked every bit of it."

He felt the warmth of her breath as she exhaled against his skin—once, twice and then she was melting into the bonelessness of heavy sleep.

And Julián… Julián was feeling, once again, what it felt like to fall from a great height. He wasn't just smitten, as Doña María had said over breakfast only a few days before. He was well and truly in love with this woman. Desperately so, with a hunger and a tenderness that made him ache to take her into his arms and brush kisses over each of those tantalizing curves.

Julián had always known that love wasn't meant for

men like him. Love was for the stalwart and the upright, not for worthless scoundrels like himself. He had never done anything to deserve such a thing, but for the first time in his life, he wanted to—even if it came at the expense of his own heart.

Chapter Seventeen

Amalia had never arrived anywhere early in her life, and her sister's wedding was no different.

Upon their return to Puerto Plata, it had taken them a matter of minutes to find out in which church the wedding was being held. Leaving Julián outside, Amalia had bent low over the saddle and touched her heels to the horse's flank, guiding it into a straight gallop up the church's steps and right into the nave.

The gasps of over a hundred people almost drowned out the thundering of hooves on tile as they raced to the altar. Along with the reins, Amalia held the pair of pistols Julián had bought from the planter that morning. Without so much as a waver, she kept one trained on Victor and the other on the pew where her uncle sat next to Julián's father.

"I do hope you weren't planning on starting without me," she said, shooting her sister a reassuring grin.

Lucía, whose mouth had fallen open in a gape, recovered enough to smile back at Amalia.

Out of the corner of her eye, she saw Don Reynaldo stand. "What is the meaning of this?"

"This," Amalia said evenly, "is a kidnapping. Give me the girl and no one gets hurt."

"Amalia?" That from her uncle, who had been a trifle slower on the uptake. "But how—?"

"If you're asking me how I escaped your own attempt to have me abducted by ruffians," she said in a loud, clear voice, relishing in the instant murmurs from the crowd, "I can tell you it was easier than you might suspect. I really hope you didn't pay them in advance."

Tío Francisco's eyes narrowed. "I don't know what you mean by this, young lady, but I suggest that you—"

Nothing could have persuaded Amalia to let him finish that sentence. "It's as you told me yesterday," she said. "I have an obligation to this family. It just doesn't involve selling myself or my sister in order to fill your pockets."

Tío Francisco's face was turning puce with fury. "You want to ruin your sister's prospects, and her life with it? Do it, then. I won't stand in your way any longer. I wash my hands of you."

Her nerves were taut—no, they felt stretched to their absolute limit, as if they would snap any second. She couldn't keep her foot from jiggling in the stirrup, though it made the horse snort. "I don't just want my sister. I want our money, too."

He blanched, but recovered quickly enough. "So you can spend it all on dresses and hair ribbons?" he snapped. "You know nothing about managing finances or property."

"You're right—I don't know anything about it. Which is why I plan on hiring an estate manager who can run things while Lucía and I learn how to do it ourselves."

"Do you know how many people are cheated by unscrupulous managers? You'll be fleeced."

"And fortune hunters will ply us with poetry and flowers, and pickpockets will run off with our bags." Amalia shrugged. "I feel sorry for you, if that's what you truly believe the world is like. If you truly think that people are lining up to take advantage of you."

Julián's father, who had stood up from his spot in the front pew next to her uncle, made an impatient gesture with his hand. From what Julián had told her, nothing would have angered him more than being embarrassed in front of his fashionable friends. And she was definitely giving them cause for gossip. "I've had just about enough of your insolence. I command you to remove yourself and this filthy beast from this church at once."

"Happily. As long as my sister comes with me."

"Touch a single strand of her hair, and Francisco will have you charged with kidnapping," Don Reynaldo said. The gray in his temples glinted like steel in the light pouring in through the stained-glass windows. "You and my son both, though I can't help but notice that the scoundrel has finally done what he does best—give up."

"You don't know anything about what your son can and can't do," Amalia told him. "Lu, will you come with me? There's nothing here for you or for me."

Tossing her bouquet to the floor, Lucía took a step toward the horse—and was stopped in her tracks as Victor's hand closed around her arm.

"My betrothed is not going anywhere," he said coldly. "Much less with you. I swore to protect her from harm, or I will very shortly, and that includes bad influences like you."

Lucía tried to tug her arm out of his grip, but even from her perch Amalia could see that he held her too tightly. "My sister's the only person who's ever looked after me," she protested.

Amalia felt her heart squeeze with guilt and remorse and a hot flash of anger. "Let go of her, you brute."

She swiveled the barrel of the pistol a fraction of an inch, but Victor had placed himself so that Lucía stood between him and Amalia. The damn coward.

It was a good thing neither of the pistols had a single bullet in it.

"I'd just as soon it doesn't discharge by accident," Julián had said earlier when he'd checked the chamber. "And in any case, neither of us has a taste for violence."

"Speak for yourself," Amalia had growled, but Julián had been right. She wasn't going to shoot anybody, not even Victor, no matter how much he deserved it.

And oh, how he deserved it.

Moving quickly, Victor had seized Lucía and was holding her in front of him like a shield. Lucía hunched her shoulders against the unwanted touch, but she didn't move away, making Amalia think Victor must have some sort of weapon.

The question was, what sort of weapon? Did a man like Victor wear a knife? That was the one thing she and Julián hadn't counted on when they'd made their plans.

She didn't have any time to figure it out before Victor started talking. "What do you think will happen if you try to ride out of here with my fiancée? Do you really believe that my uncle won't send the entire Civil Guard after you both? How far do you think that poor beast can carry you?"

For all that he was hiding behind Lucía, he had managed to inject a calm, almost smug tone into his voice. He sounded just like Amalia's uncle did when he was trying to reason with her, and as always, the sound only made Amalia feel even more furious.

"I had a lot of time to make plans when my uncle and your father had me abducted," she bit out.

All too aware of the dozens of guests filling the pews who were watching their exchange in rapt silence, Victor raised his eyebrows. "As far as I can tell, Amalia, the only person trying to kidnap anyone here is you." He softened his tone. "It's all right, Amalia. I know that my degenerate cousin has put all kinds of ideas into your head. He's led you to believe that he's trying to help you. But Julián has never served any interests other than his own. He's accomplished enough at making young women think he loves them, but the truth is that he will never love anyone more than he loves himself."

A glint came into Victor's eyes. "He's been lying to you this whole time. I heard it all—he plotted with my father about how to win your trust by getting rid of Francisco and persuading you to marry him. All so that he could hand over both your hands and your fortune to Tío Reynaldo. Seventy percent," he said casually in the direction of his uncle. "That's what you agreed on, right?"

Amalia looked into Victor's eyes and all of a sudden, it was a little harder to breathe. She could see in his expression that he believed what he was saying. And even though Julián had told her something similar, she was dismayed to discover that the flicker of doubt she had felt that morning hadn't been entirely extinguished.

Out of the corner of her eye, she caught a glimpse of a figure moving soundlessly behind the arches that separated the nave from the side aisle. As they had agreed, Julián had taken advantage of her attention-stealing entrance to slip into the church unseen. She cast an involuntary glance toward him, taking her eyes from Victor for only a split second.

It was a second too long.

Victor had a pistol, too, and his was loaded.

Pointing it at her over Lucía's shoulder, he didn't even hesitate before firing. The report echoed inside the church, and as the guests began screaming over the sound of shattering glass, the horse spooked and reared and Amalia found herself flying off the saddle, her arm exploding into agony.

One moment Julián was watching the proceedings from the back of the church and thinking that Amalia, at her boldest and brashest, was a sight to behold. Then she was being shot and thrown off a horse and he—

Well, the truth was that Julián had no clear memory of the next several minutes. The interval between the gun being fired and his arriving at Amalia's side was lost to the burning haze of his rage.

Amalia's sister had ripped off her veil and was using it to stanch the blood pouring from her arm.

It was every nightmare Julián had ever had—someone he cared about getting hurt because of him.

Not just someone. Amalia.

He looked her over quickly but thoroughly, a detached part of his mind matching up the single shot he'd heard fired with the runnel it had carved through the fleshy part of Amalia's upper arm.

Most of the guests seemed to have fled, but a few men had remained, and two of them were holding Victor back. A third was declaring something about having the Civil Guard fetched, though most looked uneasy at the thought of involving the law in what was clearly a family affair.

That, Julián thought, was exactly how Victor had come to be the man he was. The world they lived in made men like him think they were above justice, or even consequences.

"Has someone gone to fetch a doctor?" Julián heard himself say, his voice cold and distant.

He didn't hear the answer, focusing instead on Amalia.

Her eyes had fluttered open, and though her face was ashen, the snapping fire in them made him almost faint with relief.

Julián bent to brush his lips against her forehead. "I told you, Your Highness—everyone who gets close to me ends up hurt."

"There you go again," she said, looking irritated, "blaming yourself for something that is most decidedly not your fault."

He let out a laugh that could have passed for a sob. "You're going to be all right."

"I know *that*," she said. "It's just my arm. Pity you haven't any nice underclothes for a sling."

"I'll give you the shirt off my back if you want it," he said.

A sound from behind him drew his attention to his father. Don Reynaldo looked furious with Victor. Julián couldn't tell if he was angry over the fact that he had tried to shoot a young woman, or that he'd done it in full view of his fancy society acquaintances. At any other time the doubt might have saddened him—but Julián no longer cared.

After making sure that Amalia was all right being left with her sister for a moment, Julián strode to meet his father, who was advancing toward them with a flinty look in his eyes.

"I've had enough of this," Don Reynaldo said when he was close enough, taking care to avoid being overheard by the other men. "I humored your little attempt to pull the wool over my eyes because I was pleased to see you taking initiative for once, but this has gone on long enough. You will abandon your attempt to take the girl, or I will have Francisco declare her sister to be mentally unfit to handle her own affairs. Leave now, and you might still be able to persuade her to marry you."

Julián felt his face going very still, very suddenly. "I'm afraid you didn't understand. We didn't come here to negotiate with you. We're following your example and taking what we want with no regard to anyone else."

His father regarded him with disgust. "I should have disowned you long ago."

"I'm fine with being disowned," Julián said calmly. "Shooting at Amalia, on the other hand—that I have a problem with. Oh, and with being murdered. Although I'm not sure you were apprised of that particular plan of Victor's."

A slight flare of his father's nostrils told Julián he was right. He glanced toward where his cousin was being held back.

"With compliments from your cousin," he quoted, raising his voice so that Victor could hear him. "That was what the man you sent after us said. Would you like me to tell my father all the messages you had him relay? About no one knowing what you're capable of and no one appreciating all you do. He had plenty to say about Amalia, too, and none of it pleasant." He turned toward his father. "Don't tell me you're surprised to know that Victor was doing things behind your back. I thought you liked initiative. Or are you wondering what else he was involved in?"

His father looked at Victor as if he were seeing him through new eyes. "Is this true?"

Victor didn't look at him. "Look at you," he spat at Julián. "Roaming around the island like some sort of bandits, riding horses into churches and driving respectable men to desperation. No one can fault me for trying to protect my bride and my business from the pair of you."

"*Your* business?" Julián's father said in a low, dangerous voice that made the men holding on to Victor's arms take an unconscious step backward.

Victor seemed to realize his mistake. "Tio Reynaldo," he said and licked his lips. "It's not as it sounds. You know I would never dream of—"

Julián's father turned away. "Call the Civil Guard," he said over his shoulder. "I'm done with this business."

Julián would have sworn that the snarl that followed that remark had been made by an animal. His mouth fell open as he watched Amalia's uncle burst into sudden motion, seizing the pistol Victor had dropped and pointing it first at Julián, then at his nieces, as if he couldn't make up his mind who to shoot first.

"I'll be damned if I let you ruin this for me," he said in a hard voice.

He won't have me hurt. Amalia had said that, over and over again. Clearly, she'd been wrong.

Julián's eyes narrowed and he began to stride forward, directly toward the wavering barrel.

"Go ahead and shoot me," he said, advancing quickly toward the older man. "Just know that if you do, you had better kill me on the first try, because the second I get my hands on you, I will make *you* wish that you were dead."

Dropping the hand holding the pistol, Francisco tried to edge away, but all he did was back directly into a column. Julián put on a burst of speed and closed the distance between them, pinning Francisco to the column with nothing more than the menace in his stare.

"Come to think of it," Julián said, "that's one way to get past the will, isn't it? I wonder what provisions their father made in the case of your death."

"You won't kill me," Francisco said, but his eyes were wide and his chest heaving with one unsteady breath after another.

"Probably not," Julián agreed. "But like I told you a few days ago—I will make you regret everything you've ever done to your nieces. My lawyers will be paying you a visit later today. You will work with them to sign everything over to Amalia and Lucía."

"But—what am I to do?"

"Have you considered a job?" Julián said dryly, watching with amusement as true panic flashed over Francisco's face at the prospect. "I discussed the matter with Amalia, and she is prepared to give you a yearly allowance."

Greed flickered over his expression. "They owe me—"

"We," Julián said severely, "owe you nothing. Not even gratitude. Everything you've done has been for your own financial gain. Not for their father. And definitely not for them."

Francisco took a swing at Julián.

Nimbly, Julián stepped back from the older man, leaving him to crumple to the floor. Nobody went to help him up, and the church was very quiet as Julián strode back to Amalia's side.

Chapter Eighteen

Amalia must have drifted out of consciousness. She was aware of people around her, and of being gathered up into a pair of strong arms. Then there was nothing but disorienting flickers of something that might have been dreams, interspersed by an amorphous darkness.

When she managed to force her eyes open, she was so relieved to find Julián at her side that she let out a sob.

At the sound, Julián immediately lifted his head. "You're all right, Amalia. You've been seen by a doctor and your arm has been bound. You lost some blood, but he says you're going to be all right."

"I thought you had left me," she tried to explain through her tears.

"You can't get rid of me that easily, Your Highness," Julián said, the corners of his eyes crinkling with humor though he still looked worried.

Amalia tried to sit up, and found that she was able to haul herself upright without too much effort. Her entire body felt bruised, and her upper arm was in agony, but that was all. They were still in the church, and she had been laid on one of the pews. Julián was kneeling on the floor beside her, Lucía sitting at her feet.

Shifting her gaze behind them, Amalia saw a resisting Victor being hauled away by a pair of men in Civil Guard uniforms. Don Reynaldo appeared to have vanished.

And her uncle…

"Don't let him leave," Amalia told Julián. "I have something to say to him."

Julián helped her to her feet, which to her surprise were fairly steady under her. Tio Francisco, who had resentfully been talking to a guardsman, turned to watch her approach with obvious dislike in his eyes.

Amalia looked steadily back; after a moment his gaze slid away from hers.

"What is it?" he asked sullenly.

"I was thinking the other day, that it was a curious thing that you never married. I'm sure plenty of women would have liked to be courted by a man who commanded so much wealth and power, even if it wasn't his own."

"What of it?"

"Nothing, really, only I wondered… Were you so intent in keeping us isolated that you didn't dare bring another person into the household for fear that she would take our side? Or do you just abhor parting with money so much that you would have rather stayed alone all these years rather than support one more person?"

He shrugged. "Why would I need a wife when I already have everything?"

"And now you have nothing." Silence stretched between them as the truth of what she had just said sank into him. "Was it worth it?" she asked softly.

"I don't have to explain myself to you. I did as my brother asked me, and no one, not even your paramour, can claim that I have been profligate or careless with your inheritance."

Amalia's lips twitched mirthlessly. "That's always been the problem, Tio. You've always thought that managing our inheritance is about tallying up columns on some ledgers and watching numbers grow into inflated figures. But it was never about the money for us. All we wanted was our freedom."

Looking at her uncle's expression, Amalia realized that her explanations were pointless. He was never going to understand what she and Lucía had needed all these years. And he was never going to care about them the way they wanted to be cared about.

There was no more to be said. Amalia stepped back, searching out Julián, who was standing next to her sister like a guard, though his eyes were firmly on Amalia.

Maybe Amalia was slightly more overcome by her wound than she'd admitted to, because her knees went suddenly weak and she found herself being gathered gently into Julián's arms.

In the course of the next hour or two, he had not only managed to procure them a carriage to convey them to his house, he had also sent someone to the Europa to fetch their luggage, and had called for a doctor to attend to Amalia's arm.

The sun was still high in the sky behind the dark shutters when Julián helped Amalia into a freshly made bed whose carved posts were twined with mosquito netting. Her arm was freshly cleaned and bandaged, and the tonic the doctor had administered was making her eyelids impossibly heavy. So it was very likely that she imagined the glint in Lucía's eyes when her sister proclaimed that she needed to freshen up and hastened out of the bedroom, whisking the door closed behind her.

And then it was just Amalia and Julián. She reclined exhaustedly on the lace-edged pillow while Julián tugged a light cotton blanket over her.

"Have you always been this—this—"

"Handsome?" Julián filled in helpfully as she groped for a suitable word. He was as disheveled as Amalia felt, his shirt smeared in blood and grime, and his hair in complete disarray. "Dashing? Irresistible?"

"Competent," she said, offering him a drowsy smile. "For someone who continually calls himself a useless wastrel, you certainly know how to get things done."

"Allow me to let you in on a little secret, Your Highness—sometimes I have been known to make myself useless on purpose. Mainly to avoid anything having to do with my father's business. Though perhaps if I'd been obedient and diligent like Victor, my father would have appreciated me more."

"Affection shouldn't be earned through obedience, and you, Julián—" she reached for his hand "—you should be loved for your own sake, not for what you can do for other people."

"I'll try to keep that in mind," Julián said, the corners of his lips twitching upward as if Amalia had said something amusing. Or as if he didn't believe her.

Amalia frowned. At least, she thought she did. As important as she knew it was to convince Julián of the truth of her statement, the tonic was proving to be too strong and she could feel herself drifting into what promised to be a heavy stupor.

"Will you stay with me?" she murmured, making a valiant effort to keep her fluttering eyelids open.

The mattress dipped as Julián climbed in beside her. Amalia's head landed heavily on his shoulder, her eyes already closing.

The last thing she heard, before sleep finally pulled her under, was Julián's voice as he spoke softly into the shell of her ear. "I wouldn't dream of leaving you."

Amalia had been up for over an hour when Julián finally began stirring. She had awakened with her head pillowed in the crook of his arm, their faces close together as if they had sought one another's lips in the depths of slumber.

Sometime in the night Julián had kicked aside the light cotton blanket they had slept under. He lay sprawled over it now, the long, lean planes of his body golden against the bedsheets even in the faint blue light of early morning. Still asleep, he turned his head slightly, and Amalia saw that his arrogant profile was softened by the suggestion of a smile.

She loved him.

The thought came as suddenly as a lightning bolt.

She loved him with such a sudden, fierce strength it felt as though she *had* been struck by lightning— seared and electrified and dazed.

Julián's eyes blinked open, and he smiled in earnest when he saw her.

Her body's response was as swift as it was strong— unbridled delight danced through her limbs, and she couldn't hold back her answering smile. She would have kissed him—she wanted to, so deeply her heart clenched inside her chest—but she had a feeling that kissing Julián would no longer be the fun, reckless lark it had once been.

After everything that had happened, kissing Julián would be nothing but a straight descent into the near desperate need and longing she had spent most of her life trying to avoid.

He, on the other hand, was looking at her as if there was nothing remarkable about waking up next to a woman.

Because it wasn't, Amalia reminded herself. Not for someone who was always embroiled in one affair or another.

"Good morning, Your Highness," he said in a raspy voice that made the knot in her stomach tighten, reaching to run his fingertips over her cheekbone. "How do you feel? How's your arm?"

"I'm all right," she said, letting her gaze roam over the room as if by doing so she could escape his scrutiny.

Two mahogany wardrobes, their doors inlaid with mirrors, flanked a chest of drawers whose surface was littered with small bottles of hair oil, cologne and what looked like a sepia-tinged photograph in a silver frame. By the shuttered window was an armchair, a folded newspaper forgotten on its seat, and next to it a small table laid with a silver tray bearing a decanter and a single glass. It occurred to her that this must be Julián's bedroom—and his bed.

Whatever foolish fantasies Amalia might have once harbored about spending another night in Julián's bed vanished abruptly in the reality of the situation.

The sudden prickle of tears behind her eyes made Amalia sit up and swing her legs over the side of the bed. "I should make sure Lucía's all right," she said with her back to Julián.

"I don't know where you think you're going," he told her, his voice rich with amusement, "but I don't think you'll get very far."

Amalia cast an annoyed glance at him over her shoulder and found herself averting her gaze at the sight of his bare, muscular back.

To her profound irritation, he was right—she was still unsteady enough on her feet that she was forced to let him help her first to the washstand, and then down the stairs and into the dining room. Lucía, who had always been an early riser, was already at the long table with a cup in one hand and a bun in the other.

She bounded up from her chair, insisting on helping Julián as he lowered Amalia into a padded armchair. Amalia felt her heart soften as she let her sister dote over her.

The table was piled with a platter bearing all kinds of pastries, as well as a porcelain pot full of hot chocolate spiced with cinnamon and ginger, a silver one with coffee and smaller containers that held milk and sugar. Lucía puttered around it, putting together a plate for Amalia and exchanging teasing remarks with Julián as if he was the older brother she'd never had.

Back in the Hotel Europa's courtyard, when she had learned the devastating truth about his identity, Amalia had watched Julián transform before her very eyes. But what she had taken for him dropping a pose had actually been him assuming one—the cynical, amused, detached mask that he presented to his father and cousin. There was no trace of it left now as he made Lucía giggle into her *café con leche*.

Maybe Amalia did know the real Julián, even if he didn't.

He *was* handsome and dashing and irresistible. Or maybe it was just that Amalia didn't want to resist him, though she could think of a dozen reasons—maybe more—why she should.

Her father had done his best to protect his daughters, and all he'd accomplished was locking them in a gilded cage. Julián himself had tried to keep her from being hurt by their association and broken her heart in the process. However well intentioned their actions, they had both caused her pain.

But the difference between her father and Julián was that Julián was still here—and, having seen how she had suffered, he knew better than to trample over her opinions and wants and dislikes. He was the kind of man Amalia had never known existed, the kind she never knew she could want.

And now that she knew, how could she give him up?

Her gaze shifted to her sister, and Amalia felt her resolve firming. She'd give up *anything* to avoid thrusting them back into the situation they had fought so hard to escape—including Julián.

"I hope you know how grateful I am for everything you've done for us," she told him later, when Lucía had wandered into the kitchen to beg some honey for her bun from Julián's housekeeper. "I'm afraid we'll have to impose on you a little longer, at least until we're able to finish settling matters with our uncle. And then…"

"And then?" Julián echoed, lowering his cup.

As much as she wanted to keep her gaze fixed to the

painted flowers decorating the rim of her saucer, Amalia had never been a coward. With some difficulty, she looked into Julián's eyes. "And then Lucía and I will leave for Vienna."

She tensed, half expecting Julián to try and change her mind. All he did was nod slowly, though, and say, "I'll be happy to help you in any way I can."

The emotion that unfurled inside her wasn't relief, but disappointment.

She pulled herself together long enough to give him a carefully blank smile and thank him politely. Then she pled a headache and asked to be returned to bed.

Chapter Nineteen

"The first thing I'm going to do when we get to Vienna," Lucía said dreamily as she gazed out the carriage and up at the steamship she and Amalia would be boarding in a quarter of an hour, "is buy sheet music and sit in a café in the Ringstrasse and eat *sachertorte* and *apfelstrudel* and—"

"And give yourself indigestion," Amalia said, giggling. "You do realize we're going home to San Pedro first, right? It'll be a few weeks until you'll be able to while away your days in cafés like a Viennese *fraulein*—or eat like one."

To Amalia's amusement, Lucía refused to let this shred of logic dampen her dreamy smile. "I will dream about cakes every day until then."

Amalia snapped open the clasp on the powder blue leather traveling case she had purchased the day before. "You won't have to wait that long."

She lifted out the small box she had nestled in the blue silk lining, alongside their steamer tickets and money for the journey. Lucía looked intrigued as Amalia lifted the lid and showed her its contents: half dozen little cakes that looked like jewels, topped as they were with glittering sugar crystals, glazed nuts and pieces of candied pineapple and ginger.

It had only been ten days since the two of them had left Julián's house and settled into a hotel. Amalia would have charged into a steamship immediately after the events at the church, but Lucía had begged her to spend a few days recuperating. Amalia had always found it hard to deny her sister anything, but in truth, the main reason she'd agreed to it was Julián.

He had been the rock she and Lucía had never had— he'd spent the past few days dashing around the city, fetching doctors to see to her healing arm, and lawyers to start dismantling their father's will and even magazines and newspapers and endless sheafs of sheet music to keep them entertained. He'd accompanied them on shopping expeditions and to concerts and shown them the sights of the town, including the colonial-era fort he and Amalia had glimpsed from the ship on their arrival.

Through it all, he had made no demands, or asked any questions, or indicated in the slightest that he wanted anything from her. But Amalia couldn't help but be aware of the unresolved business hovering overhead.

He hadn't come to see them off this morning. Amalia couldn't blame him for wanting to avoid the awkwardness of parting.

That was a lie.

She had waited until the last possible second, blinking back the sting in her eyes as the clock above the front desk counted down the minutes until she had to leave. She'd been seething by the time she had finished distributing tips to the bellhops and climbed into the hired carriage that was conveying her and Lucía to the port.

Maybe she *should* have felt relieved that he was sparing them the difficulty of having to say goodbye. But all she could think of was all the things he had said that night at the planter's hacienda, about never wanting to be apart.

He had meant it—she knew that with all the certainty in her body. She no longer had any doubts about his intentions, or of her feelings toward him. So what, then? What had stopped her from asking him to come along with them?

Was it just that she wasn't as brave as he wanted to believe she was?

The coachman guided the carriage into a spot next to a cart loaded with wooden crates. Amalia felt the carriage move as he jumped down from his perch and began unloading their luggage.

What the devil was she doing? Was she really going to leave without Julián?

"Lu," Amalia said suddenly, turning to her sister, who was absorbed in sampling each of the cakes. "Would you mind terribly if I asked the coachman to turn back? I think I may have forgotten something—"

"Something? Or someone?" Lucía asked, looking impish.

Amalia nodded wordlessly, feeling her throat constrict with emotion.

Lucía dimpled as she raised a finger to point at the crowd milling outside their open carriage. "Looks like he hasn't forgotten *you*."

Amalia followed Lucía's finger, her heart leaping.

It *was* Julián, walking toward them at a vigorous clip that made him stand out from the milling crowd.

She turned back to her sister to see Lucía's gaze on hers. "Don't deny yourself love, Amalia. Not for my sake."

Then Lucía was hopping down lightly from the carriage, saying that she would oversee the porters as they transported their luggage into the ship. Before Amalia could follow her, Julián climbed into the seat Lucía had just vacated.

He was in a very fine suit, the kind he had worn all through the past several days. But he was bareheaded even though the midday sun was at its fiercest, and his hair wasn't smoothed back with pomade like the other men's. Amalia drank him in, lingering on the details. His chiseled jaw was shaded behind at least two days' worth of bristles. His tiepin looked like it cost more than her entire considerable wardrobe. And there was no denying that his longish hair, curling around his collar, was badly in need of a cut.

Neither bandit nor aristocrat, he looked wholly himself.

Hurricane-force winds couldn't have held back Amalia's smile. "What are you doing here?"

"I realized I still had something of yours, and I couldn't let you leave without it."

Amalia's smile faltered. "Oh?"

She'd supervised the packing herself and made sure that the things she and Lucía had brought to Puerto Plata—not to mention the many, many they'd bought since then—were neatly placed in their trunks and valises. She'd been very meticulous about it, out of a desperate need for distraction from the confused snarl of thoughts about Julián and her future.

Julián was reaching into his inner jacket pocket. "I never intended to keep it this long. I meant to return it as soon as we got to Puerto Plata."

Amalia glanced down as Julián took her hand, though not to clasp it, but to place something on her palm.

"My mother's necklace," she said softly. "You didn't pawn it."

"How could I, when I had more than enough money to pay for our passage and I could see how much it meant to you?"

"Thank you for keeping it safe for me." Amalia slipped the bright links into one of the small velvet pouches in her leather case where she kept the rest of her jewelry. As grateful as she was to Julián for not having forgotten about the necklace, she felt a little hollow. Was that the only reason he'd come?

"I know it was only in my custody for a handful of days, but it became something like a talisman," Julián continued. "Looking at it made me think of your courage. You didn't just part with something that belonged to your mother and clearly held a lot of sentimental value—you used it to fight for a better future for yourself and Lucía. I'm ashamed of how many years I spent wasting my time and my life because I didn't think I could change my circumstances."

Julián leaned forward. "I meant to be at the hotel to see you off this morning, but I had to stop by my father's office first. He asked me to run his company this morning. Not out of any excess of appreciation toward me, I don't think, but because Victor is now useless to him and he needs a second-in-command."

"What did you say?" Amalia asked.

"I told him that if he had changed his mind about disinheriting me, I was still more than happy to disown *him*. In the short time I have known you, Amalia, you have shown me a side of myself that I never wanted to admit existed. It was too easy to dismiss myself as a scoundrel and a wastrel when it seemed so unlikely that I would ever get what I wanted. I don't want to be like my father or Victor, but neither do I want to be the man I was before we met."

"Oh, Julián." Amalia reached for his hand. He held hers in his larger one, thumb idly stroking her knuckles.

"This is the right path for me. If I'm to make something of myself, I'd rather do it on my own." He took a deep breath, and Amalia's heart began to pound. "But not by myself." He traced a fingertip over her cheekbone, his touch so soft it was like being stroked with a rose petal. "I want you, Amalia. Not for a dalliance, or a moment's pleasure. For always. And though I would never dream of telling you not to go, I am asking if I can come with you."

Amalia didn't have a chance to answer.

"I know you already gave me an answer. That night in the planter's house, when I begged you to love me, and you said you couldn't. And I respect it. I also haven't forgotten that you swore off marriage," he added in a rush, his hand tightening on hers. "I'm offering myself to you with the understanding that I won't make demands of you. It doesn't matter if you won't marry me, or if you don't love me, as long as you don't make me live without you. It's been a long time since I've actually wanted a future for myself, and I'll be damned if it doesn't include you, Your Highness."

Placing her other hand on top of his, Amalia said, "I think I could be persuaded to make an honest man out of you."

Julián looked startled. "You changed your mind about marriage?"

"Not entirely." Amalia threaded her fingers through his, saying lightly, "But I have recently come to the realization that I would be bored to tears if I had to go through life without you." She offered him a tentative smile. "I love you, Julián. Loving you is one of the most terrifying, exciting things I have ever done. Who's to say that marriage won't be as exciting as it is terrifying?"

"Are you sure about this, Amalia? Because I wouldn't dream of—"

"What was it that you told me a few days ago? That there is nothing I can't do? Well, I'm determined to prove you right."

Julián looked stunned.

"Also," Amalia said, because it seemed that, at the moment, speaking was beyond Julián, "I have everything I could ever hope for now, save for a bandit of my own. Would you be interested in being mine?"

He caught her into a crushing kiss, heedless of the crowds moving around the open carriage. Amalia could hardly lay a claim to propriety after everything that had happened, so she let herself be deeply, thoroughly debauched.

He lifted her bodily from the seat and placed her on his knees. A surge of joy rushed over her as she wrapped her arms around his muscular shoulders and caressed the back of his neck.

The rasp of his whiskers filled her with an equal measure of lust and delight. His mouth was languorous and unhurried as it ranged over hers, his tongue gentle when he probed the indentation on her top lip. It was the kiss of someone who knew he had a lifetime's worth of them left, and that made it all the more precious to Amalia.

Julián was smiling when they finally pulled apart, their hands clasped tightly together. "Well, then, Your Highness. Only one thing is left. What would you say if I officially, formally, asked for your hand in marriage?"

"That I could imagine nothing more thrilling than to spend the rest of my life at your side," Amalia said at once.

"Then I have something else for you. It was going to be a parting gift if you refused me, but either way, I've known from the moment I saw it on your finger that it was destined to be yours."

Amalia caught her breath when he pulled out his mother's ring. It was just as lovely as it had been when she'd first seen it, diamonds glittering like ice as they caught and reflected the morning light.

She forestalled him by raising a hand. "Not now." He froze and she hastened to add, "You can put it on me tonight—when we ask the captain to marry us."

Amalia caught a quick glimpse of the gleam in his eyes before he bowed his head. She couldn't resist drawing it to her and holding him against her. Brushing back the dark, untidy curls tumbling on his forehead, she placed little kisses around his hairline.

"That was almost more terrifying than leaping out of a moving train," Julián mumbled.

"I found it invigorating, actually," Amalia remarked. "Wouldn't mind doing it again."

Julián lifted his head and grinned at her. "That, Your Highness, is exactly one of the reasons why I love you. Allow me to enumerate the rest."

He actually started to do it, and looked like he could have spent the rest of the day at it. Shaking her head, Amalia seized his hand and pulled him down from the carriage.

They were halfway to the ticket office when Julián bent down to whisper one last item in Amalia's ear. "And above all, I love you because when you're near me, nothing seems impossible."

They were married by the captain as soon as the ship had been steered out of the bay and into open waters— Julián was ready to insist on being married the instant he, Amalia and her sister were on board, but he grudgingly allowed that the captain did have more important things to attend to.

The sunset blazing behind them, the deep blue waters of the Atlantic Ocean spreading before them, Julián and Amalia stood on the deck and pledged themselves to each other.

Amalia was wearing another ensemble that looked like it had been made in a Parisian confectionery; this one a pale, muted green with a froth of lace, garnished with gold jewelry and topped with a modish hat. Just before they'd boarded, Julián had pressed a small fortune into the hands of a steward who had procured an indecent amount of flowers. Amalia and her sister had covered themselves with blooms, weaving them into their hair and tucking them into their clothes, and dozens more waited in the luxurious cabin Julián had arranged for himself and his new bride.

The wedding reception took place in the dining room, where Amalia's sister and the rest of the ship's passengers, all strangers, celebrated their union with flute after flute of champagne.

"An unconventional wedding for an unconventional bride—and groom," Lucía said as she toasted them, her dark skin flushed with champagne and good cheer.

Julián turned to look at his wife—he would never tire of that word. She sat with her back to the dining room's window, the countless lamps reflecting on its pane making her look like the embodiment of the light that had come into his life when he met her. Julián took her hand and kissed it, and when she turned her sparkling, luminous eyes toward him, he kissed her lips with his heart in his mouth.

At long last, Julián managed to spirit his vibrant, beautiful wife into their private cabin, where he meant to whisk her straight into bed.

First, however, he spared a moment to enjoy her delight. The same gardenias, camellias and tuberoses that adorned her hair and dress were crowded into the silver-and-faceted crystal vases on every surface. They had turned their cabin into a fragrant garden, but their perfume was no match to the delicate saltiness clinging to her skin.

Julián swept Amalia into his arms and nibbled at her neck, recalling the last time they had stood together in a ship's cabin.

"Remind me to take you into the bath later," he murmured into her ear. "So that I can lick every drop from your skin."

"Oh?" she asked, sounding intrigued. "Please say more."

He shook his head, tightening his arms around her. "Later. I want to devour you first."

Taking her hand, he kissed each one of her knuckles before turning over her hand and laying another kiss on her palm. Then he twined his fingers through hers again and tugged her toward the bed.

Lying back on the satin coverlet, she reached for the fastenings on her dress, but Julián brushed her hands away.

"It's my turn to undress you, Your Highness," he told her and turned his head to press a kiss to her thumb when she stroked the side of his face.

"Undress me slowly," she quoted, leaving off the second part of the sentence because there was no need to hurry anymore, not now that they had forever.

He took his time with every hook and ribbon, tracing each lace-edged border with his tongue and caressing each inch of skin as it was revealed. He tasted the salt that had collected in the hollow of her throat and the slight dip behind her ears, returning again and again to the sweet warmth of her mouth.

It was where he belonged.

"I have never loved anyone as much as I've loved you," Julián told her. "I will do everything I can to deserve this trust you've placed in me."

Amalia laid the back of her hand against his cheek. "You already have. I hate that I ever doubted you, even for a second."

"I think we needed every one of those seconds, Your Highness. To find our way to each other and to ourselves."

"I had no idea I was marrying someone so wise," Amalia said teasingly as she reached for his shirt buttons.

"Not wise. Just...in love."

"And lovable," she added, sliding his shirt off his shoulders. "And deserving of love. Not because you're useful, or obedient, or because you're handsome or clever or good at business, even though you are all those things. But because you're you, and that makes you worthy of all the affection you have ever needed and longed for."

Braced on his forearms, Julián let her slowly and thoroughly strip him bare, both in body and soul. If Amalia had once worried about losing control if she married, to Julián it was an opportunity to surrender himself to her and make her the guardian of his body and his heart.

Hours later, as the dense night began to lighten into dawn, Julián was drifting into sleep when he felt Amalia rise from the bed. To his chagrin, not even the tantalizing thought of licking droplets from her smooth shoulders could make his heavy eyelids stay open—but he managed it several minutes later when she opened the door of the lavatory, softly so as not to disturb his sleep, and paused to turn on the electric lamp.

Her fine lawn nightdress billowed down to just an inch above the floor. It was suspended by a delicate tracery of lace or crochet—Julián couldn't tell the difference from a distance—that left the length of her arms bare.

And then there was her hair. It rippled down her back like a miniature ocean, cresting and swelling with dark waves, all the way down to her waist.

Feeling as dazed as if he'd been struck upside the head, Julián watched from the bed as she padded to the vanity and poured a few drops of some sweet-smelling oil onto her hairbrush. She cast a glance at the bed, and Julián saw her mouth curve when she noticed he was awake. "You wouldn't mind helping me, would you?"

Julián let out a laugh as he walked toward her. "Are you trying to flirt with me?"

Amalia smiled up at him. "Did it work?"

"Always."

Gently moving her hair to one side, he dove into her neck for one kiss after another, making her squeal. He didn't pull back until they were both breathless with laughter.

Her sterling silver hairbrush was part of a set, with a swirling botanical design on its back that matched the small hand mirror she had laid on the vanity next to a leather jewelry box. Julián drew the brush through her curls, watching as the strands separated and reformed in the wake of the bristles.

Only a few minutes went by before Amalia spoke again. "I have something for you."

After opening her jewelry case, she extracted a folded scrap of paper from beneath the curled links of a necklace and half turned to hand it to him. "When I met with your lawyers several days ago, I asked for their help finding someone. They sent a messenger with this just before I left the hotel this morning."

Julián set down the hairbrush.

"Miguel?" he asked, gazing down at the words written in the neat hand of a clerk. "You had them track down Miguel?"

He'd thought about doing the same thing so many

times over the years, but he'd never quite dared—out of worry that the horseman wouldn't remember him or worse, that he would resent Julián for costing him his job. And heaven only knew if that was the only thing his father had done to the man.

"I hope I didn't overstep. The way you talked about him… I thought you might want to get back in touch with him. I want you to have people in your life who care about you, Julián. Other than me, I mean."

"You have no idea how grateful I am." Julián folded the piece of paper like the valuable thing that it was and tucked it into the pocket of his jacket, where it would be safe. He'd scrounge up some stationery and write to Miguel the next day. "I don't know if I'd ever have had the courage to try and find him, but as always, you're so much braver than I could hope to be."

"Your and my childhoods were similar in a lot of ways, but at least I had Lucía," she said, looking earnestly up at him. "For Miguel to have been one of the few people to have shown you kindness, and for you to have been blamed for his being cast out—the way you were both treated fills me with rage. I wish I could make right all the times your father wronged you, Julián."

"I don't think even he can do that," Julián said, kneeling between her legs and sliding his arms around her waist. "But I refuse to dwell on the past when for once in my life, I have so much to look forward to. Like renewing my friendship with Miguel and escorting you and Lucía to Vienna and setting up my own business." He dipped his head to kiss her wrist, dragging his lips higher up her slender arm. "And making love to my extraordinary wife. You are incomparable,

Your Highness. And thoughtful and beautiful. And if I'd paid better attention to my tutor, I'd probably have more words at my disposal."

"I know one more," Amalia said, bending over him and touching her lips briefly to his forehead. "Yours."

Epilogue

Less than a fortnight after their arrival in San Pedro, Amalia found herself on her way to another outdoor excursion. She had planned this one as well, though this time her main goal was to provide Lucía's friends with an opportunity to say their goodbyes.

After quick greetings all around, Amalia stepped away from the throng to survey the tables of food she herself had helped set around the *anacahuita* tree. One of the first things she had done upon returning home was persuade her uncle's housekeeper to leave his employ and preside over the house she and Julián had bought together. The older woman had agreed at once, and after a few days back and forth with Lucía, had produced a feast that would not have looked out of place in the Royal Palace of Madrid.

Amalia admired the spread as she nudged silver trays into place and brushed fallen leaves off the white tablecloth.

Her pale green dress, with its ivory trim and panels of delicate lace, was utterly unsuited to an outdoor romp. Though Lucía had twined lilac ribbons through her dark curls, Amalia had chosen to weave hers into a coronet, adorned with tiny white flowers. She was intercepting one of the flowers as it fluttered off her head and toward a tureen filled with hard-boiled quail eggs floating in a pink sauce when she felt someone step beside her.

"Amalia, there you are," said Paulina de Linares warmly, leaning in to press her cheek to Amalia's in greeting.

She had not given up on her gentle but insistent pursuit of a friendship with Amalia, and Amalia couldn't have been more grateful for another chance at letting herself open up to friendship. It felt almost as risky as opening up to love, if in an entirely different way, but Paulina was a motherly soul and she had seemed really concerned over Amalia after the way she'd gone missing from their last outing.

"I was just speaking with your sister. She says you're leaving town soon?"

Amalia nodded in confirmation. "We're going to Vienna so that Lucía can work on her music and I… Well, at my husband's urging, I'm looking into starting a charity to provide legal services to women and children who are in the position Lucía and I were in."

Amalia was a woman of means now, and she also wanted to be a woman of influence. In the meantime, Julián was devoting himself to teaching her and Lucía how to manage their properties and finances. These days Amalia's neatly balanced checkbook was her biggest source of pride.

Paulina nodded in understanding. "If you could keep just one person from experiencing what you and

Lucía—and I—had to go through at the hands of our relations…"

Amalia felt a rush of warmth for her new friend. Of all people, Paulina would understand her drive to help others. They had talked for a long time when they ran into each other outside Don Enrique's store more than a week before, and Amalia had learned that Paulina had gone through an experience similar to hers after her parents had died and left her in the care of her horrible brother.

"We'll have a chance to talk more about it when I stop by tomorrow for coffee," Amalia promised, having spotted a familiar figure at the edge of the gathering. "Will you excuse me for a moment?"

She waited for Paulina's nod and smile before hurrying over to the palm tree against which lounged the bandit who had stolen her heart.

He didn't cover his face with a kerchief these days, and there were few rusty suits in his wardrobe. But his rakish smile made her pulse gallop as hard as it had when he'd raced away with her.

"Enjoying yourself, Your Highness?"

"Not as much as Lucía," Amalia said as she stepped into Julián's arms, tilting her head toward where her sister stood, surrounded by a gaggle of chattering young women. Without their uncle's influence—and without the prospect of marriage hanging over her head—Lucía fairly glowed with good spirits.

"She's in her element," Julián observed.

"Just wait until she pulls out her violin." Amalia's sister had been practicing all week for what she laughingly called her first concert.

Julián smiled, his gaze returning to Amalia. "Will

you come with me for a moment? I have a wedding present for you."

"Another one?" Amalia asked fondly. Every day since they had disembarked, Julián had presented her with baubles or sterling silver hairbrushes or articles of clothing that consisted of barely more than scraps of lace and silk and were not meant to be worn outside their bedroom. "You're spoiling me, Julián."

"No such thing." He tugged at her hand, nodding at the path half-hidden behind the palms. "Come on. They won't miss us for a little while."

Amalia half expected his horse to be hidden among the greenery. The path was empty, though, and they strolled along it arm in arm until they came to a wooden structure that didn't look nearly as dilapidated as it had a month ago.

"The shack?" Amalia asked, tilting her head.

"I bought it, and the two acres of land surrounding it. I thought we could use a little refuge. In case we ever decide to take up banditry again and need to run from the law."

"We own four homes," Amalia protested, laughing. "Five, I think. Or more?"

"Definitely more," Julián said. "And they're all so large and grand. Don't you sometimes wish we had a cozy little hut just for the two of us?" He trailed a deliberately slow finger down her spine, which he knew never failed to make her shudder. "A place in the middle of the wilderness where no one could find us...or hear us?"

His lips met the juncture of her neck.

"The location does have its advantages," Amalia was forced to concede as her knees gave way and she melted against Julián.

"The interior, too," he said, laying a kiss on the corner of her lips. "Come and see."

Amalia didn't know how he had managed to fit a four-poster bed inside the small shack, but she deeply approved of it. Draped with mosquito netting and piled with embroidered cushions and feather pillows, it looked delightfully comfortable.

She sat on the edge, and Julián bent at once to remove her shoes and stockings before joining her on the smooth white sheets. From her vantage point, Amalia could see the shelf on the other side of the room, laden with a private spread he must have filched from the party—and quite a few bottles of *aguardiente*.

Filled with searing, effervescent delight, she rolled over as Julián molded himself against her back. "I'm not casting aspersions on all of your other lovely presents, but I have to admit that this one is by far my favorite."

Julián blew a cool gust of air into the back of her neck, which already felt damp from the morning's heat, and Amalia squirmed pleasurably again. He had been holding on to her waist, but now he relaxed his arms so that they rested on her hips and thighs, and devoted himself to exploring the curve of her earlobe with the delicate tip of his tongue.

Amalia nestled back against Julián, feeling herself growing molten from the warmth of his touch. If she'd been standing, she wasn't altogether sure she would have been able to remain upright.

His fingers dove into her hair, eager as always to release it from its pins. "I'm glad you like it, Your Highness. We should come as often as we can before we leave for Vienna."

"We'll come every day," she promised, rolling over to lightly bump his nose with hers before capturing his mouth in a kiss. She'd asked him not to shave that morning, and she took a moment to nuzzle his bristly cheeks, enjoying the pleasant prickle on her own soft skin.

"Don't be surprised if I have this place disassembled and packed into crates. Europe is rich in history and culture, but I have a feeling it will be severely lacking when it comes to wooden shacks. And after all," he added, "we'll need to find a way to keep ourselves occupied while Lucía is busy with her music lessons."

Amalia had several ideas, and she wasted no time in brazenly whispering them into Julián's ears.

"You, my dear," Julián said, fiddling with the pearl buttons running down her back, "are the most incredible woman I've ever met. Remind me to add this moment to my list."

"One of these days you'll have to let me see this list of yours. If only to prove that it does, in fact, exist."

"Oh, it does," he assured her. His hands had reached the last button at the small of her back and she could tell he was lingering over it. She arched into his touch, inviting his hand to trail lower and knead her bottom.

"By now, it's probably as long as your…arm," she said.

"Wherever did a gently reared heiress like you learn such filthy innuendo?" His attempt to look scandalized gave way to a smirk, and Amalia couldn't resist kissing him through her laughter.

She reached for the placket of his trousers. "You're a terrible influence on me. Then again, you know what they say about keeping company with bandits."

Julián's lips grazed her neck. "I don't, actually. What do they say?"

Amalia grinned. "That it's damned exciting."

* * * * *

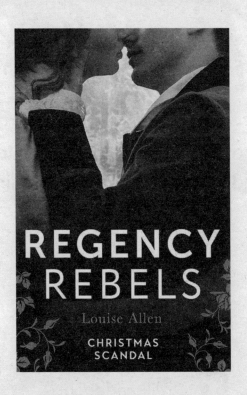

LET'S TALK
Romance

For exclusive extracts, competitions and special offers, find us online:

- **f** MillsandBoon
- **🐦** @MillsandBoon
- **📷** @MillsandBoonUK
- **♪** @MillsandBoonUK

Get in touch on 01413 063 232

For all the latest titles coming soon, visit
millsandboon.co.uk/nextmonth